PERSON OF INTEREST

SHIRLEY DAY

First published in 2023 by Bloodhound Books.

www.bloodhoundbooks.com

Print ISBN: 978-1-5040-8697-4

With special thanks to the Escalator scheme at the National Centre for Writing, without their encouragement, I'm not sure that this novel would have ever been written. With special mentions to Ellie Reeves, Holly Ainley, Flo Reynolds, Isobel Martin, Gill and my mentor Owen Nicholls.

1

APPROPRIATE OCCASION

Despite what the fashion houses tell you, not everyone looks good in black. Me, I can pull it off. People say I have a Mediterranean look. Dark hair and a sunbed will do the trick – at least till I open my mouth. Then it's pure Scouse. Although, over the years, I've managed to muscle that under control. Five years, to be precise. It's amazing what you can fix if you find the right YouTube channel. I get to the church last minute. In all the time I've been doing this, I've found last minute works best. There's a balance to be struck. You need to be late enough, so bored eyes don't notice you coming in, but not so late so's you draw attention. As it turns out, I'm not sure I've attracted so much as a sideways sniffle; the congregation is already whispering like a boiling kettle without me. I have taken to wearing black most days now, which could seem like a fashion front cop-out for a woman barely grazing twenty-six, but I like to be ever-ready. I never know when I'll get that call. This one came totally out of the blue. I'd been preoccupied with my brother, AJ. So, I must have missed the obit in the papers. First I heard about it was an eight-word text from Marco, who's also in the 'business'.

– *Influential woman on the island suffering the usual.*

Influential is about the size of it because the church is packed. *Packed* is always a good sign; popular people tend to live extravagantly. Extravagance equals debt. Debt results in a hasty offload on the property front. It's get in now or never because these people have the sort of recently emptied real estate that sells fast. The island sits around twenty-eight miles off the coast. Technically speaking, it's not actually one island, more of a clump, an archipelago. The aerial shots are seriously worth a gander; because this is not the kind of place you imagine sitting a hop, skip, and jump away from cold old Blighty; a scatter of green, frilled with bleached white sand. In truth, there is only one proper island. By *proper,* I mean *working* – somewhere that can boast a church, a pub, a post office and more than a handful of people. One less person as of today. Not that I'll be needing a hanky to wipe away any tears. It's the bricks and mortar she's leaving vacant that's holding my interest. Good stuff on the island doesn't come up every day. It's near impossible to get planning permission outside of the harbour town of Kernow. So, in the rural areas, people cling to their beachside properties. Even when the owners kick the bucket, they'll want to go passing those sea views on to their kids, or maybe even the kids of their kids. It's one hell of a good deal if you're in the supply chain.

'There's a space to the right,' a thin, sombre guy in black whispers as he pushes an order of service into my hand. He's giving me the standard so-sorry simper as I move past him into the church, a small, respectful tight twitch pulling his lips together. I mirror what Thin Sombre is doing with my own mouth. Mirroring always works a treat. It's the easiest way to slip under the radar, which is just where I like to be.

My oh-so-tastefully-low court shoes barely make a sound as I glide a few packed pews down the aisle. Nobody is interested, so I get the chance to enjoy the majesty of the high ceiling as that cool incense smell tweaks hard at the top of my nostrils. I may not be religious, but that doesn't stop me appreciating the architecture. I'll enjoy the singing too, once it gets started. As I glide, I turn off my phone. I don't like doing it; I'm waiting on a call from my brother, but the switch off can't wait. The last thing I need is to have my marimba playing its bright, sparky tune into the hushed silence of the service.

I don't always do the church. I can normally tell from the state of the congregation's shoes as they clatter through the lynch gate if it's worth direct contact. But I knew even before I got one whiff of shoe leather that on this occasion, I should go with whatever is on offer. Besides, I'd already made an effort. I'd had to catch the ferry to get here, and the hasty bit of background research I'd pulled up on the family made me keen as a cat to grab myself a closer snoop.

Once installed safely behind my pew, I take a quick look at the order of service. It's nicely done: card, not paper. Expensive with a faint vanilla smell. The relatives didn't just spew this out on a home-office inkjet. Everything about it has the professional touch. Someone has taken the time to set it out, consider the GSM, ferry it down to the printers, and then collect it all in a box they can barely lift. It bodes well when you're impressed by the stationery.

'Still can't quite believe it,' a bottle-blonde woman in her seventies, hisses at her angular husband. He nods demurely.

What can you say? I could tell her it's always a shock, no matter what the circumstances. I've listened in on enough of these conversations. But nobody likes a smart-ass. Instead, I turn my attention once again to the order of service.

A picture of a smart, hard-looking woman stares out at me from the front page; her white hair tonged in a steam-ironed bob around an angular face – Carolyn Millford. I know this not only because it's on the front of the order of service in tastefully burnished gold letters and a clear font. But when I googled her name, the face came up. Not the same picture, but that bone structure is unmistakable. I stare hard at the image, trying to unpick just who the woman underneath might have been. She's older in this photo than in the images online. I glance at the dates – 1964 to 2023. If this is a true impression, all credit to her; the woman's done a stellar job of stopping gravity from driving away with her looks. Although, being in the higher income bracket will have helped. Ms Millford was an important lady. She'd clung onto the *Millford,* despite a brief marriage. Or maybe she changed her name back to her maiden name after whoever it was she'd tied her fortune to popped his clogs. Did he die? Or did he leave? I don't have all the details, on account of this event being so last minute. But I do know about the Millford name. Everyone does in the South West. It used to be important. The island is small. We're talking four thousand people sticking it out for the 'overwinter', and the Millford family used to be one of the key landowners. One of the two big names – the Millfords, and the Fordhams. All massive fish in a very tight pond. As far as I know, Carolyn's 'clan' were the only ones still standing, apart from Carolyn, of course. As of last week, Carolyn has found herself horizontal.

'Carolyn's greatest contribution to society...'

The priest's voice seeps into my brain.

'...saw Carolyn become one of our greatest celebrities.'

There are a few rock stars clustered on the smaller islands. They might take issue with this. Then again, Carolyn was born here. The celebrity status the priest's angling after is of the home-grown variety: local girl gets lauded. I suppose it is impressive; living on this far-flung bit of sand and sea and still managing to make a national name for yourself. Carolyn Millford was a child psychologist. She wrote the go-to parenting manual that gave the first part of the 21st century the answers to just about every aspect of bringing up kids that they might happen to hanker after, or at least that's what it said in *The Times*.

'She became a staple figure in households across the country.'

The priest tells us helpfully, but I'd have to disagree with him there. We'd never had her on our shelves. Maybe it would have all turned out differently if we had. I doubt it. Some problems take more than a few thousand words to fix. I didn't even know about the book until this morning when I'd caught up with the papers.

'Her contribution to island life was considerable.'

I phase out. Carolyn, God bless her, holds no interest for me. I focus my interest where it matters now – the front pew: the living. These are the people I need to target, but they're difficult to read. As you would expect – I'm only getting backs. That's okay. This is a slow game. I'll get myself a better look when they do the readings.

But there are no readings. Apparently, that was the way Carolyn wanted it. We all file respectfully out to our cars. There are a few sad nods, a reluctance to head too quickly for the doors. I take a middle ground, losing myself in the body of the crowd. I don't always visit the graveside. But I'm itching for faces, not backs. Besides, this could be a big deal, and the ferries aren't running from town till later this afternoon.

Despite the rain, I follow the slim snake of cars as it winds out towards a wind-blown cemetery. A small church of rest waiting patiently above a scraggly strip of beach; its stone tower standing triumphantly above a chaos of cracked headstones. I eye the graveyard suspiciously through the wet windscreen, the image outside smearing constantly. It's strangely reassuring, being dry and warm. Basking in the synthetic orange smell of the complimentary freshener from the car wash. The noise of the wipers providing an oddly comforting harmony with the slow tick of the indicator. The graveyard has no walls to keep the dead in. Instead, the land around the stone markers falls casually away into crumbling cliffs on two sides and a narrow strip of tarmac at my end, a strip that's being made narrower every minute by the constant procession of cars shunting themselves awkwardly into some kind of parked line in front of me. I wait my turn, glancing at the bent, tortured trees outside, their twisted arms frozen towards the east as if trying to get out of the wind. It's a bleak setting and not helped by the slate-grey sky. Even the sea, which is most days as blue as a cornflower, is going for coal-pit grey, as though it's had all the life drained out of it. A figure in funeral garb jostles awkwardly along the line of cars, rain dripping over the man's body, leaving him shining like a seal as he waves one wet arm of his coat in front of my windscreen, ushering me into a wedge between a Merc and the Audi in front.

I pull my umbrella from the boot as the fresh salt air engulfs me, kick-starting my senses after the dull, warm fug of my car. Is it the occasion that makes me feel so alive? Or simply close proximity with the elements; that hard cold sting of rain against my skin? Could be either. Yet, despite what the trees are semaphoring, the wind isn't too cruel today. My coat is in the boot beside my brolly. It's all standard-issue black, so there's no problem with pulling it on over my neat M&S cashmere cardi. I am layered for the occasion. Slamming down the car boot, I glance around me as my umbrella flaps seamlessly into place above my head.

The congregation has dwindled, which is just as well. The smattering who have braved it out here to the ends of the earth have managed to do a great job of chewing up the lane with their expensively thick tyres.

'Beastly weather,' the usher manages.

'I'm well prepared,' I shout back. But he's not interested; other cars need to be parked.

My shoes sink into the sandy soil as, using my free hand, I button up my coat, not taking my eyes off the gathering. It's still sad faces, one-and-all. Genuine? That's always a fifty-fifty kind of a thing and beyond my remit. Bitter is the expression you need to be wary of at a funeral. At best, it's tedious. At worst, get on the wrong side of someone with a bitter streak, and you'll never get any business. You might even secure yourself an inbox full of hate or possibly a slapped cheek. But it's difficult to tell who's bitter, and who is genuinely sad when everyone's keeping their heads down out of the rain.

I strike away from the cars towards the graveside. I've been to a lot of funerals over the past five years, and my take on it is that you can't do better than a drizzly day for a burying. When I *go*, I'm not wanting sunshine. Give me that 'drip, drip, drip' on large black umbrellas, and I'll be happy. Well, not happy, difficult to be 'happy' when there's a plank of wood sitting inches above your face. But I'll feel like everything is as it should be. Blazing sunshine would be too painful to leave. Spring funerals are the worst, but everyone to their own. Besides, it's not as if you get much choice.

As the wind battles with our coats, the priest does another speech, the normal – ashes to ashes, dust to dust, mud to squelch. He's pinched his pauses and is keeping a lid on his diction; the speed of Carolyn's last public engagement is the only thing anyone is going to appreciate today. Trying not to look too obvious, I scan the mourners. There are two women clutching handkerchiefs to noses and eyes. The first is tall, willowy and lacking all curves. Her brown hair piled up under a dark felt hat which hugs her skull a little too tightly. She's the *fabulously famished* type, so thin she's more coat hanger than human. I'd be willing to bet that the only fat on her will be coming from a needle. She's maybe early thirties. Carolyn's daughter? The second sniveller is standing right beside her: a younger woman. A redhead, the copper tones looking murkier than burnished in the drizzle of the day. This one has to be younger than me, less than twenty. Probably a student still, studying something useless and unspecific. Wealthy people can afford to be qualified for nothing. They always land on their feet.

My guess would be that the redhead is a grandchild. That would explain the age gap. I continue running my eyes along the line till I come to a tall, weaselly-looking man that I could swear I've seen before. I'd peg him at late sixties. Not a pleasant-looking guy, a little Dickensian. He's stooped over the grave, neck bent low, with the proprietorial air of someone involved in the proceedings, someone deeply inside the mourning hierarchy. Carolyn's lover? I'm not sure. She'd have been batting way below her weight if she was seeing old Weasel Features. Besides, he doesn't look sad enough to have been a lover. I study his face carefully, trying to place it. But it won't fit neatly into anything within easy access. Having said this, he is unusual-looking, the kind of face you might easily register without actually *knowing* a person. Maybe I just saw him around?

I don't get too close. My position is watching benignly from the back. I do a good *benign*. It's just as I'm congratulating myself on my *benign*, that I get this odd sensation, the hairs on the back of my neck pulling vertically away from my skin. It's not the cold; underneath my tights, there are thermals that Scott would have been proud of. That prickly sensation at the back of my neck has to be about more than temperature. I run my eyes over the congregation, looking for clues. There it is – somebody watching me, watching them. A man. He's tall. I'd give him six foot, maybe just over, with a shock of dark, wavy hair falling in front of his eyes. 'Cheeky', that's what I'd say if I had to sum him up in one word. He's thirty or so, a handful of years older than me but so absolutely my type. As I clock him, he smiles. But I don't smile back. This is a funeral, not Speed Dating Saturday. Even I know that flirting at a funeral is bad form.

There's another guy in front of the 'looker'. He'd be a little older. The eldest brother? Almost forty maybe. He's not weeping, but he's got that genuine heartbroken, crumpled look weighing down his features. The face, it has to be said, is falling well below Floppy Hair's mean-standard. Heartbroken is shorter for a start. Not that there's anything wrong with short. I'm short myself. It has its advantages. But standing next to Floppy Hair is not doing Heartbroken any favours. I get the feeling that might be the story of Heartbroken's life.

The priest is winding up. The umbrellas are starting to twitch. Droplets catching on unwary bare flesh. People are beginning to move away. I fall back a little, pretending to look in the small, black leather bag I always have slipped over my shoulder. This is not a greyhound race. If I bolt for the gate, you can bet everyone'll notice me, and if they notice me, they'll start asking questions. *Who was that woman at the funeral? Do you think Dad/Mum was having an affair?* Or perhaps even more worrying... *Do you think Dad/Mum/the deceased could have had an illegitimate child?* Oh, yeah, that's not my deal. I don't want to go haunting anyone's life. Vague acquaintance, kind and supportive. That is what I want them to think when they remember me; the sort of young woman you'd trust. Trust is important in my line of work.

Despite the rain, Heartbroken has decided it is his duty to stand at the gate and see us all out. That normally works out okay. They remember you were the respectful one, dressed all in black despite the modern trends. They remember you were there to give the family support.

'Thank you for coming.' He's saying this like he's on a loop.

He's public school, but then this is the island; every square foot is pricey. All of these people have money.

'Thank you for coming.'

Rain's dripping down his face. He's not brushing it away.

'Thank you for coming.'

People clasp their pale, luminous hands with his as they pass or rest their fingers lightly on the dark jacket of his arm. I'm not sure what to go for. I think a brief, reassuring top-of-the-shoulder brush is probably best. I push my fingers out in order to deliver this gesture of support, but he grabs my hand between his and stares straight into my eyes.

He looks so sad. 'I'm sorry, I don't think we've met?'

'No.' This is awkward.

There are two ways you can take this kind of *awkward*. You can pause and let the other person fill the void with story, or you can grab hold of an end and follow where it goes. Seeing as it's cold, I jump in.

'You must be the son?' It's a stab in the dark. Stupid really. I should know better. But luckily, it lands.

'That's right. Oscar. And you're part of Mum's...' He hesitates, 'Bridge club, I expect?'

Bingo. 'That's me.'

I don't know the first thing about bridge. I'm more of a snap person myself. But for now... bridge it is.

'Please do come back to the house. Julia's put on a wonderful spread.'

Julia? Who the fuck is Julia? Daughter? It must be old skinny-pants. With starvers, it's often eating by proxy. In which case, I'll bet the food will be the good stuff. Fortnum and Masons all the way. I shouldn't, but... I glance out towards the car park. The umbrellas are going down. Car doors are creaking open for the mourners. People are disappearing gratefully inside their vehicles, escaping the elements. I can see Floppy Hair. He's putting down his umbrella, shaking out the rain. I know he can sense my eyes on him. There's a little flow of electricity in the air between us, the kind that makes every inch of your skin feel as if it's been cut out by a cookie cutter so that it tingles with life. But he doesn't look up.

'Okay,' I turn to broken-hearted Oscar and lay on a thick dollop of sincerity, 'of course I'll come.'

2

THE HOUSE

'I'M NOT sure I'll be back tonight. This looks promising.' I say, as my BMW follows the bobbing red tail-lights of the cars in front. We're heading out to the east of the island. I've got my mobile tucked under my chin. We're going so slow I can't see that the not driving whilst phoning rule applies. Besides, it's only boring old Janice from the office, so I think I can manage the two things at the one time.

'Well, all right then,' Janice's telephone voice is ridiculously high and wispy, making her sound permanently apologetic, 'I'll tell Jasper.'

Jasper's the boss. Although it's difficult to call him that seriously. He's got that silver-spoon, born-yesterday vibe. If he hadn't inherited money, I doubt *Jasper* and *boss* would have been two words seen in close company.

'Oh, and Kirstin?' Janice's wisp breaks through my thoughts. 'You fancy seeing that new horror film? I've got no one to go with.'

This doesn't surprise me. 'I don't like scary films.' Actually, I do. It's Janice I've got the problem with. She's all right. She's just... Oh, I don't know... not enough.

When Janice talks again, she sounds like she's trying her best to keep her voice upbeat – putting a little too much energy in. 'That's a pain. It's supposed to be really good, but... Have to go on my own then.'

One thing I do admire about Janice, she is pragmatism personified. 'I'll see you tomorrow. You can act it out for me.'

She laughs. Probably too much. I'm getting that uncomfortable desperate-for-friendship vibe, so put the phone down on her. Well, I am driving, although I do manage a quick, curious flick to the prison app, but there's still no word from my brother. He's waiting for the parole board meeting. It's a long boring story, but the gist of it is that he got caught out. The Tate were unloading some paintings. AJ and his mate got in the driver's seat and drove away with them. A prank? The gallery got all the pictures back; no harm done. Well, okay, not all the paintings came back. But he has no idea where the missing one is. But for now, it would appear that all is quiet.

I throw the phone on the driver's seat next to the order of service. Carolyn's in memorium photo is burying into the seat upholstery whilst the family crest on the back is facing up; a great, grey beast standing on its hind legs as if ready to attack. It looks a bit like a dog, but I know for a fact it's a wolf. That would be because the island myth is all about wolves. I'm working within the context of island mythology here, rather than artistic integrity. The image is not exactly Dutch masterpiece material. A quivering red tongue lolls down over a set of five sharp teeth. Every inch of this wolf says – mess with us Millfords, and we'll bite. Personally, I prefer crests with flowers. Flowers are an easy sell. Who doesn't love a bouquet?

The gravel driveway stretching out ahead is more road than drive. Even though the Millfords had to let go of most of their acres over the years, the name and the estate still pack a powerful punch of kudos. You can't even see the house from the large metal gates. Instead, there's a grumpy gamekeeper standing beside the high stone wall. His hat may be off, but there's a scowl supporting the man's thick, bearded jaw. Disgruntled staff, I think to myself as I pull past. Perhaps the *lady of the house* keeled over before she'd had time to settle his last pay cheque. Any problems, I have a crack team I can send in. 'Staging' a house is all part and parcel of the sale these days, and this place will provide one hell of a 'stage'.

The long drive meanders leisurely through landscaped grounds as if it had all the time in the world. There's no doubt that I'm heading in the right direction. We're moving caterpillar fashion; a line of four black cars dragging us along in their wake, followed by an impressive collection of Mercs, Teslas, and even the odd Bentley. I'm not worried. My BMW usually fits the bill. You can take a Beemer anywhere. A Beemer is kind of like the little black dress of the car world, from drug pushers to neat suburban semis or the backyards of the rich. It's so normal it's virtually invisible. This queue of cars, however, is taking forever.

I grab my phone from the passenger seat. I want to get hold of Marco. He's the one who tipped me off about this gig, and I really could do with a bit more info. I punch in his number. It's engaged. Typical. I switch to WhatsApp and record a message.

'Marco, it's me, Kirstin. I've been roped into attending the wake. Any more details you've got would be great. I'm working in the dark here. Wealthy old bird. Bridge player. Wrote a book. I'm reckoning...' I do a quick headcount, trawling through my memory: Sad Oscar, Floppy Hair and Fatally Thin. 'Three kids and maybe one granddaughter?'

The red hair is a problem; no one else had the red hair. All the other key players are almost as dark as me. But the tears? She has to be a high-profile relly, so, granddaughter.

I stare out of my window, watching as a large oak slides gracefully past as if it's on casters. We're going so slow I can almost see it growing.

'Haven't got to the house yet, but it's looking promising. Reckon you've earned your commission on this one.'

The house does not disappoint. I'm going to say Georgian, though I think something must have been there before. It's big, but not too big. Despite what people think before they win the lottery, *laughably big* is not as desirable as it sounds. It's almost impossible to make something too big feel like a home. Nobody wants more than eight bedrooms. Nobody has enough friends. You get the big house and you'll be constantly reminded of the fact that, when it comes down to it, there are only a handful of people you want filling your spare rooms. The Millford house does sit a little too close to the cliff edge for comfort, and that can be a problem when you're in the two million and under bracket. People are nervous of their 'life's savings' slipping into the sea, but when you're luxuriating in the four million and above mark, seriously, these people don't give a fuck.

'Funniest thing. You know that property we bought in Cornwall? The one on the island? Well, it just upped and fell over the cliff.' A snip at four mil when you can use it as a talking point. And I don't even have to stick my foot over the door of the Millfords' house to know that we are comfortably in the 'Don't give a fuck' price bracket. Besides, Phil and Kirsty, and every single one of those turn-it-quick property shows were right about one thing – location. You want to build somewhere on this island, you have to buy four walls and knock them down. So, a property's potential cliff-top hara-kiri might even be a selling point. I can't wait to get myself a peek inside. Nearing the large, open door, I can hear that Sad Oscar's got himself a new mantra.

'Welcome. Please hand your coats to Julia. The fire's on in the drawing room.'

I glance around the vast entrance hall, waiting my turn to be told about Julia and the fire. The place is smartly turned out. Cathedral-style candles give off dense spiced aromas that speak of opulence. There's a lovely black-and-white marble floor like a chessboard leading the eye beyond the doorway. So far, I'm getting a good vibe. Despite the size, the house still has that genuinely lived-in feel, and the statement staircase is impressive but not too in-your-face. Equally so for the chandelier. It's large and sparkly but not gauche or too bling. So far, everything is on track.

I look around for 'Julia'. But Ms Fatally Thin is nowhere to be seen. Perhaps she's standing sideways. Then I see a small, round-faced woman struggling under an enormous pile of coats and realise my mistake – this must be Julia.

'Let me help you there,' I say, loosening myself from the cluster of mourners beside the door and taking a few coats from the amply upholstered, flustering woman in her late fifties.

She eyes me, all appreciation.

'Thank you,' she says, relieved, as she hands over even more wodges of expensive, damp material. 'I'm all behind,' she admits breathlessly, her green eyes darting awkwardly around the room and the constant in-fill of people.

'How can I help?' I say. I love that phrase. It's the best phrase in the entire world, especially when you want to get something. You say that short, sweet sentence and people just open up. The woman that must be Julia looks at me as if she just might plant a powdered, pink kiss on my cheek.

'I'm still getting the food out,' she blusters before lowering her voice. 'I didn't expect you all back so soon.'

'The rain,' I offer. And she smiles a small, hurried smile, understanding, but not a whole heap interested – there's just too much going on. 'It chased us out of the churchyard,' I offer for context. 'Where shall I take the coats?'

'I'm putting them in the blue bedroom. It's upstairs at the front, overlooking the drive.'

I don't need a second invitation. I sling more rain-wet fabric over my arms and mount the stairs.

As I climb, people continue piling into the hallway beneath me. This is a seriously big 'do'; at least two hundred friends and mourners. I'm impressed.

I get a bit 'lost' on my way to the Blue Room. I'm keen to get the *lay of the land*, and this seems like an ideal opportunity. I'll need to come back and do a full recce. Mike will have to bring his camera as well. We'll do preliminary even before we get to the drones. If it's under one million, I do the photos myself. I've got a wide-angle lens and a tripod. I'm pretty good with Photoshop too, can switch a sky around from grey to blue with just a few clicks of the old mouse. But something like this place, there'll be a glossy brochure to fill and there's no point in being cheap. My absolute favourite thing is writing the copy, and I can still do that. Paint a picture with my words. In truth, I'd have loved to be a journalist. If I could pick any job in the whole wide world, that would be it. In the meantime, without a fairy godmother or a parallel universe in the side wings, writing copy is the next best thing. But I'm getting ahead of myself; for now, I just need to get the listing.

The first room I peer into is pink. The wallpaper hand-painted; those miniature budding roses might look identical, but up close, minor differences betray the human element. There's an en suite. This is a good sign. Sometimes, with these old places, the bathrooms are a bit of an afterthought. Thankfully, it looks like the house has been adapted for comfort. A row of silver hairbrushes are laid with military precision across a gleaming walnut dressing table. I let my fingers slip over them. They're beauties, but I know my limits. Things like these, floating across the surface of a room, they're treasured. Somebody dusts around each and every item at least once a week. Take something like this, and alarm bells will be ringing before I've scoffed down half a canapé. It's the forgotten treasures you need to seek out. The ones that people have misplaced, the things that have been put somewhere up high, or on a shelf, or forgotten in a coat pocket and slipped out of everybody's mind. But I don't do that anymore, I remind myself. I haven't done that for years. I've got bigger fish to fry, and everything I do now is legal. Almost.

The room smells of freshly sprayed scent. Coco Mademoiselle, if I'm not mistaken. Someone youngish then. There's a lipstick on the dressing table next to the brushes, and a case tucked beside the bed. A pink silk scarf lays abandoned on the Queen Anne chair, and the pillows aren't sitting exactly straight. There could be nightclothes tucked underneath. Someone must be overnighting here.

Still carrying my cargo of coats, I slip into the en suite. It smells of lavender. A little too aggressively. Perhaps someone's having problems sleeping? There's a wash bag open on the sink, its contents spilling out. A concealer stick standing ready and waiting directly beside the mirror. Whoever it is, they've been trying to cover up tears or spots. Given that this is a funeral, I'll go with the former. The bathroom is too small to be impressive, and Carolyn, or her project manager has seriously overspent on the taps. They'll never get that back, but then they don't care. That's when I hear it, and my heart sinks – footsteps thundering along the landing outside. If I was in the bedroom, then I could plead incompetent navigation, but I'm in the en suite. I am so obviously snooping, not using the *facilities* – the armful of coats is a dead giveaway.

Nothing for it; I pull the door to the bathroom closed. Well, not completely closed. With Marco not picking up his texts, I'm still in the dark as to the family layout, and I am a firm believer in the usefulness of a little eavesdropping.

From the crack in the door, I can just about see a slice of the room and the young redhead as she storms in. She's reflected in the dressing-table mirror. Tracks carved by tears run over her cheeks. I seriously hope she's not going to start looking for that concealer. Then it hits me. It's not heartbreak that's written on those features; it's anger. I reckon if you were to touch her forehead, your fingers would burn. This woman is steaming mad.

'Not good enough,' she spits angrily.

Someone I can't see pulls the door to the room shut; this conversation is clearly private. Since my view is obscured, I have no idea who she's talking to; whoever it is, they're just out of the reflection. Without a reply, they throw something across the double bed towards her – an A4 brown envelope. It must be stuffed with something pretty heavy because it gives a resounding thud as it falls onto the flowered coverlet. The redhead glances down at the package as if it's something disgusting, but the tears stop. The anger stops. She doesn't pick the thing up straight away.

'If they knew about you…' she says bitterly. 'Bastard. Absolute bastard,' she hisses through gritted teeth as she grabs the package and storms back out.

I don't move. I've got the nasty feeling that whoever she was just talking to is still lingering. I hold my breath. I can't afford to let the aforesaid *bastard* in the room know that I'm here.

The floorboards outside the bathroom creak. I flatten back against the tiled wall. It sounds as though someone is stepping cautiously over the floor towards me. Through the crack in the door, I glance again into the mirror. My breath freezing like a lump of cold porridge in my throat. Shit! You can see me. Not in the main part of the glass but in the bevelled edge; I just saw my own ghostly, pale, scared-shitless face. They must be able to see it too. I need to come up with an excuse. Another creak. I need to have some reason for being here. I look at the toilet. That would do, but why the coats? I need to put the coats down, sit on the loo, flush it. Create a new beginning; that's what my brother AJ would say. If a scenario's not working for you, spin it from fresh. But why would I be sitting on the toilet with a pile of coats and the door open? Why would anyone? Suddenly my phone buzzes; an incoming text! I drop the coats. Catch my breath and expel a rush of air through my lungs as I pull myself on top of the situation.

'Sorry,' I say loudly. 'I'm in here.'

I pull the door back, but the room is empty. No one. The radiator creaks loudly as relief floods my body. This is an old house. It makes noises all on its own. It doesn't need people. Whoever it was must have gone out with the redhead. I glance towards the coats I'd flung haphazardly over the bath. There's a mottled grey expensive fur dangling an arm wantonly into the tub, its sleeve crumpled and wet from the dripping tap. I need to get on with the job in hand before I end up having to fend off an insurance claim for a coat that costs more than my annual wage packet.

I put the coats in the Blue Room just like I'd said I would. The room is a beauty. It must be the guest room – proper. No expense has been spared. I lay my bundle gently over the coverlet in a series of neat coat piles before glancing out of the window at the long drive leading back to the main road. Lovely. I twist my body slightly to take in the other side of the property and the crumbling cliff edge. What would it be like to wake up to this every morning? How would that feel? I think of my childhood home back in West Toxteth. The windows that mostly streamed with condensation. The absent mother, the all too present father. Some people don't know they're born. There's a buzz in my pocket. I glance at my phone as a text comes through. My brother. The message is on the app. He's there now. Bugger. I would love to talk to him, but… I've already been gone from the party for too long.

Kind of busy.

I text into the app.
Straight away, a message pings back.

Sure. Don't do anything I wouldn't.

Well, that leaves a wide-open field.

3

THE SENTIMENT

THE HALLWAY HAS EMPTIED by the time I get down. There's a small cluster of coats that someone's parked on a chair. I could take them up, but I'm tired of that game. I follow the sounds of voices through to the left side of the house and into what must be the drawing room. It's full of people dressed in shades of black, standing in small groups, glasses in hand. An older couple have planted themselves directly in front of the open fire, their clothes letting out wispy ghosts of steam. They must have got a soaking at the service. Never leave your car without an umbrella, even if you are out on the coast and it's windy as hell. They get no sympathy from me; they're old enough to know this. Now they'll stand hogging the heat for the rest of the event. Not that it's cold in here, but I would have liked a closer look at the fireplace. It's jet black with small rinds of white set into it – fossilised marble if I'm not mistaken. Very unusual. Very expensive. Very nice.

The room's open at either end, so there's a drawing-room bit, a sitting-room bit and what looks like a dining-room bit. There's a big table in the dining room, pushed up along one wall and pinned down with more food than your average family would get through in a year. I glance from end to end of the three interconnecting rooms. This is a lot of square footage with a good flow. Shame it's not on the mainland. That extra bit of water between the house and Cornwall will probably put the London contingent off. It's that step too far on a Friday night. Unless, of course, you've got a helicopter.

I scan the room, trying to work out relationships. Most of these people aren't of interest. It's only the immediate family I want to focus on, the decision-makers.

'So glad you made it back to the house.'

I feel myself jump out of my sensible black courts, turning to find Oscar at my elbow, and having to readjust my features quickly from curious to respectful.

'And thank you for helping Julia. We're all finding this... overwhelming.'

'Of course.' My voice sounds sincere, reassuring. I have so totally mastered *empathy*.

'It was so sudden,' he says sadly.

I'm still not up to speed on the precise details of how the *sudden* came about or its exact shape. I rest one hand pragmatically on Oscar's arm, hoping he'll give me a little more juice to go on. He doesn't, so I pull one of my go-to favourites out of the kitbag. 'How are you and the family holding up?'

He does a quick sideways shrug, as though it's difficult to get to grips with the absolute shitshow of the situation, but he'll do his best. 'It's hit Miri – Miranda – hard.' Oscar inclines his head towards the pretty, young redhead, who is now standing beside the man and woman drying out beside the fire. Miri's shoulders are held a little too high, her face a little too fixed. I get the feeling she's still set to mad-mode from her interaction upstairs with the envelope. Chances are that the person who slipped her the manila wasn't family. It could have been a friend. Although not a very good friend, to be hassling poor Miri at her grandmother's wake.

'And Erica's sunk herself into hostess role.'

He doesn't need to point Erica out. Erica is the painfully thin woman circulating the room with a silver tray packed full of state-of-the-art canapés.

'There's nothing Erica likes more than organising us all.' He smiles a small, strained smile. 'She has her own way of doing things, and hers is, of course, always the *best* way.' There's a touch of sarcasm colouring the word *best.* 'And as for Luke, well, as usual, my brother will just breeze in and breeze back out again.'

Luke has to be the looker. Flashy eyes, floppy hair, crooked smile – all of that says *breezer*. I glance around the room. Luke must be *breezing* elsewhere because he's not visible.

'And Tim. Well, he's...'

'Tim?' I've missed someone. Unless Tim is the Dickensian weasel guy that I thought I recognised. But that doesn't seem right. Sad Oscar had been listing off siblings, blood relatives. The Dickensian guy was... well, from somewhere else, and I don't mean like last century *somewhere else*. Different genealogy. I scan the room again, this time with a great deal more care, on the hunt for Tim.

'Oh, Niamh. You two must know each other,' Oscar announces brightly.

I glance over my shoulder and realise, to my horror, I'm being introduced.

In front of me stands a neat, wry-looking woman who could be anything from late fifties to struggling towards seventy. Her hair is streaked wiry grey with small flecks of in-for-the-long-run black and manacled at the top of her head in a series of tortoiseshell clips. Despite the sad occasion, Niamh has chosen to wear a dark purple kaftan and each of her fat, flabby arms are adorned with silver bangles. The rings are something else. This woman is jewelled to the knuckle on most fingers. Costume jewellery, I would have said, unless her surname is Windsor.

Oscar smiles graciously. 'This...' Suddenly, he squirms. 'I'm so sorry.' He turns to face me. 'I didn't catch your name?'

Not surprisingly – I hadn't got to that part yet.

'Kirstin,' I say simply.

'Yes, of course.' There's a smile in his voice like he knew this all along. I get the feeling Oscar suffers from a crippling case of good manners.

'Kirstin is part of the bridge club,' he continues.

Niamh gives me a long, hard stare, and my heart falters. This could all start going downhill rapidly.

'The online group?' Niamh asks helpfully.

'That's the one.' I smile.

Niamh's face softens. 'Carolyn did love that group.'

'Yes,' I say enthusiastically.

'But you're all so scattered geographically?'

'Actually, I live locally.' This is all shaping up.

'Surely not on the island?'

Hmm, there may have been a touch of inverse snobbery there. But then again, for all her flamboyance, Niamh has a kind face and the kind of fashion choices that you could pick up at a charity shop.

'A bit above my budget.' I laugh sweetly. 'I work on the mainland.'

She gives me a genuine smile. This is all going so well. I cannot believe my luck. 'I'm a...'

And I'm just about to tell her – within Oscar's earwigging range – that *I'm an estate agent by trade,* that *I specialise in big properties* – the million-plus market, that *I have clients itching to snap up places on the coast. Places like this,* is the part I would leave out because it's there by implication. But just as plan A is about to steam effortlessly into action, there's an almighty crash. The sound vibrates through the room like a clap of thunder followed by the splintering of glass. A lot of glass. Everyone stops talking. They stop moving as well. Frozen to the spot and listening out into the nothingness that the sound left in its wake. Listening till our ears buzz and cutting through the silence we hear a male voice, loud, angry and oh-so bitter.

'You think I don't know what's going on here?'

Oscar's face pales. 'Sorry,' he whispers painfully as the voice from the other room continues.

'Shut up,' the voice growls. 'Isn't that what you want? You want everyone to just keep quiet. Keep their mouths shut. You hated her. Everyone did.'

Without another word, Oscar dashes towards the shouting. Trying not to look too obvious, I follow. Everyone else is far too polite and well-bred to join the train. They stand transfixed in the drawing room. But on a scale of politeness to curiosity, I'd say I'm right over there on the curiosity side, especially when I have a vested interest. And I'm pretty sure that's the case here. Because I'm willing to bet the voice I heard insult-slinging from the hallway will belong to the mysterious Tim. And it only takes one *Tim* contesting a will to get the whole property sale grinding to a halt. This house could easily take a dive into the sea long before things got sorted. Goodbye, big bonus.

But when I get to the hallway, all my wheeling-dealing schemes fail me. There's a man sprawling in the middle of the hall, lying in a sea of glass across the chessboard tiles. His face pressed against the cold marble as if it's too heavy to lift. Above us, dangling from the ceiling, is what looks like the chewed-off tail of a large cable – the rope that was holding the chandelier.

Miranda runs shrieking from the party towards the prone figure. She's not just crying now; the tonal quality has worked itself up a notch or two till it could shatter crystal all on its own. Her kitten-heeled shoes grind to a halt at the halo of glass, as a new, clipped voice comes from behind me.

'Get the doctor.'

I know who that voice belongs to even before I set my eyes on her. It has to be Erica. *Good in a crisis*, that would be Erica.

'My God, Timmy,' she says, an underlying exhaustion to her

voice, as if this whole little scene is par for the course and just a tad tedious. As though Poor Timmy gets through a chandelier a week.

I just continue to stare, wishing I could get a glimpse of his face. Why isn't he lifting it?

'Erica,' Miranda wails. 'How dare you snap at him?'

'Calm down, everyone, please.' Oscar waves his arms like a conductor in search of an elusive harmony as he simultaneously attempts to usher us all out of the scene. I'm not sure if it's the glass he's worried about or more what might come out of Timmy's mouth. Everyone wants to be prime mourner at a wake. Everyone thinks they're the one with the 'special' relationship. Everyone wants to say, *'You all hated... whoever'*, and stick themselves at the centre. Maybe that's Timmy's thing? Or maybe he's right, and nobody did like Carolyn – they're all just acting a part. He's still not lifting his head, though.

'Please go back into the drawing room,' Oscar continues, dropping his arms slightly, turning his back on poor Timmy.

'Has anyone even asked if he's all right?' I can't help myself. It's out of my mouth before I have a chance to staple the damn thing shut. That's a Liverpool childhood for you; there's no laying low. If it's on the tip of your tongue, it's out in the room.

Everybody's staring at me, so there's nothing for it. I don't normally like attention, but something needs to be done, and I'm the nominated first aider at the office. It was a two-day residential with catering. I can't remember that much, but the one thing I did get was that the first thing you do is check the body for vitals. Carefully I pick my way over the glass. It crunches under my feet like sugared cracknel, but there's nothing sweet about this; take my shoes off and it would bite. When I get beside Timmy, I brush a patch of shards to the side and kneel. Timmy's bigger than the other brothers, wider and with a thick neck. It might have been a rugby player's build once, but that's gone. What was once muscle has idled itself into folds of unneeded fat. This sort of *lumpen* comes from not being active enough. He's let himself go. I'd say he's got at least five years of *one-more-burger-for-the-road* under his belt. I stroke his hand gently, still not getting why he's not moving. I can't see that the thing hit him anywhere.

'Timmy, is it?' I say gently.

There's an affirmative groan.

'Are you all right?'

'Hmph.' He gives an ironic snort.

I glance around again at the field of glass. 'Okay,' I say, 'that was a bit of a stupid question.'

He's conscious. He's breathing. He's alert. There are no cuts on his head, so the chandelier must have missed him when it came down. 'I don't think it hit you,' I say softly. 'Do you think you can move?'

'No,' he growls. His voice sounding strangely irritated.

I glance around me again. This is not a good place to be. Some of those glass splinters look vicious.

'I think it missed you. We should get you up. There's glass everywhere. You can lean on me.'

'No,' he barks.

'For Christ's sake,' Miri screams.

They're all standing outside of the chaos, looking in, which is irritating: we need to get him out. 'Lean on me, Timmy.' I shift forward, offering my shoulder. He's a heavy-looking bloke. I'm going to need all of my body weight to balance pulling him up.

'No,' he snaps again.

It's then that I see it out of the corner of my eye. I hadn't taken it in at first because it didn't look right. Normally they're pretty easy to spot. But this one is on its side and partially crushed. Shit. It's a wheelchair.

'For God's sake.' Luke's on the scene, not so much *breezing* now as lunging forward.

Thank goodness for that, I think. At least someone's got a bit of momentum.

'The doctor's on his way,' Julia says, her voice sounding genuinely concerned. She's working towards Timmy with a large broom, creating a small path in front of her. 'Timmy,' she says kindly, kneeling beside me and searching for his eyes. His face is still down. He doesn't move it. The glass is everywhere.

'I need to get out,' he moans. 'I'm not safe.'

He sounds scared. I shoot Julia a look – I'm out of my depth here. Why isn't he safe? Is it just the glass? Is he even properly aware of it with his face pinned to the floor? Julia just shakes her head sadly.

'It's okay, love,' she says reassuringly. 'Just stay where you are. Help's coming.'

I feel my shoulder twisting around as someone pulls me gently back. Luke's hand circles mine. 'It's all under control,' he says simply, as the Dickensian man I saw at the funeral pushes past.

'Timmy? Dr Meerson here.'

So, the Dickensian man is a doctor. Maybe that's where we've met? He's not at the practice I go to. Not that I'm sick much, but maybe he just steps in occasionally. A locum?

'Well, this is a bit of a mess.'

I can't help it; I don't like Dr Meerson. His tone is patronising. It's as if he's speaking to a child. I glance around me, looking for irritated faces, but no one else seems to be taking offence. Suddenly it feels like I'm done here. It's under control. I push my toes underneath me, readying myself to stand, but as I do, Timmy shoots out a blood-soaked hand, a hand studded with fragments of glass, and grips hold of me tightly. The action is so sudden, so unexpected, my heart jerks and I let slip an involuntary gasp. Transfixed, I stare at him as, with every sinew in his neck straining, he raises his head just an inch from the floor. His piercing blue eyes bore into mine. It's that same, good-looking face that Luke's carrying around so casually. Only, on Timmy, it's all different. There's no floppy hair, no sense of fun. Timmy is crew-cut, his style more mercenary than fashion, but that isn't the disturbing thing. What disturbs me most is that when I look into his eyes, it's like looking into a storm. They're large, a troubled blue, scared-looking and constantly shifting. It's hard to imagine that his mind would ever get much rest.

'I'm in danger,' he chokes.

I don't understand. I try to pull my hand away, but he won't release me. Instead, he fixes me with those crazy blue eyes, and squeezes me hard. 'And you, you're in danger too.'

That's when I realise; it isn't just the wheelchair – Timmy's not entirely *all there*.

'Are you okay?' Luke's voice is full of concern. We're sitting in the kitchen, away from prying eyes. Julia's made me a hot chocolate. I don't know why I feel so shaken, but I do. Timmy may be disturbed, paranoid, out of his mind, but there was something so elemental and haunting about his sense of panic.

'I'll live,' I say.

'I hope so. One coffin a day is my limit.' Luke smiles.

'How did that thing come down?'

'The chandelier? That I can't tell you. It's checked every year. I think it was restrung recently. It might still be insured. No doubt Erica's onto them as we speak. Not that that's the main concern here. My sister has a habit of missing the point in favour of logistics. It was bloody lucky it didn't squash anyone.'

'Apart from Timmy.'

'Yeah. Thank Christ it wasn't a direct hit. Poor bugger.'

I take a sip of the chocolate. It's real, not powdered brown sugar. This is the proper stuff, rich and creamy. Only, after what happened, my stomach can barely take it. 'What's wrong with Timmy?' I ask.

'You mean, normally? When chandeliers aren't dropping on him?'

I know I shouldn't, but I laugh. 'Sorry.'

'No, please, don't be. It's been a tough day. It's great to hear something...' he hesitates, 'unguarded for a change.'

'When he looked at me, he looked...'

'Mad?'

The brutality of the statement hits me like a punch. 'No. No, that's not what I saw. Disturbed.'

Luke glances down sadly. I get the feeling this story is not an easy one to tell.

'It started with the legs.'

'Was he in the army?'

Luke's mouth creases at the edges with a small, ironic lilt. 'Nothing so worthy. He was bumming around Cambodia. It was a landmine.'

'Shit.'

'No kidding.'

'Then the paranoia kicked in. It was as if he had to make it worse. Grab himself a little PTSD while he was at it. I'm not saying what happened wasn't tragic, but Timmy had to make it terrible. Make it mean more. Does that sound cruel?'

I shrug. 'I don't know.'

'Mum dying, that's knocked him for six. Knocked all of us, apart from Oscar and Erica. Oscar has a way of addressing things, compartmentalising. And Erica, I'm not sure she allows herself to feel emotion.'

'Oscar looked heartbroken.'

'Yeah?' Luke chews over the thought, his hair falling down over his eyes. 'Sorry, my scepticism is uncalled for.'

'Siblings,' I say, trying to keep my tone light.

'More death us do part than a marriage. I prefer friends. Friends you choose. Siblings you have to carry.'

'That's a bleak view.'

'Poor little rich kid.'

I nod, eyebrows raised. He said it, not me.

'Okay, yeah, we are insanely privileged. I know that. We can afford not to bicker.'

'It would be easy enough to take yourself off to another room.'

He laughs.

'It must have been amazing growing up here.'

This stops the laughter short, and I get the sneaking feeling that Luke wouldn't have described his *growing up* years in quite that way, but I don't need all the details; I have an agenda. He might be a truly lovely chunk of eye candy, but the conversation needs to move on. 'Will you keep it? I mean, keep the house in the family?'

'Now there's a question.'

'Well,' I say, taking a casual sip of my chocolate as though mulling things over, 'it was your mother's house and now...' I don't like to push, but I'm not here for the buffet or glass juggling.

'I think we should sell.'

One point for me.

'But... You know... families. And of course, there's Timmy.'

'Things might be better for him on the mainland.'

'Better for who?' Luke mumbles.

And for a heart-stopping moment, I think he's onto me. 'Sorry?'

'Oh, nothing.' He flashes me one of his smiles. 'It's complicated.' He draws the words out as if they might last forever. But they're shot down too soon.

'Luke?' Erica's crisp, clear voice calls down the stairs into the kitchen.

'That would be my cue,' he exhales, with more than a little of the condemned man about him. 'Which is a shame because I would rather stay here with you. If one more person tells me what a wonderful woman she was...'

'Wasn't she?'

He pauses for a moment, sifting back through his memories, before simply shaking his head. 'I couldn't even begin to sum Carolyn up. A dark horse, I'd say.'

'Of your own mother?'

But he's standing. 'I should go help.'

I get the feeling that if there is a direct answer, he has no intention of giving it to me.

So, Carolyn was a 'dark horse'. Women can be anything. Far too many end up baking cakes and wiping their children's backsides. I know I probably shouldn't, but I always admire the dark horse variety. I realise I'd love to be able to say that of my own mother. In fact, I'd love to be able to say anything about her.

I sit for a while in the warm basement kitchen, gazing out of the high windows, watching as the rain chases down the windowpanes like thick silver worms. The kitchen is cosy, comforting despite the fact that it's in desperate need of an overhaul. Not a problem, as far as securing a sale goes. Even if a kitchen doesn't need an overhaul, at this end of the market, it will invariably get one once a new occupant steps their expensively clad feet over the welcome mat.

'You were very brave up there.'

The voice cuts through my thoughts and I turn to see Julia's kind face, realising instantly why this space makes you want to stay – this is Julia's domain.

'I did nothing. I thought your tactic with the broom was genius.'

She laughs, then stops herself guiltily, remembering the

circumstances. 'Genius, well I'm not sure anyone's ever described me as that.'

'I should go,' I say, pushing back my chair.

'No, please.' She reaches out to touch my shoulder. 'Don't let me chase you away. Please stay. It's all under control upstairs, and I find I don't really want to be left alone.' There's an air of sadness to her posture, her shoulders slumped, her body seeming to have aged in only a few brief hours. 'I've been working for Carolyn for over forty years.'

'Wow. Long time.'

She nods sadly, taking a seat for herself opposite me.

'How old were you when you first started?' I ask.

'Twenty.' She smiles with a girlish innocence. 'Well, nineteen, if we are being strictly accurate.'

'The end of an era,' I offer. It's a bit trite, but people love to think of their lives in that way: end of an era, new chapter, etc., etc. 'Will you stay on?'

She glances sadly at her hands. 'You know what families are like.'

That didn't answer my question.

She smiles kindly at me. 'You have siblings yourself?'

'No,' I lie. I always feel guilty denying my brother, but he'd understand. In fact, he'd encourage me to do just that. I'll ring him when I get home, assuage my conscience with a bit of sisterly banter.

'Only child,' I tell her.

She gives me a hard stare.

'Mum and Dad still alive?'

'Never really knew my mum. She died...' I could kick myself. I don't have to tell Julia this. But now she's looking at me, waiting for more. Best get it over quick. 'She died early on. My dad...' Even the word 'dad' makes me prickle. Julia doesn't miss a beat.

'He played a hard hand with you?'

More than once, if she really wanted to know. But that's my

story, not hers. 'He was wonderful,' I lie. It's the easiest way. No one is interested in *wonderful*. 'But I should be going,' I say brightly. My abandoned brolly will give me an excuse to get back in touch. I am done for the day.

Julia nods. 'It's getting late. Leave now, and you can catch the six-thirty ferry. I think they've cancelled the next two. There's talk of a gale force eight.'

4

MEDDLING

JULIA LETS me out of the basement door, and as I climb the stone steps into the dark, damp air, I feel one of AJ's well-worn superstitions flapping around my brain like a frantic seagull that's discovered a dropped chip in the crack of a pavement. I have no truck with superstition. I'll walk under ladders, never acknowledge magpies and don't care how many black cats choose to avoid crossing my path. If I had any influence at all over the universe, each and every superstition would be neatly expunged from the human brain. Although, perhaps there is some kind of logic to this one – *enter at the front door, leave as a tradesman, that's where you'll stick.* But as I scurry up the steps into the damp blanket of night, I remind myself that I do not have time for superstitious rubbish. Besides, there is no way I'd go back into the house now. The last thing I want to do is draw attention to myself. I've done the groundwork.

There's only a handful of cars parked up on the gravel illuminated in patches of light thrown from the wide house windows. There's another red BMW, though it's much newer than mine. This last straggle of vehicles must belong to the family. The guests probably heard about the bad weather. Most of them will be heading for the same ferry I'm trying to catch myself.

I grab my coat from the back seat of my car and slip it on. I want to make sure that when I arrive at the terminal I'm not last in the queue if there's any hint of a bun-fight for tickets.

Pulling out onto the drive, I leave the house lights glimmering behind me. The place is lit up like a wedding cake. Even in the darkness, you can tell it's something special. I hope to God I get the instruction. Maybe I won't leave the umbrella thing for two weeks. Maybe I should go back in after seven days? I'll put an alert on my phone. My car slips out of the iron gateway onto the darkened road. It'll be like this all the way into town. There are no streetlights out here. The trees arch above my headlights like witches' fingers clawing at the moonless night. I lean forward in my seat so I can stare up into the sky, and something scratches at my skin. I know straight off what it is. It must be a tiny sliver of glass from the shattered chandelier sticking to my jumper. I pull over. There's no need for indicators. I'm the only person out here. Slipping off my coat I glance down at my cardi. A trace of silver sparkles catches my eye – glass. I'll have to take the cardi off, even though it'll only be bare flesh and bra underneath my coat.

Surprisingly, the silk lining feels lovely against my skin. Seriously nice. I should do this more often. I belt back up and put the car into gear. I know I'll have to welly my foot down now if I want to make that ferry. Luckily, the roads are clear. The engine kicks in, the car rolls forward, but then there's this odd splutter. More fart than fuel connection. The peddle dies under the ball of my foot.

'Can you give me your location?' the lady from the recovery service asks.

I stare out of the window, facing off a wall of featureless darkness. 'I'm on the main island. Probably a few miles from the Millford Estate. It's quite a way out of town.'

'There's a garage in Kernow. We'd have to call them. Are you on your own?'

'Yes.'

'Okay. Do you have charge on your cell phone?'

I glance at it. 'Thirty per cent.'

'You say it's not the car battery that's the problem? And you haven't run out of fuel?'

'The headlights are still on, and I filled the tank earlier today.'

'Okay. I'll call you back.'

The phone goes dead. Suddenly, I feel very alone. There's a lay-by just a few feet in front of the car. I slip off the handbrake and let the wheels roll into it. Then sit back and wait.

Luckily, within minutes, my phone vibrates. I hit answer.

'Ms Conroy?' It's the same woman from the recovery service, her voice tight but efficient. 'We've spoken to the garage on the island. They've got another emergency. They say it'll be two hours.'

'I'm a single woman. On my own.' I play the fear card.

'Can you go back to your friends' house, wait there?'

This is a chilling thought. 'They're not really friends.'

'I'm sure they wouldn't mind.'

'No.' But maybe I would. Besides, it's a long driveway. 'I think I can walk to the ferry. That might be my best bet. Hopefully, they won't have cancelled the nine thirty. I'll leave the key on the tyre. The vehicle's in a kind of passing place, so it should be fine. Can you get the garage to tow it to the terminal? I'll grab it in a couple of days.'

It's not a perfect plan, but it's better than no plan. Besides, I'm a fidget. I hate sitting still. So I change my shoes for the pair of flats that I always keep in the car before going to grab my umbrella, and remembering with a wave of irritation that it's back at the house, waiting for me to retrieve it with the old *'Oh, so sorry, but I think I forgot...'* Just my luck.

Locking the car, I put the key on top of the driver's wheel. Luckily, the rain has dropped off so I set out into the darkness, wishing I'd left the wake a damn sight earlier, my shoes making a lonesome squelch on the tarmac. I'm not using my phone as a torch because there's not enough battery. So, it's dark, really dark, the sort of dark that makes you want to talk to yourself. A couple of times, I find myself wishing I'd stayed in the car, wondering if I should turn back. Then, suddenly I think about that stupid dog/wolf on the order of service. Who in their right minds would have a snarling symbol of a wolf for a family crest, even if it does tie in with the local stories, the ones that like to 'claim' this small island is where the wolves live?

In reality, wolves don't live anywhere anymore. Maybe the outback of Russia, but certainly not here. They're an endangered species. But okay, so there used to be wolves all over the country; great snarling beasts, bigger than dogs and nastier with it. Legend has it that at first, the humans and the wolves lived alongside each other okay. Sometimes they even worked together. If there were troublesome predators, they'd join forces – the wolves rounding the predators up and delivering them to the people so the people could finish the pesky beasts off with an axe. The wolves were okay about the people. In fact, the wolves thought the people were funny because they wore clothes and worried about houses. But the people didn't like the wolves. The people said that wolves could shape-shift. They could look human if they chose, and when the wolves took on human form, they loved nothing more than to play tricks on the people. For instance, you might cosy up next to your husband one night, only to discover the following day that the warm body in bed beside you couldn't have been your spouse – he'd been working late. You'd been shacked up with an entirely different kind of beast. According to the legend, the wolves used to absolutely love that old chestnut. Unsurprisingly, the humans didn't find it funny. Not one bit. So the humans started to systematically kill all the wolves. It was difficult because of the shape-shifting thing. You had to keep your wits about you, but gradually, over time, the humans figured they'd got rid of every last wolf. Only there was this one woman, she'd slept with a wolf, and she didn't tell anyone because she liked the wolf better than her husband. He was gentle in her bed, and his breath sounded like music. At least that's how the legend goes. So, when she felt the wolf's baby growing inside her, she knew she had to act. She knew the humans would find out, and when they found out, they'd kill her and the child. So, she made herself a raft out of ash and willow and rowed out to the island. People say – and this is ridiculous because the story is from way back when, before electricity and everything that makes life normal – but people still like to say that she lives on the island even now with her wolf child.

And this is the thought, the ridiculous thought that keeps hammering around my brain creeping me out as I walk. It is stupid and irritating and complete fairy-tale fiction, but it's easy to tell yourself that from the comfort of your sitting room, not so easy when you're out in the middle of nowhere, trudging through the darkness, with only the wind and the beating of unseen wings for company.

My phone vibrates. I glance at the screen. Someone is calling – Marco. I may have very little battery left, but I'm desperate for a human voice. I pick up.

'Marco. Bloody hell. This is a nightmare. I'm on the island. My car's broken down.'

'What, Wolf Island?'

'Nobody calls it that anymore,' I say, trying to suppress a shiver. 'I'm walking to the ferry terminal in town.'

'Bugger.'

'You're telling me.'

'How did it go?'

The fear starts to drop away. It feels so good to be back in the *normal*. 'Well, the house is amazing.'

'Marco does it again. Don't I always get the good ones for you? Although this one came through a...' I can almost hear the smile. 'Let's just say... an odd route.'

'Oh?'

There's a crackle on the line. His voice is breaking up. There are lost words that I can't fill in, so I carry on taking the weight of the conversation. 'I tell you what. If we land this, we'll be made up for life.'

'Will they sell?'

'That I don't know. You can't just slip your business card into a person's hand over a coffin.'

'I never ask how you do it,' he says, with a note of wry amusement.

'Yeah, well, I don't do it like that.' The road narrows slightly. There's a stone marker that I just manage to avoid banging my foot against; an old signpost. I need to take more care. 'It's early days,' I say, moving on past the marker. 'There's a lot of players on the field.'

'That can slow things...' Again, his voice breaks up. I lose the end of his sentence. It doesn't matter. I got the gist.

'I know. But...'

SMASH.

I am flying through the air, sweeping through the darkness. There's a pain in my head that shoots down my left side like a volcano of fire, as my brain rattles like jelly inside my cranium. It hurts. It all hurts. My God, it hurts. In the bushes, bushes that are suddenly right in front of my face, I see movement. Eyes. I can see the staring whites of eyeballs. Staring, staring before one solitary bloodshot blink. The lids close wearily and some great hairy creature slips away into the undergrowth. I'm going to die.

Suddenly I'm standing in a square, people all around me. I know this place but can't figure out why. The ground is white. The sky is white. Is it snowing? I'm not sure. Behind me, I can hear a voice. It sounds as if it's been squashed through a cheese grater. 'That's the way to do it. That's the way…' says the voice as the white ground beneath me is sucked into a plughole of darkness. Nothing. There is nothing but pain. I am going to die. A lightning bolt shines right through my retinas into my brain, making me wince back to reality and the damp, dark road stretching out forever.

'Kirstin?'

It's a torch, a beam of light. I squint and push it away. The pain in my left arm is unbelievable.

'Sorry. I'm so. Christ, I'm so…' It's Luke. 'But… what the fuck were you doing in the road?'

'My car…' My voice sounds mothballed and cracked, as though it hasn't been used for years. 'It broke down.'

He glances along the road to where my car must be. 'I didn't see it.' Then he turns back towards me. He's bent so close I can feel his warm breath on my face. 'Fuck. Are you okay?'

'No. You just hit me.'

'I couldn't see you,' he says, a defensive note of panic in his voice. 'You're all in black.'

'I was at a funeral.' A cough rises awkwardly in my throat. 'I need water.'

'How many fingers am I holding up?'

'Seriously? I need water.'

'Kirstin, how many?'

'Three.' I can't do this. Exhaustion overwhelms me.

I'm lying in a puddle of mud. The edge of my iPhone can be seen bobbing forlornly in a rain-filled pothole a few feet ahead of me.

Luke grabs it and gives it a good shake. 'Come on.'

We stagger towards his car. The lights are monstrously bright.

It's a beast of a vehicle, a four-by-four, complete with bull bars. He hit me with this! His door is still hanging open where he pushed out through it. The engine is still on. Even the windscreen wipers continue rocking manically side to side.

'Were you heading for the ferry?' I ask, as I belt myself into the warm car.

'Everybody's trying to get off the island.'

'Thought this was home?'

'You shouldn't talk so much. Try and rest,' he says, flipping lots of buttons in the car.

'I'm not sure that's right. If I am concussed, I should talk.'

'Okay.' Luke sucks in a breath. 'Then maybe I should be asking you questions?'

I'm not keen on that. 'I'll do the asking. It'll keep me focused.'

'Fine,' he says, pulling the car out into the night.

'Do you live on the mainland too?'

'I live in London.'

'London? That's a long way from home.'

'That would be the way I like it. You're not from around here?'

'No.'

'Are you Irish?'

I laugh, then wince, because it's painful to laugh. 'No.'

'Sorry. Thought I detected a burr.'

'A burr cos I'm so bloody cold, burr.' My teeth chatter.

The heating's on full blast, but I'm still shivering. Luke tries to turn the dial up another notch, as the tarmac slips away beneath us.

'And you're not going to tell me where you're from?'

How did the conversation bounce back to me? 'It's a long, boring story.'

'Your parents?'

I want to come clean: tell him that they're like scabs, both of them. Scabs I don't want to pick. But no, that's wrong. My dad was a scab, with his drinking and fists. My mum is a wound, a gaping hole because I don't remember her. Not one moment, one lullaby, one brush of her skin against mine. She jumped out of my life, literally. And when she did, she took a part of me with her. I don't know what part that would be, but I do know something big and vital is missing. As a kid, I'd tried talking to my dad about her, but he was carrying some chip on his shoulder about their relationship, or us kids. I wasn't sure. So I stopped asking. Besides, AJ had it covered. He had a shoe box under his bed with photos inside of a smiling dark-haired woman and a baby. AJ didn't need to lie to me. I made the link myself; it was Mum and me. I must have been about thirteen when it dawned on me that there was something off about the images. That the dark-haired woman wasn't always the same. Even the colour of the baby's eyes seemed a little too prone to change. They were cut-outs from a magazine but, bless him, AJ had gone the extra mile, sticking the flimsy images on carefully cut rectangles of an old cereal packet so's they felt proper. I loved my brother even more for that – making the effort. Nobody else did.

When we cleared up the house after Dad died, we didn't find anything personal. Not one keepsake from my mum, not even a school photo of his lordship; just bottles and pills and long-forgotten grubby Y-fronts in places you couldn't quite believe anyone would ever in their right mind put a pair of pants. One thing we did find that was strange, apart from the location of the underwear, was this Polaroid of a painting. You couldn't see the frame or anything but could tell it was oil on canvas from the hairline trace of brush strokes through an all-consuming wash of dark paint. It reminded me of one of those Rothko's from the Tate, only not half as interesting. And written on the back of the photo in time-forgotten cursive were the words *The true cost*. AJ and I mulled that one over for years. We had photos of it on our phones and would pluck the phrase out from time to time, talk it over. But we never came up with any answers. We knew it wasn't my dad's handwriting. He didn't do cursive or cryptic. We wondered if it was Mum's; the flowery script was kind of girly. But the question that burned us both was, could this be the thing she left behind before she jumped? Her final note?

Whatever *the true cost* was, I always had the sneaking feeling that it was me and AJ who ended up paying. Not surprisingly, I don't want to tell Luke any of this. Thankfully, Luke breaks through the silence with that age-old banker of a question:

'What do you do?'

There's no point in lying. 'I'm an estate agent.'

He laughs. I have no idea why. 'You don't look like an estate agent.'

'What does that even mean?'

'Normally, around here – buck teeth, tight lips. The slightly dim child of the family. The public-school numpty.'

He has a point. In fact, he's just described my boss, Jasper.

'Is that what you always wanted to do?'

This is the kind of thought that comes courtesy of a privileged upbringing.

'Kirstin?'

He's trying to keep me awake.

'I worked in an art gallery once. I liked that.'

'Nice. Gallery assistant?'

'In the café. I was on the coffee station. I wrote the menu up on the chalkboard. I loved it.'

He probably can't get his head around the thought – working in a café and loving it. Not exactly a career. Sadly, not somewhere I'd ever be able to go back to either. When AJ got banged up, I thought it best to hand in my notice. Everyone had figured out we were related. The suspicion I could cope with, but the sorry looks, I couldn't be doing with those.

Despite the rain, Erica has the door open and an anxious look on her drawn, pale face as we lumber towards her.

'What the hell happened, Luke?'

She doesn't bother to ask me.

'Kirstin was in the road.'

'In her car?'

Why are they talking over my head?

'No, she was walking in the road.'

'What?' Erica steps back, and I stumble through the door. 'Good grief, she's a mess.'

'Is Meerson still here?'

'Only just. I asked him not to leave when you phoned.'

'Oh, my Lord,' says a warm voice. Julia. 'What happened?'

Erica slips into organising mode. 'Find her something warm and dry, Julia. Not mine. She'll stretch the living daylights out of my clothes. Ask Miri; she must have something the girl can wear.'

I want to say I'm not a girl; I'm a woman. But I don't feel much like a woman. I feel like a crumpled bird with its wings broken. Every inch of me is screaming in pain.

'Come on, love.' Julia leads me towards the stairs.

'This is the sort of staircase you want your daughter to walk down when she gets married,' I mumble. It's the trite old patter I trot out every time I'm doing a hard sell. My job seriously has sunk way too far under my skin. I don't even know how to talk to people anymore. But if Julia thinks it's odd, she doesn't say.

'Wouldn't that be lovely?' she says wistfully, brushing a strand of hair from my face as we continue to move up the steps, talking to me like every blessed thing that comes out of my mouth makes perfect sense.

'What the hell?' I hear Oscar's voice, sharp and shrill, from downstairs in the hall.

I'm not sure I can take one more family member. I'm beginning to regret ever coming out to this island. And the ringing in my head... Luckily, the voices of the family trail away below me. We are on the landing, hobbling towards the front end of the house.

'Let's put you in here.' Julia pulls the door open. This room is pale yellow. All the rooms must have a colour theme going on. Yellow is my worst colour. It reminds me of vomit and egg yolk. But I am a professional. I am absolute tact, even when my mind is ringing with nonsense.

'It's a beautiful room,' I say. 'Double aspect with an original picture rail.'

Julia looks worried.

'Sorry,' I say. 'It's like the top of my brain's all on show. I seem to have lost my filter.'

I can hear someone outside running up the stairs, taking them two at a time. I don't want any more people. I just want to go to sleep. I certainly don't want Meerson, but he bursts through the door anyway, bag in hand, taking my shoulders and sitting me down on the bed.

'Well, what have we here? You're the bridge player?'

Oh dear. I hope he's not going to ask me to play bridge.

Meerson pulls my eyelids back and shines a torch at my eyeballs. I wince.

'You brought that to the party?' I say, trying to keep the note of irritation from my voice.

'The wake,' Julia corrects me gently.

'Always keep my bag in the car. Did you hit your head?'

I shake it. Boy, does it hurt. I make a mental note not to shake it again. 'I think the car hit the side of my body. I was flying for a minute.' I shiver. I get the feeling that if the car had hit me one tiny bit harder, I might not have ever come down. 'My left arm feels like someone tore it off.'

He lifts my left arm. I cringe in pain.

'Can you flex it?'

I do. But not much.

'Almost impossible to tell without an X-ray. It could be a

fracture, but in all probability, it's most likely badly bruised. I can give you something for the pain. Julia, can you keep an eye on our young patient?'

'Of course.'

He takes a bottle of pills from his bag and shakes two into my palm. I go to swallow them, but the doctor reaches out, stopping the rise of my wrist. He says nothing, just glances up at Julia. She seems to understand.

'Water? I'll get a glass,' and she bustles out.

Then he does something odd. He crosses to the door and closes it tight shut.

'I'm glad we managed to get this little chat, Kirstin.'

I'm not. There's something aggressive about his attitude. 'Oh?' I say. It's like AJ always tells me – don't feed them information; let them feed you.

The man fixes me with his beady eyes. 'I think I might know what you're up to.'

'I've just been run over by an SUV built like a rhinoceros.'

'Not that,' he says dismissively. 'The funeral.'

'Yes?'

'It's not your first.'

Why is he looking at me like that? 'I won't be celebrating twenty-five again. You'd expect a few funerals along the way.'

'I've seen you at three recently.'

That stops me short.

'I'm a doctor. Very sadly, funerals are part and parcel of my occupation. But you...?'

'I'm a...'

'I wasn't actually asking, Kirstin. I looked you up.'

'It's not illegal what I do.'

'No, but it's not exactly... ethical. You might want to think of quitting while you're ahead.'

The door starts to open. Effortlessly his conversation changes tack. 'Take two tablets tonight and again in four hours if you need it.'

He even manages a smile.

When he's gone, Julia runs me a bath. She says I can close the door, but she's going to sit outside. Julia wanted me to have a shower, but I am so cold my teeth are rattling my jaw with such unremitting force it feels like they'll shatter my skull. I have to make them stop. Only a hot bath will do. My iPhone is resting on the radiator in a bowl of rice. Does that really work? I'll soon find out. I lie in the water, as my body blossoms into patterns of large purple bruises. Tomorrow it will be worse. Maybe I'll stop trying to pull get-rich-quick schemes after this. It's too exhausting. AJ always said I was the brains of the family because I made long-term plans. I could see the legal ways you could make money out of a scam. If I do get this sale, it can be my swan song. Time to do something that I actually want to do. Maybe take a degree in journalism. Maybe. I let the water wash over me and, I don't know why, perhaps it's the near-death experience, or it could be the pain. Maybe it's just that reality is all closing in a bit too close for comfort, but I start to cry. I don't sob. I'm quiet as a mouse. Another skill I learnt from AJ – hide your emotions. If people see raw emotion, they'll use it against you. Old habits die hard.

5

WOLVES IN THE HOUSE

A SHARP STAB of pain wakes me. It feels as if someone's plunged a cleaver through my head. I have no idea where I am. None of it makes any sense. This place is so much bigger than my flat, and all the scrawling shapes over the walls? Dark flowers? Patterned wallpaper? Groping to the side of the bed, my hands fix on a nightstand and lamp. I put the light on. My head! I can't switch the thing off again quick enough. There was a pill on the bedside table. I saw it. One doesn't seem enough, not with the size of the headache. But I'm in no state to fuss. I toss it gratefully through open lips.

Then I wait, head banging, as the memories come flooding back: the funeral, Luke with his floppy hair and playful eyes. That's all okay, but it soon gets worse. There's the chandelier freewheeling through space onto this guy trapped in a wheelchair pushed aside by images of me on the road, in the dark, talking to Marco. I'm laughing, then SMASH.

Shit. I need to phone Marco. I was talking to Marco when it happened. He's going to be worried. I throw back the thick blankets, heavy and expensive. So heavy, it feels as though they were pinning me down. I need to get out. I need air. I need

Marco. I reach for the bowl of rice that I'd left on the radiator. My mobile is sticking up out of one side, trying to invite a little alchemy. The thing feels dry, but none of the buttons respond to my persistent fingers. It's dead. When I look closer, there's a hairline crack running down the side. I need to call Marco. I have to tell him that I'm okay. A place like this, they have to have a landline. Carolyn was old. Old people always keep at least one landline. It takes them forever to wake up to the fact that they don't use it anymore; that the only calls they're getting are junk or the pesterings of other old people.

I swing my legs out of bed. I'm wearing something. Pyjamas? I don't usually wear pyjamas. These are white. I never wear white. They're too long for me. I roll up a cuff on each leg and pad across the thick, velvety carpet towards the door. I'm amazed Marco hasn't called the police. Does he even know where I am?

The landing is dimly lit; a series of lamps dotted in corners, dappling the hallway in warm orange pools. It's the sort of thing I'm forever telling vendors – get your lighting right, and the rest will follow. I'm irritating myself now. I need to get a different job before my brain liquefies. I scan the landing. The lights may be on, but the house is in silence. It could be midnight or four in the morning. I need to find a clock and tie myself back into reality.

Walking barefoot down the staircase, I can't help but cringe as I remember what I'd said to Julia; the thing about watching your daughter come down these stairs in her wedding dress. Shit, I'm such an idiot. I talk too much, and a good eighty-five per cent of what I say is absolute rubbish. If I could swap myself out for another, quieter version, I seriously would. My head is still hurting. My left arm feels like someone's chewed it off. A phone, I must find a telephone. Hallways. People usually have phones in hallways. I search all four corners of the entrance hall, the cold marble of the chequered floor biting into my toes. There are a couple of recesses but no phone. So, maybe there's a snug or an office? There's no point heading to the drawing room. That was far too fancy, so I split off in the other direction, moving to the right side of the house. The first door leads to what would be listed in the property details as The Snug – cosy, no TV, and sadly no phone. Instead, the room is lined with shelves ram-packed with books. I see Carolyn's book straight off – *The Parenthood Jungle,* propped against the others showing its face rather than its spine. Pausing for a moment, avoiding Carolyn's unsmiling bobbed headshot on the cover, I flick to the index. One chapter title leaps out. *The six styles of motherhood.* Curious, I scan the contents. It's a simple list: i) Overprotective. ii) Sacrificial. iii) Lassitude. iv) Ineffectual. v) Destructive. Loving has a chapter all on its own, but it's a seriously short chapter. I get the feeling that in Carolyn's book loving always comes with an adjunct. Loving but ineffectual, Loving but overprotective, that kind of thing. And it's so obvious that she's missed one core 'style' completely – absentee. What about the mother who decides she can't be arsed to stick around? Who decides that the life she's left you in stinks so much that it's not for her? Is that simply a bad case of *Lassitude*? I feel my heart sink a little. Every time I think of my own mother, I get this hollow feeling inside. Hollow or angry. I'm never sure which one is best. Tonight it's hollow that's hitting me. One thing's for sure, suddenly I'm in no mood to talk to Marco. I put the book back on the shelf and go for something else. Something pretty. Plumping for a spine embossed with flowing gold lettering on cobalt-blue leather. It's Kant, the philosopher. Normally with books like this, they're pristine. Open the spines, and you can see they've never actually been read, but Carolyn obviously knew her Kant. Each page has been broken into, bent back and pored over. One page has even had its corners turned down with a block of text underlined. I flick through the rest of the book. There are no other annotations, just this one. Normally people who scribble do so from cover to cover, but not here. Not Carolyn. I peer at the letters, trying hard not to let them dance in the low light. *'One who makes himself a worm cannot complain after if people step on him.'* Even with the headache, I smile. You have to admire Carolyn's sense of style, reducing Kant's entire body of work to just one line that fits her needs. I slip the book back onto the shelf, suddenly tired of my dead host and her quirky penmanship. I still need to get word to Marco.

Going back out into the hallway, I try the next door. Success; the 'home office'. It's fancier than most, with not a whiff of MDF. This is all solid wood, dark and expensive. The curtains are open, hanging idly down over large windows, looking out over a corner of the gravelled car park towards the silhouetted cliff edge. Despite the constant drizzle of rain, the moon has reappeared; just a sliver, but enough to cut a thin, wobbling path across the dark waves. Despite the moon, there's not much light filtering in through the windows. Luckily, the polished, wooden surfaces reflect whatever they can get hold of. AJ would love this room. It's the sort of set-up where easy pickings can be found – forgotten items on the bookshelves, or lost, wedged down upholstery corners. I glance at myself in the long mirror over the mantelpiece. What a piece of work. Even with a splitting headache and a damaged body, I am still trying to find an angle. Switching on a desk light, I carefully fold my body into the high-backed leather chair, ready and waiting at the desk. I'm still unclear what time it is, but Marco is a nightbird. He'll be awake.

Within minutes my call is ringing out into Marco's curiously Gothic hallways. An odd building, that's got even stranger in the four years that Marco's been running the place. Every time I visit, it seems to have acquired another gargoyle or a curious, vaguely disturbing, piece of taxidermy. I have to hope he's not working on a body. If he's working on a body, I know for a fact, he won't pick up. But I'm in luck. The receiver clicks, and I hear his voice, loud, clear and always professional.

'Penzance Funeral Services. How can I help?'

'Marco, it's me.'

'Kirstin? Honey, you know what time it is?'

'Actually, no.'

'Three thirty in the morning, crazy Kirstin. I was just heading up the stairs.'

'Sorry. I thought you might be worried about me.'

There's a brief silence; he wasn't worried, not one bit.

'Oh, sure. Yeah. You got cut off.'

'I got run over.'

'Oh my fuck! Shit.' There's concern, but also, I wonder, is that an excitement for gossip in his voice? 'What happened? Are you okay? Are you in hospital?'

'My car broke down.'

'That I got earlier. On the island?'

'Yeah. I mean, it was really dark.' I glance around me, suddenly feeling awkward. Wishing I was home. 'I probably shouldn't have been walking, but then this SUV came out of nowhere and...'

'Fuck.'

'Exactly.'

'But you're okay?' Now there's genuine concern.

'Bruised and sore.' I rub at my temples. 'My head's throbbing, and my left arm...' I start to lift the offending arm slowly. 'I don't think it's broken, but it's... ouch.' I stop. I've raised it too far.

'So, where the hell are you?'

'The Millford Estate.'

'No?'

'Yes.'

He laughs. 'Well, that really is getting your feet through the front door.'

Suddenly his amusement strikes me as irritating. I'm tired. I'm wounded. I could be dead. 'I don't want to be here.'

'Ahh.'

'I just thought you might be worried.'

There's a pause. 'Oh right, sure... yeah.'

He hadn't even noticed. I had been run down, and one of the people I'm closest to was oblivious.

'Right, well.' It's late. I'm tired. 'I better get back to bed.' I try to hide the sorry-for-myself wobble in my voice.

'Sounds like a plan for both of us.'

I'm about to put the phone down when suddenly I remember. 'Oh, and Marco, you said something about this lead not coming through the usual route.'

'What?'

'The lead on Carolyn Millford?'

'Oh right, 'course. Yes, she wasn't on my slab. Normally the leads I give you are my fresh meat; only this was someone else's.'

'Who told you about it?'

'Oh, Kirstin, now you're asking.' I can imagine the eye roll. 'It was a bit of a wild night.'

When Marco isn't working, he can be found on the *wild-night* circuit.

'Can you think for me?' I'm beginning to feel there's something odd about this whole thing. There had been two accidents in one night. First Timmy, then me.

'Umm. It was a party. Lot of people. Lot of conversations. One of the Millford sons? That must be it. The good-looking one.'

'Luke?'

'You're asking me for names?' There's a wry, mocking humour in his voice.

'He's gay?'

'Kirstin... You know we don't do that. You want to find out if someone's gay ask them yourself.'

'He didn't seem gay.'

'We don't carry signs and wear T-shirts.'

'No.'

'Done with the homophobia?'

'I wasn't...'

'Teasing, Kirstin. Love getting on that high horse.'

But I'm in no mood.

I sit there in the room, phone in hand, facing the facts. There was no chemistry between Luke and me, not one watt of electricity. That was all faulty wiring on my part. I was hooking up wires that weren't even there. No doubt it was in Luke's interest to keep that impression going. Maybe the family were homophobic, and he'd just got so used to pretending, he couldn't stop himself. Besides, I'm sure I could sue him for driving without due care and attention. He may even have been drinking. It does seem bizarre though. This whole mess had started because Marco had been partying.

As the phone goes down and my connection with the mainland is cut, I realise that my circle of friends, my world, is incredibly small. I've been concentrating so hard on getting rich, working a scam, running my life along one track, that maybe I've missed the point. Perhaps I should have been working harder on opening my life up so that, in the event that I did ever get run over or hurt, someone would be concerned. When I return to the mainland, I'm going to get my priorities sorted. And as I walk from the room, I wonder how Janice got on at the cinema. It was a horror film that I had heard about, one of those grungy, independent things with lots of story and an odd twist. I do want to go and see it, only not with Janice. Janice is the intern, for Christ's sake.

The clock hanging on the kitchen wall tells me that it's almost four. I grab myself a glass of water and go through the drawers in search of medication. Eventually, after losing myself in some bizarre car-boot-sale-style mess of long-forgotten kitchen gadgets, I manage to find a half-empty bottle of Night Nurse and stick it in my pocket, just as my head screams. I need something stronger. Something targeted. Then it strikes me – Timmy. Timmy must surely have something stronger.

I find his room just past the office, opposite what must be the mechanism for the chandelier: a series of ropes and pulleys held fast with a large metal clip. His door stands open just a crack, revealing a space bathed in blue light and adapted to suit his needs. There's a rail around most of the wall, and his bed is more mechanical than luxury, with a series of prominent metal levers and pulleys waiting ready for action, but all is quiet. Timmy lies under the sheets out cold, a hydration drip feeding into his arm. I'm feeling so exhausted I half want to crawl in under the blankets with him. Instead, I sink into the hard seat beside the bed. His features look different in the blue light. Earlier in the day, they were contorted in fear and anger; now, they're loose, relaxed, kind.

'You wouldn't begrudge me a couple of high-strength paracetamol?' I ask, my voice low.

He says nothing, of course. I hadn't expected him to.

I glance around the room. It's minimalist, but there's one of those digital photo frames sitting on top of a low sideboard, along with what looks like a baby monitor. The light spilling from the frame is providing the source of the blue illumination. I sit, mesmerised by the photos as they slip past. One is of a younger Timmy. I'd put him at around eighteen – nineteen. He's not only younger; he's standing. Standing beside a sign and loaded down with a backpack. There's a big smile spread unchecked across his eager, young face. The sign behind him reads, 'Welcome to Cambodia'. It must have been taken shortly before his accident.

There are other photos. Some of Timmy as a child with the whole family. Erica still sneering. Luke acting the fool – a hand waving at the camera, a mouth wide open in a joyful holler. Oscar looking neater than the other siblings – collared shirts when the others are in round-neck T's; trousers with a pleat when the others are in shorts. His stance is always the same; hands at his side. A small smile on a face half buried under the beginnings of a worried frown. There's no Miri in the early ones. Miri was a later addition to the family. There is, however, a baby. Its head covered in red fuzz. Miri? She must be Oscar's child. Perhaps there was a divorce.

There are no photos of weddings or couples or wives, although there are some earlier photos. The old-school variety – pre-digital. They have a yellow quality as though the past has a different colour. The protagonists all wear shirts with overwide lapels. The images must be from the seventies. Most are of a haughty young girl with a knife-edged geometric bob. She looks miserable and angry. Even though the last time I saw that face (in another photo), it had forty years on this one, I know who it is – Carolyn. The image dissolves again. Carolyn has aged another ten years or so. Her face still has that – *mess with me at your peril,* look. She's standing next to another young woman. The features are similar, but the other woman is more rounded. Her face smiling. Her hair darker. She looks familiar. It could be a relative, a cousin perhaps. Although I can't remember seeing the dark-haired woman at the funeral. Then again, she would have changed. It's not always easy to spot people once age plays its hand.

I yawn. I need to get back to bed. But my head is still hurting. I slide open a few drawers till I find what I'm looking for. Timmy has a whole pharmacy of delights but I'm only after paracetamol. I grab a packet and push it deep into my dressing-gown pocket next to the Night Nurse.

'Okay, that's me,' I whisper to the sleeping Timmy. 'I do appreciate this.'

Then I do the oddest thing. I lean forward and kiss him gently on the forehead. Stupid, I know, but it's been a bugger of a day for both of us. Suddenly, his eyes blink open. It's a pure horror moment, they're wide and staring. The pupils lost in a golf-ball of white. My breath catches tight in my throat.

'Danger.' He stares straight at me with those burning eyes. 'You're in danger.'

Then, just as abruptly, the eyes snap closed, as sleep pulls poor Timmy back under its covers.

6

THE FULL ENGLISH

I WAKE to golden rays of sun sliding opportunistically through a thin slit in my curtains, Timmy's words still ear-worming through my brain. Poor sod, I think to myself, pushing away the heavy eiderdown in search of a little cool air. The man's mind is sadly on a different planet. Although, I pause for a moment, the silky blanket still wrapped around my feet, maybe he was onto something; there had been *'danger'*. In the form of one very real, very stupidly reckless driver – Luke. Which reminds me, I'm still reeling from Marco's intel. I could swear the man had been flirting with me. The more I get to know this family, the more confused I feel. I slide my legs from the mattress, stepping across the room to the window and peeping out through the narrow crack. The rain's stopped, and my headache has, thankfully, drifted off with it. I use my good arm to draw back the heavy drapes. They're a sickly yellow to match the walls. In the full unforgiving light of morning, I can't help wondering if perverse old Carolyn hadn't taken her inspiration from Perkins Gilman's *Yellow Wallpaper*. It's a story of a woman slipping slowly but surely into madness. Going there willingly or given a helping hand from her medic of a husband, that's unclear. It's only the insanity which isn't up for debate. From what I've gleaned so far about my curious dead host, some kind of perverse gameplay could be right up Carolyn's street. I stare around me at the constantly shifting swirls and vow that, if I do get the listing, the first thing I'll do is slap a couple of coats over it. Yellow wallpaper in a bedroom, it's an absolute no-no. If I don't Dulux it out, some bright spark is bound to bring it up as we mosey through the property, sale particulars in hand, and release Ms Perkins Gilman's never-welcome ghost. Besides, this could be a nice room. It might not be a principal bedroom, but it's set at the corner of the house. Double aspect, as I so cringingly pointed out to Julia last night in my catatonic but creepily observant state. Out of one *aspect*, you even get the sea, which this morning is no big deal. The water looks brutalist, as cold and unforgiving as concrete. Although the rain has indeed gone, the sky is still that unattractive battleship grey. Yet despite the colour scheme, inside and out, credit where credit is due – this bedroom has a view.

There's still a handful of cars parked up on the gravel outside; Luke's beast. A smart Mazda sporty thing – my guess is that one has Erica's name stamped on it. Oscar's got to be driving the red BMW, the overly sensible saloon. That would leave the little electric-blue Golf for Miri. There's also the country-house, standard-issue knackered Land Rover weighing down the gravel. It wasn't there last night. It could be one of Carolyn's leftovers, waiting to be tidied away. The dead have a habit of leaving their possessions scattered.

I have a quick shower. It's always a good sign in a property when even the shower cubicle has space for a family of four. I let the soap slip over my body, finding more sensitive areas than I'd noticed last night; some haven't even got a handy bruise to mark the spot. What would have happened, I wonder, as the water chases over my skin, if Luke had been travelling just that little bit faster? I was lucky.

Clutching the snow-white towel across my chest, I open the door to the bedroom bringing a small billow of warm steam out with me. In my absence, the bed's been made. The coverlet stretched tight till the satin gives off a soft, fresh gleam. In the corner of the room, there's a pile of clothes set neatly on the Liberty-patterned armchair. Julia must be in the building, still tidying up like a house elf. I hope they pay her enough. Every extra body must add to her already packed schedule. I look through the neatly folded clothes. It's nothing I would normally wear. Nothing black, not even a charcoal grey or dark navy. Instead, there's a white strappy vest along with a soft green V-neck jumper. The jumper is gorgeous, with the silkiest feel ever. I glance at the label and discover it's a merino wool mix. Ralph Lauren. Even as I flatten it out across the bed, I can tell the cut's flattering, tapering slightly at the waist. There's also a pair of purple slacks. Purple? I remember the funny old bird at the wake: Niamh. Maybe purple's in fashion? I'm not up with the trends. My wardrobe is all basics, everything work-adaptable, very little that says fun. I turn the slacks over curiously in my hands; these clothes aren't Niamh's, of course. The sizing is all wrong. And the green – well, it's a dead giveaway. This has to be the wardrobe of a redhead, Miri. It's all size twelve, so at least I'm in the right ballpark.

Pulling on the clothes, I instantly feel like a different woman, a more wealthy one certainly, but curiously also more demure. It's as though, in these clothes, I wouldn't have to fight so hard: doors would open, and respect would be heaped on by the shovelful. Riches are built into the marrow of the Millford family. I glance at myself in the long mirror. I could seriously get to like this. Behind me, on the swirling yellow wall, I notice a painting, and turn to get a better look. It's a simple bowl of flowers. Unlike the wallpaper, this small picture is a masterpiece.

So intricate. So beautifully captured. It has to be Dutch. Even the frame must be worth a small fortune – carved antique wood holding a delicate gold leaf inlay.

I give myself a mental slap. Artwork was my brother's downfall. The impromptu job change had proved a step too far for AJ. The rules were different. It's easy to sell a lorry full of bricks, but a valuable bit of artwork? Well, that's another story. It was a Lowry that caused all the fuss. An oil on canvas called *Punch and Judy*. Something triggers in my brain. *'That's the way to do it.'* That same mocking voice I had heard as I lay delirious in the road. Shit, I'd actually thought I'd been standing inside the painting. I sigh wearily as I throw my weight down on the corner of the bed. Stupid. I'm becoming obsessed. I need to let it go. Tricky though, when that painting is what's keeping my brother from getting out. You can still see the thing, only now it can only be viewed online and digital. The real Lowry is nowhere to be found. I'd loved that thing even when I was a small kid. Got an A star in an essay I'd written about it for school. Perhaps that wasn't such a good thing. The whole experience had swelled my head. I'd dreamed of writing books about art, painting, anything. But reality soon cramps all dreams. You need an education for that kind of thing. It didn't stop me loving that painting though.

Just as you'd expect, the scene is packed full of people, Lowry-style and right at the back of the canvas, there's a Punch and Judy show in full swing; the distant candy-stripe of the show's canvas tent a muted dull red. The puppets resting on the line marking out the stage are just blobs of paint, but then, despite the name, the pocket-handkerchief of the theatre isn't the important bit. As always with Lowry, the masses are the real show. The red that the holidaying workers wear is vibrant and bright. There are prams with babies and men with pipes. There are groups of people and solitary figures. The world is Lowry's stage. You find something different in the painting every time you look. But centre stage is the thing that haunts me. It has haunted me since I knew that myself and that picture would end up linked forever because of one bungled AJ project. There's a woman standing in the middle of the canvas staring at something just out of the scene. Lowry's paintings are a bit like that, everyone looking in a different direction. But this woman in black and brown is staring directly at the viewer, and there's something heavy about her. Her shoulders are slumped as though she knows all of this is an illusion, and she doesn't want to be there, trapped like an unwitting butterfly pinned into a dead world, forced to fit into somebody else's story.

I sometimes feel that me and the woman in the picture have a lot in common. Neither of us can move on. It's that one painting that's stopping us. AJ says he doesn't know where it is, but it's not me he needs to convince. It's the parole board.

From the corner of the bed, I glance at my face in the mirror. My eyes have sunk sullenly to a murky grey. I have some make-up, a lipstick, and a tiny dab of concealer, but nothing for the full-on overhaul which is called for. Normally, I wear make-up like a mask, but beggars can't be choosers. Besides, the look might even work in my favour; a sympathy vote is always a card worth keeping in the back pocket.

Despite the size of the house, it doesn't take long to find the action. Standing in the hallway, the chequerboard tiles under my feet, I hear the echoey clatter of silver cutlery on china plates, punctuated with a scanty mix of morning talk. I walk through the drawing room to the far end of the house, and I know as soon as I set my foot through the archway – this is the view that will sell the house. In fact, this could be a 'one image' kind of a deal.

The perfect green carpet of lawn outside the long windows levels out briefly before dropping gently down to the sea. But before the sea, there's a beach, one of those white, sandy affairs that the island's famous for. The sky's shifted a little since I woke. The sun braving its way through the clouds, allowing the ocean to shake off that industrial concrete look. Now it sparkles coyly in the morning light. The water surrounding the island has to be the best in the UK. A clear fifteen feet visibility when you look down and sapphire-blue all the way. The first time I'd seen it, I was gobsmacked. I'm a girl from Liverpool, growing up with the dishwater Mersey and New Brighton for a bathe. I'd only ever seen water like this when checking in with David Attenborough, but when I ended up in the West Country, I suddenly had *Blue Planet* paradise right under my toes.

I don't need to ask if the beach is private. It will be. There are no roads out here. As I peer from the windows, I notice what looks like a beach bar to the left side of the cove, nestling invitingly in the shelter of a high rock. A home-grown, shabby-chic shack, complete with a rickety jetty of faded wooden slats, reaching out into the sea. I feel pound signs whirring through my brain. The beach access has just added another million. Jeeze, I want this house on my books. Actually, I'd love this house in my life, but that's not going to happen, and the best thing after owning something is being in on the sale.

Suddenly, I'm aware that it's not only the house under intense scrutiny here. Erica and Oscar are staring up at me. Erica has her white china coffee cup stranded halfway between the table and those cold, pale lips. I realise I've been doing an inventory with an audience.

'Not sure the outfit suits you.' Erica sniffs, placing her coffee cup down gently on its saucer.

From the old-person wardrobe she's wearing, I'm not *sure* she's a reliable arbiter of fashion, but I choose not to go there. 'Well, I'm grateful for it.'

She slides a distasteful look down her angular nose and I dread to think what she'd have me dressed in.

Oscar's a different story. He's on his feet, pulling back a chair, ready to shake out my napkin. He's so full of bluster it's making me feel dizzy. 'I am so sorry, Kirstin, about last night. I've rung Pope.'

I look blank.

'He said he was aware of the situation.'

In my head, I'm thinking Vatican. Then I realise – Oscar must be talking about the garage.

'Pope's already towed your car back to his yard. He's giving it the once-over now.'

'Thank you,' I say, perching on the chair Oscar's so thoughtfully pulled out for me.

'We've got a lot to do today,' Erica says briskly. 'So, we need to get this little mess sorted asap.'

I do kind of resent being referred to as *this little mess* but have no intention of going there. 'I'm sure you're flat-out,' I say, making a mental note not to bring up the property sale with Erica. I need to attack this from an easier aspect.

'Oh, my goodness. All the clothes fit,' Miri exclaims warmly, breezing into the room.

'The jumper's lovely, Miri,' I say, smiling, running my hands over the wool. 'Thank you.'

She gives a dismissive shrug as if to say *that old thing*.

In the morning light spilling in through the windows, Miri looks older, certainly over twenty. Not a school leaver then, a woman. I scan Oscar's face. Does that work? To be her father, he can't have been much more than a teenager when he got caught out.

'I'll text Julia for drinks. Tea or coffee?' Oscar asks, slipping into his own chair.

I try to still my mind for a moment, to stop calculating family trees in my brain and organise my breakfast order. 'Black coffee, please.'

'Make that two,' Erica adds, but there's a mixed message here because she's standing as if she really hasn't got time for all this top-of-the-morning banter.

Oscar picks up his phone and starts to tap. 'We always text now,' he explains. 'So much more civilised than hollering through the house or ringing bells. The kitchen's downstairs. In the basement.'

I smile innocently as if this is all news to me.

'So, we really did have to shout,' he adds, half amused.

'Or ring,' Erica states dryly. 'But I think we all preferred the hollering. Not all progress is *progress*.'

I'm not sure she's right about that, but she's leaving anyway. There's a dab of the napkin on those tight, pulled lips and a screech of her chair as she pushes past it.

'Make sure to get this mess sorted before lunch, Oscar.' And she's gone.

At least she's dropped the *little*.

'I'm guessing I'm the mess, not the breakfast detritus?' I say.

Miri snorts with amusement.

'You'll have to forgive my sister, Kirstin.' Oscar shoots me a sincere look. 'It's a tense time for us.'

'Oh, come on, Uncle Oscar. She's always like that. Unbearable.'

Uncle?

'Miri, we don't speak ill of each other. Families don't do that.'

Miri raises her eyes heavenward, and I decide it might be best if we get off the subject of Erica. 'I'm sorry to have ended up back here. I know you do absolutely have enough to be getting on with. But I appreciate the clothes.' I stroke the arm of the jumper as if it's a Persian cat. 'If you give me your address, I'll wash…' I stop myself, 'dry-clean everything and get it back to you.'

Miri waves her hand dismissively. 'Honestly, don't bother. It's all old stuff. Keep it. And it's hardly your fault you're here. Just do us all a favour and don't sue Uncle Luke for running you down.'

'Miri.' Oscar's face colours, a shade of repressed vermillion.

'Uncle Luke clearly didn't mean to...' he hesitates, 'be involved in an accident with our guest.' His words are as carefully balanced as a lawyer on a unicycle. 'She wasn't supposed to be there.'

Ah, nifty. So it's all my fault. 'Could have happened to anyone,' I say, magnanimously.

'Especially...' Miri raises one perfect sable eyebrow ironically, 'when somebody is driving *that* fast. He tore out of here as if he was on a racetrack.'

Some people need no rope to hang themselves or anyone else unfortunate enough to be standing close by.

Oscar fixes Miri with a hard look. 'Nobody was supposed to be on that road. Everyone had left. Now, let's put an end to this, please. What time are you leaving, Miri?'

'I'm going to catch the 5.30. That should get me back in London before midnight.'

'Great,' Oscar announces as Julia arrives with the coffees. 'Julia, could we do two more for lunch and maybe supper as well? Just in case.'

Julia nods. 'And Miri, I know your breakfast order. Same as usual with a protein shake?'

'You absolute star.' Miri reaches over and gives Julia's hand an affectionate squeeze. 'One day, I'm going to steal you home with me.'

Julia beams, Miri is so obviously a favourite. 'And Kirstin, would you like cooked, or are you happy with cereal?'

I don't hesitate. 'Cooked. I mean, if it's no trouble.' The trousers are a bit tight, but my belly is hollering *'feed me'* so much louder than it's shouting *'cover me up'*.

'No trouble at all.' Julia clears Erica's plate. It looks clean. It's only Erica's coffee cup that has evidence of use.

'Sorry about all the extra work, Julia.' Oscar just can't help himself from apologising.

'Nonsense. Lovely to have the house full. Must admit I'm dreading you all driving away.'

Miri jumps up and gives Julia a big hug. 'Oh, I'm going to miss you.'

There's an awkward pause. This seems to be a sore subject. What is going to happen to Julia with Carolyn off the scene?

'Well, there's still Uncle Timmy,' Julia says brightly, though her eyes are beginning to water.

'Of course. I always forget Timmy.' Miri sounds suddenly guilty. Her moods appear to be intense but, like the weather around this island, blow over quick.

'Right, well, I shall leave you ladies to it.' Oscar edges his chair back from the table, crumpling his napkin and placing it beside his empty plate. 'Kirstin, make sure to find me and say goodbye before you go.'

I nod. I most definitely intend to find him; I want to discuss their plans.

'Julia...' He smiles towards her. 'We're expecting a phone call from Pope. Get him to bring the car over here on the low-loader if necessary. Kirstin's going to need those wheels back.'

'Where are you from?' Miri asks as the room clears.

'The mainland.'

'You don't have the accent.' She pulls her words out in true West Country fashion.

'Would you?' I shoot her a cheeky smile.

She laughs. 'Actually, I love it, but... Oh, I can't wait to get back to London. I've had the shittiest six months, and now this. It's been so stressful, and...' she hesitates, glancing sadly down at the table, 'I miss Gran.'

'You got on well?'

'Oh yes. I mean, the others all say she was an ogre.'

'Really?' I decide to play dumb.

'Absolutely. Surely you've heard?'

If there was dirt going, I was more than happy to add a bit more to the pile.

'You must have noticed.' Miri arranges her cutlery so that it sits to one side of her place setting in a sparkling row. 'Noticed the lack of partners?'

'I...'

'Nobody's married anymore. I mean, me, that was a tragedy.' She sniffs.

I'm not sure what she's talking about here. Luckily, she doesn't stop.

'But the others, that was Carolyn. They all blame her; *Carolyn put a wedge between us.*'

Miri's good at voices. That last one was a dead ringer for Oscar. The words tumbling out dry, uptight and, defensive.

'She tied everyone up in these ridiculous pre-nuptial agreements. Oh, and she hired a private detective to ruin Aunt Erica's marriage. He was cheating. Not the private detective, the husband. But, let's face it, if you were married to Aunty Erica, wouldn't you?'

'I...' I can see her point. Luckily, she's happy in monologue mode.

'Luke, of course, is a darling. He would have snookered his own marriage anyway. You know he's got that...'

Marco's conversation comes back to me – the good-looking brother in the gay bar.

'That over-sparkle thing going on. Can't help himself,' she says, her eyes glittering playfully towards me, and I wonder if there's a warning in there somewhere.

'And Oscar. Well, he is seriously sweet, but you'd die of boredom if you married Uncle Oscar. His wife went off with an accountant. Can you believe that? And she was an accountant herself, so that must be double the boring. I mean, it's almost so bad it's good. And Timmy...' She hesitates. 'Poor Timmy. So odd how life turns out because, of course, it was no secret he used to be Carolyn's favourite. But that's what a landmine will do for you. Savage. You heard about the landmine?'

'Luke told me.'

'Life-changing gap yar.' She pronounces the year with a true Sloane tone. I think she's taking the piss out of the gap yar idea rather than being serious, but I'm not sure.

However, I am getting confused. Nothing is stacking up here. 'And your parents are…?' I have to ask.

She shrieks with laughter. 'Oh, shit. Couldn't you tell? None of *them*. I'd have Uncle L if he were on offer but… I'm adopted. That's why they sometimes call me their niece, rather than *sister*.'

I don't bother to inform her that I hadn't heard any of them say either. I'd just made the cognitive leap all on my own.

'Though *officially* I'm the grandchild. Not very observant, are you? The hair is a dead giveaway.'

I don't know what to say to this. I could actually give her an inventory on the valuables in each of the rooms I've staggered across during my short stay and the square footage, but…

'To be honest, I think the fact that I'm not a blood relative is why Carolyn liked me best. It's the whole wolf thing. You've heard the stories?'

'About the wolves and the baby?'

'Yes. The baby from outside the clan. That's me. Well, obviously I'm not a wolf. Not even part-time. It might be easier to think of me as the spanner in the works.'

'Sorry?'

'Well, it's irritating when a mother has favourites, right?'

I smile as if I understand, but in truth, I don't have any first-hand experience of mothers.

'Favourites were Carolyn's thing. *The Golden Child* and all that.'

I'm completely lost now. She must see it.

'Carolyn's book? The favourite son or daughter? *The Golden Child*. So…' Miri continues. 'It's all in her book. After all that bit about the six types of motherhood.'

I should have kept reading.

'Not a joyous read. She was in the middle of a new project, no doubt that would have been equally controversial. Just imagine how irritating it is, how insulting, if the favourite isn't even from the same gene pool. How can you compete then? She was complex, Carolyn. I mean, don't get me wrong, I love complex. But I watched her play them off against each other for years, even poor Julia. Give Carolyn your heart, and she would origami it into a different shape. Only…' Miri throws her large green eyes up towards the ceiling as if trying to capture the exact right thought. 'Only a heart that was far less pretty. That didn't function properly anymore.'

I remember the quote I'd found underlined in Carolyn's copy of Kant. If you act like a worm, you deserve to be treated that way.

Miri yawns, stretching into a beam of sunshine as it pours through the long windows, lighting up her hair like a torch.

'I always kept my distance,' she says, bathing her face in the glow. 'That's how you survive in this family. Ah, Julia.' Miri turns towards the door just as Julia comes through carrying a tray.

'Sorry. Everything seems to take me twice as long these days,' she says sadly, setting it down. 'If only your brother hadn't got rid of Rose.'

'I liked Rose,' Miri says lightly, before turning towards me. 'Rose was Timmy's carer before someone took it into their heads to get rid of her. Now poor Julia has to do everything.'

Along with the breakfasts, there's a tall glass containing what looks like a protein shake. No doubt it cost a fortune. Its promises will be youth, vitality and the guarantee of a glowing complexion. Even though I know all of this is just hype, I'd dearly love to take a gulp.

Julia places the plates in front of us. Mine is weighed down with just about everything that goes under the heading of 'breakfast'. It looks delicious. My instinct is to bury my face in the thing and gobble it down in a few large bites without the aid of chewing. Miri's plate, on the other hand, looks like the breakfast you might eat if you were stuck on a space station: a thick gloopy shake and a single green apple cut into segments.

'I started this amazing diet,' she says, looking down at the plate in rapture. 'I have to let the camera put on the pounds these days rather than rely on true calories.'

'You're a model?'

'No.' She looks indignant. 'Please. An actor. I'm up for this huge part at the moment. It's a Marvel sequel? Prequel? To be honest, I don't care. It doesn't even make sense. And now they're messing up the Marvel timeline the terms *prequel* and *sequel* have to be redundant, don't you think?'

I smile sweetly. In truth, I have no idea.

'The storyline's bonkers. That's kind of par for the course when you can do anything you like with time. And they can.'

'The Marvel people?'

'Exactly. Imagine having that power.' She sighs wistfully, lifting a slice of apple with her delicate pale fingers. 'I have to admit I have absolutely no integrity. Just as long as they send me to boot camp. Those places are amazing. You come out sculpted. Seriously. They can do it to anyone.' She narrows her eyes a little, running them over me.

I pull the jumper down lower over my stomach. I don't need anyone to tell me that I'm in need of a boot camp. Time. It's time. I don't have enough of the stuff. 'What's the part?' I ask, deflecting the attention.

She sucks her cheeks in thoughtfully. 'I'd be playing the mother and the daughter. Only I'd look exactly the same when I'm playing both. Which is good because I don't want them messing with my hair.' She coils a thick wodge of it around the fingers of her free hand. The piece of apple, in the other hand, still not getting anywhere near her mouth.

'Sounds complicated though, two different characters?'

'Three years at drama school, I can handle it.'

So, she is older than she looks.

She shoots me an apologetic grimace. 'Look, I'm so sorry, Kirsty.'

No one has ever called me that, not in years. But it feels nice, friendly.

'Don't think me rude, but can we cut the chit-chat?'

I wasn't aware that I'd been doing that much.

'I don't talk between mouthfuls,' she explains in an exaggerated apology, waving the apple slice through the air as if to underline the point. 'It's all about digestion.'

'Fine,' I say simply, trying to stop the amused smirk creeping across my face.

And so we continue to sit whilst Miri chews loudly. I'm not sure if the exaggerated munching is an affectation from the chi-chi diet she's got herself hooked into? Or perhaps she's sporting one of those teeth-trough things that straighten everything up and whiten everything out. It doesn't matter. I'm left in peace, working through my egg and meat feast and staring out of the wide windows. I could sit here forever, and as we sit, I realise there's a strong chance Miri will have inherited something. I bet she knows that too. I make a note to get her address before I leave. I'll send her the jumper and slacks back along with a thoughtful *thank you* for the clothes. It's not just Carolyn who can work to a game plan.

After breakfast, I grab a coat and a pair of wellingtons from the back porch and then set off for the beach. It's odd not having a phone. Normally I would just hole myself up in a room and happily twitch and scroll through the wide worldly web. It's Sunday, so there won't be a lot happening, but I like to keep an eye on the obits. Although ideally, this will be the last time I need to chase a hearse. I seriously am going to do something different. Although I'm not sure I'll be able to wean myself off in one yank.

Maybe I could sub-contract to Janice? I think of her open, honest face. Her clueless manner. No, Janice would mess it up. If I'm out, I need to be completely out. Besides, I realise, as I stride across the perfect strip of grass towards the sea, raising my face to the bright October sun, letting the salt breeze run over my body – this is what I need. More days like this. More interfaces with reality where there are no schemes.

The beach sits in a small cove. To the left is the little makeshift bar I'd seen from the house and a coastal path winding up over the headland. To the right is a sheer cliff, birds nesting all the way up the rockface. It looks like a precarious way to live. Surely, they must lose some of their eggs, but then again, up there at the top, there are no predators. Is it better to lose something because of carelessness or because it gets stolen away? I'm not sure.

'It's beautiful, isn't it?'

I turn to see Luke wrapped in a sludge-green Barbour. His floppy hair doing some mad wind-blown dance around his face.

'It's an amazing place.'

'Yeah. I'll miss it.' He stares out at the wind-chased sea. 'How much do you think it's worth?'

I laugh.

'Oh, come on. You're an estate agent. It's in your blood. Give me a price.'

I bite down on my lip, so my smile isn't too wide. 'How many acres?'

'Hmm, not that many anymore. Probably eight to nine-ish. Most of it around the house.'

'I'd say ten million.'

'Hmm.'

There's a moment's silence. I'm hoping he'll say something more, give me some reaction. But he's not giving anything away.

'Is that what you expected?'

'To be honest, I don't know. I try not to think of it. Mother liked to dangle the house like a carrot in front of all of us. I've made my peace with the fact that I may well be getting nothing.'

'Oh?'

'Miri was her favourite.'

'But "favourite" doesn't mean Miri's going to inherit it all.'

He gives me a hard look.

'Did she tell you the story about the wolf?'

I nod.

'Miri likes to mythologise her place in all of this.'

'She also said your mother ruined all of your marriages.'

He smiles a wry smile as he tugs at his hair, trying, despite the wind, to flatten it back into shape. 'I'm not sure that's entirely true. Seriously, I think it only takes two to ruin a marriage. I did a pretty good job on my own.' He glances at me, and I swear his eyes twinkle. He may be gay, but this man is a top-level flirt.

'Well,' he grins, 'if Carolyn does leave the house to me, which is unlikely, I owe you something. You can flog it.'

Job done. Only we both know that pigs will sprout wings before Luke gets the house all to himself.

7

FALLING

Back at the house, Julia's been busy; a fire glows in the snug. Luke tells me I can wait there till Pope arrives with my car. Yet again, I find myself running my eyes across the room's reading material. Apart from Carolyn's book, her severe headshot facing out over the room, all other titles stand backbone forwards, regimented in height order, with the shelving straddling three of the snug's walls like an iron-firm embrace. It is a lovely room: the soft upholstery, the heavy rust drapes, the crackle and warm blush from the fire. It should be cosy, restful, but there's an odd tension sandwiched between the shelves, a pressure. It's almost impossible not to feel sergeant majored into reading something, and the choice is drier than a 1930s dust bowl. The books are mostly academic stuff, Carolyn's go-to on mothering, the copy of Kant, and very little fiction. Not one glossy magazine or even a self-aware uber-lush Taschen title blatant as a fluorescent Post-it Note on a posh person's forehead – I AM CULTURALLY AWARE. There will be no flicking through photos going on in this room. It could be that the owner is encouraging you to improve your mind. Alternatively, more likely, the motive could be one of intimidation. There's a couple of knick-knacks forgotten on the inch of wood left vacant beside one row of book spines. A random screw. Why is there always one screw too many? There's also a solitary earring somebody must have pulled off and abandoned. Carolyn's? Possibly. It's overlarge, with a rectangular blue stone shouting out from the centre, hemmed in by a gaggle of diamantés. I discover a small, barely perceptible rind of dust beneath it. No doubt it's been here for a while. If I were AJ, I'd slip the earring into my pocket. Although I'm hoping he's changed. He says he has, but this lone piece of lost treasure would test him; so easy to reappropriate.

Ignoring the forgotten jewel, I pull down a copy of Machiavelli's *The Prince*, the sort of thing you'd expect to find on Carolyn's shelves, and settle myself into the big leather armchair by the fire, flicking idly through the pages. I can see how Carolyn might have enjoyed something like this; she'd been building her own dynasty, one she fuelled with grandstanding one-upmanship. Worms are asking to be trodden on. Those without a plan deserve to have their will bent until it serves your own. Not my kind of thing. I like to wander in, wander back out again, always helpful, practically invisible. The doorbell goes, cutting into my thoughts. The noise making me feel oddly self-conscious as it echoes through the house. Hopefully it's the much-talked-about Pope with my car on his low-loader. I glance out of the window. There's an old wine-coloured Volvo parked on the gravel, no sign of my BMW, no trace of a low-loader. I hear the heavy door opening in the hallway and voices – female.

I put *The Prince* back on the shelf just as the door to the snug pushes open, and Julia peers in.

'You can wait in here,' she calls back to someone in the hall, with a quick smile of acknowledgement towards me. 'The fire's on. Erica won't be long. I think you two have met?'

My heart sinks when I see Niamh, the bridge player; I hope to God she doesn't suggest we go for a game. I try and wrangle a little more happy-to-see-you onto my face than I feel. 'Hi,' I say brightly. 'We met yesterday. Kirstin.'

The large greying woman is still wearing purple, a different outfit but the same shade. I wouldn't be surprised if her entire wardrobe is made up of purple. Not that I'm one to throw stones, mine's equally short on variety.

A smile flickers across her face. 'Online bridge. I remember. Still here?'

'My car,' I offer. 'Problems. And you?'

She lets her large frame sink down onto a massively forgiving sofa. 'Just wanted to see how they were all doing. It's quite a shock.'

I realise I don't even know how Carolyn died. I'd heard *sudden*, and *shock*, and putting the two keywords together had come up with heart attack, but I could be way off the mark.

'Wasn't it?' I say, hoping Niamh will fill me in as I navigate my way back to my leather chair.

'Brutal,' she replies, and her eyes begin to well.

Bugger. I've got this all wrong. I'm not sure anyone would describe a heart attack as *brutal*. 'Actually, I'm not too clear on what did happen?'

Niamh squashes her purple skirt further back into the wide cushions. Luckily, the sofa is green, so she's not too much of a clash. She's a good-looking woman, a little heavy perhaps, but probably once, she was a beauty. The nose is angular, the cheeks high. And her eyes are a soft, kind grey.

'I'd always told Carolyn not to walk up there alone.' Niamh tilts her head sadly down. 'There's a cliff path,' Niamh explains. 'It goes up around the coast to the family church. It's truly beautiful. A little windy this time of year.' She glances out of the window. 'But the cove next to this one is spectacular. The path's well established. Always been there. Although since the land is mainly private property, the council don't check it. There's no fencing of any kind. No barrier.' She takes a moment to pull a tissue from her bag but doesn't use it, just holds the thing ready and waiting in her purple lap. 'All the children were coming home for the weekend. If Carolyn had just waited another hour, Miri and Luke would have been with her. Maybe somebody could have...' Her voice trails away, lost in a sense of hopelessness. 'At least they could have raised the alarm.'

Mourners are fond of their '*if onlys*'. As if there are multitudes of possible universes branching away into infinity, but Niamh's comment does make me curious.

'I thought the family were just back for the funeral?'

She shakes her head. 'It was a classic case of bad timing. More so because it was unusual for the whole clan...' she raises her eyes awkwardly, a little embarrassed by the description, '...to be back. Even Miri was heading home, and you know what Carolyn was like about Miri?'

I nod. Miri had left me under no illusions. 'And you didn't approve?'

'Oh, that's not my place. I loved Carolyn dearly, but she could be a cruel woman sometimes. In fact, the more you loved her, the crueller it made her.' Niamh smiles bitterly. 'Maybe there is some truth in the old legend. Perhaps Carolyn was the wolf child. Hard as nails and with very sharp teeth.'

It seemed as though quite a few people in this family fancied themselves in the wolf role. 'Why were the family all coming back? Was it a birthday?'

Niamh shakes her head, forcing a tuft of wiry hair to come loose and curl around her large shoulders. 'No. Carolyn said she wanted to get things straight. I don't think they knew... but...' The hand with the tissue starts to rise towards those large, soft eyes.

'But?'

She stops in her tracks, eyeing me curiously over the rim of her handkerchief, then melts. 'Oh, what harm can it do now. Carolyn was dying.'

'Ah.'

'Cancer. They said it was inoperable. She opted out of chemo. Money can buy you everything but life it would seem.'

'Do the family know now?'

'Hmm, I'm not sure. I don't think so. Not convinced she had the time to tell them. Would it matter?' Niamh takes a deep intake of breath in an attempt to settle herself, slipping the tissue back into her pocket. 'Maybe it was all for the best. I just hope there was no fear. Fear is such a terrible thing. I hope it was so quick Carolyn didn't even know what was happening.'

I remember the car hitting me last night, the pain, the panic, the terrible sense of darkness. Was it better to have death creep up on you? I wasn't so sure.

'Are you all right?'

I realise she's staring straight at me. 'Yes. Sorry. It's been an emotional time.'

'For everyone.'

She fiddles idly with her right earlobe, and I remember the earring; it has to be Niamh's. Today she's wearing different ones, a vibrant jade green but easily as large as the lone earring on the shelf.

'Do you come up to the house a lot? You play bridge here?'

'No. No, the bridge group hires a private room at the Ship.'

Then maybe the earring's not hers? I'm about to ask when the moment is lost. The door opens, and Erica appears. Despite the soft low sofa, Niamh is on her feet, pulling the brittle Erica into a giant jangling hug.

I sneak out. There's no place for me here. I shouldn't be involved in any of this.

I go to my yellow room, throw myself across the bedspread, stare up at the ceiling and wonder how long it would take to go insane if you were to stay staring at this wallpaper. I figure a week should do the trick. I need to get out. The beach is too obvious. It can be seen from the house. Someone will come and offload something about Carolyn that I seriously don't want to hear. I have my own family troubles. They can keep theirs. But... oddly enough, I realise there is one place I do want to go. I want to find the footpath. I want to see the place where Carolyn went over. I reassure myself that this is not voyeurism, no. I'm interested in the logistics. Because this is a woman who knew she was dying. A woman who liked to control things. Could Carolyn have thrown herself into a possibly neater, certainly more immediate end?

Back in wellies and a waterproof, I walk quickly down the side of the path to the left of the beach that skirts up onto the cliff. There's no signpost standing sentry, pointing out the way. As Niamh had told me – this is private property. They all grew up here; they know the route. I didn't bother to tell anyone where I was going. They aren't interested in me. I shouldn't even be here.

The wind may have dropped, but once I get out onto the path, it starts pawing at my coat. Another month or two and this same walk will be too bitter to enjoy. I slant my face down towards the ground, pushing through the oncoming assault as I climb steadily towards the cliff, thinking to myself about families and how odd it is that even with all the money, there are still problems. Would money have made any difference to my family? My mother was depressed, so perhaps nothing could have knocked her out of that, and my father might have drunk himself under the table and into the emergency ward just that little bit quicker if money had been no object, but AJ? Would my brother have bothered straying from the straight and narrow if there had been cash in the bank? When AJ got banged up, I was an adult. Old enough to look after myself. Sixteen. I took the 'emergency tin' from the top shelf in the kitchen. It was a laugh really that we had an emergency tin because when you looked back on our life, it was pretty much emergency all the way, but I took the tin and went to the train station. I decided I'd go as far as possible, so that was Land's End or John o'Groats. The first train through was on its way to Birmingham, and I kept heading west. Now it feels as if I've travelled just about as far west as it's possible to go.

Niamh was right about the second cove. It's awe-inspiring, steep-sided and stretching out ahead of me. More expansive than the cove by the house. The water is deeper, less graduated and shines like a brilliant blue sapphire. I make a mental note that if I do land the sale, we'll need a shot from up here. On one side, the house is laid out beneath me, standing as it does beside a strip of white sand that leads off into shallow azure waters. Face out the other way, and it's the clean-cut second cove, filled with deep ocean, clouds and soaring seabirds.

Past owner falls off crumbling cliff path is a bit of a downer in more than one sense. Maybe it didn't hit the papers. Perhaps Carolyn's death had been newsworthy enough in itself. I hadn't seen the headline. I make another mental note to check on the details. Hopefully, I can be vague about it if the sale ever does get off the ground. Mysterious deaths can seriously damage the price of a property; twenty per cent or more can get sliced off before the details come out of the printer. Suicides and murders are the worst. Curses and ghosts are an even bigger put-off than landfills. Accidental death is okay if it looks like a one-time kind of a thing, so no obvious hazards. The path is in good nick, a two-foot-wide stretch of hard-packed sandy soil cutting through the short wiry grass. There's no barrier, even in the narrow places, but this is understandable. Any form of fencing would cost a fortune, and if Carolyn was dying anyway... A cold shiver passes over me. Those rocks look hard. The drop is steep. My own mother jumped in front of a train. It was quick. So they said. Jumping from a cliff is a whole different story. You'd have way too much time to think as you went down. Suicide says *unhappy house*. Was Carolyn the kind of woman who might be able to throw herself off? Niamh didn't say what kind of cancer Carolyn had. I peer over the edge. The waves below me crash into the waiting rocks. Pulling the rigid arms of my borrowed waterproof tighter around me, I press on up the hill.

The path cuts through some gorse bushes. It's a little more sheltered, and I'm thankful for that. I'm not sure this outward-bounds idea was the best activity after what happened last night. My headache is lurking around like a rain cloud, full of threat. Nonetheless, on I go looking for a recent collapse on the path, a strip of raw sandy soil – the point where Carolyn stepped out of this world and into whatever lies beyond. I'm disappointed though. I can't see any fresh crumbles, no comic skid-marks. If I want to know exactly where she went over, I'm going to have to ask.

After a good forty-five minutes of battling against the wind, I look up and see the crouched shape of a church, sitting in the shadows of a bank of dark clustered trees to my right. It doesn't look inviting, but I feel an overwhelming sense of relief. Twenty minutes inside four stone walls will hopefully be enough to melt my poor frozen ear canals. From a distance, the church looks small, a forgotten lump of dark-grey patchwork stone, but as I draw closer, I realise it's the real deal, not just some folly. This is a mini-church, at one time a working place of worship. I come around the side of the building, the long grass tangling damp around my ankles as I move out of the wind and towards the heavy oak door. It smells different here. A metallic, earthy taint masking the salt of the sea. A smell that seems almost pagan. In the shadow of the building and the clustered woods, I suddenly get the strangest sensation, as though I'm being watched. Peering into the dense green foliage, it all seems dark and eerily silent, but the harder I stare, the more convinced I become that there is something just beyond the thick line of trees. I remember last night just after my body went hurtling up into the air, the fall, the eyes in the woods. Someone was following me then, and they're following me still. My breath catches in my throat as I take a step back, ready to turn, ready to run. Something is moving in the shadows. I'm suddenly aware of how alone I am: no phone, no people, no witnesses. A crow rakes the sea air with a cold harsh rasp. I take another step away from the woods. Carolyn was up here alone. If Carolyn had waited for the others, she might not have been dead. A branch snaps.

'Hello?' My voice sounds ineffectual, lost. Another movement. My heart thumps as a branch of leaves dances into action and a muntjac deer dives across the netted undergrowth. What an idiot.

I step towards the stone building, take the rusty iron ring on the church door in both hands and turn. From inside, I hear the muffled reassuring metal scrape as the lock on the latch goes up. I give the damp wooden door a push with my right shoulder, and it slides open belching out a thick musty cloud of trapped air. It's dark inside. The only windows run along the wall that backs onto the trees, throwing the church into perpetual shadow. There are no windows on the cliffside of the building. Perhaps it's too exposed. Whatever the reason, the result is gloomy darkness. The church is simple inside; just a single room, around twenty-four feet by eighteen, with four rows of dark, hard wooden benches lying either side of a thin aisle. There's a carved stone font at the back and a small altar at the front with a large rectangular painting hanging above it. The church smells of seawater and rotting wood. I glance around me. Each of the heavy stone walls is engraved with plaques honouring the dead. I wonder if Carolyn will get herself a plaque. Probably. Walking close to the wall, my footsteps echo across the floor. The sound bounces, amplified by the hard stone, making it seem as though there is more than just me in here. Perhaps there is; there are certainly enough people carved into the wall. It's difficult to make out the names in the half-light. I scan the uneven plaster for Millfords. I suppose they will all be Millfords. The hasty bit of homework I'd managed before arriving at the island informed me that the house had been in the same family for a couple of centuries. I can't help wondering what it would be like to be able to trace your history back through the ages. Would it make you feel more secure? Grounded? My family tree is more dead ends than branches. My mother eloped with my dad. God knows why. Dad's family must have been from Ireland; the name Conroy is a bit of a giveaway, but he never mentioned it, and his accent was pure Scouse. He worked at the docks. Though 'work' is a bit of a misnomer. The man was a drunkard, one that liked nothing more than a good strike and a bit of time off sick. Sadly, he took the wrong day off and ended up having a fatal encounter with a steel girder. He was out of his head, so at least that's one mercy – he probably didn't feel much. If it weren't for AJ, I'd have ended up in care. Only four years older than me, but AJ managed to keep the wheels on my life turning. We had nothing but each other. These people have everything. I move down the aisle towards the altar with its wide rectangular painting hanging overhead. The picture is kind of weird – very dark. Even in bright light, it would be difficult to tell what's going on in the painted strokes of the canvas. Half of it is cast in complete swirling black. In the left half, I can just make out, emerging from the darkness, a few figures – a man standing in the background, a young woman and four bright-yellow birds flying off into the dark heavens. Then I notice something odd. I peer closer into the black well of the painting. The woman looks a little like...

'There are lights.'

The voice comes from nowhere, accompanied by a familiar buzz of electricity spritzing through the air. Warm, yellow light fills the room. I turn to see Oscar standing in the doorway. 'You gave me a shock when I came in.' He laughs. 'Didn't think anyone would be here. Admiring the family portrait?' He extends his arm out towards the picture.

'Sorry. Yes,' I bluster. 'I needed a walk.' I turn back towards the canvas, pointing to the figure of the woman emerging from the darkness. 'Is that Carolyn?'

He nods. 'Indeed. My mother had it retouched when she was in her forties. I don't remember that. But I do remember when she put Miri in.'

'Miri?' I stare back at the picture; there's no Miri. It's just Carolyn and an older man.

'The birds.'

Now I get it. 'They represent you all?'

'Exactly. The old guy at the back, the one with the stern face, that's my grandfather. The *children...*' he looks a little embarrassed, 'that's us; we're the birds. Miri came along later, so that is how I remember her being added.'

'Why birds?'

He takes a deep breath. 'To do with the island legend. The wolf; the only way to get away from its jaws is to fly.'

I can't help myself. I laugh.

'Yes,' he smiles, 'it is all totally over the top. No doubt now Carolyn's dead, someone will paint us in. As people, hopefully. Not that it's currently a priority.'

'Speaking of which, has there been any word on my car?'

Oscar shakes his head gravely. 'Pope always takes his time. I'd like to say he does a good job, but... no. He's just slow. No doubt there'll be word when we get back.'

'Who are all these people?' I gesture with my good arm up towards a wall that's carved with names.

'The Millfords and the Fordhams. They owned two of the biggest estates. The families joined in 1897.'

I smile. 'That's very precise.'

'Sorry.' Even in the darkness, I see him blush, embarrassed. 'I can be overly precise. The 1890s would have sufficed I expect.'

He's kind of sweet. Bashful.

'I was married here,' Oscar says, glancing around the church, taking it all in.

I feel a sudden pang of defensiveness for him. I know more about this than he thinks.

'And christened here too. My father's memorial was also held in this church.'

'When did he die?'

'Oh, a long time ago. I was around eight.'

'And you didn't want to hold your mother's memorial here?'

'The guest list was too big. There were a lot of people who wanted to see her buried.'

Does he mean what he just said?

'And... under the circumstances...'

He leaves the words hanging awkwardly for a moment. 'It was close to here that my mother...' he hesitates, 'lost her footing.'

'Oh,' I say apologetically.

'Fitting in a way. She loved this place. It's part of who we are.'

I don't know how to respond to this. I'm still not sure what the best exit plan for Carolyn was but, if she loved this spot, perhaps dying so close is what she would have wanted?

I glance up at the engravings. Then notice, hidden behind the carvings, there are eyes. They're everywhere, on the wood and carved into the stone. All slightly different shapes and sizes, but each and every one open and staring. 'Are those gargoyles?'

Oscar follows my gaze. 'Technically, yes, but they're actually wolves. It's to do with the legend. Again. This is where they say the wolf was born.'

'This spot?'

'That's right. A silly tale, no truth in it, but part of the island's history. Don't get me on the subject.' He smiles, glancing awkwardly down at his hands. 'I can bore you for England. The others are always teasing me.'

I smile kindly. I'll bet they're always teasing him. Out of all the siblings, he's the one with the thinnest skin, and people do love to poke anything they think will squirm.

'We should go,' he says. 'It feels a little morbid being here after...'

I'm exhausted, my ears still ringing from the cold. I don't want to go anywhere. I just want to sit, but that's not an option. 'Well, it might be easier with two of us, battling through the wind.'

He laughs. 'True, but...'

I note a playful glint of mischief in his eyes.

'I do have the car if you'd rather.'

8

TWO DOWN

THERE'S a small car park outside the church, enough for maybe four cars if parked carefully, but there's no need for careful parking today; the knackered old Land Rover sprawls proprietorially across all spaces. I clamber into the passenger seat, inhaling the smell of dried mud and wax jackets, as I pull the rattling metal door shut behind me.

'I appreciate this.' I tug the seat belt across my body and buckle up.

'I was hardly going to leave you there to walk back. Besides, I'm not sure that cliff path is safe.'

'No,' I say simply, not wanting to unpick any raw wounds Oscar may be carrying. We both know it's not safe. 'I just needed some fresh air. I feel like I'm kicking my heels a bit back at the house. My phone's still not working.'

'We can probably find you a spare. There's a drawer in the kitchen dresser. Mother used to keep all her old mobiles there. Have yourself a root when we get back. Something might work. Modern technology.' He smirks. 'Where would we be...?'

As we pull away from the small church, I can't help feeling

glad to see the back of it. The building seems to be crouching in the shadows behind us, grimy as a rat waiting to pounce.

'Do you live at the house permanently?'

Oscar bumps the car over the track towards the main road. 'None of us exactly lives here anymore. Officially, I live in Bristol. But I spend a lot of time here visiting Timmy. He's a worry, you see. Especially now. He had a live-in carer but…'

'But?'

He grimaces, clearly something happened here, but he's not entirely comfortable about spilling it to someone not in the inner circle. 'It didn't work out.'

'What will happen to him now?'

Oscar hooks his bottom lip under his teeth, thoughtfully. 'I think it's best if he stays here. I mean, it's not just Timmy; it's Julia as well.'

'But the house is so big.' I gaze out of the window at the rolling landscape. 'And a little cut off.'

'True. I can see how that might worry some people, but this is Timmy's home. We have to think of what's right for him. We're so fortunate, Kirstin. I know that. I'm the first to admit life has been good to us, and not because we've worked for it. It all fell at our feet – Erica, myself, Luke, even Miri. An easy start in life works wonders. And now we can all support ourselves. Apart from Timmy, we all have jobs.'

I'd been so seduced by all the rich trappings I hadn't even thought about them having professions. 'If you don't mind me asking, what do you all do?'

'Erica's in PR. She's done well for herself. Who would have thought? PR?' He seems genuinely amused. 'Luke's done okay. As *okay* as is possible for anyone in publishing to do.'

This has all the hallmarks of a back-handed insult, but I say nothing.

'I think he struggles a bit. It's one of those businesses; all or nothing – money to burn or eating beans on toast. I'm in sales.

Cars. I've always loved them. The Mazda's mine,' he adds proudly.

'Nice,' I say, more because I feel appreciation is expected, than from a desire to be driving the Mazda myself.

'And this,' he taps the wheel of the Land Rover, 'I just keep this here for running around. I'd be happy to do you a deal on something?'

I laugh. 'I'm not sure I'm in your price bracket.'

'Ah, I have something for every pocket. You come and see me when we get back. I'll make sure you're all right.'

Once a car salesman... 'Bristol's a long way.'

'I have a dealership in Taunton.'

I get the feeling it's going to be easier to just agree. 'Great. Count me in.'

'And even little Miri's been doing fantastically, considering.'

'Considering?'

'Well, you know. We all have our trials. She's had a testing time recently.'

I think of the brown envelope I saw handed over at the wake. I remember her tears.

'Car crash,' he says.

'Oh.' For a moment, I'm taken off guard.

'Rather bad, I'm afraid. She wasn't driving. Luckily, she was thrown from the car. The driver died.'

'Oh, no.'

'About six months ago, I'd say.'

'Was the driver a close friend?'

'Fiancé. Malcolm Tanner.'

Odd. The name rings a bell. Oscar gives me a sideways look in the mirror.

'He's a...' Oscar hesitates. 'Not sure what they call it anymore, a social media sensation?'

'Ah. That Malcolm Tanner. The YouTuber. He does reviews?'

'Exactly.'

This is big. Malcolm was the poster child for the zero-to-hero culture. I'm not even sure what he was worth anymore. He had a massive following. I even followed him myself for a bit. From what I could remember, he reviewed everything and anything. He had this cheeky, fun style and was always cropping up: selling things from sofas to beard clippers. Companies showered him with products to test and there were regular appearances on chat shows. He may have even done *Dancing on Ice*, but I'm not sure. Dancing or not, everyone had a soft spot for Malcolm, till it went wrong. 'He was good. I used to watch his stuff. Sometimes.'

Oscar clears his throat apologetically. 'Not my kind of thing, I'm afraid. Although I did watch a few of the car reviews.'

I glance out of the window, trying to hone in on the memories – the headlines from six months ago – the crumpled, burnt-out shell of Malcolm's car. 'That must have been difficult for Miri.'

'Exactly. We should have been having a wedding this autumn, not a funeral.' Oscar threads the large steering wheel carefully through his hands as we take a corner. 'So, Miri, *buoyant*? Hmm, sometimes, yes. Other times, not so much. You can never tell. Although I have to say, on the work front, Miri's nailing it. She wanted to act and that's a hard gig to break into.' *Gig* sounds uncomfortable coming out of poor Oscar's mouth. I get the feeling he knows this because his shoulders stiffen just that little bit more. 'Then after Malcolm's death, well she's been swamped with work offers. So that at least helped take her mind off things.'

'She told me she had a big audition coming up.'

'Yes. Very big. America big.' He grins. 'So, fingers crossed. She could do with a break.'

'Everyone could do with a break.' Miri wasn't exactly *struggling actress* material. I find myself wondering what she'll get in Carolyn's will. Most likely, a heap more money than she needs. I wonder if she got anything when Malcolm died. Probably not; they were both too young to realise death might be driving towards them full speed. Either way, I don't have any doubts that Miri's going to be more than comfortable.

'She used to do a few voiceovers; would you believe?' Oscar seems genuinely amused. 'People paid her to talk.'

'What did she say?'

'Oh, anything. One day she'd be talking about gin; the next, she's selling time-shares, or what do you call it... those dating sites?'

'I wouldn't imagine Miri had any shortage of offers on that front.'

'Exactly. And that's what they want. They wouldn't want someone like me.'

There's a pause, one that changes Oscar's comment from something which could have been funny to something which only manages to be sad. 'Anyway,' he blusters on, 'the American thing's pretty much in the bag. The movie people want her, and she won't need to do any of those chicken-feed fill-ins if she lands it. Cross fingers.' He lifts his right hand momentarily from the wheel and does just that.

'And Luke?' I can't help myself. 'I'll bet Luke doesn't need dating sites. He must be quite a hit with the ladies.'

I know this is all wrong; Luke isn't really interested in me. He's more Marco's type, but I'm curious and so fishing. There was the strange conversation I'd overheard between Miri and that mystery man with the stationery. *'If they knew about you.'* Those were her exact words. Had Miri been talking to Luke? Was she referring to his sexuality? In this day and age, would anyone even care? And if it was Luke, what was in the envelope? Who had dirt on who?

'Luke?' Oscar drags me back from my thoughts. 'Oh yes. Luke is an absolute flirt. Please don't take it personally if he's been flirting with you.' Oscar shoots me an apologetic look before angling his eyes back towards the road. 'It doesn't mean anything.

He does it with everyone, even me sometimes. It's his moods. Just the way he blows.'

Now I am completely lost. The more time I spend with this family, the less I understand it. Then again, maybe that's the way all families work.

Either way, I'm relieved when we pull up outside the house. Oscar is sweet, but he's somehow hard work. It's not that he doesn't talk, or ask questions, or isn't amiable enough, but even fifteen minutes in his company leaves me feeling desperately sad. He's one of those people that just tries too hard.

'I expect Julia will have sorted something out for lunch by now,' he tells me brightly.

'I may just skip it. Would you mind if I headed up to my room? That walk almost finished me off.'

'It's the sea air.' He smiles kindly. 'Gives the lungs a run for their money.'

It's probably more likely to be the fact that I got hit by his brother race-tracking his tank of an SUV, but none of that is Oscar's problem. Besides, it's in my interest not to rub people's feathers the wrong way. 'You're right, sea air.' I smile. 'I might just try and get a bit of shut-eye.'

'Good idea. I'll ask Julia to make you up a cold plate.'

We head towards the large front door. I can barely keep my eyes open. I cannot wait to get into my room and crawl under that satin coverlet when suddenly a scream rings out.

There's a moment of absolute stillness when the shrill note hangs in the air, as we stand dwarfed by the tall battlement walls of the house, confused. Even the sea and the birds seem to have shut up. Then time seems to fast forward. The other sounds come flooding back in, accompanied by the roar of the wind. Oscar sprints forward with me following as we dash through the large front door. Then more screaming. So much louder now. It's a woman. The shrill sounds, seemingly torn from her body, bounce across the marble hall like an out-of-control tennis ball. Every drop of blood appears to have drained from Oscar's pallid face. He hesitates, then stares up towards the landing; the sound must be coming from upstairs. We speed up the steps, taking them two, three at a time.

Once on the landing, Oscar dashes towards a room. It's the one that I'd hidden in during the wake – the room with the pink flowering wallpaper. The door's standing open. The screaming, thankfully, has stopped; only the ring of it echoes through the house accompanied by the sound of someone sobbing. Every bit of sensible in my head is telling me to run back down the stairs, out of the door and down the long gravel driveway. Whatever is in that room is not for my eyes. But like a sleepwalker, I find myself following Oscar through the door, my body pulled towards the inevitable.

'Shit.' Miri is sprawled across the bed. Her eyes staring, glazed and wild, towards the ceiling. Dried foam oozes from her mouth as her body hangs down, head towards the floor, red hair dangling in a macabre tangle. Everything about the way her body is abandoned seems unnatural. No human being should be lying like that. Broken. I stand frozen in the doorway, a good ten feet from the bed. I don't need to get any closer to know that Miri is dead.

'Oh no. No. Please, no.' Erica collapses back against the wall, her mouth twisted open in shock. It must have been Erica who was screaming. Julia is slumped on the floor, actually on her knees, clutching her stomach as if she's in physical pain.

'Fuck.' Luke's arrived behind me. He pushes past. 'I know she was struggling, but... has anyone checked her pulse?'

We all know there's going to be no pulse. Reluctant for confirmation, everybody hangs back.

'Why would she do this?' Erica wrings her hands helplessly. 'Call a doctor, for Christ's sake. We should do something. What should we do?' Erica lurches aimlessly forwards, her body loose, helpless as a rag doll.

A wave of panic grips my insides. Before good sense can get hold of my brain, there are words chundering out of my mouth. 'I'm not sure we should touch her.'

They all look around at me. They'd forgotten I was there. I wish to God I'd kept quiet – animosity, shock, bewilderment, it's all there in their faces.

'Miri wasn't... well.' Oscar draws the fire. He sounds heartbroken. His words barely audible.

But I'm shaking my head. Everything about this feels wrong. 'We shouldn't touch anything.'

'I just didn't realise she was this...' Luke mumbles.

'It's suicide.' Erica's face is white as a sheet.

'I don't think so.'

Erica turns her ghostly features towards me, her lips a curious dried slit. 'You wouldn't know anything about this, but Miri's been having...'

'I mentioned to Kirstin that Miri was having problems.' Oscar stares guiltily at his feet. Awkward at having been found airing the family laundry to a stranger.

'Problems?' Erica hits the word back hard. 'Miri's fiancé, and then mother's death. It destroyed her.'

We all stare at the body, apart from Julia who is still head down, weeping, a low continuous moan.

'She seemed fine this morning,' I mumble.

'*Fine!*' Erica swings her body around so it's facing mine. 'How could you possibly tell?' Erica's moving towards me, her face a picture of open hate. I have no idea what Erica intends to do. I just want to get out.

'I'm sorry. I shouldn't be here,' I say, stepping back.

Luke grabs Erica's arm as she reels past him, slowing her, holding her, pinning her like a butterfly in place.

'Look,' I say and point towards the edge of the bed. They can't see it from where they're standing. They're too high, too close. But I've got a wider view. I can see why Miri's body looks contorted. She was trying to write something. There are letters scrawled across the carpet in the shadow of the bed. A dark stain of liquid.

HELP.

The next words to come tumbling from my mouth are ones that I never thought I'd be saying in a million years. 'I think we need to call the police.'

9

THE INVESTIGATION

I DON'T WANT to be wearing Miri's clothes anymore. The purple slacks, the vibrant green jumper, it feels so wrong. As we wait for the police, I try and give the family a bit of space. Keeping my black coat firmly buttoned over my dead-girl outfit as I wait up in *my* room. Once, I brave it out into the hallway and hear someone sobbing like a banshee. A woman. Has to be Erica. I don't go out again. I still don't have a way of texting anyone, and there's no word on my car. I feel trapped in someone else's life, and, despite all the fancy trimmings, and even without the murder, I seriously don't want to be here. The yellow room is still unfamiliar, making me feel more trespasser than guest. It smells of expensive lilac air fresheners and sheets so over-laundered they've retained that generic cover-all of washing powder, as opposed to anything personal, anything genuine. This is not my world. I look out through the large windows onto this strange landscape, like a bird in a cage – my life on hold. Outside, the day is still and grey, the trees in the grounds not even bothering to rustle, the sea barely breaking foam. Even the gulls are unnaturally quiet.

I have never been so relieved to hear the wail of a siren and catch a glimpse of a flashing blue light. Though I have to admit; the response is underwhelming. We get two police cars and a couple of paramedics. Personally, I think we should get a whole lot more. This has to be a murder investigation. No doubt Oscar will have played it down. He'll have bigged up poor Miri's depression. The tragedy of the fiancé she'd had to watch burn to ashes in his super gadget car. The loss of the beloved 'grandmother' – the woman who saved Miri from the care system: all of it could point to a strong possibility of suicide. Perhaps the pitiful police presence doesn't matter. It's all too late now. As soon as I hear the sound of the guys in blue coming through the door downstairs, I head out of my room and onto the landing. This time, thank goodness, there's no wailing Erica within earshot. Although I've had experience with the police, I realise that I don't know how any of this works. When they came for AJ, they just carted him off. They weren't interested in me. They didn't even ring the doorbell, but it would appear that a murder in a country house is a more civilised affair than a raid on a council flat. The doorbell is rung, no warnings are issued. Not one person is shouting out rights as they stumble in a group cluster-fuck through the doorframe. I can't help thinking they've got the legal procedure arse-over-backwards here. AJ didn't kill anyone.

It was art that snookered my brother. He'd never dabbled in the art world before. Usually it was just small stuff off sites, the sort of thing anyone could have taken if they had a transit, working biceps and a full quota of light fingers. But there had been an exhibition at the Tate and a delay getting the pictures in. A golden opportunity: that's how it had been pitched to AJ. He insists it was just a bit of a prank. Either way, AJ and his mate Jericho were in over their necks. They'd been rounded up within twenty-four hours, and the paintings were back on the wall. Well, most of them. One of them never got back to the gallery: the Lowry, the Punch and Judy. And that one single painting just will not get its claws out of us. It's the reason why parole keeps being pushed back, but next week there'll be another hearing, and this time AJ's got a pretty good chance of getting out. But, like I said, murder in a country house, it's a different ball game.

'Mr Millford?' There's a detective standing in the hallway, addressing an ashen-faced Oscar. He may be plain clothes, but I could spot him a mile off. He has a wallpaper look, as if he's trying to blend in. With his ruddy, round face and just enough dark, wiry hair clinging to his scalp to cover the skin, he's doing pretty good on the *blending in* front. He's over forty, which always helps if you want to be invisible. Nothing about his demeanour says, *'notice me'* or *'boss'*, but his eyes are sharp as grit. I'm willing to bet he misses nothing.

'We're both Mr Millford,' Luke explains, stepping forward, hand outstretched for the shake. His eyes are rimmed-red as if he's applied a scouring pad to the lids. 'But I called it in.'

The detective takes Luke's hand. 'I'll be your officer in charge. I'm DS Graham. We'll need the medical team to identify the body.'

'She's my niece,' Erica says. Her ironing board posture is crumpled.

'We all know who she is.' There's a note of irritation threaded through Luke's voice.

'Just a formality.' In contrast, DS Graham says this calmly. For him, this is just routine.

'It's suicide.' Erica sniffs. 'My niece wasn't the most stable of people. She's not a blood relative, you understand. Miri was adopted.'

I can't help wondering if Erica wants to imply that, genetically, the true family bloodline is not at all on the fruitcake scale. That Miri had her own sweet Looney Tunes thing going on.

DS Graham doesn't reply. Instead, he shoots Erica a small,

curt smile. 'Is there anywhere I can conduct interviews? I'll need to get statements from all of you.'

'I'm not family,' I say, hoping he can let me go early.

'Were you here when the body was discovered?'

'Well, I...'

'Kirstin and I got back to the house just as...' Oscar hesitates. 'As my sister discovered...' he falters again, unwilling to spell it out, '...as Julia and my sister made their discovery.'

DS Graham fixes me with those hard, grey eyes. 'Then, yes, Ms...?'

'Kirstin,' I offer in the pause he's left. 'Kirstin Conroy.'

'Yes, I will need to question you.'

Suddenly, I'm not liking any of this. I've gone from being a nobody to providing alibis.

DS Graham takes over the snug, whilst we take our seats in front of the cold fireplace in the drawing room.

Oscar gives the empty grate an irritated look as he comes through the door. 'I'll get that started.'

'What's with the coat?' Luke asks.

How did I get myself mixed up in this?

'Kirstin?'

I pull open the top button on my coat, so Luke can see what I've got underneath – Miri's green jumper.

'Ah.' He leans towards me, so he can keep his voice low. 'When it calms down, I'll sort you something.'

I try to look grateful, but I'm not. I want to be hightailing it out of here at the first opportunity. I'd go naked if it meant I could get out faster, but I can't help feeling sorry for them all.

'Are you okay?' I ask, my voice barely breaking above a whisper.

'No.' He shakes his head. 'Miri was the best breath of fresh air around this place.'

Even though I'd only met her briefly, I could tell that's exactly what she was, but was that all an act? Was she still traumatised by the death of her fiancé? Then there was the envelope. What was in that envelope?

We sit huddled on our respective sofas like shipwrecked sailors. There's a sense of relief when Oscar does get the fire burning. Now we have a gentle, continuous flicker to hold our attention and a soft crackle to fill the silence.

It doesn't take long for the coroner to come back down the stairs. He's old, greying, balding, and slow, way past retirement age. Somewhere, woven into the fibres of his white coverall, he carries with him the sad, faint whiff of bleach. He doesn't want to be here, not doing this, not looking at the bodies of young women who should have years of life left stretching ahead of them.

'I'm sorry,' he says gently.

Julia lets out a little sob.

'How? Why?' Erica jitters, her voice shrill and unwelcome.

But the coroner shakes his head. 'We'll have to do tests.'

I'm still wearing my coat when DS Graham finally calls me through. Julia was in with him for at least forty minutes. It must have been slow work getting anything out of her. The room feels completely different than it did earlier. Even with the fire glowing in the grate, there's an uncomfortable residue of tension. Though, hats off to him, DS Graham's face is neutral; he's not giving anything away. I get the feeling he finds it difficult to smile, even when he's off duty. He's too used to being serious for a living. Humanity's suffering is absorbed daily through his brain before being passed on to the relevant department.

'I shouldn't be here,' I say after confirming my name. 'My car broke down.'

He says nothing.

I've been in this sort of interview situation before. When I was growing up, there were a lot of questions about AJ. The failed art heist was just the end of the line. So I'm familiar with the format. When I was small, there would be biscuits and tea. I ate the biscuits. I drank the tea, but however long they kept me in, I didn't spill: not a crumb, not a drop, not a word.

'Why are you wearing a coat?' DS Graham asks.

'Miri lent me her clothes.'

'The deceased?'

An involuntary cold wave slips over me. What a horrible description. 'She had a name,' I say, correcting him. 'My clothes got wet. Miri lent me some things. It feels wrong wearing them now.' I flap the ends of my coat, awkwardly. 'So...'

'How did you get wet?'

'That isn't important. I'm not supposed to be here.'

He says nothing.

'Okay.' I draw in a deep breath. 'If you insist. I had an accident. I was heading for the ferry. It was after the wake.'

'Carolyn Millford's wake?'

'So far, there has only been one, so, yes.'

I know I shouldn't let it rile me, but it drives me up the wall when the police ask the obvious. It's all part of their strategy, but it gets to me. I have nothing to hide. Why interrogate me?

He says nothing, just looks at me shrewdly, knowing I'm rattled.

I need to keep calm. Just the facts, Kirstin, I think to myself. Just give him the facts. 'My car broke down,' I say simply. 'I started to walk. I got very wet.'

'You've got a fresh scar under your left eyebrow.'

My fingers reach towards my face. 'That was the accident.'

'*Accident?*' He runs his teeth over his bottom lip. 'And can you tell me what this *accident* involved?'

'It's not related.'

He shrugs, as though he has all the time in the world, and why not tell him anyway.

'My car broke down.'

DS Graham nods dismissively, as if to say *yes, we got that far.*

'It was dark. I was walking along the road. I was on my phone and this other car came up fast behind me.'

'It hit you?'

'Yes. But it was dark.'

He leans forward slightly in his chair. I'm not sure if he's genuinely interested, or just ticking the boxes. 'Who was driving?'

'Luke. He's one of the sons. The taller one.'

'We've met.'

Of course they have. 'He brought me back here.'

DS Graham eyes me curiously. 'You've seen a doctor?'

'Yup. I have, but look, this is going nowhere because it's not related. I don't know anything about Miri. I'm not supposed to be here.'

'So you keep saying. Where's your car?'

'Good question.' But he doesn't look amused. 'Apparently, it's at Pope's.'

'Can you check that, please?' DS Graham calls out over his shoulder, and one of the men in blue goes out.

'You don't like the police much, Ms?' His eyes are blank, unemotional.

'I didn't say that.'

He nods, slowly. 'But even though you don't like the police, apparently you're the only one who thinks the death may be suspicious.' There's a pause before he continues. 'What would make you think that?'

'The way the body was angled. It was awkward, as if she was trying to get up. And the message on the floor – *HELP*.'

'Apparently, she wasn't a well young lady.'

'I'd only just met her.'

'Depression.'

The word sits there in the room for a moment. I don't do anything with it, making it sound even more final.

Graham glances down at his hands, breaking eye contact for just a moment. 'Did she seem unwell to you?'

I think about this long and hard. My experience of Miri had been fleeting, but even in the brief time we'd spent together, she'd struck me as doing okay. She was upset about her gran but optimistic about the future. Naïve? Yes. A little too silver-spoon for her own good? Definitely. But unwell? Depressed? I still didn't get that. 'No,' I say. 'No, she didn't seem unwell. She seemed to be coping okay, under the circumstances.'

He flicks one hand over his trouser leg, as if removing a speck of dust. I have no idea if he thinks I'm way off the mark here or if he agrees with me. He's impossible to read. 'And how did you know Carolyn Millford?' he asks, fixing me again with those flint eyes.

'Bridge,' I say shortly. In for a penny, in for a pound. 'Online bridge. So, can I go now?'

Graham sucks at the insides of his cheeks as if thinking it over. 'Yes.'

'And my car?'

'We're checking on it.'

Suddenly it hits me – the thing that's making me feel that this isn't suicide. It's not the dead fiancé. It's not the dead gran. It's not even the 'HELP' scrawled on the carpet. There was a tension in the Millford family – a secret. 'This may mean nothing,' I say hesitantly. Immediately he's scrutinising me hard again. 'But… I saw something at the wake.'

Now he's interested.

'I was putting away the coats. I was in the bathroom, the en suite in Miri's room.'

'You were putting the coats upstairs?' He looks puzzled.

'Actually, I kind of got lost.' None of that is important. I sigh. 'The point is, I was in the en suite, and then Miri came into the bedroom. She didn't know I was there, but she was with someone else, and they were having an argument.'

'About?' he says, straight back in there.

I shake my head. 'I don't know. I only heard the end of it, but I think someone was blackmailing her.'

His features remain blank. 'What makes you say that?'

'This person, whoever it was, they gave her an envelope, a large A4 brown envelope. She wasn't happy about it. She said something like *"If they knew about you"* and called the person a bastard.'

'And you don't know who this other person was?'

I shake my head. At the time, I hadn't even known who Miri was. 'I didn't see the other person.'

'And you've no idea what was in the envelope?'

Again, I shake my head.

'Okay.' His tone is brief, final. 'That's it for now. If you leave this house, Ms Conroy, please keep us informed of your whereabouts.'

I should learn to keep my mouth shut.

10

CAR TROUBLE

BACK IN MY YELLOW BEDROOM, Luke brings me a pile of clothes.

'Sorry,' he says in an embarrassed tone. 'It's a bit thrown together. I avoided everything of Miranda's. Most of this stuff is Mum's, and the jacket's mine.'

I take the clothes from his hands. I can't bear to be in Miri's signature green any longer.

'Thanks, Luke. I appreciate it,' I say, moving to the bathroom.

Behind the door of the en suite, I pull off Miri's green sweater, holding it limply between my fingers. Should I throw it? That seems so wrong but, seriously, who is going to want the thing? I can't imagine Erica's the sort of person to lug stuff to charity shops, and Julia's in no fit state to do anything. I press the pedal on the waste bin and pack the green jumper firmly inside.

'Any news on my car?' I call through the closed door. 'If I want to make the ferry terminal to catch the 7.30, I should be leaving about now.'

'The police are chasing your car as well. That should light a fire under Pope's backside.'

I pull Carolyn's silk shirt over my head, wincing when I try to get my left arm through the armhole. 'How are you holding up?' I ask, as I tackle a pair of Carolyn's jeans.

'To be honest,' Luke replies cautiously, 'I wouldn't really describe myself as *holding up*. They're searching Miri's room at the moment.'

I stop, mid-pull on the denim. 'Oh.'

'Yeah, something about an A4 envelope?'

I say nothing, hoping Luke doesn't know that it was me who spilled the beans on the possible blackmail.

'This whole thing is a nightmare,' he continues. I hear the sound of the bed sinking under his weight. 'Mum was bad enough, but Miri? It's such a waste.'

There's a pause. We both know he's right. I draw up the fly on the jeans and catch the top button. I'm in. I wouldn't be winning any catwalk parades for the island's best dressed, but at least the clothes are warm, dry and not off someone who's died within the last twenty-four hours. I slip on Luke's jacket. It's one of those baseball ones, a dull red with cream stripes down the arms. This, I like.

'I just can't see how it could be murder.' Luke's voice intrudes from the other room. 'Why would anyone murder Miri?'

'The "HELP" thing,' I say. I feel like I'm going around in circles here. 'Why write "HELP" if you don't need it?'

I give myself a once-over in the mirror. I am completely out of make-up. I look a sight, but there is absolutely nothing I can do about it. I pull open the door.

'Wow,' Luke says, his eyes literally popping out of his head.

That gets me. I know I shouldn't. This is not the time, but I burst into laughter.

'Sorry. Was the *wow* too much?' He smirks.

'Just a tad.'

'It's sort of the eBay look.' He smiles appraisingly. 'And I have to say... you rock it.'

'I'll give you a rocket if you don't stop with the sarcasm.'

He smirks again. 'Fair point. But the murder thing, Kirstin.' A frown creases his face. 'I just can't see it. There are two big problems.'

I take a seat beside him on the bed. 'I'm listening.'

'For one, who do you think would do it? Oscar's afraid of his own shadow. Erica's all bark no bite. Julia hasn't got a nasty bone in her body. And Timmy?'

'I think we can safely rule Timmy out.'

'So that leaves you or me.' He shoots me a wry smile. 'Your being here is a total fluke. If it hadn't been for the car breaking down, you'd have been on that ferry.'

It's even more of a fluke than he realises. I shouldn't have even been at the funeral. I'd never met Carolyn, but I don't bother to fill him in on all the missing details. 'So, I guess it must be you then.'

'Hmm.' He's not looking worried. 'That's kind of bound up with the second problem. Why? Why would anyone murder Miri? I've got no reason. I liked her. There has to be a motive.'

'Money?'

'Yeah, but she had nothing. Not really. Not more than any of the rest of us.'

'So, you – the siblings – you all stand to inherit the same amount?'

'The will hasn't been read yet, we've got that next week, but I think that's pretty much the gist. Miri probably got an equal share. She wasn't blood-related, but she is "family" and mum's favourite.'

I eye him cautiously. 'Does that hurt?'

'Not really. If I had to choose a favourite, Miri would be pretty far up my list too. I can be…'

'Yes?'

He shakes his head. 'Doesn't matter. This is not about me. We all loved Miri, favourite or not.' He laughs bitterly. 'Maybe my mum failed on that front. I always got the feeling she was trying to play us off against each other. Then Miri came into the family and stole our hearts.'

'Was she depressed?'

He tugs at his bottom lip. This isn't easy for him. 'Sometimes. Malcolm, her fiancé, dying; I mean, she had to watch the car burn with Malcolm inside. It can't have been more than six months ago.'

'What caused the accident?'

'Not sure. The car went off the road. It's just...' Luke glances down towards his hands, unable to meet my eyes. 'We couldn't afford to lose her. She added a bit of... something.'

'Something?'

He smiles sadly. 'Something nicer.'

'I am so sorry, Luke.'

'You knew she was adopted?'

'She told me.'

'My mother called her Miranda, after *The Tempest*.'

'*"Hell is empty, and all the devils are here"*,' I quote. I did *The Tempest* for GCSE.

'That wasn't the line Carolyn was always pulling out of the bag.'

This surprises me; I would have thought that one was right up Carolyn's street. 'Go on, then,' I say.

'*"O brave new world, that has such people in it"*.'

I pull myself up from the bed. 'I've always found humanity is a bit of a mixed bag, myself.'

'I think the Bard would agree with you there. But Miranda, she was a treasure.'

He looks away, dabbing at the rims of his eyes, and I wonder if he's crying, but when he turns back to face me his eyes are dry. 'So my mother was not actually her gran; she was her adopted mother. They just did the gran thing because it felt like a better fit. We don't know who her birth parents were. Not even my mother knew.' He hesitates. 'At least, that's what Carolyn told us.

It is possible that Miri had a genetic disposition for depression. She probably had an attachment disorder.'

'You think so?' She had seemed so upbeat, so happy, so secure in herself.

'Think it goes with the territory.'

'Not always.'

'I'm not a doctor, but I know for a fact – *normal* in the morning and *suicidal* in the afternoon, well, it can all be done.' Wearily, he pulls himself to his feet.

'I am sorry,' I say yet again. I feel like I must have said it a thousand times.

Luke takes my hands between his and gazes into my eyes, but his look is no longer playful; there's something deadly serious about his expression. 'This whole claiming it was *suspicious circumstances*, Kirstin, it's not helping. We're a family in crisis here. Could you cut us some slack?'

I should have kept my mouth shut. They knew her. I didn't. 'I don't think the police believed me anyway,' I say, hoping, yet again, that he doesn't know it was me who hammered the point home by mentioning the envelope.

Luke smiles sadly as he drops my hands, and I wonder why all the best men have to be unattainable, married or simply not interested, till a sharp rap at the bedroom door makes me jump.

'Ms Conroy,' someone calls from the hallway. Not a voice I recognise; the tone sounds official.

'Yes?'

'It's about your car.'

DS Graham is still installed in the snug; only the tea tray has changed. There's evidence that he's been tucking into sandwiches, and what looks like the remnants of a cherry cake are crumbled across a white china plate. I enter the room, not sure if the smile on my face was appropriate under the circumstances, but I just want my car back.

'Ms Conroy.'

'Is my car outside?'

'No.' His reply feels like a punch to the solar plexus.

'Sorry. I don't understand. Is it beyond repair? It's not even that old. I mean, it wasn't brand new, but I think it's still under guarantee.'

'No.' DS Graham coughs. 'The car is not beyond repair.'

Now I'm confused. 'Then…?'

'It's evidence.'

This doesn't make sense.

'Ms Conroy, your car has been tampered with. The brake cables are damaged, and we've had confirmation of a foreign substance in the tank.'

'I'm not sure I understand.'

'Someone,' he says, his words much slower, presumably so I can keep up, 'has meddled with your car.'

'But...'

'In your written report…' he cuts through my words, flicking through the pages of notes that I'd scribbled down earlier, 'it says you had pulled over to put your coat on?'

I hadn't bothered to say I'd pulled over to get my cardigan off. That seemed too odd. So, I'd just kept it short, sweet and accurate enough. 'That's correct.'

'Why put your coat on when you were in the car?'

'It's a… an odd story.'

He glances back at his notes. 'Seems like that coat's a bit of a charm for you.'

'Sorry?'

'If the car hadn't stalled, the vehicle would have gone out of control.' He stops looking at his notes and fixes me with those flint-like eyes. 'Ms Conroy, do you know anyone who might want to harm you?'

For a moment, words fail me. All the breath in my body seems to exit in one swift, sharp blow. It must be a full minute at least before I realise he's deadly serious.

'Do you know anyone who has a grudge against you?'

'What?'

'Have you been threatened by any persons recently, however insignificant that threat might have appeared?'

My mind is whirring. Why would anyone threaten me? The doctor: Doctor Meerson. Our snatched conversation comes flooding back:

'You might want to think of quitting while you're ahead.'

Was that a threat? If I tell the police what Meerson said, I'll have to tell them what I do. Hearse-chasing isn't illegal, but the truth will most likely cost me my job. Even though Jasper, my boss, knows exactly what I'm up to. Someone will have to be thrown under the bus.

'No. No one's threatened me. And look, I'm sure I'm wrong about Miri. I spoke to the family. I hadn't realised how disturbed she was. I didn't really know her. And I'm absolutely positive that my car is…'

I trail off as DS Graham's words flood back in a sickening wash. *'If the car hadn't stalled, the vehicle would have gone out of control.'*

AJ. Could this have something to do with my brother? Maybe somebody thinks AJ knows where the missing Lowry is, and this car thing is a warning that, when AJ gets out, unless the painting ends up in the right hands, there's going to be trouble. Fixing the car of a loved one is the sort of intimidation tactic that AJ's associates would love.

'No, I don't know anyone who would want to hurt me. I've never been threatened,' I say. But my mind adds two words extra: *I've never been threatened – until now.*

DS Graham looks back at his notes. 'The autopsy should show

up anything suspicious on Ms Millford,' he says calmly, as my mind continues to spin.

With a sickening chill, I remember Timmy's words as he lay in the middle of a shower of glass.

'I'm in danger,' he had choked. *'And you, you're in danger too.'*

'Sorry?' I look up to see DS Graham's beady eyes staring intently at me. I'd spoken the words out loud. What an idiot.

'Timmy Millford,' I bluster. 'The brother, the one in the wheelchair. The chandelier came down.'

'What?' DS Graham looks at me intently.

'The chandelier must have come loose because it fell.' I feel the colour rising in my face. A sense of panic. 'It crashed down at the wake.' No, that was wrong. 'No…' I look deep into DS Graham's eyes and can tell from the way he's leaning forwards in his chair that we both know I've dredged something up which could be important. 'Timmy Millford must have thrown himself out of his wheelchair,' I say slowly. 'He got away from the chandelier, but maybe… maybe the thing crashing down like that wasn't an accident. Maybe someone was trying to kill Timmy.'

11

ESCAPE

It doesn't take the police long to figure out that Erica and I drive the same car, even though Erica insists her car is nothing like mine. Luckily, Oscar is on hand to convince her that although her BMW might well be the latest model, it's the same colour, the same make, and even the same basic shape. The fact that it was probably dark when the tampering happened and that the car had been parked outside Erica's family home, all points to the same thing – whoever it was, they were after Erica. With the new evidence about the car, events take a paradigm shift. The idea that Miri's death was suicide starts to seem naïve. How many accidents can one family have? There's an added tension in the house now, one which wasn't here before. I wouldn't say fear exactly. It's difficult to be afraid when the lights are on, and the place is crawling with police, but everyone is on edge.

No one was surprised when DS Graham asked if the police could search the house. They whipped through my room in ten minutes flat. There's nothing personal in there, so it was easy to navigate. I didn't even bother to supervise. The other rooms take longer. Erica's is by far the most time-consuming because she insists that she watch their every move. I could hear her from my room, giving out instructions; *mind that, be careful with this,* her voice sounding increasingly stressed. Sadly, the envelope I saw being handed to Miri is nowhere to be found. After a good two hours, the police are empty-handed, and Erica's nerves are boiling over. I don't blame her. Somebody tried to hurt her. She's exhausted, grieving over Miri and becoming increasingly paranoid. Everyone takes a sigh of relief when she decides to retire to her room. The search is over. The doors to the house are secured. Two policemen are going to be staying the night.

'So, that must mean you're free to go?' Luke asks.

Apart from Erica, we're all standing in the hallway like the cast of an Agatha Christie. I have no intention of staying in the house any longer than I have to. The place is like treacle – one foot over the threshold, and you're stuck.

I hoist the strap of my handbag over my shoulder. 'I've been told I can leave the house, but they've asked me to stay on the island. It's just red tape. Not sure my boss is going to be happy.' I glance over at DS Graham, who's giving instructions to the two police officers on duty tonight.

'Tell your boss it's an order,' Graham says without looking around. 'You're helping with enquiries.'

I hate that phrase.

'Right.' Luke runs a hand through his hair, making it stand on end a little more than it's supposed to. He looks weary, out of kilter with the world. 'Where are you staying?'

DS Graham appears to have all the answers. 'We've booked Ms Conroy in at the Ship.'

'It's okay. Clean, at least.' Luke approves. 'I could drive you over while they tie everything up here.'

'I think not, Mr Millford.' The DS turns towards us, called into action. 'It's best to keep the family's movements limited.'

'Blast. That's my escape plan up in smoke.' Luke smirks, his tone suddenly playful.

'Do you take anything seriously?'

He fixes me with his blue eyes. 'The fact that you're leaving before we've had a chance to get acquainted.'

He may have lowered his voice, but I have no doubt DS Graham caught every word; Oscar certainly has.

'Have some decency, Luke. Mother is dead. Miri...' The words dry on Oscar's tongue as if he's unwilling to commit. 'And...' He starts up again before fully knowing where he's going. 'There's most likely been an attempt on Timmy and Erica's lives.'

It's then that I remember my phone. I'd put my damaged phone in my handbag. The rice had done diddley-squat to dry it out. But Oscar had said there was a kitchen drawer full of old mobiles.

'Sorry.' I turn back into the hallway. 'If it's okay, I just want to grab something from the kitchen.'

'I can get anything you need.' Julia starts to move zombie-like towards the stairs.

'No, please don't worry, Julia. You stay here. I can manage.'

She looks towards DS Graham, who clears his throat. 'Probably best, Ms Catalow. I'd like to run through protocol before I head off for the night.' He turns his attention back to the room, taking in what's left of the key players. 'We will be leaving two officers...'

I slip across the hall and down the steps into the basement kitchen. I don't need to hear any of DS Graham's briefing. I've done my part. All I need now is a phone, a slice of cake and a police car back into Kernow. Luckily, Oscar was right. There's a whole shopful of old mobiles in the drawer, even the latest iPhone, with barely a scratch, but that would be too cheeky. A replacement on my old model will do just fine.

I get Graham to drop me off in Kernow. Who knows how long I'll be stranded here. The local store is hardly fashion central, but

I manage to pick up something fresh to wear. It's just a short walk to the Ship Inn from the store. Kernow is prettier by streetlight. During the day, it can look a bit scrappy. In the wake of the pandemic, a couple of charity shops have managed to work their way to the front, along with a single, garish betting store. At night, all of that is somehow softened. The cobbled streets catch the lights, and fishing boats bob peacefully, throwing sulphur-coloured splashes across the water. Nothing bad could happen here, or at least that's the impression the place gives.

The Ship lives up to its name. Okay, so. It's not actually floating on the water, but it's right beside the quay. According to a folded card propped up on the reception desk, most of the beams in the Inn came from salvaged sea vessels; none of this is surprising – there's that trapped saltwater smell in reception, and you can almost hear the creaking framework, as though the beams are reluctant to give up any maritime memories. Nothing in the reception area is symmetrical, not even the receptionist, whose dark-brown eyes are a little too close together. She glances down her long nose at me with a curious, tight expression on her face. The police had made the booking. I don't suppose that happens every day.

'A double on the first floor,' she says, handing me the keys. 'Will it be for one night or two?'

It's a natural question, but I can't help feeling as though I'm being mined for information.

'One, I hope.' Any longer and I'm not sure how I'm going to get it past Jasper, my boss.

She writes something in her book, flicking the pen across the lined, white page in a satisfied manner. I wonder if she feels a one-night stay is more palatable. That perhaps, one night indicates I'm only a bit player in whatever it was that went down at the Millford estate.

The room they've given me is in the annexe. It's a 1960's-style extension: rectangular, small and neat, with not one beam. There's nothing tasteful about it, but I'm more than happy; I don't want the ghosts of old sailors hanging around. I've had enough spooks recently to last me a lifetime. I'm hoping to be back on the mainland by morning, the afternoon at the latest. Either way, it's not going to be a nine o'clock start at my desk. There's no point in putting it off. I pick up the landline, dial nine and ring the office. It's the answerphone. Janice's bright, overly sparky recorded voice tells me to leave a message, and they'll get straight back. I don't go into detail. I just say there's a problem. I've been held up. The police have asked me to stay on the island and help with enquiries. I'm not personally involved. I should be back at my desk at some point tomorrow.

I strip off Carolyn's clothes. It can all go to the charity shop tomorrow. Then I turn my attention to Luke's baseball jacket, letting my fingers run over the heavy sleeves. It's odd how some clothes hold a sort of energy, as if the owner is never far away. I noticed that with AJ. When I left the house after he'd been arrested I 'borrowed' his scarf. I swear it kept me going when I left Liverpool. Every time I felt nervous, every time I felt alone or lost, I'd just touch the scarf, and it was like he was there, willing me on. Even though I know there's no future for Luke and me I can't help but savour the energy his jacket gives off. I give myself a sound shake. I have to stop this. Never mix work with pleasure, especially when there's a murder investigation on the slate.

Being a Sunday night, the restaurant at the Ship is only half full. I'd intended on bolting down my food and heading back to my room, but the dining room is stunning. For want of a better word, it's been glassed. There's not a trace of beam. The whole back of the building's been taken out to create a transparent wall looking out over the water. I order the Chardonnay. A carafe – why not? – before texting Marco, just in case he's interested.

I'm in the Ship Inn at Kernow. That last lead – basket case.

He must be sitting on his phone because a text flies in.

Tell me more?

I start tapping back:

Not sure I can sum it up.

Commission for me?

Is that all you think about?

Hmmm…

Still a tad irritated that the brother is gay.

Sorry, honey. Your loss. 

I put down the handset and take a large slug of my wine. It's wonderfully cold.

'Booking for Millford,' a woman's voice filters across the

room.

I'm not sure if her voice is extra loud or my ears are just hypersensitive to the M-word. Whatever it is, the question seems cut-out and clear over the background chatter.

'Ummm.' The maître d' scans the booking list as I shift around in my chair, trying to get a better view of the action.

'Rachel, Rachel Millford,' states the high, sharp voice.

'Ah, of course.' Slicker than an oiled cog, a waiter grabs two menus and waltzes across the smooth, wooden boards of the dining room, followed by a smartly-dressed couple weaving their way behind him.

Rachel Millford? I scan her face. She's a small, bird-like woman, her hair tied back like a ballerina. Her features, sharp. In a similar vein to Erica's, yet on Rachel, everything seems to be working in harmony. I don't remember seeing her at the funeral. The man in tow is on the large side. The kind that stuffs out his expensive suit like a barrel, his oblong face topped with a salt-and-pepper-style halo. As luck would have it, they're heading to another seat in the window. The couple wait until they've been handed their menus, ordered their wine and the maître d' has waltzed away before starting to speak.

'Who did you say told you about the tax loop?' Rachel asks, her eyes narrowing shrewdly.

'Geoff Caster,' the barrel man replies. 'One of my golf buddies.'

'Well.' Her features tighten as she shakes out her white linen napkin, placing it squarely on her dark above-the-knee skirt. 'It's not anything I've heard of before. And you need to be careful.' She lowers her voice slightly, and I find myself leaning towards their table. 'Cheat the taxman with something that's not legit, and he'll only come knocking for it later.'

Of course, I think to myself. Oscar's ex-wife – the accountant. She's obviously kept her last name. Understandable, the name has clout on the island.

'Just look into it for me, will you, Rachel?'

'I won't get involved with anything I'm not one hundred per cent comfortable with.'

He clears his throat. 'Speaking of which, did you hear there was another death at the estate?'

She looks blank. 'I knew Carolyn had gone. Not that I'll shed any tears.'

'No, it was the young one. The redhead. Melanie?'

'Miranda.' Rachel's face pales.

'That must be the one.'

'Oh, no. That poor child. How?'

'Not sure,' the man says, helping himself to a bread roll and a knife full of butter. 'But a lot of police cars.'

'That place is toxic. It was all Carolyn's fault. She was always playing the siblings off against one another. Making them fight for her attention. Meddling.'

'Well, you're out of it now.'

'Thankfully. But poor, poor Miranda. She was a little spoilt, but the best of the bunch. My ex-husband.'

'The *Snivelling Worm?*'

'I'm not sure I said *worm.*'

Barrel Man raises one eyebrow ironically.

'*No backbone* is what I said.'

I can't help thinking that somehow, she's wound up at the same place.

'I mean, who doesn't stand up to their mother when she systematically belittles the person that they are supposed to be in love with?'

'Meaning you?'

'He said it all at the altar. *Till death us do part*. That was the deal, and then he lets that woman tear strips off me.'

'None of them ever disagreed with her.' Barrel Man puckers his lips. 'I guess they didn't want to be written out of the inheritance.'

'She ruined Oscar's career. I swear that's why he gave up. I mean, I didn't marry a used car salesman.'

Rachel pauses for a moment before indulging in a hearty slug of the blood-red wine that the waiter's just poured. 'I suppose they weren't all bad. Luke was charming.'

I wouldn't argue with her there.

'Erica. So superior.'

'Even by your standards?'

'Don't tease. Remarkable really. Not even a mother like Carolyn could knock Erica down a peg or two.'

'Wasn't there a third brother?'

'Timmy.'

'Had that unfortunate accident?'

'Tragic. Only a young guy. Went on some holiday of a lifetime and then...' Suddenly she looks puzzled. 'I never completely understood Timmy. He was a bit of a wildcard. The others, it was obvious enough what motivated them.'

'Oh?'

'Carolyn – power. My ex – biding his time, waiting for his boat to come in. Luke – fun. Erica – lording it over everyone and anyone. It wasn't about the money for Erica; it was all about the status of being a Millford.'

The man's eyes narrow, amused and I detect a wry note in his tone when he speaks again. 'You did keep the name yourself.'

'I earned it...'

'And the other one, Jimmy? What motivated him?'

'Timmy. I think he was one of those people who like to throw a spanner in the works.'

Barrel Man laughs. It's a big, warm guffaw. 'Well, I'll drink to that.'

Back in my room, I slip off my clothes and sink onto the mattress, pulling the laptop I'd borrowed from reception towards me. I have a little research to do. Luckily there's a historical society for the islands, and the Millfords certainly have *history*.

According to the webpage, at the turn of the last century, there were two big estates on the island: The Millfords' estate and the Fordhams'. The society's website has all the details and even a few photos. The Fordhams' place was called the Grange. Both houses had been modified over the years, but the Fordham estate remained in the Tudor style; brick, beams and diamond, leaded windows. The Millfords carried on with the modifications, ending up with, what was pretty much, the house that I'd stayed in – Georgian. Both estates had around the same acreage, but it wasn't all neatly squared off. There was a panhandle of land, a strip that ran along the coast. At the edge of the panhandle, one of the families, at some point in time, had built a church. The church I visited? Who had ownership of the church and, therefore, the panhandle of land was hotly contested, but the families merged in 1897. This must have been the union Oscar alluded to. It was a marriage between Marianne Fordham and George James Millford. So the church should have come under the Millford estate. The marriage didn't last long. Within twelve months, Marianne was dead. There had been some rivalry. The ownership of the church had been contested again, this time in court. The case was inconclusive. Eighteen months later, the Fordham estate had been razed to the ground. A fire. There didn't appear to be any record of what happened to the court case. Most of the Fordhams had perished in the blaze. Maybe there was no one left to argue with? Since Marianne had no children, Oscar, Luke, Erica and Timmy must be pure Millfords. There's a picture on the webpage of James Millford. He has an angular jaw and an overproud face. A touch of the Carolyn's, perhaps?

Oscar's words from the church come back to me: *'There were a lot of people who wanted to see her buried.'* Had he meant a lot of people wanting to pay their respects? Or something more voyeuristic?

12

KERNOW

WHEN I WAKE, it's eleven. I'm amazed. I'm usually an early bird. I check my phone; there's nothing. Not one concerned *are you okay*? Or even an aggravated *where the hell are you?* I have a quick shower. I've missed breakfast, but that shouldn't be a problem. I'm in the swinging port of Kernow. There's a note of sarcasm to the thought. The only thing that's ever swung in Kernow is a gibbet. Kernow is what you might call *behind the times* and not in a quaint way. There's no Starbucks or Costa. That might be just about okay, but this time of year, I'm not convinced there'll be any proper ground coffee machines either. It will have to be Captain Jack's for my morning refuel. The island's infamous full-monty provider, where the bacon swims in fat and the bread shines brighter than the picked-clean bones of pirates.

I grab a paper from the newsagents, *The Island Journal.* It comes out every day, which is a miracle as most days there's no news, but today we have hardcore headlines. *Tragedy Strikes Again At Millford Estate.* I run my eyes over the article. It says nothing about murder. 'Tragedy' is a bit of a cover-all. Are they hedging their bets? Was it murder? Was Miri being blackmailed? That A4 envelope could have contained anything, and the other 'accidents'? Perhaps that's all they were. The car 'sabotage' was odd, but maybe it was kids messing around? I try to think back to the wake. Were there kids there? No. No one odd. The disgruntled gamekeeper by the gate, but everyone else looked like they were meant to be there. Even the chandelier could be explained away. It had recently been rehung. Maybe they'd messed up when they put it back. In the morning light, the idea that Miri's death was a murder seems crazy. The Millford family had all been on the same page – Miri was emotionally unstable, given the circumstances, wouldn't anyone be? Watching your fiancé burn inside a vehicle that you've only just managed to pull yourself out of, that's not exactly something you can walk away from whistling into the future. No. Suicide must be a strong possibility, and the word 'HELP' written in Miri's gloopy protein shake on the carpet? Most suicide attempts are exactly that – a cry for help.

Captain Jack's is full to the brim when I get there, a mass of bulky bodies, burbling voices and the sizzle and spit of breakfasts laid out over a grill.

'Ruin the island if they stick another port in,' some salty sea-dog ruminates over his mug of tea to a waitress, who's leaning idly beside the grill. She's sporting a stained name tag that reads 'Barbara' and looks as if she may well have been standing there since the sixties. She wrinkles her nose at the sea-dog's comment as though he's talking bollocks. Then gives her hooter a quick brush with the back of her hand, leaving an inadvertent dab of bacon fat glistening on her cheek. 'If it makes those bloody ferries more reliable,' she sniffs, 'you ask me, it's the best thing.'

The salty sea-dog grumbles as if to say Barbara's opinion

doesn't count for much. I get the feeling they'll be there disagreeing for what's left of the year. Fortunately, two other waiting staff are circling the tables, their eyes on the job.

I walk through the café, inhaling a lungful of fry-up that could keep me going all day. The deck outside looks pretty empty – two old guys playing cards and three women with babies. The babies are all asleep. Perfect. It's not exactly warm out there, but the sun's shining. I open the glass door and step out onto the wooden slats. Oddly enough, it's the summer months you want to avoid for *al fresco* dining at Jack's. You only need one clueless tourist with an outboard diesel engine, and you can end up ingesting almost as much carbon dioxide as you'd get from a weekend on Mars. Mars is ninety-five per cent carbon dioxide. A fact AJ picked up on one of his courses. I have no idea which course because the information doesn't seem to fit into any brand of *useful* that I can think of. Maybe HMPS are thinking of developing prisons on Mars. This would not surprise me. But then again, *this* is not my problem because AJ will be out soon, and there's no way I'm letting him go back in.

For now, the deck outside is blissfully quiet. The mothers look tired rather than perky, which is good. I'm not in the mood for perky. The water is clear, and the sun shines. The air has that salty taste tinged with lobster pots, damp wood and rusting metal. I pull up a chair and give the headline article a closer inspection. There's a picture of Miri on page two. It must be one of her acting headshots. Her face is pale and ludicrously well lit, her lovely features stranded in a sea of inky black. What a waste.

'I thought that was you.'

I look up. Someone's standing in the sun. The dark figure obligingly takes a step to one side. It's Luke.

'Hi,' I say, as my errant heart gives a quick flutter, and my on-the-ball brain calls me an idiot. He may be my type. But I'm not his. 'Julia not cooking?'

He raises a concerned eyebrow. 'Julia's... well, she's taking this whole thing very badly.'

'I'm so sorry.'

He glances down at the newspaper laid out over the table, the violent headline appearing to shout aggressively into the quiet October air.

'To be honest, I needed a trip out.'

I can believe that. 'It is tragic,' I say, referring to the words in the paper, trying to soften them a little.

'Yeah.' Luke's voice catches in his throat. 'You mind if I...?' Without waiting for an answer, he pulls out the chair next to me.

I don't mind. For once, I'm glad of the company. 'How's it going back at the house?'

'Lot of police.'

'I'm sorry if I made things worse.'

He looks blank.

'By implying it... well, that maybe there were suspicious circumstances.'

Luke smiles sadly. 'I'm not sure it could be made much worse. In fact, in some ways, it was good having you there. You diluted the Millfords in a good way.'

The waiter takes our order. We both go for the Big Breakfast, then sit soaking in the sunshine chatting. Avoiding talk about the family. Instead, Luke tells me about his publishing business. He publishes biographies. He's met some truly amazing characters. A guy whose father was, like, this Chinese Schindler. A saxophonist who taught music to tribespeople way out in the Amazonian jungle. They taught him a few things too. Luke also deals in rare books and spends weeks looking through house clearance sales, trying to pick up forgotten antiquarian gems amongst the junk. On some levels our jobs seem to have a common thread, only Luke's passionate about his work, and I can't help but think there's something wrong with my own. All I've been interested in is turning a buck. That's how the whole *hearse-chasing* thing started. There weren't enough properties on the market. The big ones secure the largest commissions. The person who gets through the door first normally nails the deal. And all the old favourites – Savills, Fine & Country – well, they always managed to get themselves through that doorframe before anyone else. Jasper's agency is independent, not some national chain with a well-worn name and backing that gets handed down through the decades. My boss might do a good impression, but he's not from the sort of old money that can keep things afloat when times get bad. So, I had to make it work, drag in my own punters, and I did. But, I realise, as Luke natters away, I'd like to be passionate about something, not just because of the cha-ching in the bank account at the end of the day, but because something genuinely excited me.

'You're so lucky,' I say, taking my teaspoon on yet another tour around my coffee. 'Knowing what you wanted to do.'

Luke smiles. 'I'm not saying it was easy. When I finished uni, Carolyn was pushing me into banking. She knew I hated it, but she liked to have us all…'

'Tow the line?' I offer helpfully.

He takes a deep breath as if chewing the thought over before he replies. 'I would have said… *dance to her tune* was a more accurate description. She was an unusual woman. No doubt brilliant, if you weren't related. You've read her book?'

'Bits,' I say.

'She was working on another one.'

'Oh? More *Golden Child?*'

He laughs. 'As if she'd tell. No. I have no idea what it was about. I asked her if I could publish it, but… she refused. Hadn't decided who she was going to go for. Not even her agent knows where she stashed the manuscript, and now the damn thing's lost. Sometimes you can keep things too close to your chest.'

I get the feeling that beneath Luke's chiselled jaw, there could well be an expensively white set of gritted teeth. Had Carolyn refused to give Luke the rights because she didn't trust him to get it published properly, or perhaps there was something in it, something that she knew he would try and change.

We sit there in silence for a moment as Luke stares out over the wrinkled blue water. A boat chugs across the harbour. We watch as it drags the sea behind it. I'm not sure what I'm supposed to say to any of this. I have my own family problems. I'd like to say that Carolyn's behaviour doesn't matter, but my gut feeling is that the ripples left over from this strange, controlling woman will probably keep cropping up for the rest of Luke's life. She's infected all her children with a fierce insecurity. What a waste of a relationship. When he turns back towards me, the irritation has gone. That playful quality is there again.

'Look.' He leans in, tilting his face towards me. 'I know this is going to sound odd, but…' He laughs.

'But?'

'When we first met, Kirstin, it was…' He smiles again but glances down at his feet, shying away from direct eye contact. 'I'm feeling like a schoolboy here.' He takes a deep breath as if hoping it will buoy him along. 'When I first saw you, I swear, there was this connection. I seriously wanted to get to know you better…' He raises his eyes to mine. His sparkling eyes.

My heart sinks. Why, when even the merest hint of romance happens, does it have to be so complicated? Luke is blissfully unaware that my best mate and himself happen to go to the same gay club. Luke's free to feel all the electricity and crackling air he likes, but for my part, I've put a circuit breaker on. Maybe he is bi, but I'd need him to be more upfront about it.

'I'd love for us to get to know each other better,' he babbles excitedly.

'Right,' I reply with a little too much breath. My words sounding unsure.

'Look, Kirstin, I know it's been... more than tense.'

His mother's six feet under, his sister's in the mortician's drawer; tense is the understatement of the year.

'But...'

The waiter arrives with the bill. Whatever he was about to say is lost.

'I'll get these.' He jumps to his feet, the true gent with a credit card. 'Look, I'm back off to the house now, but maybe we could meet up again? Can I put my number in your phone?'

Hmm. It's his mother's phone, so that's a little awkward. Will he notice? It's been lying on the table. I stare at his face, looking for a tell. Is this some kind of double bluff? But his face is the picture of innocence.

'Sure,' I say, picking the phone up, but hiding the back, just in case it's got any identifying features that might give it away. Oscar had said I could take it, but that doesn't stop me from feeling somehow guilty about taking the dead woman's phone. As Luke tells me his number, I tap it in, filing it under work contacts. If the family do sell, he'll most likely be my way in. When I look up again, he has this odd look on his face. It's like he's sizing me up and realising I'm somehow different than he thought. Maybe he does recognise the phone?

'Great,' I say as I slip the damn thing into my pocket.

'Just... do me a favour, Kirstin and think about it – meeting up again. I'd love to get to know you better.'

I smile. But my heart is beating like a flat tyre driven over tarmac. If I take a punt on a relationship with Luke, and he is bi, and he doesn't come clean, we're already off to such a shaky start.

On my way back to the Ship, I decide to call in at the station and see if there's any news on my car. DS Graham isn't around. He's most likely up at the house but the story seems to be the same;

they don't want me leaving the island, so I head back to the inn and check the booking on my room will hold for one more night. It will. Feeling as much enthusiasm as a condemned man, I go to my room and fall back into a deep sleep. The past few days must have taken it out of me. My body feels like a bag of chicken bones that someone's been shaking hard, every inch painful and jarred.

When I wake, it's already late afternoon. My phone is ringing. My eyes barely focused, I grab it.

'Yeah?' I mumble into the glassy rectangle. I haven't linked phone numbers with my address book yet, so everybody will be coming up as 'unknown'. Only this time I've got a good enough idea as to who it might be.

'Kirstin?'

It's work. More specifically, my boss, Jasper.

'Yeah?'

'We've got a problem.' I swear to God he loves saying that.

'I left you a message. I'm stuck on the island. It's the police. There's nothing I can do about it.'

'No, not that. We've had a complaint.'

I feel my breath catch in my throat. 'About me?'

'Kirstin, keep up.' His voice is all irritation. 'Why else would I be calling you?'

'I just...'

'Apparently, you've been acting unethically?'

When put in a corner, it's always best to deny everything. Indignation is a great ally. 'What, how dare...'

'Stop, Kirstin. Save yourself the angst.' Jasper sounds weary. 'We all know it's true. You seem to have an uncanny knack for finding properties just before they're about to go on the market.'

'It's called *doing your research*.' I hold on to the indignant tone.

'I think it may go a bit deeper. Sometimes the corpses are still warm.'

Technically speaking, that would not be possible. But I feel it's best to let it slide, besides, he's got a point; often, it's not just hearses I'm chasing. I also have a contact in intensive care.

I take a different tack. 'Who complained?' It can't have been Marco. He always got a cut. 'Was it bloody Janice?' I'd always thought she had a snail inside her skull rather than a brain. That'll teach me to underestimate people.

'Janice?' He sounds genuinely surprised. 'Look, stop mud-flinging, Kirstin. Poor bloody Janice is too friggin' loyal. You're the one who did the deed.'

'I got you six million-plus properties in the last year. Six properties that went within a week of us advertising.'

'And that's why I'm not going to sack you.'

But all that holier-than-thou crap is not washing with me. 'And... hand on heart,' I bluster, 'if you're perfectly honest, you knew what I was up to.'

There's a pause. But not for long. Jasper's already sorted his game plan. 'We need to wait for this to cool down. The person who reported you, they'll want to see action's been taken. Give us six months, and we can re-employ you in the Taunton office.'

'And my wages?'

'I'm not exactly going to pay for you to swan around doing sweet FA.'

'But you can't do that.'

There's a pause. 'Kirstin, I can.'

Suddenly, I know exactly who it was – Meerson. 'That bloody doctor.'

'Language.'

'Oh, come on, Jasper.' I pull my hands through my hair. 'It's obvious. I reckon he's doing the same. You know how many funerals I've seen him at? I bet he's working for an estate agent too.'

'Stop. For Christ's sake, Kirstin. He's a doctor; that's why he goes to funerals.'

'Well, he's not a very good doctor then.'

'Look, you just disappear for a bit.' Jasper's voice sounds tired. 'Call me in six months, and we'll look at Taunton. You're a good worker. If I could keep you on, I would, but you're too hot.'

I cannot believe it. Six-month sabbatical – that's going to eat right into my savings. I am so mad I could spit.

I grab Luke's jacket. I need to walk this off.

I head down to the port. The boats bob lazily on the water, flagpoles rattling in the wind. Most of the day's activity has come to an end. There's just one fisherman sorting out nets and lobster pots on the quay. I lean out over the metal barrier, watching the lights of Kernow twinkle and dance across the dark, crinkled water. I have no idea what I should do. Tomorrow, I'll have to go to the police station again and say I've got to get back to the mainland. I guess I could sublet my flat but then where would I go? I can't live on my savings for six months. With AJ about to come out of prison, I need to sort myself out – find that passion for work that everyone else seems to have. Do something real.

I decide to walk up to The Point. It's a war memorial on the coastal footpath just outside of town. It's almost dark now, but the moon's bright enough, and there are no clouds. Besides, the memorial is lit; a small circle of light has it shining out like a beacon into the darkness. As I walk, I run everything through my head. When I stumbled on my little property scam, I thought I was set up for life. But everything comes to an end. If I'm careful, I'll have enough money to set myself up in something else. I'd always wanted to try my hand at journalism. I did all the copy for the office. Writing has genuinely always been a passion. Maybe I could write about the property market? But that seems like a pipe dream. There are a million people already doing that. I know I've just got to keep thinking, the right plan will come up, but I do need a plan.

The war memorial's smaller than I expected. It's a Celtic cross. You see them all over the West Country with their intricate angular patterns. This one's a beauty, carved with a web of threads that feed into one solid structure. I've never walked all the way to The Point before. Previous visits to the island have been mercenary. I'd view a house, try and strike a deal: no time to miss that last ferry. But as I stand, hand on the stone, looking out into the night, I realise with a touch of sadness that this might be the first and the last time I'll explore this part of the world. The lights from Kernow look small and insignificant from the cross, but they've meant something to me. They've seen me set out on my career, carve a life for myself. But just as I'm beginning to gather a little strength, feel hopeful about the future, the clouds shift, and the moon disappears. Apart from the small halo of light surrounding the cross, I'm in darkness. It's time to go back. Tomorrow will have to look after itself. Tonight, I'm going to treat myself to fish and chips from the shop on the quay, and, if the rain doesn't start up, I'll eat them out in the square sitting on a bench.

It should take me a good fifteen minutes to walk back. I shine the torch from my phone out in front of me. The path is well cut, and no vehicles are allowed, so I'm safe. Instinctively, I rub my left arm, remembering my run-in with Luke's bonnet. It's then that my heart gives a sudden thump against my ribs. I heard something. Something odd. At first, I don't understand what it is. I'm walking pretty fast, but the sound of my footfall has changed. It sounds wider somehow. Then, with a sickening sense of dread, I realise – there's someone else walking behind me, falling into my steps. I quicken my pace; there's a slight telltale mismatch on the footfall, before the other footsteps sync once again. My first instinct is to run. But scouring the cliffs ahead of me, I can see that I've still got a long way to go. Besides, whoever is on my tail doesn't realise I'm onto them yet. Run, and I lose that element.

On this part of the walk, I'm pretty safe. It can be seen from the town. Okay, so it's dark up here, but still, chances are that the moon will come back out, and someone will see me out here walking. The danger is when I get to the point where the footpath funnels into town. There's a narrow lane. It's unlit, and there's no way of seeing into it from the outside. Once I'm in there, it's just me and whoever it is that's following me. If you were going to attack someone, that's where you'd do it. But that's ridiculous. Why would anyone want to attack me? Yet still I can hear it, the sound of the footsteps behind me. I need to stay calm, not increase my pace. Then, when I get to the lane, I leg it. I glance at my phone. I could call the police, but by the time I explain where I am and what's going on, it will all be too late. I've just got to hope that, on the sprint through the bottleneck, I'm faster than whoever it is I've got following me. The lane is fifty metres. Not long. Surely, I can put some distance between myself and the person falling into my step. I wrap Luke's jacket tighter around my body and try to keep my breathing regular, try not to panic, try to move slowly. And when I get to the narrow strip of lane, I run.

There's no doubt now; someone else is running behind me. It sounds like a man. The footsteps are heavy, the breath coming out in short, hard bursts, like a slobbering dog. I run and I run. I know I shouldn't scream; I need all the energy I can muster. I have to get out onto the quayside, right out. If I get only a few metres outside of the lane, he'll pull me back. But the footsteps are getting closer. He's gaining ground. My arm still hurts from last night. Pain shoots down my side. And suddenly his hands are on me. They're rough. They're pulling me back. His face is beside mine. Horrible and slobbering, coarse and hairy. He stinks of beer and yeast and damp and some odd spice-style smell that I can't place. His eyes are wild. He's too close now. It's impossible to get free. He's all bristles and dirt and flecks of saliva with rough hands pulling me back. We topple to the damp, hard ground. I'm on the rock-hard concrete. I scream. Suddenly his body is yanked away.

Standing peering down at me is DS Graham.

13

THE FORDHAMS

EVERYONE at the station could not be nicer. A doctor checks me over and I end up having to give the police more info than I'd like. On seeing my bruises, DS Graham is particularly interested in the run-in I'd had with Luke's car, asking me if I want to press charges, but Luke hadn't meant to mow me down. For now, all I'm interested in is Martin Fordham. That's my attacker's name. He's the guy I saw skulking outside the gates of the estate the day of Carolyn's funeral. I'm also beginning to wonder if it could have been him that I'd sensed watching me when I visited the church? Though maybe I'm being paranoid. Oscar was the only other person I saw up there, and why would Oscar be snooping on me? Fordham is a much better fit, besides, he has a connection with the church; it sits on the parcel of land shared by both families.

It turns out – the Fordhams didn't all die out in the fire that razed their property to the ground, and neither did their resentment towards the Millfords. The feud carried on down the generations, giving itself a fresh coat of paint and problems with every turn of the calendar. There had been tensions for most of Carolyn's life. When Fordham had been a bit more presentable, a little less bottle-dependent, smelly and bearded, there had been letters to the press, accusations, insinuations. There hadn't been any court cases, seeing as that would take money, and the Fordhams had lost all of theirs, but Martin Fordham was a man with an axe to grind. He was the last of his line and wanted that church back. He claimed there was an altruism behind his demands; he wanted it back so it could become public property – an accessible part of the island's heritage. But Carolyn refused. Fordham had no track record of altruism and Carolyn had a reputation for never giving an inch. So, Martin Fordham's sense of injustice festered. He managed to keep it under control unless he'd had a few drinks. Fordham lived in a small place just outside Kernow but was well known in the town. When sober, he could put his hand to fixing pretty much anything apart from his family's fortunes. But for the past twelve months or so, Martin Fordham had been kicking things up on a Friday night. He'd been barred from the Globe, a pub by the docks, and there were a couple of other places where his face no longer elicited a smile.

Fortunately for me, the police had started getting suspicious when they rang the company that fixed the chandelier. Fordham had been a last-minute addition to the team. He wouldn't have known the BMW was mine. He'd have thought it was Erica's. And poor Miri? The stain on the floor was written in berry juice. The man had a reputation for foraging. The police were still waiting for the pathology report, but it seemed likely he'd somehow put something in the shake. I'd been wearing Luke's jacket when I went out for my walk. The police figured Fordham was most likely being opportunistic. He wouldn't have expected to see Luke in town. He'd been drinking in The Vulcan, the only pub where he was still welcome. He would have seen me as he stood outside in the pub yard. Watched me as I cut across the cliff path towards The Point. He was drunk as a skunk, probably seeing double. So, the jacket would have been enough for him to think he'd got Luke marked. The police were beginning to wonder if Carolyn's fall from the cliff had been an accident, or could it have been something more sinister. DS Graham had gone to the Ship, to give me an update on my car when he'd seen someone running across the coastal path.

'I thought you deserved to know the whole story,' he tells me as he walks me back to the inn.

But it's a lot to process, and I'm still not one hundred per cent sure how all the bits of this puzzle fit. 'How did he get into the kitchen to spike the juice?'

'Julia Catalow leaves the door open.' Graham stares out over the sleepy town. 'Most people do here. Although no doubt it'll be locked windows and doors in Kernow tonight. And...' he hesitates, dragging his teeth over his bottom lip, 'if you do talk to Ms Catalow, best not to mention the door. She's devastated.'

'Poor Julia. Do you think Fordham intended to pick the family off one by one?' I ask as we arrive at the Ship.

'Maybe.'

I step through the glass door into the warm reception, Graham following me through. The desk is unmanned, the lights dim. There's soft music playing somewhere. I wonder if this is one of the bars where Fordham found himself no longer welcome. Despite the warmth of the building, I shiver as I remember his thick arms around me. Even allowing for the cheap aftershave, the smell had been disgusting; damp slept-in clothes and musty armpits. The first thing I intend to do when I get to my room is take a shower.

'And you'll be heading back to the mainland tomorrow?' Graham asks, his question more of a probe than general conversation.

I get the feeling he's still trying to work out how I fit into the picture and coming up empty-handed. 'Is that okay?'

'Provided you give us a contact number.'

'I left one at the station already.'

He smiles. 'All sorted then.' He turns to go but then stops, twisting his body back towards me, the light from the porch casting half his face in shadow, so I can't fully see his expression. 'And, just remind me... you knew Carolyn how?'

'Bridge,' I say. I need to keep my story straight.

'Ahhh.'

'Online,' I add, just in case. Online should be harder to trace.

'It's great, isn't it.' He smiles, glancing down at his hands. 'So much stuff online these days.'

'Yeah.'

'I play a bit myself. What's the app called?'

I feel the colour drain from my cheeks, and my smile slip. 'Bridge,' I say, 'plain and simple,' before going for a wide yawn. 'Sorry. I'm just...' I indicate behind me into the building, back to where the stairs will take me up to the safety of my room.

'Course. Night, Ms Conroy.'

'Night.' I turn my back on him and stride quickly through the foyer. But even though I hear the door swing shut behind me, I get the uncomfortable feeling that he's standing just outside, watching through the glass.

I wake, just as it's starting to get light, and feel an overwhelming sense of confusion, finding it hard to place where I am. It's not the different location. No, that's easy. I'm in the 1960's annexe at the Ship Inn, Kernow. I'm feeling lost because I'm not sure what my role in the world is anymore. I'm out of a job. Time stretches ahead of me, and I have no idea how to fill it. Is there any point in hurrying for the ferry? Should I start looking for employment? What am I even good at? I need to find out how I want to move forward with my life and commit. It's Tuesday. AJ has his hearing on Thursday. That's something concrete to hold on to. I feel a swell of excitement. We've waited for this for so long. If the decision does go our way, which it should, it could be up to two months before his release. But that's okay. It'll give me time to work things out, time to set up a small business. I wonder if I should tell AJ about Fordham and the attack. I want to. In an ideal world, I'd tell him everything, but I've learned over the years that telling someone who is incarcerated too much about life outside can be a special kind of torture. So, I decide I'll tell him nothing.

On my way over to Captain Jack's I grab a newspaper from the newsagents. I'm relieved to see that my run-in with Fordham is not headline news. There's no mention of him attacking me. If I'd been murdered, it would have been a different story. FUNERAL GATECRASHER FOUND SLAYED FOR JACKET or something. Okay, so perhaps that is a little on the melodramatic side. Tabloid journalism is clearly not my thing. Then it hits me, but what if I were to find Carolyn's latest manuscript? Perhaps it was still at the house. If I could just get to read the thing, I could write a column about it. She was a celebrity. The papers would pay well for even the smallest hint on Carolyn's missing masterpiece, and maybe I could get my foot in the door on the journalism front. They'd get the article if they gave me a job. Hadn't I always wanted to write? I just needed to get myself a head start.

The bell rings above me as I push through the door into the steam-filled café. Barbara gives me a smile of recognition. Not a big smile, just a curve-up at the corners of the mouth, as she tugs her American Tan tights back into place around an ankle and slips a low plastic shoe back onto her foot. It's a quiet day; no salty sea-dog, no mums with babes. I'm not sure if I'm too late or too early. I don't care. I order everything, sit back and relax. This afternoon I'm going to draw up a plan, how can I get myself back into that house, but this morning I'm just going to soak in the idea of freedom.

'Kirstin. I just heard. You were attacked!'

It's Luke, of course. Okay, so I probably knew deep down that if I went to Captain Jack's, he'd find me.

Today he doesn't ask if he can take a seat; he just does. His eyes, every bright blue pixel, is showing concern. 'Are you okay?'

'I'm fine.'

'That stupid jacket.'

'The jacket is also fine. But I will most definitely be giving it back.'

His face is wracked with guilt. 'Fordham thought you were me?'

'That appears to be the case.'

'Fucking Fordham.'

'Yup. Do you know him?'

Luke exhales a thin stream of air. 'Oh yeah. The man's a nutter. I mean, he was always ranting about the family – bitter shit. But I thought it was just a case of a *chip on the old shoulder*. I didn't think he'd go this far. I mean…' he bites his lip, 'Miri?'

I lower my voice to a whisper. 'And maybe your mother?'

'It's impossible not to start linking all the events together. But Miri, she wasn't even involved in all this Fordham-Millford shit, for Christ's sake.'

I reach out my hand, touch his, and there it is again, that flow of electricity. I grab my hand back, not sure he noticed.

'We are so definitely selling the house now. If the others want to buy me out, fine. I'm done. The place is nothing but trouble.'

'Actually, I'm having a few problems with the agency… my boss,' I say, trying to keep it vague.

'You could set up on your own.'

I sigh. Somehow, I don't feel like I've got the energy for it anymore. I should be doing something I love, like Luke. Like the others?

Luke fixes me with his clear blue eyes. 'I'm so sorry about everything.'

'Yeah. How's Julia? I hear she's taken Miri's death badly.'

'Devastated. She thinks that it's all her fault. She left the back door open. But how could she have known?'

'Exactly.'

He clears his throat, awkwardly. 'Actually, Kirstin, I already heard through the grapevine that things aren't going well so well for you, and that you're taking a…' He coughs. 'Sabbatical?'

'That bloody doctor. Wow, news travels fast.'

'He didn't say what it was all about.' Luke waves his arms dismissively. 'To be honest, I didn't ask, but I just… I hope it's nothing that any of us have done that's got you in trouble.'

'No,' I reassure him. 'The blame's squarely on my own shoulders, but that doesn't make it any easier.'

'Tell me about it.' He smiles, knowingly.

I glance out over the water. 'I'm feeling a bit stuck. I can't afford to take unpaid leave.'

'No.' He looks guiltily down at his hands. I get the feeling not having to work isn't a problem for a person like Luke. Suddenly his eyes light up. 'Hey. I've got a great idea. Look, if you are at a loose end, it would be great to have some company back at the house. Free bed and breakfast. I…' He falters, trying to find the right words. 'I could call other people, other friends, but I don't want to have to explain to everyone what's happened, how we all feel. You were there. You know.'

He reaches out and brushes my hand with his. I seriously have no idea how to read this man. Is it just friendship that he's after? Then again, maybe it doesn't matter. Going back to the house is, in fact, just what I'm after. I want to find that manuscript. Besides, I never turn down the offer of a fridge-load of food.

'Sure,' I say. 'Why not.'

14

HOME

'YOU HAVE GOT TO BE JOKING.'

Not everyone's happy to see us, and Erica's not the sort of woman to hide her emotions. We're standing in the grand chequerboard hallway, just inside the heavy front door, the amputated chandelier cable dangling somewhere above our heads. If there were a stage trapdoor under my feet, I'd be praying someone would push the lever and magic me out.

'Erica.' Luke's voice is nothing but absolute calm. 'I invited Kirstin here. She's my guest.'

'It's the timing, Luke,' Erica seethes.

'Timing.' His face twists into a sneer. 'Oh, come on. This house has always been difficult. There's never been a *good time*. You know that, Erica. Mother took absolute delight in ruining everyone's relationships.'

'Please,' Oscar stutters. 'Let's not speak ill of the dead.'

'Oh, come on, Oscar.' Luke rakes his hands irritably through his hair. 'Mother destroyed your relationship with Rachel. And Erica, Kenneth didn't stand a chance.'

Erica draws herself in, serpent-like, in an attitude reminiscent of somebody about to spit or bite. 'Mother didn't drive Kenneth to the roulette wheel.'

'She got him a job at a casino,' Oscar points out helpfully. His voice might be quiet, but his diction is surprisingly clear-cut. 'Mother knew Kenneth had a problem.'

'Don't be ridiculous.'

At this, both Oscar and Luke throw up their hands.

'He was a weak man,' Erica blusters. 'Selfish,' she adds as she storms away.

'Personally, I rather liked him,' Oscar states quietly. 'And, Luke, you're right – there's never been a good time to bring anyone into this house. So, welcome, Kirstin. I don't think you'll find us majorly changed since your last visit. No doubt Erica will stop venting by tomorrow and fix her attention on someone else. The best approach with my sister is to smile, nod and then ignore her. You can have your old room back. That way, Julia won't have to change the sheets. The domestics are on a bit of a go-slow. I'm sure Julia would like to see you though. When you have time. She's taking all of this badly.'

Back in my yellow room, Luke deposits my bag on the small metal suitcase stand that's tucked beside the ornate, oak wardrobe. The canvas bag might have been the biggest they had in the Kernow boutique I'd plundered, but it still looks lost. It makes me realise how underprepared I am for all of this. Perhaps Erica was right; it is all too much too soon, yet Luke seems oblivious.

'We're taking it in turns on the cooking front,' he says casually, sitting down on a corner of the bed. 'Just to help Julia out. I'm on the rota tonight. I hope you like pasta?'

'Love it.'

I walk to the window staring out at the landscaped grounds,

framed to the left with an edge of sparkling sea. I suddenly feel very small. Like a pawn on a chessboard, out of the action and not entirely sure why Luke's invited me here. Is it just to detract from the game, the family game that's been going on for years?

'Kirstin?'

'Sorry.' I glance back towards him. 'Is Erica always so harsh?'

He smiles, sadly. 'She loved Miri. So, it's a big loss.'

I remember the wailing I'd heard coming from Erica's room the last time I was here.

'My sister finds it difficult to make friends. She got teased, bullied as a kid. It's just her defence mechanism. I should have stood up for her more at school but… God, that was all a such a long time ago.'

'You're all grieving,' I say. 'I guess tempers are bound to fray.'

'Well, hopefully, having you here will keep us all on better behaviour.'

So I really am here to keep the peace. 'I was wondering…' this seems like a good time to get things back on track, 'about Carolyn's manuscript.'

'The one she was writing? I guess we all will be now.' Luke says, a wry smile flickering across his face. 'What happened to *The Golden Child*.' He shrugs. 'Who knows.'

'You haven't seen it?'

'I've turned her office upside down. Maybe she wasn't writing anything. I wouldn't put it past her. Inventing a new manuscript and then saying she wouldn't let me publish the damn thing just to spite me. She was…'

'A complicated woman?'

He laughs. 'You're getting it.' Pulling himself from the bed, he ambles slowly back towards the door. 'Julia's room is to the left, down that way.' Luke points back out into the hallway. 'And up the stairs. The small flight. She's got a whole suite-type thing up there.'

'Sounds fancy.'

He shoots me a sardonic look. 'It's years since I've been up there, but I'm not sure *fancy* would be the right word. To be honest, it's a bit basic. We were always on at Carolyn to overhaul it. But... It's certainly a different world up there. Yeah, if you could talk to her, that would be...'

'Sure.'

'You know that female empathy thing.' He gestures awkwardly, rounding his hands through the air.

I nod. I'm happy to pull my weight. Besides, I like Julia.

'Great. Then I better go chop garlic.'

'Luke, I know you said about me selling the house, but if I'm not going back to the agency I wouldn't seriously be able to help you...'

'So?' he cuts in, before lowering his voice. 'Commission on a place like this – set up your own agency.'

Then he's gone. Could I do that? It's certainly a possibility. What with the commission on the house, and the inside story on Carolyn's manuscript, I could seriously set myself up in style. As I'm musing, my phone buzzes from my bag. I pull it out and glance at the screen. It's Marco.

OMG I just heard. They sacked you?

How come everyone gets to know my business at light speed? I've barely had time to digest it myself.

Not sacked. A sabbatical.

Hmm, so... a slow sacking?

Sometimes Marco is infuriating. I'm about to switch him off, but I can see him typing.

Oh, and I found this. Photo of the good-looking, gay brother.

There's a file attached. I click on it. Why am I doing this? Do I seriously want to torture myself? Whatever is going on here, I'm convinced for all his flirting Luke isn't seriously interested. I'm just here to defuse. The file downloads as I watch, expecting the photo to confirm that Luke is simply a flirt. Only, that's not what I see. Sure, there's a picture of Marco and a young man. The man in question has been ringed helpfully in red 'pencil', and Marco's right – the guy is great-looking. Fit with dark hair and an easy manner. But it's not Luke. In fact, I have no idea who it is.

'Anyone caught up with Julia?' Luke asks as he ladles mounds of steaming pasta onto our plates. It's a creamy red sauce and smells delicious, of rosemary and garlic and the fresh, meaty tang of slow-cooked tomatoes. He's set the table in the dining room beautifully, small side plates bursting with brightly-coloured salad leaves and four balloon-style glasses standing open-mouthed and waiting for wine.

'I did knock on her door,' I say, feeling guilty. There was no answer.

In truth I hadn't tried very hard. Even from the top of the staircase I could tell this was seriously a different world – forgotten, damp and dusty. Luke had been right, Carolyn should have overhauled the attic.

'I told you, Luke.' Erica toys with her fork. 'I saw Julia earlier. She was absolutely fine, just tired. We're all tired.' Her voice sounds bitter and clipped and okay, yes, tired.

In fact, Erica looks exhausted. I'd changed into a fresh crew top and a pair of cheap jeans that I'd got in town. I'd brushed my hair, put on a dab of make-up that I'd managed to grab from the Co-op. Freshened up. Luke and Oscar had also changed, but Erica's still in the exact same crushed tweed outfit I'd seen her in earlier, only now it's looking even more crumpled. I remember Luke telling me about Erica's lack of friends, her fondness for Miri. The bullying at school. I bet she was an easy victim. Suddenly I feel an overwhelming sense of sadness – poor Erica.

'Will Julia come down tomorrow, do you think?' Oscar unfolds his napkin, laying it over his legs.

'Of course,' Erica sighs, 'we're all in the same boat here. You can't just remove yourself from life. She was worrying about funeral arrangements, catering and things.'

'Oh, for Christ's sake.' Luke says wearily. 'We can't do all of that again.'

Erica rolls her eyes in an irritated fashion. 'We have to.'

Oscar sniffs as Luke pours wine into the glasses. 'We do need to do something. Maybe London?'

Erica eyes her brother with irritation, rapping her fingers on the table. 'This was Miri's home.'

'All her friends were in London though,' Luke says, as he tops up my glass and slides it towards me.

Erica shoots him a dry look. 'And, of course, you would know?'

Oscar's not eating, toying at his food with his fork, twisting the tendrils of pasta around and around on the silver prongs. 'There's Malcolm's parents.'

I glance towards Luke. He catches it. 'Miri's fiancé, Malcolm Tanner. His parents, they'll want to come. Poor sods. London would be better for them.'

After supper, we clear up together. Nobody speaks much, but nobody bickers either. This is an improvement. When the plates are packed neatly in the dishwasher, the pots rinsed, and the kitchen cleaned, I make my excuses, telling the others I'm going to pick a book from the snug, but I have no intention of doing this. No, I'm trying to piece together where a person like Carolyn might leave a manuscript in a house that's the size of a museum.

15

TIMMY

ACCORDING to an article on the web, Carolyn Millford wrote everything by hand. I snoop around the house as much as I can, without drawing attention to myself, but Carolyn's manuscript is nowhere obvious. I can find – scribbles, notepads and lists galore, but a manuscript? Her next thesis? If it does exist and it's still in the house, it's not in any of the normal places. Irritated, and too wired for sleep, I decide to check in on Timmy. I half-hoped he would be awake, but whatever medication they've got him on must be strong stuff. It's only around nine, but Timmy is motionless as a carved icon, lying in the near-darkness on his hospital-cornered medical-style bed, the lights off. The only illumination leaking erratically from the digital frame; the flicker of photos transitioning memory to memory. I get the feeling no one's bothered to check on him, or at least no one's bothered since it got dark. Without Julia playing ball, Timmy could be in trouble. It smells acrid in the room, of trapped bodies and sleep-sour breath. It might seem harsh, but I can't help feeling he'd be so much better off in a nursing home. Maybe it was okay when he had Rose, the full-time career. I can't help but wonder what happened there, Julia had said one of the brothers had dismissed her. Then maybe after Rose left, perhaps it kind of worked when Julia was on the ball, but what if Julia doesn't come back down? I make a mental note to talk to Oscar about it in the morning. Luke might be easier to approach, but I get the feeling he's the type of person who's full of good intentions, but action is not really his bag. Oscar, on the other hand, probably has 'sensible' for a middle name. He'll be able to put a plan in place, or even sort a replacement for the carer that walked out.

'Hi,' I whisper, after I've finished going through all the drawers in Timmy's room. Needless to say, the manuscript is not there. I pull up a seat beside the bed, glancing over his features; there's no movement. No signs of awareness. I find myself curiously wanting to touch him as if somehow a little humanity might wake him from this spell. Reaching out with my right arm, I brush my fingertips gently across his forehead. But there's no reaction. Perhaps he is genuinely asleep. I pull back my hand, letting it slide onto my lap. What right do I have to touch anyone without their permission?

The light from the frame continues to dance over the room. I glance at the image on display; a wind-blown shot of all three kids playing on the beach, broad smiles, spades held at triumphant angles. Happier times. I keep watching as the frame transitions through to the next image. This time it's a shot of Erica standing beside a short, dumpy, piebald pony. She must be around ten or so, but she's unmistakable. Her limbs are thin as twigs. Her pale face looks gaunter than ever, framed under a shock of hair almost as dark as my own, scraped back in angry bunches. There's a curious look on her face as if she's trying to bite back a smile; her features are somehow too long, her cheeks pinched. It seems as if Erica is an uncomfortable character at any age. I realise I'm snooping. This is not my home. These people are not my family. I have no right to be sitting here judging. I glance around the room. It's tidy – nothing on the floor. No drink or food detritus to take out. I can't see that there's anything I can do for Timmy. Then I notice the baby monitor. It's got the handset with it. Julia must have left it lying there, hoping someone would take on the responsibility. I pick it up, slipping it into my pocket. I might as well earn my keep.

'Night then, Timmy,' I whisper softly, moving towards the door. As expected, he says nothing.

Back in my room, I put the receiver beside the bath and start to run water into the sparkling white ceramic tub. I could do with a soak. I want to check over those bruises, and my left arm still hurts. The warm water might just relax my taut muscles. There's a knock on the door. I'm still decent, so I call out over the sound of the gushing taps. 'Yeah, come in.'

It's probably Luke. We didn't have a debrief after I got here. In fact, it felt more like he was avoiding me. But to my surprise, it's not Luke.

'I wanted to apologise.' Erica hovers just inside the doorway.

This is a real shocker. I had her marked down as one of those women who have no idea how to say the word *sorry*.

'Yes.' Her voice sounds a little breathy. I get the feeling she's not used to admitting she's wrong. 'I didn't mean to be…' she hesitates, 'hostile. It's just that it's been a very stressful time.' She holds her hands, awkward and limp, across the same plaid skirt she's been wearing all day; like a child who finds her limbs an embarrassment. It's not every day you lose a mother and a sister, or niece, or whatever it is they called Miri – a best friend? I wonder sadly.

'I know,' I say. 'I'm sorry. I didn't mean to impose. Luke thought it would be a good idea – dilute things. Maybe he was wrong.'

'No. Not at all. We've talked it over. We've all decided, we'd like you to stay. Julia's very keen as well.'

I hadn't heard anyone go upstairs, but then I had been in with Timmy.

'So please, just stay as long as you like.'

After my bath, I get into my PJs. I have to pull off all the labels. Everything is new. I've never done that before – walked into a shop and bought myself a whole new wardrobe. Sadly, my *Pretty Woman* moment was not exactly satisfying. Island fashion is about twenty years behind the rest of the world.

I glance around the room. It's understated and old-fashioned. The wallpaper is a mess, but the space itself has everything you could need laid out and waiting – comfy chair, long mirror, even a little chaise. I run my eye over the bookshelf. I haven't read a book in years. How does that happen? When I was a kid, I used to love curling up with a good story, but somehow, when I got myself on that work treadmill, I hadn't known how to get back off. Reading for pleasure became a casualty.

I run my fingers along the bookshelf, disappointed when I realise that mostly it's philosophy; this house seems to have a theme going on. I recognise Plato, but most of the other books are beyond me. Not exactly the best route back into casual reading. Then I notice there's a thin notebook tucked in between all the others. The spine is unmarked. Carolyn's manuscript? My heart skips a beat. I give it a tug. It's a little brown moleskin book, the cover soft between my hands. I open it. Instantly I'm juggling. Things are falling out left, right and centre. Not the pages, but scraps of paper that have spent their days sandwiched inside: tickets, the coaster from a bar, a matchbook. I grab all the bits, trying to stop the avalanche. They're leaking out from specific pages as if marking territory. Cautiously, I attempt to push everything back into the right spot. Maybe they're bookmarks? Or perhaps they are wedged in systematically. I give one of the paper scraps a closer look. It's a boat ticket to somewhere called Cát Bà Island. I have no idea where that is. I look closer. Lan Ha Bay, Vietnam. Then it hits me. This isn't Carolyn's manuscript, no, this is something far more curious – Timmy's travel journal.

16

A TRAVELLER'S STORY

Hanoi – day one

I arrived late, eight o'clock in the evening. It was already dark. The taxi dropped me off at Hanoi Lake with its temple standing like some ridiculously ornate golden beacon. And so many people! Couples, families, groups of kids. The air was warm, scented even. Same stuff as you get in the Buddhist centre – incense. Not even the mopeds were diesel-fuming that sweet smell out of existence, which is incredible because the mopeds are mad. So many, and all loaded down. Five people, six people – everyone squashed onto one scooter. And animals. It made me laugh. At first, I couldn't even work out how to cross the road, just stood on the pavement, scared shitless to step out. The roads were that dense with traffic. I could imagine being stuck there on the same side of the street for my entire trip. Nuts! I'm eighteen, not knowing how to cross the road. Mad. Then this old woman came over. She thought I was German at first. The muddy-blonde hair maybe, and I'm tall. Well, compared to the Vietnamese, I'm like some giant. Which was maybe making me even more nervous about crossing that road – there's much more of me to hit.

'You step out,' the old woman said. 'They will part like fish.'

And then she started gesticulating with her arms as if shoals of fish were being budged over to the side.

'Only rule... No sudden movements. Keep moving one direction. Slow, but sure.'

I couldn't see how it was going to work. The traffic was seriously not stopping. There was barely enough room for a size ten trainer on that street, let alone one with a body attached. But... this whole trip, it's about being brave. Doing things differently. Out of my comfort zone. So off I go, one step at a time. Sure and certain, no hesitation, no backtracking – and to my absolute and utter amazement, the moped-creatures of Hanoi, they just part all around me like they're choreographed. My first day, and I've learned a new skill – how to cross a road. Not sure they'll be impressed back home. Doesn't matter, must send postcard tomorrow. Can't have those funds running out. I am so bloody lucky. This whole trip was booked and paid for, a present from The Wolf.

The Wolf? I don't understand. Who is The Wolf? Miri had told me that day at breakfast that she was like the wolf – coming into the family from the outside. But Miri would have been a child when Tim set off on his travels. No way could she have paid for his trip. It didn't make sense. There was the coat of arms. The Millford symbol is a wolf, so I guess any of them could have used The Wolf as a name. I close the journal and stare up at the ceiling. The Wolf. I know Carolyn was odd, but would anyone seriously call their mother The Wolf?

There's a knock at the door. I jump out of my skin before quickly pushing the scraps of paper back between the covers of the journal and sliding it onto the shelf.

Just in time – Luke pokes his head into the room.

'All okay? Thought I'd check on you,' he says, with one of those twinkling smiles.

'It's like Grand Central in here. I've already had a visit from Erica.'

He looks mock-scared. 'No battle wounds?'

'No.' I smile. 'Actually, she was really sweet.'

He nods. 'Told you. She can be. We talked it over. We all agreed we need to try and cling onto some kind of normality.'

'I'm not sure how I feel about being held up as a paradigm of normality.'

Luke takes a seat at the bottom of my bed. 'I hate this wallpaper.' He glances around the room. 'I always see things in it.'

I wish he hadn't said that. It's the last thing my imagination needs.

'It used to be Timmy's room. Carolyn decorated it after the...'

'The accident?' I offer helpfully.

'Yeah.' He glances down sadly, as if the weight of the memory is all too much. 'Timmy was a great guy.'

'He is still around.'

Luke shakes his head, sadly. 'Not the same. At first, when he came home, Mum kept him up here. He was bedridden. When he got a little more movement back, she set up a room for him on the ground floor. He could get around a bit. But lately, he's been...' Luke hesitates. 'According to Julia, he hasn't been doing much of that. Mostly he stays in his room.'

'So, at the wake? That was unusual?'

'Unusual and bloody bad timing. He's on some pretty heavy meds now.'

Luke glances up at me, his eyes intense. 'We haven't told him about Miri yet. He's not going to take it well.'

'Is that why he's so heavily sedated?'

Luke breaks eye contact, and I can't help feeling that he's not happy about the sedation.

'Meerson thought it was best.'

'You're going to have to tell Timmy sooner or later.'

'I think...' Luke stares down at his hands. 'I think we need to accept it first, and that's going to take time.'

'What will happen to him now?'

'Oscar's going to look into a few places on the mainland. We all agree it's too much for Julia, and Rose, the help that we had, it...' He hesitates. 'It didn't work out.'

'Oh?' I can't help but pick.

He looks awkward. 'I don't know, some run-in with Erica.'

This story is never sitting straight, Julia had said it was one of the boys who got rid of *the help*.

'There are going to be some changes,' Luke says, taking in a long, deep breath. 'And... so that you don't feel like the outsider, Oscar's invited a friend to stay.'

'Sounds like a good idea, and Erica?'

There's a brief pause.

'I'm not sure Erica has friends.'

'She must have some friends?'

He shakes his head. 'Miri. But... Erica's one self-sufficient lady.'

I think of the picture of the young girl and the pony; the one I saw in Tim's room. 'Animals, then? Does she ride?'

Suddenly, he looks more attentive. I get the feeling I've stumbled on something, and he has no idea how I got there.

'You think she looks the type?'

'No. I can't believe you said that.'

He smirks. 'Truth be told, Erica did love horses. As a small kid, she was terrified of them. I mean, they're pretty big. Then Carolyn bought her one. I'm pretty sure it was her tenth birthday. A scruffy little brown-and-white thing. Cute. I think my mother bought it just to scare Erica. Only it backfired. Erica adored it, but she knew better than to let on. She managed to cover up her joy in the thing for a year, but as soon as Mother realised Erica's fear was gone, and that passion had crept in, the pony got sold.'

I remember the bitten-down smile I'd seen in the photo. 'Seriously?'

Luke shrugs. 'That's the family myth. You know, I can never make up my mind. Is this family cursed? Or did Carolyn stack all the cards against us all? Tragedy seems to dog us. Cursed or stacked?'

'Either sounds a stretch. Can we go with *unlucky*?'

He smiles a small, thin smile.

'Ah, superstitious?' He lets out a little chuckle. 'Me, I'd go with the stacked. Carolyn was an odd woman. I certainly wouldn't put it past her, lining us up like dominoes for a fall. I often wonder what we would have been like without her. Oscar would have his…' Luke pauses. 'He'd have found his own relationships. Most likely, Erica would have avoided the whole romance thing. Maybe she'd have been an animal lover. But she's missed the boat now. I think she's afraid to love anything.'

'And you?' I ask. 'What would you have been without your mother's influence?'

'Interference, you mean?' He thinks about it for a moment, then fixes me with those clear blue eyes. 'Better.'

'Not safe.' The words creep into my sleep-filled brain. *'Get help.'*

I wake. It's dark. Someone is in the room with me! I peer into the blackness, finding it difficult to identify the rules of the room – where the solid objects should be. I should have left a light on. The bedroom is filled with uncertain shapes that seem to twitch and move under my half-asleep eyes. I remember the strong arms of Fordham. The beery breath. The darkness.

'Too close.' The voice crackles from beside my bed.

Then suddenly I realise it's the baby monitor, the one that belongs to Tim.

I throw back the blankets and hit the light. I'd left the monitor by the sink in the bathroom. Dashing towards it I can see blue lights on the handset flickering as it picks up a noise from downstairs.

'Not safe. Sister,' Tim's cracked voice repeats.

Is he talking about Miri? Or could this be a warning? Perhaps Erica is not safe? Whatever he was trying to say is lost. The handset has gone silent.

Grabbing the waffle-style dressing gown that's hanging up behind the door, I tear quickly down the stairs. But, by the time I get to Tim's room, all is quiet. The light from the photo frame is the only thing offering action. I put one hand gently on Timmy's forehead. He feels a little hot. Fever-fuelled dreams can chase a person anywhere.

17

ARRIVALS

A BELL RINGS OUT, high-pitched and loud into the still, morning air. Streaks of bright yellow sunlight needle their way persistently through cracks at the edges of the curtains as I pull a soft, plump pillow from behind my head, sink back on the mattress, and bury my face beneath it. Doorbell, I think. Not my problem. Someone will answer. It goes again. I grope towards the nightstand, taking a swig from the water glass. Any minute now, I'll hear the clatter of feet on the landing, but there's nothing. The bell rings once more. There are no footsteps, just the empty echo after each chime of the bell. With Julia out of action, who is supposed to be answering the door?

'Ms Conroy?' DS Graham's voice has a hint of surprise to it as I pull back the front door. A blast of morning air making every inch of my exposed skin feel just that little bit too vulnerable.

'I thought I'd stay on the island for a few days,' I mumble. I don't like having to explain myself; I like it even less when

Graham silently runs those hard, beady eyes over me, sizing me up. 'I was going to ring the station later, fill them in.'

There's another pause, longer this time. It's a pause in which I feel so awkward I wish I could rewind time and let someone else get the door or, alternatively, leave the DS to hammer it down. It's not just that I'm in the wrong place; I'm also in my night stuff.

'Well, this is awkward,' I mumble. 'I have no idea where anyone is. I've just woken up.'

'Then you'll do,' he says simply.

Reluctantly, I let him in, feeling relieved that my PJs are more tracksuit than temptress.

'Can I get you tea?' I offer, moving back through the hallway, the chequered marble tiles feeling icy under my bare toes.

'Tea would be good.'

'You better come down to the kitchen, then. Not sure my waitressing skills are up to much. I'm a kettle-to-table sort of person,' I call back as he follows me through the house. 'Julia's having some time off.'

'Ms Catalow?'

'Yes. She's not taking things well.'

'Oh?'

I stop in my tracks, turning back on the detective perhaps a little too quickly; he's being insensitive. 'They're grieving. They've lost their mother and Miri. That might not be a big deal for a copper, but for us mere mortals...' I'm certainly finding it hard enough to process.

In the warm kitchen, I get the kettle on and pull out a couple of mugs from a rack beside the Aga.

'Looks like you're making yourself at home,' Graham says.

'I didn't want to go answering the bell.' I try to keep the

irritation out of my voice. 'But no one else was getting it. I'll wake them as soon as I've got your tea.' I put the bags into the pot. The kettle seems to be taking forever to boil. I should have just offered him a tumbler of juice; I'm keen to be out from under Graham's microscope eyes.

'I looked you up,' he says as he takes a seat at the table.

I laugh. 'You wouldn't be a very good copper if you hadn't.'

'I hear you've lost your job?'

'Sabbatical,' I blurt, probably a bit too quickly. 'I'm on a sabbatical.'

He draws in his cheeks as if to say that's not what he's heard. 'Your colleagues aren't too sure if you're coming back. Apparently.'

'I don't suppose you chatting to them helped much on that front.'

He says nothing, just takes a long, good look around the kitchen, filing all the details away.

'Once I rouse the family, I'm sure they'll take you to one of the fancier rooms.'

'Actually, out of all the rooms I've seen so far, I think this is my favourite.'

I smile. 'Yeah. Funny. I felt that way too. Why is that, do you think?'

He pauses, drawing in a long breath as he mulls it over. 'It's a bit like a hotel upstairs.'

'It's certainly big enough.'

'No, it's not that.' Tilting his head to one side, he searches his brain for the right word. 'It's impersonal.'

'I guess it feels like home to the family.'

He nods, but not in agreement. I get the feeling he's mulling something over. 'There are no photos of anyone.' His eyes narrow. 'This place has been in the family for generations.'

I send my mind back through the rooms and realise he's right;

there are no tastefully lit masterpieces of Great-Great-Grandfather Millford.

'Maybe all the Rembrandts got sold off. Hard times,' I say, pouring the water into the pot and giving it a quick stir.

'That's not what I meant. There aren't even any photos of the family: not Carolyn Millford, not the kids, not even young Miri.'

I stop stirring, place the lid firmly on the teapot and let it stand for a moment as I digest what he's just said. To my mind, the Millfords have more than enough *family* stuff going on. 'There's a seriously bizarre painting in the church. The kids are all painted as birds.'

'Birds?'

'Yeah. I can't explain that one either. Maybe it's like some sort of rite of passage thing.'

He looks as confused as I feel.

'And there's also a digital photo frame in Timmy's room.'

'He's the youngest son?'

I laugh. 'You're asking me? Seriously, I only met them all a few days ago.'

'You seem to be making up for lost time.'

'I'm a guest,' I reply, one eyebrow arched.

He leaves a pause before his next question. I know what that pause is: space for me to sweat in.

'And you knew Carolyn Millford from online bridge?' He gives me a long hard look.

Has he rumbled me, I wonder? Does he know the real reason I happened to be standing at the graveside? But I'm too good at this. I don't miss a beat.

'Exactly.' I pour hot tea into a mug and push it towards him across the naked wood of the table.

He takes a sip. 'What did you think of her then?'

Now there's a question.

'I think… I think she was a woman who kept her cards close to her chest.'

He smiles, and I get the feeling that's tickled him. It's probably the bridge/cards analogy. I'm left under no illusions – he knows there's no online group. Or at least, not one that I'm involved with.

'Anyway, it's not me you're after,' I remind him. 'I'll go and knock up the others.'

I move towards the stairway, keen to get out of the firing line. This is feeling a bit too much like an interrogation for my liking.

It doesn't take me long to find the others. They're sitting out on the back terrace. Erica's voice floating into the house like a slap through the open door.

'There are people who know she was working on it. Her agent for one.'

As soon as I step out, there's absolute silence. Were they talking about Carolyn's manuscript? As far as they're concerned, it's none of my business, but the thing is clearly valuable. Her last book made a mint.

'DS Graham's downstairs in the kitchen,' I say.

Erica throws up her hands and hollers, 'The kitchen!'

But I don't take offence. With Erica, whatever room I'd parked Graham in would have been the wrong one.

'Does he want us all?' Erica says sharply.

'That I don't know. The only thing I do know is that he's not after me.'

Once I've changed out of my PJs, I decide to visit Julia. My motives are all about self-preservation. This family can't even open the front door by themselves. They're going to drive me nuts. That missing manuscript is still niggling at the back of my mind. Julia might have more insight into how Carolyn worked. The thing might not be in the obvious places, but maybe she'd taken to working in a different room in the house. Julie would know. Besides, I figure someone responsible needs to be looking after Tim. I'm pretty sure people who are bedridden need to be moved and fed.

I climb the small, narrow staircase to Julia's room and knock lightly. 'Julia?' I call softly. 'Just checking to see if you need anything.'

No reply.

Should I go back downstairs, leave it an hour or so, but then, that's not really my style.

'Julia?' I push open the door.

Luke was right; it seriously is a different world up here, dark and musty. A lumpy couch that looks like it's made out of horsehair, and a chipped sideboard. There's a photograph propped up on the flat surface, just one – a baby, chubby-cheeked and smiling. I know it's rude to stereotype, but if a person were to stereotype, they'd pretty much come down on Julia as being cut from spinster cloth. She's been so busy caring for everyone else I'm willing to bet she left herself out of the get-a-life picture. These overtired living quarters say exactly that. The photo on the sideboard is most likely a niece. I cross to the picture and hold it to the light. The smile's cute, whoever it is, they're pretty. I put the frame down. There's a small door to my right, just behind the TV. She must be through there.

'Julia, it's Kirstin. I was just…' I push open the door, and what I see almost floors me. Through the door is another attic room. Only this second room is a whole different story; a second apartment. The furniture is small but tasteful; plush fabrics, soft colours. A living room, with all the twenty-first-century bells and whistles; a large flat-screen TV, a stereo system, no horsehair antiques or wobbly-looking carpentry. Designer stuff, by the looks of it.

Photos of the family are lined up along a modern console. I take a step towards them, casting my eye quickly along the images, then realise: I've got it wrong. These are not photos of the family. The images are all of one family member: Miri. There are a couple of framed acting headshots, not the one from the paper, but the same style – an illuminated face against an infinite well of black. Miri looks amazing. It's star-quality stuff, but most of the photos are less formal: snapshots. Some of them look as if they've been taken in secret. One is of Miri standing on a kitchen chair, chubby arms, curly red hair, a mixing bowl on the table and a wooden spoon with creamed butter heading towards her open mouth. Professional shots, or hastily taken snaps, there's one thing that unites them – all of these images have been framed with such love and care. Miri's pretty, green eyes dance out from the pictures. What a terrible waste. Then suddenly, my brain dries. It feels like the tide is rushing out, taking all my thoughts with it, emptying everything from my mind till I am left with one single realisation: Miri is Julia's daughter. Julia has those same green eyes. I sink onto the cobalt-blue sofa, the sofa that's set before the console and photos. Set as if placed there to honour a shrine. No wonder Julia was heartbroken; she'd lost her child. Even worse – Julia's own hands had served Miri up the poison.

Frantically, I hammer down the stairs. I have no idea where to look for Julia. Has she done something stupid? Could she be planning on ending it all? I hope to God DS Graham is still around. He'll know what to do. Do the others have any inkling that Miri is Julia's child? I get the feeling, not. If they had known, they'd have been a bit kinder to Julia and probably not so nice to Miri.

I soon find Julia, she's standing over Timmy's bed. Her short, round body is wrapped in a smart, blue wool coat. The old-fashioned type. The type people used to wear for church or to go on long journeys. This one has a line of muted silver buttons running down the front. Every one of which is fastened in place, ready for action.

'Julia,' I gasp. 'I was so worried.'

She glances towards me, confused.

'Miri was your daughter?' I blurt.

She looks defensive.

'I didn't mean to pry, but...'

'You've been in my room?'

'I'm sorry,' I say. 'I went up to look for you. I was worried about Timmy.'

She glances sadly down at her charge, gently picking his hand up from the bed and resting her own over it.

'He's getting so much worse,' she says sadly. 'They should never have let Rose go. Nice young woman. Just before Carolyn's funeral as well.'

'Why?'

She shakes her head. 'Oh, some problem. I wasn't told the details. One of the boys had an altercation.'

'Luke?'

She pauses for a moment looking thoughtful, before shaking her head. 'I'm not sure. I thought it was Oscar. It doesn't really matter. They just need to sort out what they're going to do. Sedating Timmy this much, it can't be good.' Her eyes start to water. 'You're right, of course; Miri was my daughter.'

'I don't understand: why pretend she was Carolyn's?'

Julia smiles a small, sad smile. 'All of this.' She indicates around the room, meaning the Millford estate in all its grandeur, not Tim's utilitarian, hospital-style annexe.

'I couldn't offer Miri the things that Carolyn could. I couldn't offer her anything. I've worked for the Millfords most of my life. I don't have a house of my own or any real savings. Carolyn had everything. She knew about children. Adoption. Timmy was her favourite, of course, but after the accident... Carolyn wasn't good with imperfections. The children are all good people in their own way. But she wanted to mould things in her image, control them. She said, if I gave up my claim to the baby, she'd bring it up as her own. It would be a whole fresh start. I knew she could do it. She'd give the child everything. In her will, it would all go to Miri, this, her last child. Carolyn promised me.'

'I don't understand.'

'Carolyn was going to cut the others out of the will. They'd have an allowance, but Miri would get most of the inheritance.'

'Did they know this?'

Julia shrugs. 'Carolyn would threaten them with it, but I think they all thought it was just talk. Only...'

'It wasn't?'

'I witnessed the will.' She glances back down towards the bed and the sleeping Tim. 'But, oh, if I'd only known the cost would be this high. I thought it would all be for the best.'

Tears roll down her cheeks.

'I'm so sorry.'

She wipes her face with the back of her hand. 'My greed, my obsession that my daughter should have a better life, tripped me up. Miri's gone, and now it's time for me to leave.'

My face must have paled because she smiles sadly, half-amused. 'No, Kirstin. I shan't do anything silly. I just mean it's time for me to go from this place.'

'Have you told them?'

'I was hoping...' She picks up a small, neat blue handbag from beside her feet, the old-fashioned type with a golden metal clasp over the centre. 'Since you're here.'

From her bag, she takes two letters. For a split second, I don't quite catch on. Then she pushes the envelopes towards me and, with a sickening lurch of dread, I understand; she wants me to play postmistress.

'I was going to leave the letters in the hall, but... I'm scared they won't find them. They're not terribly observant.'

The first letter is addressed to Erica, Oscar and Luke.

'I've said my goodbyes in there, told them where to find everything. And Timmy's routine. Just until they get someone else in.'

The second envelope simply reads *DS Graham*.

18

JULIA

'SHE TOLD you she was the birth mother?' DS Graham eyes me shrewdly. We're standing on the gravelled driveway beside his car. I haven't told the others yet. When Julia drove off, Graham happened to be coming out of the house. It seemed a good time to hand over her letter.

'She didn't say birth mother. She just said mother.' I try to keep the snappiness out of my voice, but I seriously don't want to be playing Chinese whispers with anybody else's life.

'And she'd seen the will?'

'Witnessed it. That was what she said.' Curiosity gets the better of me. 'Is she right? Have the siblings been cut out?'

He glances down at his polished shoes. 'The will is being read tomorrow afternoon. They could be in for a shock.'

'But...' I frown, trying to work out the implications. 'I suppose that doesn't matter anymore. Miri's dead. They'll get the fortune.'

He shrugs. 'Maybe. Either way, it's one hell of an insult.'

'I think Carolyn was like that.'

He narrows his eyes, wanting more, but I feel I've got nothing else. I'm still reeling from Julia's news. Did she honestly think that giving her child away to a rich, cold woman, could ever bring anything good?

DS Graham gives me a long hard stare. 'You okay?'

'I like Julia,' I say because it's the simple truth. Out of all the people I've met at the Millfords, she's the most honest, the most normal. 'Don't grill her too hard.'

He smirks. 'I'm a real pussycat when you get to know me.'

Somehow, I doubt that. He pulls open the car door, giving a small, middle-aged grunt as he lowers himself into the driver's seat.

'I've still got a lot of questions.'

'I don't snoop,' I tell him firmly.

'Now that is a shame, because you always seem to be in the exact right place at the exact right time.'

'It's a habit I'm trying to wean myself out of.'

He pulls the door to, starts the engine and away he drives.

Pussycat? Is he for real?

'But she can't just leave.' Erica's standing in the drawing room, Julia's second letter hanging loosely from her thin white fingers. Going by the scowl on Erica's face, it's clear she'd rather be clutching a candlestick, a rope, a dagger and a bit of lead piping, than something which would be hard-pushed to offer up a paper cut. I can see why Julia opted for a handwritten socially-distanced exit.

'She's probably just taken some time off.' Oscar lifts the note from Erica's hands and starts scanning through Julia's, school-girl cursive.

I can't make out the words from my view at Oscar's elbow, but knowing Julia, I'm certain each line will have been carefully chosen. This letter is something from a different generation, one where words weren't disposable and tapped out with the aid of a thumb and the concentration of half a brain cell.

'But to leave us now...' Erica collapses onto the sofa in a defeated heap.

I'm pretty sure the letter can't have gone into details about Miri. Erica's reaction is every bit histrionics, as opposed to genuine emotion. If there are no details about Miri and the fact that she's Julia's daughter, that would also mean there's no mention of the will. It must just be a letter of resignation, pure and simple.

Luke takes the thin sheet of paper from Oscar and skims through. 'I'd say this is pretty conclusive. Julia won't be coming back.'

Erica sniffs, tapping her hand in a repressed fashion on her knees as if trying to control a more powerful impulse to run out of the door and slap the poor woman. 'I told you she was disloyal.'

But the men seem more thoughtful. Oscar stares sadly out through the window at the sloping green lawn and the sullen, grey October sky. 'This place won't be the same without her.'

'Let's face it,' Luke adds cryptically, 'this place is never going to be the same, full stop. Mother, Miri, we're losing someone every day.' He points to the bottom of Julia's letter and a line of neat ink near the end. 'She's left an agency number for someone to help with Timmy.'

Erica flicks imaginary fluff from her tweed skirt. 'Maybe Rose will come back.'

There's a moment's silence.

'Doubtful.' Oscar shoots Luke a surreptitious glance.

I can't for the life of me work out what the story is here. Who was it that sacked Rose, and why?

Erica shivers. 'Well, I can't handle more strangers in the house. Not at the moment.'

Oscar's shoulders slump in resignation. 'I could help with

Timmy, I suppose.'

This seems like such a bad idea but, incredibly, not one person protests.

'Fine.' Erica ejects her angular body from the sofa. 'Just don't bother me with it. I'm absolutely snowed under with work at the moment, and these last few days, I haven't been able to get one thing off my desk. I need to catch up. I'm taking over the study. Nobody's to disturb me. If the house falls into the sea, if aliens land, if...' she flicks her eyes between the brothers, 'if you two both drop down dead...'

Luckily, I seem to be invisible.

'I'm not interested,' she continues. 'I just want everyone to leave me alone.'

As she struts from the room, her narrow court shoes clicking across the floor, I get the feeling she's probably safe on that front. I wonder if she takes after Carolyn. Somehow, I don't think so. Despite her cruelty, Carolyn had friends. Erica is simply more bristles than a porcupine, so difficult to get close to.

'I'd better check Timmy,' Oscar announces. 'We've got the solicitor coming around tomorrow. In the morning, around eleven, I think?'

I make a mental note to be well out of the way for that.

'And Gareth will be arriving this evening,' he adds. 'Thankfully. I need a little normality.'

'Gareth?' I ask Luke after Oscar's safely cleared the room.

'Oscar's friend from the mainland.' Luke folds Julia's letter neatly along its creases and puts it back in its envelope. 'Tennis partner, I think. There's a court over in the gardens, quite a nice one. Bit windy, though, this time of year. We're all trying to inject a bit of normality into our lives, apart from Erica. She doesn't mean to be so sharp; she's just not that good socially.' His forehead creases into small, fine, thought lines as he taps the envelope against his empty hand. 'I just can't believe Julia's gone. She's been here forever.'

'Did you know anything about her? Her life, I mean, outside of this house?'

He shakes his head. 'I'm not sure Julia had a life outside of the house. She worked pretty much every day. Even on the weekends, she'd do breakfast then stay up in her room. That was counted as time off. I think she only ever went on holiday once. It was years ago. But then, none of us has actually lived here for a long time, so… things could have changed.'

'You said you had been up to her room?'

'A long time ago.' He pauses, rooting back through his memories. 'When we were little. Hide and seek, I seem to remember it was pretty good for that. Not much light up there. To be honest, I always thought Carolyn should revamp it, but Mother was pretty tight where money was concerned, and to be honest, I think she took some kind of perverse satisfaction in there being servants' quarters.'

'Not anymore. Someone did revamp. It looks amazing now.'

Luke's eyes sparkle. 'You dark horse, Julia,' he says, with nothing but admiration as we stand in Julia's secret attic and he continues opening cupboards, running taps, stroking furniture. It's the sort of thing I do all the time when I inspect a property, even though the soft furnishings are not on sale. It's never a house that I'm selling; it's a lifestyle. Seeing someone else do it though, it makes me realise how shallow the whole thing is.

'Luke, I was just wondering. With Julia gone, what happens to Timmy? What about this Rose person?'

'Oh,' he sighs theatrically, 'there was a fall out with Erica.'

Another change in the story, and if it was Erica, why was she suggesting that they get Rose back?

'Besides, Oscar trained as a doctor.'

What? None of this makes any sense. 'A doctor?'

'Yeah, *trained as*. Not sure if he practised or not. I was going through a bit of a wild patch at the time and not paying much attention, but all that medical knowledge stuff, it will still be there somewhere inside that brain of his. Oscar never throws anything out.'

I'm not sure, but do I just detect a note of bitterness; a hint of rivalry?

'Besides, Oscar won't charge us anything and, I have to admit, I'm a bit short of the readies at the moment. Short-term thing.'

He smiles, and I find myself hoping he's not banking on a windfall anytime soon.

'Oscar knows Timmy's case inside out. He's helped Julia for years. He employed Rose. So...' Luke places his hands palm upwards, 'Problem solved.'

'But...' I am seriously not getting this. 'A doctor? And now he's a used car salesman?'

Suddenly I remember the overheard conversation in the Ship, Oscar's ex-wife insinuating that Carolyn had ruined her ex-husband's career. But that didn't work. How can your mother ruin that kind of thing?

'Luke, I don't understand. Why would Oscar give up all that medical training?'

Luke shrugs. 'It's a mug's game – medicine. That's what Oscar says.'

He looks around once more at the apartment, appearing to have lost interest in his brother and the logistics of poor Timmy's situation. 'But this, Kirstin,' he sweeps an arm around the expensive furnishings, the beautiful carpentry, the expensive fittings, 'this is absolutely bizarre and incredible.' He smiles. 'Know what I think? To get all this done, everything here, without any of us knowing, to do all of this – Julia must have a secret lover.' And he laughs as if this has to be the funniest thing ever.

19

THE OTHER WOMAN

TIM'S BED whirrs mechanically as Oscar lowers it into place.

'So, you just gave up medicine?' I'm trying hard to keep the incredulous out of my tone.

'I found medicine, as a discipline, overrated.' Oscar places the remote on the bedside table. 'I don't need the prestige. That's something I already have and, believe me, Kirstin, *prestige* is not all it's cracked up to be. Could you just grab that bath blanket while you're standing there?'

I glance around. There's a neat pile of clean sheets, blankets and towels piled up on the sideboard.

'This one?' I say, taking a sheet from the top.

'Please.'

I hand it to him. He unfolds it, draping it over Timmy, before going to stand at the bottom of the bed and pulling the old one down. It slips under the fresh blanket covering Tim's body. Oscar gently rolls it up as he pulls.

'Course I had to learn how to do all this. Can you just grab the blanket, so it doesn't...?'

I can see that it's slipping down. I tug it back up, resting it neatly over Timmy's shoulders.

'You can do the pillow if you like,' Oscar says.

I glance nervously at Tim's head. I'm not sure I want to. It feels somehow wrong to touch him when he's not conscious.

'It's only a head.' Oscar tuts, before gently lifting behind Tim's cranium, removing the pillow and resting the sleeping man carefully back down on the mattress. 'There you go, Timmy.' He throws me the pillow. 'Think you can manage to change the case?'

'Just about.' I grab a clean pillowcase from the pile and strip the old one off.

'Don't put it back on the bed yet. We need to do the sheets.'

Oscar's already rolling one side of the sheet in towards Timmy's body.

'Don't you worry, Timmy. She's a novice, but I think she'll manage to pick it up and pssst,' he sinks his head down towards Tim's ear, 'I think our Luke may be soft on her.'

'I'm not sure that…' I feel the colour rising in my cheeks.

'He was very insistent you should come back to the house. Mind you; our Luke is the *soft-on-women* type.' He gives me a warning look.

'Was that what happened to Rose?'

Oscar looks at me curiously. 'Rose?'

'Timmy's carer.'

He seems surprised. 'No. It was…' But whatever *it* was, Oscar decides not to enlighten me. 'This is just short-term.' He glances down at the patient. 'We'll get something in place by next week.'

'Luke's a bit of a flirt, isn't he?' I say, sadly.

'Well, at least you know what you're getting into. I didn't want to have to warn you, not over my mother's grave and my youngest brother's body.' He smiles ironically before coming over to my side of the bed and nudging me gently out of the way.

'Okay. Now for the tricky bit. I'm going to roll him. You go my side and push the bedroll as far as you can under his body. Think you can manage that?'

'I'll give it a go.'

'Luke told me Julia's been living the life of luxury over our heads.'

'I'm not sure you'd call it that.'

'Good for her.' Oscar grabs a clean sheet and places it over the portion of the mattress that I've just rolled.

'Almost done. Same thing, other side. Ready?'

I do as I'm told. When the sheets are changed, I slip the pillow back under Timmy's head. For a brief moment, I hold his face in my hands, and am struck by an uncontrollable wave of pity; he's so vulnerable. 'Julia said he's getting worse.'

'Oh, he'll be fine. He always pulls through.' Oscar raises his voice. 'Don't you, Timmy. Young Kirstin here is getting all worried about you, but there's no need.' Oscar turns his attention back to me. 'He's heavily sedated at the moment because...'

Oscar doesn't finish what he was going to say. I get the feeling that's because Timmy might not look like he's listening, but that doesn't mean he's not picking things up; hearing about Miri might prove one tragedy too far.

'But, at the wake,' I say, 'he must have got himself into his chair.'

Oscar gives me a long hard look before slowing his voice and explaining as though he's talking to a child. 'No, Kirstin. Julia put him in the chair. She wanted to take him to the funeral. That was a ridiculous idea. He's barely aware of what's going on. Besides, he's never liked people gawking at him. Sympathy can be cruel.'

Oscar bundles all the dirty sheets into a ball and carries them towards the tall wicker basket standing ready in the corner.

'But he was lucid at the wake. He spoke to me.'

'I find that unlikely.'

'Well, he did.'

Oscar glances back at his brother, lying still as an effigy. 'Well, don't keep it to yourself, Kirstin.' His gaze seems to burn into me. 'What did my brother say?'

I hesitate, flustered, trying to recall Tim's exact words. 'I'm pretty sure it was – *I'm in danger*. And then he said – *You're in danger too*.'

Oscar looks thoughtfully at his brother. 'Hmm. Well, I suppose it works. You were both sitting in a sea of shattered chandelier.'

'So, he could have said that?'

'I don't know, Kirstin. Mostly now he...'

Oscar pulls the lid of the linen basket up, then stops, staring at it, his whole body deflating. 'Oh, bugger. I suppose with Julia gone, the washing is going begging. That is so...' He looks puzzled. 'So unlike Julia. I know we are an odd family, Kirstin. Difficult, perhaps, But...' He smiles ironically. 'And I do know this sounds... awful, but it was about to get a whole heap easier without Mother.'

'She really messed everyone up, didn't she?'

'It was her speciality. She was a "cat amongst the pigeons" type of a woman, but sadly... things haven't got any easier.'

'Do you know anything about this missing manuscript?' I ask, never one to miss an opportunity. 'The thing she was writing?'

'Hmm, she was always writing something.' He glances at his wristwatch. 'Lord, is that the time? My friend from the mainland will be here any minute. Would you?'

He thrusts the bundle of sheets into my arms, and he's off, reminding me strangely of the white rabbit from *Alice in Wonderland* – always in a rush and not making much sense.

I have no intention of washing the sheets. I put the bundle down on the chair. If I put it in the linen basket, everyone will conveniently forget about it, but if I pile the dirty sheets on the chair, hopefully someone will take responsibility.

'I don't mind looking in on you, Tim,' I say, moving closer to the bed, easing my hand over his forehead. 'But if they think I'm going to tidy up their mess, they've got another thing coming.'

It's an odd way to live. I just don't understand it. I can't see why he's not in a hospital. Then it dawns on me, what if somebody wanted to keep Timmy out of the action? To do that, you would have to understand drugs. Doctors understand drugs – even doctors who only do their medical training. Julia had said Tim was getting worse. In fact, all of them had admitted this. It didn't matter why Rose was sacked; the important question was – why wouldn't you get him more help in? Could I trust Oscar? He seems sweet, bumbling almost, but that could all be an act. Then again, maybe Oscar isn't the only one I need to watch. Luke had told me it was the first time he'd been upstairs to Julia's apartment in years. But that couldn't be right, because, when Erica came to my room last night, she'd said Julia wanted me to stay. According to Erica, Luke had been up with Julia and asked her.

But this is stupid. The product of an overactive mind finding answers that I don't even need – the police have found the murderer. I should leave the sleuthing to DS Graham. I need to get my priorities right. Find that manuscript and look after my own family. Which reminds me, it's 5.30, the only time I can get through and hear AJ's voice.

'Sorry, Tim,' I say. 'I'll be back though, I promise.'

I glance at the photo frame on the sideboard just as the image transitions again into the one I keep meaning to ask Luke about. Two young women. Going by the clothes I'd say this was the eighties. Carolyn, with her geometric bob, stands beside another young woman. The other young woman has a kinder, softer face. Perhaps she was a friend. She's got the kind of gentle features that you'd be happy to have sitting beside you as you went through life. Only something about that doesn't work. Carolyn is scowling at the younger woman, and when I look closer, I see the woman is pregnant. Most likely this was taken shortly before Carolyn fell pregnant with Oscar. So who was the other woman, the other child? But the photo changes once again. Time is ticking on.

20

A TASTE OF FREEDOM

IN THE PRIVACY of my yellow bedroom, I open the prison app and dial. I can put a message on any time, and AJ can pick it up when he has access to his phone, but direct contact can be tricky. Usually 5.30 works, but not always. Tonight, I'm in luck.

'Yes!' AJ's voice sounds triumphant.

I feel a warm wash of happiness sweep over me; this is home. 'How are things?' I blurt, but I'm too excited to wait for answers. 'Everything okay? Are you ready?' I gush.

'One thing at a time, sis.' He laughs.

I take a deep breath, gripping the phone tighter in my hands as though it's anchoring me. 'Are you nervous about the parole meeting?'

'Me?' AJ's voice is all bluff and swagger. 'No way. They gotta let me out this time. I've been good as gold. So good, they have to keep nudging me to see if I'm still alive.'

I laugh.

'Seriously,' he protests, 'I'm a changed man. Swear on Mam's life.'

AJ loves that joke. It's not funny, but I've heard it so many times over the years that there's no sting in it.

'And you, you doing all right?'

I glance around the room, the opulent furniture, the wide double bed and the strange yellow wallpaper that seems to shift and twitch if I forget to fix its pattern with my eyes. 'Great,' I say because I don't know where to start. *Someone tried to murder me. Actually, strike that, somebody tried to murder me twice.*

I decide to keep it simple. 'I lost my job.'

'Why?' AJ's indignation is hardcore genuine. 'I thought you were brilliant at it.'

'You are my brother.'

'Yeah, but... You told me all about all your sales. You were on a roll.'

I can't deny it. Hearing someone state the truth makes the *'sabbatical'* insult even worse. 'My boss said that what I was doing was unethical.'

There's a pause. 'The hearse-chasing?'

'Yeah.'

'S'all legal.'

'That's exactly what I told him, but ethics and legality are two different things.'

'Tell me about it. I would have been out of here years ago if the world ran on *ethics.*'

I'm not sure that's true – you commit a crime, society likes you to pay for it, but there's no way I'm going to burst AJ's balloon. And, besides, he's probably got half a point; he should have been out on parole by now.

'Never did like the sound of that boss of yours. What was his name?'

'Jasper Moreau.'

'Bloody silly name.'

That was AJ's style. If anyone stepped on my toes, he would happily torpedo insult after insult. Jasper could have been called anything. AJ would have still said it was *bloody silly*. My brother was loyal to the core.

'So, what you going to do?'

'I thought maybe...' I sink down on the bed, pushing the soft pillows behind my body and sliding my legs up underneath me. 'Well, you know how I always wanted to go into journalism?'

There's absolute silence from the other end of the line. I'm not sure if he doesn't remember, or simply thinks it'll be too tough to get into. I don't care. I've got to start dreaming big. 'I know it might sound like a sideways step, but I've always done the copy and the press releases for Jasper. I'm good at writing. If I could get my foot in the door. Write some articles. There's a few things been going on here, odd things, and I'm kind of on the ground.'

'Odd?'

'Well, you know that posh woman's funeral that I went to?'

'On the island?'

'Yeah, that's the one. Carolyn Millford. She's the woman who wrote that parenting book.'

The line goes dead. He clearly has no idea what I'm talking about now, then again, parenting is not his thing.

I continue, leaning on the juicy bits, the bits I might pitch to a paper. 'Her daughter was murdered.'

'Seriously?' His voice sounds incredulous.

'Yeah. They caught the guy. It was some age-old family feud, but I was in the house when it happened.'

'Wow. That would be a good story.'

'Exactly. And there's more. Carolyn Millford was writing a new book. An update on her parenting manual. Only now it's been lost. If I can get a sneak peek at it I could pitch a few extracts to the papers.'

He laughs. 'You are seriously always one step ahead of the game.'

'Yeah, but...' I sigh. 'I've looked everywhere that I can in the house, and I can't find the damn thing. Where would you hide something like that, if it was you?'

'Me? I'd bury it.'

I slump my body down on the end of the bed. This doesn't seem very helpful. I can't see Carolyn Millford, posh dress on, spade in hand, digging a hole for a manuscript.

'I'd copy it first,' he says, clearly working things through in his mind. 'Then plant it.'

'It was handwritten.'

'So. She would still copy it, digitise it.'

Suddenly it hits me. Even though she was writing by hand, somewhere there had to be an electronic file, one she hadn't quite managed to send to her agent or save on her desktop.

'But it's a good pitch. The murder is probably enough to get a paper interested. You know what I'm like, always love a bit of training. You could go on a course.'

AJ loved his prison courses.

'I can do loads of stuff now. Lots of new skills. Doing history stuff at the moment.'

'What happened to the law *stuff?*'

'Got bored and I'll be out soon anyways. But the history stuff's brilliant. History's not just about kings and queens, sis. Everyone's got history.'

I smile. 'It's taken you an OU course in prison to find that out?' My own plans are dropped by the wayside.

'S'not OU. It's a lady, a lady historian.' His voice sounds all posh and snooty when he says the *historian* part. 'It's just a short course on account of the impending parole, so... It's non-vocational.'

'Woo-hoo, fancy,' I say because I know he wants me to say just that.

'The historian lady, her name's Sheila. She comes in twice a week, and we trace family genealogy. That's like trees: family trees. Who's related to who.'

'I thought you didn't see the point of all that. What happened to us being enough for each other?'

'Yeah, well. I did okay, didn't I at raising you?'

'You did great.'

'Exactly. Besides, you're all grown up now. I just like... you know... Time on my hands so... I'm doing Dad at the moment. Tracing the bugger right the way back to the old country.'

He means Ireland. We've never set foot on the Emerald Isle. As far as I know, neither had Dad. But the name's a dead giveaway. *Conroy* – there has to be Irish in there somewhere.

'If it's keeping you out of trouble,' I say.

'Me? Trouble? They love me in here.'

'I bet they do.' I laugh again. 'Just keep that nose clean till tomorrow.'

'Two months, sis. If it goes in my favour tomorrow, less than two bloody months, and I'll be out.'

I leave the call, but keep hold of the handset, as if I'm hanging onto a lifeline. AJ had sounded elated. Surely it had to go in his favour tomorrow. He's served enough time. They're keeping him back because of that one stupid missing painting. He swears he has no idea where it is. I believe him and, tomorrow, I'm hoping the parole board will too. It's good that he's busy, though I can't get my head around him looking into our family. There was no love lost between AJ and Dad. Then it hits me, an odd uncomfortable feeling; when I first met Luke, he asked me if I was Irish. Why would he ask that when I hadn't even told him my name? I glance at myself in the large, circular mirror hanging opposite the bed, suspended over the dressing table. My hair is dark, but my skin's not exactly pale. That's probably partly my fault; I love a good sunbed. AJ would be much paler than me, and not just due to the incarceration.

There's so much more to this family than I'm being told. If I could just find Carolyn's missing manuscript, it might give me more clues. Her whole bag was child rearing. AJ was right. She had to have made a copy. Then it dawns on me: her phone. There's a drawerful of phones downstairs in the kitchen. One of them is the latest model. Could it be her last phone?

Barely breathing, I creep downstairs. The house is mercifully empty. The kitchen, vacant. The drawer exactly as I left it. The latest iPhone still jumbled in with all the rest. There's even a charging wire in there. Back in my room I plug the thing into the wall. Eagerly it buzzes into action. But damn, it's password protected. Dates. I rack my brain. Would there be any important dates? There's only one I can think of, 1897, the date when the two families – the Fordhams and the Millfords – merged. When the image shifts and a grid of brightly-coloured apps fill the screen, I cannot believe my luck. I'm in. Files. I think. It has to be in files. But there's nothing, only disappointment in the files and folders; old Covid passes. A credit card. Some train tickets, first class to London. This is hopeless. I think, kicking back on the bed, easing my back into the headboard as I flick idly through the apps: diet apps, parking apps, podcasts and books. Then suddenly I see it. A scanning app. She wrote everything by hand. To get it into the phone it would have to go through a scanner. Holding my breath, my heart beating hard in my chest, I open it.

The Experiment,
the myth of successful parenting and the dominance of genetic disposition.

Shit, I think to myself, flicking on to the first page. This is a goldmine. I scan down the chapter headings. It's all academic, most of it's way too dry and formal for my taste. The kind of dry and formal that is going over my head, so I flick forward to the intro.

It's been over thirty years since my book The Parenthood Jungle made its first appearance on the bookshelves of the UK. The take-up was phenomenal. At one point, it was said that seventy-five per cent of families in the UK had the book on their shelves. The publication was stocked in libraries and translated into twenty-five different languages. Its contents were hotly debated in universities up and down the country and across the dining tables of the middle classes. The Nature versus Nurture debate has reimagined parenting for generations. Therefore, it would seem only right to come back to the table. To discuss how my theory, which I put daily into action, played out. Aware from an early age that I would be unable to have children of my own, I turned to adoption.

My eyes virtually ping out of my head. *Unable to have children?* So Miri was not the only adopted child. None of the people downstairs are Millfords. Do any of them even know, I wonder. Maybe only Julia. She'd said she decided to give Miri away because Carolyn knew all about the adoption process. At the time I'd thought it was just a throwaway comment. But now, it's clear that Carolyn knew exactly how to go about it. No wonder Carolyn kept this latest manuscript close to her chest. A sharp knock at the door derails my thoughts. I shove the mobile under a corner of the eiderdown, unready to discuss any of this.

'Yes?' I manage, my voice breathless.

Luke pokes his head into the room. 'Oscar said he heard you talking. He thought I must be with you. Clearly I wasn't, so I was worried you might be talking to yourself, that you'd finally flipped over into madness.' He smirks. 'Which in fact, would be fine – join the party.'

'No.' I laugh, trying not to look guilty as sin. 'My brother. I was just... calling in.'

'Oh, right. I didn't know you had a brother?' He looks genuinely surprised.

I remember with an awkward jolt that I'd told Julia I was an only child. Had she said something to Luke? For such a big house, rumours and gossip seem to circulate at the speed of light.

'Just the one,' I say, as if this reduction makes all the difference. 'And he's not living here. He's on the mainland.' I shift awkwardly on the silk coverlet.

Luckily, Luke appears to have lost interest. 'So tonight...' He twirls on the spot like a master of ceremonies. 'Tonight, it's a beach party.'

The pace of this seems all wrong. It's not just the deaths now. I'm still reeling from Carolyn's revelation.

Luke continues, oblivious. 'There will be mountains of food, magic, moonlight and a great fire flaming to the heavens. Jumpers, woolly hats and thermals are absolutely essential though. Don't come fancy.' He fixes me with a cheeky stare.

Going fancy would be a serious stretch for me with my limited clothes situation.

'Nobody is allowed to wimp out on account of the cold.'

'I'll wrap up,' I say, trying to keep my tone light. 'Like a mummy?'

A pretend worried look creases his brow. 'Hmm, hopefully something a little more lively.'

'Lively, sure, but Luke...' I hesitate. I don't want to bring it up, but I have to: his energy feels so out of place. Is it appropriate under the circumstances? It will make great copy for an article on the Millfords and how they cope with grief, but a party, now... 'Is it okay?'

Luke's features are blank.

'I mean... what with Miri.'

'We have to live, Kirstin,' he says in a tone of absolute

sincerity. 'Miri would have wanted that. She loved beach parties.' He smirks, all serious gone. 'Meet downstairs in thirty. I need hands.'

When I arrive in the dining room, wrapped tighter than a silkworm in my entire island wardrobe, I can see Luke was right about needing hands. There's so much food, blankets, cushions, wine. There's even a little record player with a raft of vinyl records.

'This is insane.' I laugh, nervously.

'I know.' He smiles, taking my face between his hands and kissing me on the head.

I am so confused. What is going on here? The man can't fancy me. Something would have happened by now if he did. I seriously believe he's got me here simply to diffuse the Millfords. Who, curiously enough, are pretty genetically diffused anyway. Are they all from one parent? I have to try hard not to stare.

'Insane… isn't it, though?' Luke moves towards the table, slipping effortlessly into party planner mode. Despite the tragedy, the excitement is palpable. I guess there is a good reason. They have no idea of what's brewing in Carolyn's manuscript, or Julia's will. They're under the assumption that they're about to inherit a small fortune. Fordham is also behind bars. I guess I should let them have their fun.

'Apparently, Oscar's friend has arrived,' Luke says, placing large food bags, their mouths open, onto the table. 'Our numbers keep decreasing, increasing… Hard to keep track.'

I don't like to point out to Luke that the decreasing numbers are not, in any way, good. Although Luke's on such a high, I don't think even pointing out that there's practically a coffin in the room, could dismantle his mood. I remind myself, yet again, that everyone grieves differently. I'd been to enough funerals to have witnessed some pretty odd behaviour.

'I've done this for Miri,' Luke says, carefully packing soft fruit into a large carrier bag. 'Everything she would have loved. The food, it's all vegan, in her honour.'

'I didn't realise she was vegan?' I say, wondering if that explains the shake.

'Oh, yes. And this... this...' Luke reaches across the table, fixing his hands on a bottle still clouded from the fridge. 'It's her favourite wine, Sancerre.'

'Oh, for Christ's sake,' Erica barks as she enters the room. She's swapped the tweed skirt for an impossibly smart pair of jeans, and her features are pulled into an attitude so sharp and disapproving that Luke's mood deflates in an instant. Only she seems to sense that she's gone too far. Her face crumples. 'Look, I do appreciate all the effort you've gone to, but I can't do the whole *Miri* thing. I can't have everything reduced to *what Miri would have liked, what she would have said*. It's too much. Far too painful. You understand?'

'She's right.' Oscar presses through the door past his sister. He's looking sober and sad, his shoulders no longer held straight as if he's carrying a plank under his jacket. This whole thing is beginning to take its toll. 'Let's go to the beach,' he eyes us sadly, 'but let's do it for us.'

Luke nods. 'Sorry. I... I don't know what's got into me. I'm either high as a kite or wanting to slit my wrists. I wish I could get a grip.' And suddenly, he starts to cry, tears welling up in his eyes as he sinks onto one of the high-backed dining chairs, resting his head pitifully in his hands. It's heartbreaking. I wrap my arms around his shoulders. Poor Luke.

'Sorry,' comes a male voice, the tone awkward. The voice, not one I recognise.

There's a man standing in the doorframe. I'm sure we've met before. He's dark-haired, slim, smart but casually dressed. Nice-looking. The sort of person you would notice, he looks so clean as though he was freshly minted an hour ago, but I can't remember him from the wake. Is he a police officer? Maybe he's another detective?

'I didn't mean to interrupt,' he continues. There's a light West Country burr to his voice.

'Nonsense, Gareth,' Oscar says lightly.

Of course, this must be Oscar's friend from the mainland. He's not what I expected. He's younger than Oscar for a start, more mid-twenties than thirties. With dark close-cut hair and a chiselled jawline, he looks too... and I hate myself for even thinking it, but he looks far too interesting to be a friend of Oscar's.

'This is Gareth,' Oscar announces to the room.

Luke wipes his eyes with the back of his hand. 'Sorry, Gareth. I'm all over the place at the moment.'

Gareth shakes his head dismissively. 'You've all been under so much stress.'

'Yes.' Luke gets to his feet, taking my hand between his. 'And, Gareth, this is my friend, Kirstin.'

Friend, I think. The way he's holding my hand, the way he looks at me, it must be so obvious to everyone that 'friend' is not an accurate description. There is something there. Perhaps he's holding back because of the situation. They are all in mourning after all.

'And, Erica, my sister,' Oscar says.

She moves forward a little for her introduction.

'The sensible sister,' Luke adds cheekily.

'Yes,' Oscar smiles, 'Erica keeps us all in check.'

'I'm so sorry for your loss...' Gareth's face shifts into an awkward grimace. 'Sorry, losses. I knew Carolyn. I work at Longbow and Mclean.'

Luke's blank expression incites further explanation from Gareth.

'Your mother's solicitor.'

'Oh,' Luke says warmly but a little confused. 'I thought that was all happening tomorrow – the will reading?'

Now it's Gareth's turn to look shocked. 'Oh no, sorry, that's not me. I'm here just...' he glances towards Oscar, 'just to give Oscar a little support. As a friend,' he says, looking awkward. 'It will be Josh Mclean who reads the will tomorrow. I'll probably stay out of his way, if that's okay. Might be best not to say that I'm here in fact. He... well, we're...'

It feels like Gareth's digging a hole for himself.

'It's just best.' Oscar does a good job of pulling the metaphorical shovel out of Gareth's hands. 'Best if we keep the company and our private lives separate. Easier all round.'

'Fine by me.' Luke drags one finger across his mouth, implying his lips are sealed.

'I take it then, Gareth,' the name sounds sour in Erica's mouth, 'you're not supposed to be here?'

'No,' Gareth blusters, 'my being here is okay. It's just, maybe I don't want them, the company,' he stutters, 'to... to know my business.'

Erica looks irritated, but she says nothing. Instead, still frowning, she moves towards the table and starts packing her arms with cushions, blankets and towels. 'Well, now that you are here, you'd better help. This stuff won't get to the beach on its own.'

We all dive in. I grab a small freezer-box containing salads, charcuterie and wedges of thick-cut bread that smells delicious: fresh and yeasty. A cold blast of air bursts into the room as Oscar throws open the wide French windows leading out into the dark night and the terrace; a terrace that slopes quickly down to the beach.

Our way down is truly magical, illuminated by glowing torches as the path winds towards the sand.

'And make sure you bring everything back,' Erica says as we snake along the path. 'It's all very well having beach parties…'

I can see the wood pile waiting like an eager torch on the white sand. Childlike excitement courses through my veins as the sea-wind teases around me, and Erica's voice gets broken into snatches.

'Beach parties are fine, but people need to bring everything back to the house.'

Her words are carried away by the sea air, as I marvel at this wondrous place – a place where you can step through worlds – from house to beach. If it did all work out my way, if by some fluke the siblings did end up putting the house on the market, it would be worth setting up as an independent for just this one sale. Although there would be a problem; I'd never want to sell this house. I'd want to live here forever.

As every vestige of light fades from the sky, the great fire takes over, a giant towering beacon reaching up into the dead, black web of night. Luke must have spent hours building it, collecting driftwood along the shore and piling it high. We cluster around the flames. I've taken off my shoes. The sand beneath my toes feels deliciously cold in contrast to the left side of my body; a side which is being cooked by the fire. I've managed to abandon most of my silkworm layers, which is great. They weren't exactly flattering. Now I'm down to one jumper, a baggy blue crew neck I'd picked up in town, and a pair of infamous island slacks. The world feels unreal, like a fairy tale, the sort of pixie-dust story that, only one week ago, I would never have inserted myself into. I sit beside Luke, enjoying the warm buzz circulating between our bodies. Maybe it's better this way, this 'just friends'. Maybe it's even more perfect than romance at least I don't feel obliged to tell him what I've discovered, or to keep it away from the press. I've got to remember to look after number one. No one else will.

The *'siblings'* seem much more relaxed sitting beside the fire in the fresh night air, making it a perfect time to push for more info.

'So…' I say, keeping my voice relaxed, 'I'm just curious because Carolyn didn't seem very maternal. How did that work?'

Luke laughs. 'Boarding schools.'

'Erica,' Oscar gestures towards her, extending his finger into the air, 'do you remember that one year you refused to come home?' He laughs.

Erica stares into the sky, pulling her mohair blanket tighter around her thin shoulders. 'I don't think I ever actually relished the thought of coming home.'

'But don't you remember…?' Oscar continues. 'That one time you'd barricaded yourself in your room at school.'

This strikes me as odd. Luke had implied that Erica had been bullied as a child. Then I realise, I'd put two and two together and come up with the wrong number count – maybe the bullying didn't happen in the schoolyard; perhaps home was the problem.

Despite the fire, Erica's starting to look brittle again. I get the feeling she doesn't like scrutiny.

'I don't remember the details. Luckily, Oscar,' her voice has a hard, bitter edge, 'I have you to remind me of all the awkward, embarrassing moments I've ever had to live through.'

'She always sent us away when she was pregnant as well,' Oscar says, staring into the fire.

Of course she did, I think – because Carolyn was never actually pregnant. But this tells me so much more. The 'siblings' have no idea they're adopted. Are they even from the same family? I scrutinise them carefully. They look similar enough.

Luke's brow furrows. 'You can remember Mum being pregnant? Do you remember her being pregnant with me?' He's suddenly switched mood again. Now he's so intense. But Oscar fails to pick up on it.

'Only just. More the, being sent away, and the bad moods. I remember those.'

Erica snorts. 'Mother always had bad moods.'

Oscar must feel he's gone a step too far because instantly he pulls back into silence.

'I always loved the contrast between home and school.' Luke gazes into the fire as if he can see their past lives laid out before him. 'You could do anything at school. People get this warped idea that there are strict punishments at boarding schools. But actually, the school's main concern isn't you. Their main worry, their single preoccupation, is that when you mess up your parents don't get to find out. All that *"next time this happens, Millford, we will have to tell your mother"*. That's all rubbish. You're the cash cow. The cover-up is in their interests. And the best schools,' he laughs, 'well, they do the best cover-ups.'

Even Erica smiles at this. 'You did push them, Luke.'

'That time you took all the furniture out of doors and put it on the lawn.' Oscar laughs.

'And scaling the flagpole.' Erica flicks her eyes to the heavens as if this was all so predictable. 'Every week, there would be something new flying from the top.'

'Good times.' Luke smiles.

These people might be adopted, they might come from different families even, but there's one thing for certain – they are still a family.

'*Good times?*' Oscar leans forward to push another log into the flames. 'Not good for everyone. You remember that Bristow boy?'

And it could be my imagination, but I swear Luke pales.

'Fat child? Timmy's year?' Erica's face furrows into a frown.

'No, Luke's,' Oscar continues.

'Christ, it was years ago now.' Luke sighs. 'And there were a lot of us. Not sure I can remember everyone.'

'He committed suicide,' Oscar says. 'You must remember, Luke. I think you sat next to him in…'

'Physics. Yes. It rings a bell.' Luke's tone sounds suddenly curt.

'Depression?' Oscar says, his brow creasing as he tries to search back through the details.

'Oscar,' Luke groans. 'I think we've had enough death to be going on with.' He flicks some sand onto the fire. 'Subject-change, please. Right,' Luke jumps to his feet, 'enough. Who's for swimming?'

I look towards the cold, dark waves, their frilled edges nibbling away at the shore. It's inky black out there. I'm uncertain as to where the sea stops, and the sky starts. The world just seems to merge into the dark. Luke playfully kicks a little sand towards me.

'Don't tell me you can't swim, Kirstin?'

It might be warm by the fire, but I know for sure that the water will be freezing. 'I can swim, bu...'

'That's settled then.' Luke pulls his jumper over his head, the firelight dancing across his toned body. 'Race you. Last one in is a wimp.'

I'm about to object but glancing around I see that everyone else is tearing off their clothes. Even Erica is ripping everything from her body and racing down the beach towards the sea, laughing.

It's the first time I've seen all the Millfords actually laughing, actually having fun. No way am I going to be the damp squib here. I pull my crew neck over my head, shake my legs out of my slacks and run headlong into the black night.

We're not in there long. The water is too cold, too rough. I'm keen to get my clothes back over my goose-bumped skin, but Luke is having none of it. Apparently there's an odd but unavoidable family tradition – a sand fight. Being wet means the sand sticks, and this would appear to be the point. The fight is punctuated with shrieks of laughter and Erica's constant *'No sand-flinging higher than the waist.' 'Not near the eyes.'* Then, and this is seriously bizarre, we all have to roll down the sloping shore: roll over the freezing sand into the sub-zero-temperature sea. Thankfully the alcohol and laughter must be keeping us warm because no one seems to care.

By the time we snake in a line back up the path towards the house, each one of us laden down with the empty picnic baskets, my teeth maybe chattering but it's partly with laughter. There's an outdoor shower tucked away on the terrace just outside the dining room. We take it in turns queuing to get under the lukewarm spray, our teeth chattering. Erica refuses to let anyone into the house if they haven't showered. Sadly, the barely warm water seems to make the sand stick tighter to the skin.

After saying our goodnights on the landing, I know exactly what my next priority is – getting that sand out of... well, everything. It's in my hair, up my backside, plastered all over my flesh. I go straight to the bathroom, take off my beach-caked underwear and hurry into the walk-in cubicle. My skin tingles thankfully under the gush of warm water. What a night. It seems as though before Carolyn, before the funeral, my life was on a one-way track. Now, the world has opened out with so many possibilities. I feel alive. For the first time in my life, I feel truly live and kicking.

21

A PATH TO NOWHERE

A PILE OF CROCKERY, cutlery and placemats are piled come-and-get-it-style, cowering in the shadow of a wall of garish cereal boxes – frosted rice, muesli and some kind of multicoloured oat-based abomination. I'm not sure who set the stuff out. We may be in the dining room of some grand mansion, but this particular arrangement is all about function, with zero attention to aesthetics. The siblings appear to have reverted to childhood. The milk is still in its litre container. Napkins have been abandoned, and the marmalade has a glob of yesterday's butter congealing in a slovenly sprawl under its lid. Surprisingly, not even Erica seems offended by the thrown-together nature of the table. Dressed in a dogtooth A-line skirt and twin set, she's nursing her standard black coffee, a frown fixed on her forehead. I wonder if she had a bit too much wine on the beach last night. She wouldn't be the only one. Yet the ever-persistent pulse of a hangover, and even the addition of another guest – Oscar's friend Gareth – has done nothing to quell Erica's righteous indignation; she's just got back from Julia's secret room.

'The woman must have been stealing from Mother for years.'

'You don't know that.' Oscar rolls his eyes.

'Besides,' Gareth pours himself a glass of orange juice, 'you can't say *that*. It could be litigious. Sorry...' He pauses, readying to correct himself. 'It is litigious. Even if this... Julia?'

We all nod; he's clearly not up to speed yet with all the names.

'Even if Julia,' he reiterates, 'may not want to sue you for it now, you don't want to open up any possibilities.'

Erica doesn't appear interested in the legalities, so doesn't bother with a direct reply. 'I know what Julia earned.' Avoiding the cereal, but in need of more sustenance to fuel her rage, Erica pours herself a second coffee. 'It wasn't exactly skilled work that the woman did.'

I'm not so sure that's accurate. Looking after the Millfords seems to me like a highly specialised occupation.

Erica takes a sip from her cup. It barely wets her lips, before irritation has her talking again. 'She also had a sister.'

This piques Oscar's curiosity. 'Oh?'

Luke frowns. 'I think I vaguely remember her going off for a visit.'

'Not the point, Luke,' Erica bites. 'The point is – the sister was in care. She was much older than Julia, but had some kind of meltdown. Permanent meltdown, and Julia paid for her care. A lot. So she wouldn't have had the money to renovate the attic. It's twice as big as it used to be.'

I'm pretty sure it's triple the size of the original footprint, but I'm saying nothing. Instead, I attempt something less inflammatory. 'Surely, if workmen were coming in and out, wouldn't you have noticed?'

All three of them shoot back at me as though synchronised, words which amount to the same kind of thing. 'We weren't here all the time.'

'I have to say,' Gareth glances down at his shoes, reluctant to draw any flack but, like me, he's got questions, 'Carolyn, I mean, your mother,' he corrects himself respectfully. 'She was one on-the-ball woman.'

'That's why it is so very odd.' Erica worries over a minuscule slice of cold toast, trying hard to get away with the smallest wipe of butter that it is conceivably possible to spread.

Personally, I'm beginning to wonder if the *deal* that Julia struck with Carolyn wasn't just about the will. Maybe the scope of this thing is bigger. Could Julia be the blackmailer? She didn't strike me as the type, and I couldn't quite work out why she'd be holding Miri, her own daughter, to ransom. But to renovate someone's attic without their consent? How would you even get away with that?

'None of it makes sense,' Erica says, attacking the marmalade jar. 'But one thing's for sure. I'm glad Julia's gone. I feel...' She hesitates, her knife stuck deep into orange jelly. 'I feel utterly betrayed. I'm going to take breakfast in my study.'

In fact, she leaves everything but the coffee. We wait for her to go, watching as she buzzes her coat-rail body out of the room like an angry bee.

'When did it become *her* study?' Luke frowns.

Oscar stares after his sister, looking uptight and irritated. 'If she's going to start bagsying, then I think it's only fair that I get...'

Luke shoots his brother a hard look. 'Before everyone starts putting sticky notes over things, we need to settle on what's realistic. We do not need this house but, even more important than that – we do not need to be chained together.'

This is the most sensible thing I've heard anyone say for a long time.

'We're all very different people,' he continues tactfully. 'Together, well, everyone gets suffocated. After the will has been read, and...' He drops his gaze to his breakfast bowl, turning the milk idly with his spoon. 'We need to get the house on the market.'

As I clear the dishes, a part of me can't help worrying over Erica. In some ways, we're similar, both of us locked into our work – not enough friends, not enough joy in life. That's all changing for me though. I stare over at Luke. He's sitting at the large table, chatting to Oscar. Even though I know now this is just platonic, I like him. It feels good to have a friend in my corner. Although... I take in a long, hard breath, I'm not exactly sure our that friendship will stand up once I leak Carolyn's manuscript to the papers. I can't even do it secretly because I'm after a leg up on the journalism front. I've got to make sure I don't make this more complicated than it is. Luke will land on his feet, all of the Millfords will. They may not have been born with silver spoons clutched in their hands, but they soon got hold of the necessary cutlery. They might not have got everything they wanted from the will, but it's pretty clear something will be winging its way to them. The estate is big. They'll all get something. Not so for me. I've spent my life working an angle and I can't let anything, not even my new friendship, get in my way of waltzing away with a piece of this pie.

By the time Mclean arrives from the solicitors, Erica has put around the hoover. She did it angrily, bumping the skirting boards and slamming it across the stairs, but we are probably a little more presentable than we were. I watch from my window as the solicitor parks his mink-brown Audi on the wide drive and walks towards the front door. He's old. I'd say seventy, with a slightly crooked gait, throwing one leg out awkwardly to the side. In his hands, he clutches a large, manilla envelope. With Miri gone, the siblings might well inherit the estate in its entirety, but

I bet there's some kind of kick in that package headed for each one of them. I'm pretty certain now they're unaware that they're all adopted. The comments about going away during her pregnancy suggest Carolyn was secretive about the process, which sends up red flags. I wonder if she'll have owned up about the deception in the will? I glance around at the yellow wallpaper; the swirls guaranteed to push anyone out of their mind. Of course, I think. This isn't just any mother we're talking about here. This is Carolyn Millford.

I swear I am only going to get a glass of water. Well, if I get caught, that's what I intend to say, but I'm curious as hell: desperate to hear how the 'siblings' react. So, I do the undignified – I loiter. They're in the study, so it's fine for me to haul up in the adjoining snug. And, if I hear anything, well... that's hardly my fault.

Mclean is the one doing most of the talking. There's a bit of preamble. The usual; he's sorry for their loss; how are they all coping? But no one is interested. Everyone's burning to know what's inside the envelope. I listen hard, standing inches from the adjoining wall. I listen for a good five minutes, there's lots of talk, but the one thing I'm not hearing is shock or indignation. Carolyn's obviously still keeping shtum about the adoptions and Julia must have got it wrong on the inheritance front. Finally, there's an announcement: the estate, according to Mclean, is to be divided between the four siblings and Miri. Since Miri is no longer around, Miri's share will be held in probate. They may not be surprised, but I am. Nothing about this stacks up. I need a break from the Millfords. Besides, AJ has his parole meeting today and I'd rather be out of earshot when I'm chatting with him.

After the will has been read and Mclean's departed, I find Luke on the back patio, nursing a coffee.

'So, it all went okay?' I say, pulling up a chair.

He nods.

'I was wondering…? I'm feeling a bit trapped.' I follow Luke's gaze out towards the white sand and sapphire-clear waters.

He laughs. 'Here?'

I pull my jumper tighter over my shoulders; a barrier against the light wind. 'I know. It sounds odd but I still don't have my car.'

'Of course. Sorry.' He taps the side of his head as if trying to kick-start his brain. 'You should have said earlier. You want to go into town?'

'I do. I need to…' I hesitate. 'You know, grab a few things from the shops. Chemist stuff.' That normally deters any further investigation.

He barely looks up from his coffee. 'Sure, I'll stick you on the insurance.'

It doesn't take me long to get used to the car. It may be a beast, but Luke was right; it's an easy drive. I turn on the radio. It feels good to escape, only… I'm around five minutes away from the Millford estate when I see the spot where my car stalled. There's nothing there now, not even police tape. The car has been towed. Most likely, it's at the station. I drive a little further, a hundred yards or so, but suddenly find myself hitting the brakes; I know it's odd, but I have some kind of morbid desire to see the place where I almost ended up pancaked.

Standing on the flat tarmac, the earthy smell of damp woods permeates my nostrils. It's darker here than the rest of the road. Despite the fact that it's October, the trees are still holding on to their leaves. They tunnel over my head in a canopy of green and rust. The left side of the road is packed tightly with oak and ash trees clambering up the steep sides of the hill. To my right, the land falls away into a lower valley, the sun dancing across a hotchpotch of fields. But on the road, the canopy is throwing everything into darkness. No wonder Luke couldn't see me. Even with a full moon, it wouldn't have been easy and there's barely enough space to swerve. I'd had a lucky escape. I glance back towards Luke's car standing behind me. Its wide metal grille, the definition of unforgiving. A bird calls out from the wooded bank. I glance up, scanning the trees to see if I can catch sight of it. It sounds like a crow. The noise echoes, harsh and unpleasant, mocking even. Sure enough, I catch a glimpse of a bundle of sleek black feathers; its beady eyes fix on me – an intense stare, before it flaps its wings and weaves up and off through the trees making for the sky. It's then that I notice the path, a small track winding up high through the wood.

It's a steep climb, but the track is well-established; somebody's been going up here most days. Odd, because I didn't think there were any other houses this close to the estate. The light dapples in front of me, tinged green from the criss-cross of branches above. The road had felt dark, oppressive, but as I climb, I feel an incredible sense of peace. It's almost as if I can feel the roots of the trees sucking up life.

I climb for about ten minutes until the land flattens out into a clearing. This strikes me as odd. Why would there be a track up the hill? There's nothing here. I peer further into the dark tangle of branches that edge the clearing. At first, I don't see it; it's well camouflaged. I think that the cross-hatch of brambles to my left is nothing more than that, a simple unruly knot of undergrowth. But there's something strange about the hunched, dense shape.

Stepping closer, the light shifts slightly, a beam of sunlight illuminating the edge of the clearing, throwing gold beams into the corners of the wood. There's some kind of structure in there; a primitive shelter made of rusted, corrugated iron. Someone's tried to hide it, burying the sides of the building in a chaos of dead and dying shrubs. It's a little half-hearted. It doesn't take me long to pull the tangle away. Nothing about this is making sense, because underneath I find a corrugated sheet with a handle on. I hesitate for just one moment, but curiosity spurs me on. I give the handle a short sharp tug. A panel dislodges in a cloud of mud and dust, clattering to my feet as a door swings open.

It's dark inside. The air smells thick and fetid. A thin trickle of sluggish mote-filled light oozes through a small window. I glance around in the darkness, just able to make out the layout of the hovel. There's a bed, a little stove, and a series of water buckets. On a shelf, there's an abandoned bottle of aftershave. A white bottle with a thin neck – Old Spice but that's not where the smell's coming from. A cloying, dense stench lingers at the back of my throat, stuffing my nostrils because abandoned on the table is a fetid plate of mouldering food, busy with flies.

I dash back out of the hut, filling my lungs with the fresh air outside and feeling unnerved. Everything about this place seems wrong. Then it hits me – the aftershave on the shelf: Old Spice. My dad used to wear it. I can almost recreate the smell of it without the aid of a sniff. But that's not the thing that's bothering me. I've smelt it somewhere recently. I smelt it when I was being attacked. I turn my back on the hovel, keen to get away. As I do, out of the corner of my eye, I see a large stone cross. Instantly, I realise where I am – the church. I'm at the church.

Is this where Fordham had been camping out? That would explain the decaying food; he hasn't been here for a few days. I start to walk back down the hill. I'm going quicker now. Questions buzzing around my brain; more frantic than the flies I'd just seen attacking the moulding food. The church is important to Fordham. It's the last physical claim he had on this land. That's why he was out here. I walk faster, the tall, dark trees surrounding me, closing their fingers over my head as I push quickly forward. My feet begin to slip over the wet ground. If Carolyn had come up here alone, Fordham might well have confronted her. Yes he was old, but he was big and strong from all the manual labour he did. It wouldn't have taken much effort for him to pick her up and throw her over the cliff. I slip across the wet, raked ground, barely able to keep upright as I move faster and faster down the hill, the grass seeming to pull and tangle my feet as if reluctant to let me run free. Fordham might be safely behind bars, but the wood suddenly feels menacing. All the vestiges of peace and tranquillity I felt earlier have gone. Over the years, this small pocket of land has collected malice; the warring families; the stories of the wolf baby; the lone woman walking close by on the cliff-top before falling to her death. It feels as though this place has always been biding its time, waiting for some foolish person out on their own to stray off the path and into its web.

I break into a run, crashing down the last few feet of the path and out onto the road. Luke's car is waiting. I press the key fob. Feeling a swell of relief at the reassuring mechanical clunk of the car unlocking, and sprint the last few steps towards it. When I get into town, my first port of call will be the police. If they know Fordham was at the church the day Carolyn went for her last walk, they might be able to get him to confess. I tumble into the car. With shaking hands, I pull the door closed behind me, pushing the lock down and sinking into my seat. What am I doing snooping? How stupid, how naïve. This is a murder case. I take a deep breath, before looking up out of the wide front windscreen. Suddenly my heart stops. There it is, just beyond the pothole where my iPhone sank into the muddy water. It's the path that leads to Fordham's hovel. I remember the darkness, the smack, the car, the pain, the fall, but I also remember something else. There was a face. A face staring out at me from the undergrowth. Shit. I inhale sharply. He was there. Fordham saw it all. If Luke hadn't taken me home in his car, would Fordham have dragged me up to his lair? The bile rises in my throat. I fumble frantically again with the door, unable to unlock the damn thing fast enough. It swings open as the upper part of my body jack-knifes down towards the ground and I vomit.

22

KERNOW REVELATIONS

'Let me get this straight...' The young PC eyes me cautiously from beneath her razor-straight blonde fringe. 'You believe Mr Fordham was at the church on the estate when Carolyn Millford had her... accident?'

DS Graham isn't in. PC Colbert will have to do. She's writing it all down, drawing out laboured lines with her cheap biro, but I'm not convinced she knows anything about the case.

'It really is urgent,' I say, trying hard to keep the panic out of my voice. 'If Fordham was at the church, then he could easily have attacked Carolyn Millford. If you tell Fordham you know he's got a place out there, maybe he'll confess.'

She stops writing, looking up at me once again through that fringe. 'Mr Fordham was released this morning.'

The world kaleidoscopes around me. 'What?'

'I said Mr Fordham was...'

'I heard. I heard what you said, but...' Words fail me. 'Released? He tried to kill me.'

'He claims he stumbled.'

'He was all over me. I was on the ground. If DS Graham

hadn't pulled him off…' I stutter. 'And my car. Someone tampered with my car. They thought it was Erica Millford's.'

PC Colbert remains inscrutable, which is bad because it allows me to bluster on like a runaway train carrying crate loads of live and kicking turkeys.

'And what about Miri? Miri was poisoned.'

'We're still waiting for Toxicology to clarify. I believe there are a number of questions.'

'Questions?' This is going nowhere. 'And my car?'

'I'm sorry, Ms Conroy. I will look into your vehicle for you.'

Sadly, getting the car back no longer feels enough: Fordham is out and he's dangerous.

'Ms Conroy, you've gone very pale,' PC Colbert says, no doubt keen to flaunt her bloodhound powers of observation. 'Would you like a glass of water?'

I'm not interested. This is madness. I have to get to Graham. Then I remember; I have his card.

Once outside, I throw myself down on the first bench I come to and dial. In less than a minute, Graham's voice tells me that he's not there, and if my call is urgent, I should ring 999. When it does eventually click through to voicemail, I have to stop myself from spewing words out like a madwoman; I'm so furious.

'You let Fordham go?' I blurt. 'How does that work? Call me. As soon as you get this.' Angrily, I thrust the handset back into my bag.

'We had to let him go.'

I jump five inches out of my skin. Graham is standing behind me, leaning his gnarled, pale hands on the bench, looking out towards the quay. 'It's the law.'

'He attacked me.'

'He's saying he didn't.'

'You saw him.'

Graham draws his cheeks in taut across his jaw. 'He was inebriated and very unsteady. All of this, he's admitting.'

'And what about the poison? He poisoned Miri. Why hasn't the autopsy come back?'

'Well, that's the thing.' Graham raps his fingers on the back of the bench. 'It did. Only the results were…' he glances back over the water, 'unusual. So we're waiting on Toxicology.'

'So, not poison?'

'You know I can't…' He smiles a wry, ironic smile.

'Oh, please!' The man is so infuriating. 'This is crazy.'

He raises one eyebrow but fails to comment.

'I found Fordham's little camp.' I swivel my body on the bench, so I'm looking straight at him. 'It's right by the church on the cliffs. He could so easily have thrown Carolyn over.'

'Well, he's got an alibi.'

'Seriously? You know the exact time she fell?'

'We know when she went out for her walk. We know when they found the body. So, we've got a window for the time.'

'Window! It's him. I know it's him.'

'Mr Fordham has a cast-iron alibi. Ms Conroy, we have to have evidence to charge someone, and we can't just hold a person without charging them.'

'Yeah, well, thank you for the lesson in policing. Fascinating as it is, I don't want to be the next bit of evidence on the mortuary slab.' I get to my feet, slinging my bag over my shoulder. I'm so done here.

'You still at the house?'

'Yes.'

'Which one is it then?'

'Sorry?'

'The brothers? The love interest?'

'We're just friends,' I say, irritated. Unsure as to what exactly is going on between Luke and myself. 'Besides, I'm not a suspect here. My business is my business.'

He laughs. 'You're right; you're not a suspect.'

I say nothing, just walk away, but this doesn't stop him from filling the air with his own sweet conjecture. Graham calls after me, 'At the moment, anything that family does is of interest, and that everything happens to include you.'

'They set him free?' There's disappointment in Luke's voice rather than fear.

'Not enough evidence.'

'I don't understand.'

'Makes two of us.' I've arrived at the quay. The path I'd been walking down splits in two, leading off into town or along the waterside. The ferry is just pulling out, chugging steadily over the blue-green water.

'Okay.' Luke's voice comes back, quiet but determined. 'Forewarned is forearmed. I'll tell the others to keep a look-out: make sure all the doors are locked.'

'Oh, and another thing.'

There's a pause.

'I found this shack by the church.'

'Sorry?'

'Some kind of hovel by the church. Fordham must be living in it.'

'When did you go to the church, Kirstin?' He doesn't sound angry exactly, but there's a sharpness to his voice that I don't quite get.

'As I was driving over to town.'

Another pause.

'Why though? Why the church?'

This is a good question. 'Um. Like I said I was driving. I saw the place where we'd had the accident and noticed this path. I just followed it. But Luke, that's not the important part. The important part here is that Fordham was living up there.'

'I mean, he is seriously odd.'

But Luke's missing the point. I clear my throat, there's no easy way to say this. 'It would have been very easy for him to push your mother off the footpath.'

'Shit.'

'Exactly.'

'I'll take a run out there now.' His voice sounds heavy, deadly serious.

I feel my chest rise in a wave of panic. 'Not on your own.'

'No, no. I'll take Oscar or Gareth, or both. And you told this to the police?'

'I did.' Once again, I feel so frustrated. I want to kick something. Preferably DS Graham's ankles. 'I can't believe Fordham's out.'

'You and me both.'

The British legal system is a difficult one to digest. It ties itself up in knots. How could it be right that Fordham was free? That reminds me with a sudden lurch of guilt – AJ. AJ is up for parole today. I glance at my watch. The day is slipping away. He'll most likely be in there right now, standing up straight in front of the board. A call could come through in the next hour. We are so close to freedom.

I decide to haul up in a café for a bit. I've got my own life to sort. I should read through Carolyn's manuscript; see if I can get an angle that the press might be interested in and decide how to pitch it. There's a lot to work through, and I've never done anything like this before. A written pitch is a whole different ballgame than a hastily cobbled together CV. Luckily, I know a great place for tea, cake and a slice of undisturbed peace. Look after the stomach and all will be well. There's a little café called Bunty's. Everything home-made. They serve tea in mismatched china pots, and everything's done with a smile. But as I arrive, I see someone familiar sitting in the window – Erica. My feet grind to a halt. I'm just out of sight. It's not that I'm avoiding her, and probably I should go in and tell her about Fordham, only she's not alone. She's sitting across the table from a man. I'd put him at late thirties. He's got faded red hair and a kind, honest face. The wrinkles at the corner of his eyes are sun-bleached in all the right places, the places you use to smile, although he's not smiling. His forehead is cut into a frown. Erica's upset about something. She shakes her head in frustration, her hands fidgeting on the table in front of her. The man reaches out, gently putting his own hands over hers, and I see her tight, high shoulders sink. I don't want to break this scene with bad news about Fordham. She's been through enough. This must be Erica's 'friend'. Even Erica has someone special.

It's then that my phone buzzes, not a ring, but an incoming message. I grab it out of my bag and press unlock. But as I do my heart sinks. I don't need to go into the prison app. The message is showing on the screen. It's from AJ. There's just one word.

Recalled.

Tears stream down my face. I can barely get my breath as I hurl myself into the car locking all the doors behind me. The parole meeting didn't go our way. I'm sobbing so hard my ribs are beginning to ache, but I don't care. How could they recall him?

He's only eighteen months away from serving his full time. He's behaved. It's just one, single canvas that's lost. No one got killed. He was stupid – in way over his head, but he knows he shouldn't have done it. If you asked AJ if he regretted it, he'd be the first to say he did. *Recalled.* I continue to sob, vaguely aware that I'm getting looks from people in the car park. I don't care. I want to scream. How can they do this? It's all so unjust, so unfair. For the second time in one day, the authorities have failed me. I feel utterly helpless and am blubbing so loud that at first, I don't hear it – the small tap, tap, tapping on the car window. When it does eventually permeate my brain, the hurt stops. Instead, anger floods in. Busybodies. Why can't everyone just leave me alone? I turn, pulling my bent body from the passenger seat about to hurl abuse, then see – it's Julia.

Sitting in a room at the Ship Inn, it feels as if life is taking me in ever-decreasing circles. I never seem to break free of anywhere anymore. But this is not my old room. This time it's Julia's.

'You've had a shock.' Julia pours steaming water from the kettle into one of those teacups with the ridiculously tight handles. 'It's been a hellish time for all of us.' She glances at me, looking concerned. 'Is UHT all right?'

'Sure.'

In truth I don't think UHT is ever *all right,* but this is a case of grin and bear it; the woman has been through enough.

'I didn't offer you sugar. I think you should have some. Sugar's good for a shock.'

What is it about old people and sugar? 'It's great the way it is.' I take a sip. All I can taste is that slightly metallic tang of processed milk, but I haven't the energy to complain. Nothing matters anymore.

'Now.' Julia pulls up a chair so she's facing me as I perch on her bed. 'How can I help?'

I smile sadly, letting loose a small sigh. 'I'm not sure that you can.'

This problem isn't as easy as switching on the oven or baking a batch of muffins. Which I'm sure is Julia's regular answer to anything. This goes deeper.

'Well, I can listen,' she says kindly.

Why not? I think. I know she won't say a word if I ask her not to. She's kept secrets far bigger than mine. 'It's my brother,' I say, and I sniff because it feels like I'm about to start blubbing all over again.

She reaches out a hand, laying it over mine.

'Go on,' she says gently, not once stopping to remind me that I'd actually told her I didn't have a brother.

'He's in prison.'

If it's a shock, she doesn't flinch. Her face remains impassive. I get the feeling that if I'd told her he was in Benidorm, I'd have got the same reaction. 'He...' How can I explain how he got there? Don't all inmates' relatives say *'they're innocent. They're not really a bad person; they were just unlucky?'* I have no idea where to start. I've never told anyone about AJ before, but suddenly now I want to. 'He stole some art. Got in over his head. No one was hurt, but it was kind of high profile. He got locked up.'

She nods sympathetically.

'It was his parole hearing today and...' I break off, feeling tears welling up inside me as my lungs judder, threatening to jump-start the whole weeping process yet again.

'And it didn't go well?'

I couldn't answer even if I wanted to; the tears are coming.

Julia hands me another tissue. 'Do you know what happened with the parole board?'

I shake my head. 'There's an app. I've got it on my phone. AJ can leave me messages. That's mainly how we talk.'

'And he hasn't left one?'

'Just the one word. *Recalled*. That means...'

'Parole's been refused?'

I nod.

'I'm so sorry, Kirstin. Is there an appeals process?'

'It would depend on what he's been recalled for.'

Julia smoothes her skirt across her knees, arranging her thoughts. 'It could just be an admin bungle. That happens all the time.'

I think of how they've let Fordham walk free. I have to agree with her, but I don't mention Fordham. If Julia finds out that the man who killed her beloved Miri is walking the streets again, it could destroy her.

'Kirstin,' her voice draws me back, 'there's nothing you can do now.'

I know she's right.

'You've left a message for him?'

I nod.

'Then he'll be in touch when he's ready. He's probably trying to make sense of everything. He may need time to get his head straight.' She pushes a strand of hair away from my face, tucking it neatly behind my ear. 'How are things at the house?'

Perhaps she's genuinely curious, or perhaps she just wants to move the subject on.

'I'm worried about Timmy,' I say with a sigh. 'They didn't take your advice on getting professional care.'

She shakes her head in disgust. 'For an intelligent bunch of people, they do some very stupid things.'

'Apparently, Oscar trained as a doctor?' I try to keep the sceptical out of my voice.

'He did.' She glances down at her hands, drawing in a long, deep breath. 'I'm not sure that he ever wanted to be one though. Carolyn had ideas as to what they all should do. It was always a profession. *My son, the doctor,* sounds good at parties.'

'He never practised, then?'

'For a bit, but I don't think his heart was in it. Doesn't have much of a bedside manner.'

'What did the others do, initially? I mean their jobs. Suddenly, I'm curious. Have they all switched career, and if so, what did Carolyn choose for them?'

'Erica trained as a lawyer. Hated it. Now she does something to do with marketing.'

This seems to fit with what Oscar had told me. 'Was it PR?'

Julia looks puzzled. 'I have no idea what that is. But she always seems busy. Poor Timmy was going to be a solicitor. Until…'

She must mean until the accident.

'And Luke, he got a place at Oxford studying…' Her voice trails off. She can't remember.

'English?' I offer.

'I forget now,' Julia says, her tone brief. 'To be honest, I didn't listen much. It was "Oxford" this, "Oxford" that. Carolyn wanted him to be a professor or go into banking. She was mortified when he gave it all up and went into publishing. She cut off his allowance.'

'They got allowances?'

'Yes. Still do. Well, Miri…' Julia stops. It's clear that Miri's name is painful to her; the loss is raw. She gives herself a moment before taking a run at the sentence again. 'Miri needs an allowance. Being an actor is an unpredictable occupation. I got the feeling Luke was also struggling financially. His allowance might have been stopped, but he'd been known to ask his mother to help out from time to time.'

Suddenly I seem to have so many more questions. 'On the weekend that Carolyn died, can you remember who got to the house first?'

'Hmm.' Julia tilts her head as she searches back through her mind. 'I think Miri or maybe Luke?'

If Luke was going to approach Carolyn for money, he would have wanted to be there before the others. Maybe the fact that he was short on funds also explained why, out of all the siblings, he was so keen to sell the house. 'Did Carolyn always give Luke money when he asked?'

Julia shrugs. 'Only if she could get something in return.'

Which reminds me. 'We found your apartment.'

She smiles, genuinely amused. 'You know, I wondered how long it would take.'

'It caused a lot of talk.'

'I'll bet. Blackmail and extortion?' She smiles.

'Along those lines. Did Carolyn know about it?'

Julia shakes her head. 'I only had it done around four years ago. I'd lived up there in that horrible, dark space for years. Then a…' She hesitates. 'A friend pointed out there was a lot more attic to be had.'

'So, your friend redeveloped it for you?'

'Exactly. For the major renovations, I had to wait till Carolyn was away, but most of the small alterations and furniture, well that was pretty easy to sort. I mean, it's a large house. If Carolyn heard anything going on, I'd just say I had men in fixing the boiler or whatever. Miri knew about the renovations, but the others, they weren't interested.'

'Well, that's all changed.'

'Yes,' she says, with a touch of bitterness. 'I'll bet. How did the will go down? I assume that's been read now.'

'Fine, actually.'

She looks shocked.

'It was pretty much a five-way split.'

'But that's not what it said.' The colour drains from her face.

'I guess, with Miri gone…'

'But,' Julia looks like a woman grappling to grab a life jacket when the boat sinks, 'that's not right. They would have to read the will I witnessed, which says Miri was to inherit. That was the last will. Even if Miri is dead, they should have read the correct document.'

'I think there was something in it for you,' I say gently.

She looks close to tears. 'I don't want anything for myself, Kirstin. All I want is honesty. Maybe Miri is gone, but it doesn't mean the will shouldn't have been read out as it was.'

'Well...' I flounder. 'Could Carolyn have changed it? You drew it up when Miri was born, but that's over twenty years ago. Carolyn could have...'

Julia shakes her head vehemently. 'Six months ago, when Timmy's health took a downturn, Carolyn altered her will. I witnessed it. The house and maintenance money for its upkeep went to Miri, along with royalties for Carolyn's book and other significant assets. Anything left, which wouldn't be much, went to any additional blood relatives.'

'Blood?' Suddenly, it hits me. 'Julia, did you know all the children were adopted?'

Julia tries to glance away.

She must have known, because if she didn't, she'd have classed the siblings as blood relatives. 'That's why you said Carolyn knew about adoption. She'd done it before?'

Julie leans back in her chair, her tea forgotten. 'They'll find out soon enough.'

'None of them know?'

Julia shakes her head. 'Carolyn's next book would have set everyone straight. Miri had as much of a claim to the inheritance as any of the others. Carolyn was always playing games, but this time...' Julia fiddles around her neck, her fingers lighting on a small silver chain which she draws out from her teal-green jumper. There's a key on the end. Bending forward towards a small tin box that's sitting on the dressing table, Julia slips the key in the lock and turns. 'Here.' She takes out a white envelope. 'This is Carolyn Millford's last will and testament. I know exactly what it says. Reading between the lines, I'd say if Miri is dead, that money is going nowhere. The others won't get a look-in. It's all here.' She brandishes the envelope. 'Carolyn doesn't want them to have the fortune. Not under any circumstances. She cut them all out. They're not related.'

23

TWO WILLS

My head buzzes all the way back to the house. Nothing about this mess fits together. Even from the grave, Carolyn appears to be playing games. Should I tell the *siblings* what I know, show them the manuscript, tell them about the will? But if I do that, my story – the one I'm going to build around Carolyn's manuscript – will be blown. They could leak the missing book to the papers themselves or force me into signing some kind of NDA.

As soon as I pull up on the parking place in front of the Millford estate, I check my phone. Never mind the Millford mess. My brother has to be my priority – I'm still hoping for a voice message. I don't owe the Millfords anything. It's AJ and myself that I need to look out for. Disappointingly, there's no voicemails on the phone, so I record my own.

'AJ, it's me. I know this is a setback but that's all it is. If you can tell me what happened, I'll try and figure out a way forward.'

The fact that I have no idea what this *way forward* might be makes my heart sink.

I hear the gravel crunch under the wheels of another car as it slides up beside me and push my handset back into my bag. I don't want anyone to see my texts to AJ. That's my business.

When I do glance up, I'm surprised to see DS Graham's smiling face.

'Well, well, well,' he says, lowering his car window. 'Bumping into each other is becoming a bit of a habit. It's like there's some magnetic attraction.'

'Seriously? You're a police officer investigating a murder in a house that I happen to be staying in.'

'Investigating a suspicious death,' he corrects.

'Oh, come on. People are dropping like flies.' I glare at him. 'I'd be on the headcount myself if you hadn't pulled that tramp off me.'

He holds up his hands in an ironic gesture of submission. 'We didn't have enough evidence to hold Fordham.'

'Whatever.'

I grab my bag from the seat next to me, push open the heavy door of the car and step out onto the gravel.

'Hear anything interesting when you were in Kernow?' he calls, pulling himself out of his car in a slow breathy manner that I find curiously satisfying.

'Actually, I did. The police let a murderer go free.'

'Innocent until proven guilty. We've done this, Kirstin.' He sighs. 'Anything else?'

'Not a dicky bird.'

'So how long will you be staying then?'

'No plans,' I say as I press the locking device. 'I've got nothing to go back to.' I shoot him a hostile look. 'I know that you already know that. Is this what they call investigation by irritation?' I stride towards the house, Graham keeping step with me. 'Because, if it is, I'd like to congratulate you; it is grade one irritating.'

'Maybe that's why I'm not married anymore.'

I stop, turning towards him. 'Now, I don't have to be a detective to know that's not surprising.'

'Ouch,' he says, but he looks amused. I get the feeling he likes it when people try to rattle him.

'Nothing interesting when you went to see Julia Catalow then?'

'Have you been following me?'

'Nope.'

'Then how do you know I went to see Julia? Am I under suspicion?'

'Nah.' He waves one hand dismissively.

'Then why focus all your efforts on me? I don't even know these people.' I sigh, as I continue walking towards the door.

'Seems like you're getting to know them a whole heap better.'

'Maybe they fascinate me.'

He eyes me curiously, and I get the unnerving sensation that maybe I fascinate him.

'Anyway, Kirstin, I'm not *focusing* all my efforts on you. Currently, it's a sort of even-Stevens meal deal.'

'I'm not sure that even makes sense.'

'But you understood what I meant?'

'That you're pestering everyone.'

'Then it makes sense. If I was focusing all my attention on you, believe me, you'd know. Only I am disappointed.'

'What?' I stop stock-still.

'Julia – how I knew you went to see her. I wasn't following you. Julia turned up at the station and told us she talked to you.'

'Why would Julia do that?'

'She wanted to inform us about the will. Drop off the version she had.'

None of this matters. I push on again towards the house.

'So, no, I'm not following you.'

'You are kind of following me now,' I say, ironically and the DS laughs.

Wanting Graham out of my hair, I offer to make some tea. A date with the kettle seems a sure-fire route to freedom. By the time I get to the drawing room with my tea tray, Erica, Oscar and Luke are also there. Graham has both wills spread out over the desk. Erica's bent over them awkwardly and looking like she's been slapped with a dead fish; her mouth hanging open on its hinges.

'Are you sure this is Mother's signature?' Luke picks up the second will, Julia's will, turning it over in his hands before holding it to the light, examining every curve.

Graham clears his throat, 'The bank verified it, and Ms Catalow was witness. She remembers doing it. This is her copy. Your mother appears to have made two different wills at the same time using separate witnesses.'

'Is that normal?' Erica asks indignantly.

DS Graham takes a moment. 'I wouldn't say normal. Either way, Ms Catalow's copy also contains the original signature. It's not a photocopy.'

'Which can be easily faked?' Oscar muses.

'Exactly.'

'And with Miri dead the money would be equally divided between the remaining siblings.'

DS Graham shrugs. 'I'm no lawyer, but you would think so. Only it's one hell of a motive for removing Miri.'

Oscar traces one finger over the second will. 'And this *blood relative* thing? Is that normal?'

Erica sighs dismissively. 'Nothing about any of this is in any way normal, Oscar. But I don't understand what it all means.' There's a helpless tone to her voice.

I say nothing. In fact, I hang back over the tea tray, wondering how slowly I can pour the tea without people noticing and kicking me out of the room.

'Julia must have fixed this will,' Erica says, sinking down into a chair. 'We've only got her word for it.'

DS Graham breathes out heavily. 'Problem is, with "Ms

Catalow fixing the will" – in the will Ms Catalow gave us, Ms Catalow doesn't get anything. Whereas in the will Longbow and Mclean brought over, Julia Catalow gets a cottage at the edge of the estate.' He pauses, eyeing them shrewdly. 'If you happened to be Ms Catalow, which will would you be pushing?'

I can't help wondering what would happen if they saw Carolyn's manuscript and realised that actually none of them were blood relatives. Nothing about this mess is going to get sorted anytime soon. I decide I'll check on Timmy.

When I get to his room, Timmy's lying in his bed, still as a statue, avoiding all the angst and recriminations, the photo frame still spilling out happy memories. I glance at it as the photo of a young Carolyn with the dark-haired pregnant woman appears and realise instantly that this could be one of the surrogates. Suddenly I begin to feel uncomfortable. My being here is a total fluke – a lead from a random man posing as a Millford son. Twice I've been involved in 'accidents' where I could have wound up dead. It hits me in a blinding flash of light. A searing epiphany: I may not be adopted but my mother seemed to come from nowhere, bearing children and being unhappy. Could this woman in the photo be my mother? She's got dark hair, she's short. I stare at my reflection in the mirror over the sideboard. She looks as like me as the photos AJ used to cobble together. Is that why Luke had been so keen for me to stay? Could this mystery woman be pregnant with my own brother? Are AJ and I Millfords? Lurching forward, I grab the frame eagerly, pressing the display screen and bringing up the settings. Every photo has its information date-stamped. This one is no exception, which is lucky. The dates are way out. A good five years before AJ was born. Bang goes that theory. This pregnant woman, whoever she is, is not carrying my brother.

'Sorry, Timmy,' I say, slipping the miniature flash drive back into the back of the frame so it can start up again. 'Getting caught up in fantasy-land there.'

I turn back towards him smiling, but my smile soon fades. There's something wrong. His features are alabaster white, and there's a staring panic in his wide-open eyes. Suddenly his body jerks. Jerks so hard the headboard bangs against the wall.

'Timmy!' I scream as he jerks again. 'Timmy.' But the convulsions don't stop.

Watching the ambulance pull away, I feel an overwhelming sense of relief. I'm exhausted, shattered, as if each of the convulsions had coursed through my own body. But none of that matters because things have shifted in the house. DS Graham is still asking questions. Only, now they're all about Timmy.

'And there was no warning?'

'Nothing.' Sadly, his questions are not getting any less irritating. I've told him all of this at least five times. 'I was... I went in to check on him and then it happened.'

He stares at me shrewdly.

Luke slides to my rescue. 'Timmy could have had a fit at any time. He's not well. We're just lucky it happened with Kirstin there. I hate to think of him being alone.'

Half an hour later, I watch from the window in my strange yellow room as DS Graham drives away. There's a sibling conference going on downstairs, and I have no desire to get involved. The wills may well have to go through the courts. Whatever money there is in this estate will get stuck for years, even if the so-called siblings remain blissfully unaware of the fact that not one of them is even entitled to a penny – they're not related by blood. But this is not their only concern – Fordham's release has also provoked a tangible sense of fear – is the killer still at large?

My phone buzzes. It's AJ, and this is no voicemail. He's live. I pick up.

'I am so sorry,' I blurt.

'Yeah.' His voice is barely audible.

'What happened?'

There's a pause. A big one. Have we been cut off? 'AJ?'

'They found drugs in my cell.'

I'm so shocked I can barely speak. 'You did that the week you were up for parole?'

'Bloody hell, sis, no. What do you take me for? Someone stashed it in there. They were trying to frame me.'

I have no idea if he's telling the truth. He didn't use to touch drugs, but it's been a long time. Besides, innocent or not, the outcome is the same. 'What now?' I manage.

'Nothing. We wait.'

I feel my chest clog as though my whole being is turning inch by inch into cement.

'It'll be okay,' he says gently.

I could kick myself – I've allowed us to switch positions. Now he's comforting me! 'Course it will be okay,' I say, sounding a lot brighter than I feel.

'Meantime, I'll just keep busy. Study something else. Going to be Brain of Britain by the time I get out.' He laughs, although there's a touch of bitterness to it. 'Anyway, gotta go.'

'Let's fix a time to talk,' I say, rushing in, desperate to stop him from putting down the receiver.

'This time tomorrow suit you?'

I glance at my watch. It's five o'clock.

'Perfect.'

'Great. Gotta go, things to do.'

I doubt that. More likely, he's *got to go* because this conversation is too heavy, too hopeless.

Tired of the Millfords, tired of the house, I have no intention of going back downstairs. I want to stay out of their mess. Luckily, I'd bought a couple of protein bars when I was at the shops; those will do for my supper. I get into my PJs, brush my teeth and crawl into bed reassuring myself that AJ will be out soon. This is just a setback. I need to get my life on track, and the best way to do that is to sell my story. Well, Carolyn's story. Pulling out Carolyn's mobile from where I'm stashing it in the bedside table, once again, I begin to read.

24

THE BROOD

Wolves: *'Beasts of waste and desolation.'* *(Roosevelt)*

Extract from Carolyn's manuscript: *On taking over a pride, a male lion will usually kill the cubs of his rival. Wolves tend to do the opposite. When a male wolf takes over a pack, the cubs of the deposed leader are adopted, assimilated into the pack. The logic for this is simple: numbers increase the power of the pack.*

Is this what Carolyn was doing? Increasing the size of her brood in order for it to succeed? This complex barren woman was determined for her 'line' to survive, a line she had chosen. No doubt the surrogates would have been vetted for intelligence. For looks even, the siblings all look similar. Miri was Carolyn's last grab for immortality. Julia getting pregnant under Carolyn's roof must have seemed like an invitation for Carolyn to throw her hat into the ring one last time. To try and quell the disappointment she felt when each of her adopted children came to fruition. Oscar would not have been brave enough for her. Erica was too uptight. Luke too irresponsible. For a brief moment, there had been satisfaction in Timmy, but that plan hadn't worked out. Miri came from the below-stairs working classes. There was no expectation, and yet she had brought warmth, fun and love into a divided house. Carolyn had internalised the island myth. The idea of the wolf; nurturing a feeling that there was safety in numbers and the advantages of building a clan. Then I remember Timmy's journal. The entry had said that The Wolf paid for the trip. Somehow there's something missing. I can't believe that Timmy would call the woman he thought was his mother 'The Wolf'. Did he know he was adopted?

I'm interrupted by a sharp knock. 'They're driving me up the wall.' Without asking, Luke pushes open the door, crosses the room and throws himself down on my bed, pausing momentarily to wrestle a pillow over his face. 'Erica's dashed off to the hospital with Timmy, like it was only her who could go with him. What is it about women? What makes them think they're at the top of some hierarchy on caring?'

'If it takes a seizure to prove you care,' I say, 'I think maybe you're all missing a step.'

'Okay.' Wearily, he pulls the pillow away, his features still hard, but I get the feeling my comment has hit home. 'Yeah, there's probably some truth in that.' He rakes his hair thoughtfully with his fingers. 'I feel so guilty. I'd forgotten all about Timmy. Not sure I'm entirely comfortable around sick people.'

At least he's honest.

'I probably should have made more of an effort.'

It's true, but sadly the same applies for the entire family. 'Who was The Wolf?' I ask.

'Sorry?' Luke yawns, pulling himself up from the bed, so he's sitting.

'The Wolf. Did you know somebody called The Wolf?'

His face creases into a frown as he searches his mind.

'How about Carolyn?' I ask. 'Did she ever call herself The Wolf?'

He laughs, a spontaneous sound that bounces off the yellow walls, sounding a little too loud under the circumstances. 'Oh dear. How little you knew Carolyn.'

I look at him curiously, hoping he'll shed more light.

'If you were to call my mother anything but Carolyn, it would be *no tea before bedtime*. Short answer – no, we never called her The Wolf. Witch, maybe, a couple of times when she was out of earshot.'

'So, there's no one that...'

'Ah...' His face breaks into a smile. The smile you get when you've just netted where a conversation is going. 'I know what you're talking about – the legend about the wolves being driven here. The church thing, it was supposed to be built where the woman gave birth to the last man/wolf?'

He fixes me with a slightly amused look.

'I don't think that's it. I think there was somebody calling themselves "The Wolf".'

Luke shakes his head. 'No wolves that I can think of.'

This is going nowhere. 'Do you think Timmy will be okay?'

He signs and rolls over. 'I don't know, Kirstin. This whole thing is a nightmare.'

There's a pause. A long pause. Outside the window, it's dark. I wonder how Timmy's doing. Is he still fighting for his life? This family really does seem cursed. Lost in my own thoughts, it takes me a moment to notice that the bed's shaking a little.

Concerned, I turn towards Luke and realise he's crying. 'Luke.' I rest my hand gently on his shoulder.

'Sorry, Kirstin.' He drags one arm across his eyes and nose before giving a hearty sniff and turning so he's flat on his back. His entire face is red and blotchy. 'I know I shouldn't.'

'No.' I rub his shoulder. 'It's fine.'

'I just can't cope with much more, and... and oh, Kirstin it gets worse.'

'Worse?'

He eyes me shrewdly, as though wondering if he should take the next step before, with anguish in his eyes, he continues. 'I'm adopted, Kirstin. I'm not Carolyn's real son. I did a DNA test. It was stupid. I shouldn't have done it.' He hits his head with his palm. 'It's a long story, I've got this condition.'

'Condition?'

He turns away. 'That doesn't matter, but...' He can barely talk now his breathing is so fractured. 'The point is. I'm not a blood relative. I thought this was my family, but God knows who I am.'

The next morning as a soft warm light colours my room, I wake to find Luke beside me. The sobs have been stopped with sleep. His breathing is loud and relaxed. The trauma of last night forgotten. For a moment I panic, the jigsaw pieces of the previous evening flashing hastily before me as I realise, with a sense of relief, that nothing happened. I'm under the blankets. He's on top. Fully clothed. One muscle-toned arm may be thrown around my waist, but this is not the 'love story' I thought it might turn out to be when we first met. This is friendship, pure and simple. He was distraught the previous evening as he spilled his revelations about the adoption. I could have told him not to worry – that the entire Millford clan is a cobbled together gene pool, only I didn't. I'm not ready for that. Not yet anyway. I don't want him to know I've got the manuscript. That thing could be my lifeline. So last night I talked him down, comforted him. Told him that I was sure Timmy would be okay. He was in the right place. Basically, I ladled out all the reassurance in the world while giving the problem of identity a wide berth. So wide, that if Luke hadn't been so upset, he might have smelled a rat. But none of that matters, because whatever I did say has clearly worked; this morning he's calm, sleeping like the innocent babe he truly is. Perhaps Luke's not Carolyn's biological son, but this place is home to him. His cheeks may be blotched red from yesterday's crying, but the trauma of last night is forgotten. With Luke, there's no ignoring life. Even when tragedy is hitting you from all sides, there is still laughter and love and sleeping like a child at night. A smack of bitterness hits me. Isn't that because he's so privileged? When you're privileged, you're allowed to be soft. You've got a safety blanket of wealth to parachute you to higher pastures. Julia had implied Luke's business wasn't lucrative, that he wasn't above nipping home to ask Carolyn for handouts. When you've been forced onto life's coalface and are trying to pick your way across it, you have to stick close to the ground emotionally. Because, if the life you're trying to erect crumbles, you can't afford a big fall. Despite complications, I get the feeling that money problems are one concern that the Millfords don't have.

Gently, I lift Luke's arm and slide out from underneath. I've decided to go on a bit of a wolf hunt. It'll provide a great angle for the article. I could even use extracts of Timmy's journal. The children are all part of Carolyn's cruel experiment – part of a story. A story that I can sell. Perhaps Tim had a friend; Wolf, or maybe someone called De Wolf? It could easily be a surname. These people are wealthy. Even the school kids have money. It could have been someone from school who paid for Timmy's ticket. Although, suddenly I feel the cogs in my brain start to slow, that doesn't quite seem to work. What about the island legend? I get the feeling The Wolf must be closer to home. Quietly, I grab my clothes, deciding to shower in Luke's room, afraid I'll wake him if I put the shower on in my own en suite. I need research time, and if Luke's awake it's unlikely I'll get that.

Luckily, I'd taken note when Luke had pointed out where his room was – just past the bookcase. Okay, so I'd my reasons for drinking in every word. Initially I'd thought I might pay him a night-time visit. Seriously, I have to get better at working out when a man fancies me. No wonder I rarely manage to get past first-date level. All those signals from Luke that I thought were chemistry had been way off mark. Curiously, I'm not feeling anything like that towards him either. He's a lovely guy, but way too emotional for a cold survival-fish like me.

The house feels deathly quiet as I slip across the landing, more *empty* than *sleeping*, and maybe it is; everyone's been leaving. Julia's gone. I haven't seen Oscar's friend, Gareth, since the party on the beach, so he must have left yesterday. Then Oscar drove away from the house at around six. He'd said he had business at one of his dealerships and would be staying over. I'm not sure if Erica's in the house or not. She'd gone to the hospital with Timmy. She could easily still be there. Then again, if she is in the house, she most likely got back late. She'll be sleeping.

Cautiously, I push open the door to Luke's room. Even in the half-light, I can see it's a beauty, larger than mine. A mixture of silver-grey and blue furnishings. It even has its own little snug sitting area. And yet as I stand on the threshold, I get an uncomfortable feeling. Is this okay? I'm about to wander through someone's private world. Standing there in this fresh, new environment, I realise I should have showered in my own room. Did it seriously matter if I woke Luke? But it's too late for that now.

Once in the en suite, I pull off my nightclothes, stepping under a large showerhead that hangs like an invitation in a cubicle sparkling with aqua-blue mosaic tiles. The water thumps eagerly through the pipes, steaming over my body. Even the soap is overly generous, an enormous bar that barely fits in my palm and smells of citrus groves. Delicious. Good, I need to wake up. I'm going to go into town early. I'll head to the island library first. Perhaps The Wolf was Tim's father? Though I'm pretty sure his father died when Tim was a baby, perhaps he left a trust fund that kicked in when Timmy was eighteen? No, that didn't work. In the journal, Tim seemed to suggest that The Wolf had booked hotels for him. You can't do that from beyond the grave.

After my shower, I towel down. Luckily, I'd remembered to bring the electric toothbrush I'd bought on a jaunt into Kernow. I ease a bit of paste onto the bristles, then switch the setting to on. That's why I don't hear the door open into the main bedroom, or the depression on the mattress, as someone flops down exhausted on the coverlet. By the time the electric brush has stopped its whirr, somebody is outside and already mid-sentence; talking to someone that they think is in the bathroom; a different someone.

'They just don't know what it is.'

Shit, I think to myself: Erica. She must think Luke is in the bathroom. She thinks she's talking to her brother. It's almost too late to stop her now. Besides, I feel embarrassed being there. I know easy-going Luke would understand why I'd used his bathroom, but I'm not so sure Erica would.

'Timmy seems to be stabilising.' Her voice sounds flat and exhausted. She must have been up all night. 'Even opened his eyes at one point.' A sob catches in her throat. 'He hasn't done that for a while, not since the wake.'

There's a pause in which I hold my breath, not wanting to make a sound. I wish she'd shut up, go back out. The longer this goes on, the worse it gets.

'But, Luke, don't you think it's odd? I...' She hesitates, unable to form her words, or possibly unwilling.

'He used to be okay. I mean, he was conscious, but since the wake, Timmy's been so out of it, and now he's away from the house he's getting better. I can't help wondering...'

I hear her stand and walk towards the bathroom door. Panicked, I glance down at the lock. Shit, I didn't bolt it. The footsteps come closer. She wouldn't come in, would she? It's her brother. Well, that might not be strictly true, but thankfully

Erica's oblivious to that fact. I reach out one hand so it hovers just above the lock. The moment that knob turns, I'm going to slide the bolt in place. Shit. Shit. Shit. But the footsteps stop. The handle doesn't turn. When her voice comes again, it's from directly outside the door.

'I was wondering, Luke.' She clears her throat before her words slip to a whisper. 'Why did Oscar let Rose go?'

My heart stops. I'd kind of thought there might have been some kind of inappropriate advance from Luke. But my brain is barely having a chance to catch up with the implications because Erica's not stopping. 'And what was Oscar giving Timmy?'

Is she insinuating what I think she's insinuating?

'I know...' I hear her footsteps on the soft carpet outside as she moves away from the closed door. 'It's ridiculous. I just... I'm going to have a lie-down, but maybe afterwards we should go through Timmy's room together. Check any of the medication that's in there. Get rid of it.'

It? What's she talking about?

'I'm sorry, but I refuse to be dragged down with him.'

Oscar? Is she talking about Oscar? Does she think Oscar tried to kill Timmy? I am so scared now. If she knows I'm here, it's no longer embarrassment that she's going to feel. She's going to be livid. I shouldn't be hearing any of this. Then, suddenly, I remember Oscar's friend, Gareth. Gareth works at the solicitor's. Gareth would have been in an ideal place to switch the wills. My heart is beating so fast, so hard, I swear any moment she'll hear it.

'I won't do this on my own, Luke.' Erica's voice sounds clipped, determined. 'If we are going to cover his tracks...'

His? Oscars?

'...you need to help. Timmy's going to be okay now, so it's probably all fine. But if for any reason the tables turn. If Timmy doesn't pull through, this place is going to be crawling with police sticking their noses in yet again. Only this time they might dig a bit deeper, and...' She pauses. 'I don't think you want that,

Luke. Too much scrutiny, and the police might discover your little sideline.'

Sideline?

'Anyway, Oscar won't be back in time to clear up his mess. So, it looks like it's just you and me. I won't have this family mired with scandal.' She sighs. 'I'm going to get some sleep. Wake me before twelve and we'll go through Timmy's room together.' She sighs again, only this time much louder. 'Oscar is an absolute idiot.' There's bitter irritation in her voice. 'If I ever get sick, for Christ's sake, Luke, don't let him look after me.'

I stay in the bathroom for a good five minutes after she's gone. She can't know that I was here. Is she seriously implying that she thinks Oscar gave Tim an overdose? If Oscar sacked Rose, Timmy would have been a sitting duck. Was she asking Luke to get rid of evidence? And what the hell was she referring to when she talked about Luke's sideline? When I am absolutely certain Erica's gone, I open the door and peek out. No one. Hurrying across Luke's bedroom carpet, my feet leave a wet imprint in the deep pale pile. Shit. I stop and towel-dry my soles. As I do, I notice a drawer to one bedside table has slid open. It can't have been shut properly. My movement must have disturbed it. I go to push the thing back in, glancing down into the drawer as I do. My heart thumps hard in my chest; inside are neat little packets of white powder. There's only one reason you would package powder like that. There's also a notebook pushed to the very back. An accounts book? I open it. It's full of names and amounts paid. Sometimes the amounts are in red – money owed? Other times they're crossed through. The book is full; every page containing names and numbers. I'm not sure the names are real names or secret handles. There's one entry that says *Fordy*, along with some obvious nicknames: Dog, Lofty, Descartes. I turn the page, and my blood runs cold because there it is – The Wolf.

Back in my room, Luke is still sleeping soundly. I need to get out. I've just discovered his sideline and it's not pretty. I have to get as far away from this family as I can. Luke is a dealer, and he's dealing to a man he denied he knew. He lied. I pull on my clothes from last night. Luckily, I'd strewn them on the back of the chair. My other clothes are hanging in the wardrobe. Wardrobes always make a noise, especially when they're half-packed with empty hangers. Are the clothes worth the risk? Then again, what am I doing wrong? It's okay for me to leave this house. All perfectly normal. I'm a free woman. At the thought, I feel a tinge of bitterness. AJ isn't free. One royal fuck-up did for him – AJ's problem is also drugs related. These Millfords are up to all kinds of scams, but no one's locking them up and throwing away keys. Sod it. If Luke wakes, I'll deal with it. I pull open the wardrobe door. The hangers chime, but the lion remains asleep.

As soon as I get to the vast marble hallway, I realise there's a problem – my car. I still don't have it. Luke's keys are probably in the kitchen. He tends to throw everything on the kitchen table when he gets in, but if I take Luke's car, there's going to have to be more contact. I'm not sure I'm ready for that. I don't owe that man anything and it's best to keep it that way. This latest fiasco is certainly making me feel a whole heap better about leaking some of Carolyn's manuscript to the press. I call a cab.

They answer after three rings. Apparently, there's someone in the area. Someone that can be with me in ten. Perfect. I stand in the hallway by the front door, bag in hand as the minutes pull themselves past in a torturously slow fashion. No doubt, Luke will text me when he finds I've gone. At the moment, I have no idea how I'm going to excuse my hurried exit. I can't use the drugs. I have to pretend I know nothing about that. Knowledge can get a person in serious shit. The drugs are bad enough, but then there's the Oscar thing. Had I got it right? Was Erica implying Oscar had been overmedicating Tim? And there's Gareth. Gareth suddenly seemed like so much more than a *friend*. Gareth had access to the will. Since the taxi hasn't arrived, I decide I should check out Timmy's room. Erica said she was going for a lie down. She wanted Luke to help her when she woke. Help her to remove any evidence? She probably needed to talk it through with him. No doubt there would be a lot more posturing about saving the *'family name'*. I glance at my watch. I've got five minutes. Enough time for a quick snoop.

Tim's room feels empty without him, as if it's had its heart torn out and yet the photo frame is still mechanically rotating family memories. The parade seems a little grotesque now. There's a picture of all four siblings in a racing-green pedal car, a metal one, by the looks of it. Timmy hangs off the back of the car, smiling. Luke is lying in front of the thing, as if he's been knocked down, a wide smile across his face. Erica is driving, serious as always, eyes on the road ahead. Oscar sits beside her, irritation on his face. His lips tight shut in a horizontal line. Perhaps he wanted to drive? Probably. No doubt, the story behind the image has been forgotten now. Miri's not in it. It was most likely taken before she arrived. I glance at my watch. Three minutes and counting. The taxi could easily be early. I don't have time for this. There's a brown pill bottle on the bedside. I tip it on its back and take a photo of the label, before working my way around the room methodically. I slide open the drawers of the bedside tables. Empty. I go to the sideboard. Maybe there's something in there, but no, that's empty too. I open the left drawer. Sure enough, there are some vials inside and a few pouches. The names mean nothing to me, but somebody will know what all of this is. I photograph everything. I'm about to put it all back in the drawer when I think I'll just reach inside and see if there's anything left in the corners. My fingers grope blindly, before catching on something – a sliver of foil. A vial. Again, the label means nothing to me. The word, too long to pronounce. I photograph it and put everything back. Then I do a quick scan of the room, checking there's no evidence of my being there. The image of Carolyn and the pregnant woman has come to rest on the photo frame. I wonder if Julia will know who she is. It seems odd, to have a photograph of a surrogate, if that's what it is, and why would you have only the one surrogate? Does it matter? Probably not, I have enough mysteries on my plate. I grab my canvas bag and walk quickly from the room. It's perfect timing. The cab has just pulled up. Eagerly, I open the front door and hurry towards it, unable to stop myself from looking anxiously back over my shoulder.

In the cab there's a small, squat woman in her fifties with an impossibly round face. Her blonde hair styled unnaturally like candy-floss on the top of her head.

'Falcon Taxis. You're going to Kernow?' she says, brightly, as if the world is normal and this is just another day.

'Yes, that's me.' I lower myself in, clutching my bag across my lap.

'Such a lovely home this,' the blonde, candy-floss lady says, angling the car into an unnecessary three-point turn.

I gaze up at the stark building, not entirely sure this place has ever been a home.

25

BIRD'S EYE VIEW

ONCE THE HOUSE grows reassuringly smaller over my shoulder, I go into my photo app and select all the images I'd taken in Timmy's room. I have no idea what these medications do. Maybe they're fine, then again, maybe they're not. The one thing I do know is that I don't want to go to the police. Besides, there's one person who might be able to give me a quick answer. The person who got me into this – Marco. I select the blue tick on a series of photos before punching in a line of text:

Any idea what these are?

'My name's Mavis,' the candy-floss woman says, as we drive out of the iron gates. 'Don't you worry, love. I've never had a point on my licence. Cautious driver, that's me.'

I catch my face in the rear-view mirror, then get it. I'm looking pale as a wax candle. She thinks I'm scared of her driving.

'Right,' I say. 'Sorry, it's not you. I'm… I've got a lot on my mind.' I stare out of the window, trying to calm my jangled nerves. 'Probably best having no points though – for a taxi driver.'

'Exactly.' Mavis smiles. 'Some of these young ones whip around the island like Lewis Hamilton. I have to tell them, *Lewis, he's on a track. All the action going one way. The island, well, action can go anyway it pleases. Come at you from the front, rear and sides.*'

I had been hoping for a peaceful ride, a chance to collect my thoughts. That's not going to be a possibility with Mavis.

'Sometimes, things even coming at you from above.'

'Sorry?' I say. I genuinely have no idea what she's talking about now.

'The action. Sometimes it comes from the top as well.'

I look blank.

'Falling trees.'

'Oh right. Course.' I glance out of the window, hoping she'll shut up, realising too late that Mavis probably thinks I'm scanning the woods for loose branches. The only way Mavis will shut up is if I drop dead or fall asleep. Even then, I'm not sure.

'Terrible tragedy they had with that young girl. I mean to say, Carolyn Millford, that was bad enough, but when a young one goes.' Mavis shakes her head sorrowfully. 'Just doesn't seem right.'

'No.'

'You a friend of the family, then?'

I want to say, *Actually, I was just over for the funeral,* but that's not exactly tactful. 'Kind of. Have you driven the family before?'

'Carolyn Millford, yes. Not the children. My father used to drive Carolyn when she was a child. He worked up on the estate. Carolyn and her little cousin...'

Suddenly my ears prick up. 'Cousin?'

'Pretty little thing. Orphaned, so I believe. That's why she spent summers here.'

I remember the picture in the frame. 'Dark curly hair? Heart-shaped face?'

'Yes.' Mavis beams. 'That would be her. Odd name. What was

it?' Her forehead furrows as she searches her brain. 'Maya.' Mavis snorts, as though this name is ridiculous, and *what will they think of next* on the naming front. 'Will you be staying much longer on the island?'

'No. I'll probably book the afternoon ferry.'

'Ohhhh.' Mavis draws in her breath as though if she's sucking a lemon: tight, sharp and clear. 'I wouldn't count on that.' She glances at me in the rear-view. 'Ferry's broken,' she says brightly, relishing her job as fount of all knowledge.

I feel a weary weight hanging over my shoulders. I've had enough now. I want to go home. 'Right, maybe I'll get the plane then.'

'Well, problem is, see...' Mavis says gravely, 'ferry broke down yesterday. So, it's a bit of a bun-fight at the airport. The island shuttle, it's only a small prop plane after all. An eight-seater. If I was you, I'd leave it till tomorrow.'

My heart sinks.

'There's lots to do in town though. You been to the Maritime Museum?'

I hadn't, and I didn't want to. I ask her to drop me at the library.

Since the library hasn't yet opened, I grab a coffee from Captain Jack's and head down to the front. The town is always quiet in the mornings. Taking a good few hours to wake up. A handful of trawlers chug out into the clear blue water. The gulls dance through the air; too early for scavenging, just enjoying their wings riding high on the breeze. It may be out of season, but the savvy birds know the tourists will be along later, with their carefree chips and ice creams tumbling forgotten from unwary hands. The pickings are year-round these days.

I take a seat on a bench and glance at my phone. No messages from Marco, but that would have been a bit quick. No messages from Luke either. At least that's good. He's probably still asleep. I wonder if I should be honest with him when he rings; tell him I found the drugs, but what if his outfit is bigger than a few bags of coke in a bedside drawer? The notebook with all the names suggests that it is and there's one thing that I know about criminal activity. The fewer people who are in the loop, the better. I google the island and add 'drugs trade'. A local pharmacy comes up. Not exactly what I had in mind. Pragmatically, I scroll down the search results; the net widening, losing relevance. There's nothing of interest. It's just as I'm getting to the bottom of a long tedious page that I catch sight of a government forum: Cornwall Export and Trade. Curious, I click on it. According to the link, there are plans to boost Cornwall's capacity to increase trade. The islands are included in the bid. Concerns have already been expressed about drugs getting into the small sleepy community. Although that's dismissed as scaremongering. The council's keen to develop the islands as an import-export centre. They won't be selling goods made here; instead, the island will be used as a giant warehousing facility. It's still at the proposal stage: so, far from a done deal. Things like this get rejected all the time, but then I remember my call with Janice. I can't help wondering if that's what affected the warehouse in Falmouth, the one Janice had told me about – the planning application which had switched from commercial to residential. Then again, none of this is my concern. I stare out at the blue sea. This morning the island is like a small corner of paradise. I try to imagine tankers and cranes, spanning the docks. Surely, they wouldn't allow that to happen here?

There's a shop across the road from my bench. A small tourist place selling anything and everything. Each eventuality has been thought of, from buckets to umbrellas. A hand comes out of the shadows inside the shop, reaching up to the sign on the door and flipping it from *closed* to *open*. Kernow is waking. I drain the bottom of my coffee cup. It's time to head to the library. I can ring the Ship on the way and book myself a room. Tomorrow, the ferry will be working, and I can get home but, for now, I'm curious. What happened to Maya? And who is The Wolf? I know I shouldn't have, but I'd taken Timmy's travel journal with me when I left the house. I wanted to read to the end, find out what happened. No one will miss it. No one's even looking for it. It's Carolyn's manuscript they're after. Luckily, I also have a digitised copy of that. In fact, I have one hell of a lot of reading to get through. It's going to be a long day. Walking briskly across the cobbled street, I pull my phone from my pocket and dial.

'Good morning,' comes a young voice, full of sparkle. 'The Ship Inn.'

'Hi, I'd like to book a room.'

'Oh...'

There's a pause from the end of the line: the sparkle gone.

'I'm afraid we're fully booked. There are problems with the ferry.'

'I know about the ferry,' I say, my voice sounding a little terse. I let loose a small sigh. I really do need somewhere to stay. 'Can you recommend anywhere?'

'Best head to Tourist Information. That's on Low Street. It's just past the Co-op. They sometimes advertise B & B notices. If the islanders know the ferry's not running, people often put a room up for rent in the window.'

I thank her, then ring off. This is turning out to be a first-class pain in the backside. I can imagine what the rooms they get last-minute at the tourist board are like – opportunistic. There might be an accommodation list at the library. I'll try that first. It's then that I notice a slim, red-haired man cross the street in front of me. I recognise him immediately. It's Erica's *friend,* the one I'd seen her with in the café. Before I have time to talk myself out of it, I find I'm falling into step behind him. Does he live on the island? I wonder. If I am going to go to the papers with a pitch, leaving Luke's drugs trade out of the article, I still want to have the lowdown on all family members. He doesn't look like a full-time island resident. Most people from here have a windblown look – cracked cheeks, crazy hair, walnut-brown skin, but Erica's friend is pale, suited and slick. He walks away from the quay into the shopping district. He can't be going to see Erica. She must still be at the house, sleeping or (more likely) disposing of whatever she feels can be used against the family as evidence. I follow behind the pale man, keeping far enough back so I don't draw attention. As the man turns off the high street, he takes something from his pocket. I stop on the corner of the street and fake-look in a shop window selling nothing but plastic: cheap sunglasses, phone covers and a multitude of chargers. In the reflected image of the street, I can see that the red-headed man is flicking through an oversized bunch of keys. He isolates one, unlocks the door in front of him and disappears behind it.

Once he's safely inside, I trace his footsteps to the doorway. It's an unassuming place. There's an intercom, a row of six bells and to the right of each bell, a typed description. He must work here. One of the bells is for a chiropodist. One, for a solicitor, another appears to be a marketing company. That could be it, PR. Perhaps the man is not so much Erica's friend as her colleague. I start googling the companies listed on the buzzer panel, hoping to find websites and photos of each 'team'. The chiropodist is a woman. The PR company is also run by a woman. I search all of the companies on the list. None of them belongs to Erica's mystery man. There's a unit number for the building: number five, but no wider indication as to what goes on there. He can't be a client; he let himself in. I look at the street sign. I'm on Fore Street. I google number five, Fore Street. Bingo, it's him. Mark Hitchin. As I read down the description my eyes practically pop out of my head – Private Detective. So, maybe he's not Erica's friend? Maybe Mark is on the payroll, but if so, what on earth would Erica be investigating?

'Hello, again.'

I turn sharply; the sun shining into my eyes, causing me to squint. When my retinas pull back into focus, I see Niamh, the large, purple-dressed lady from the funeral, the bridge player, standing behind me. Her bejewelled arm outstretched, reaching for mine. She's still wearing purple, though it's less formal this time. The kind of outfit that's never seen an iron.

'Niamh.' I suddenly feel awkward. What am I doing in this side street?

'Hope you didn't get stuck here?'

I glance up at the street name, trying to fight a growing sense of panic – unsure what she's talking about.

'The ferry, I mean. I hear it's cancelled. Again.' She rolls her eyes.

My body relaxes. She has no idea I was snooping. Ferry talk is as safe as the habitual, never-ending, idle discussions on the changeable island weather. 'Does it happen often?'

'Too often to be a joke.'

'Yeah.' I glance around me, at the shop windows, at the tat. Not one of these places is offering up vacancy signs. 'I have sort of been stranded.'

She nods pragmatically, as if to say this is just business as usual.

'Will it be working by tomorrow?' I ask.

Niamh shrugs. 'Normally, it's a one-day thing. Any longer, and the islanders cause a stink. Sometimes I think the ferry people do it just to give their staff a holiday, or maybe make us locals feel more appreciative. You stayed longer than anticipated?'

'Too long, it seems. Unlucky. And now, all the hotels are booked.'

'I'll bet.'

'You don't know of anywhere?'

'Only all the usual. But, you're right...' She glances at her watch. 'They'll all be full by now. Bad news spreads quick on the island.'

'A night at the terminal then.' My voice sounds flat, resigned.

'Not at all.' She throws one arm out towards my shoulder, resting it gently there, beaming at me. 'You're welcome to stay at my place.'

'I couldn't...' I flush, unfamiliar with any kind of genuine hospitality.

'Nonsense. I have a spare room, and the company will do me good.'

'You're sure?' I can't quite believe my luck – how nice this woman is. How genuine.

'Absolutely.' She smiles. 'It will be lovely to talk to someone about Carolyn. Sadly, not too many people liked her. She had a way of putting people's backs up.' Niamh nods apologetically. 'So... yes, I would love to have you. When you've had enough of town, just drop by. I'll be in all day. I have a mountain of work.'

'What do you do?'

'Writer, for my sins.'

A writer. My mind starts to whir. Perhaps she has contacts. People who might be interested in my take on Carolyn's story. I'd have to be careful not to offend, but...

Misunderstanding my silence, Niamh ploughs on. 'It's okay,' she says lightly. 'I promise I won't stick you in a story. I'm mainly non-fiction these days anyway. You're welcome to sleep over. I'm at Gull Point.'

I look blank.

'Grab a taxi. They'll know where it is.'

'Great, I was just...' I hesitate, having no idea what I'm supposed to be doing up this dead-end street. I catch sight of the shop on the corner, its plastic offerings glinting in the sun. 'Sunglasses,' I say, squinting as if to reinforce the idea. 'Who would have thought? October and I'm needing sunglasses.' And with a quick, 'See you later,' I dive into the shop.

In the end, I do actually get some sunglasses. They're only a fiver. Knock-offs, of course. They say Ray-Ban, but the metal on the arms is pure gold plastic, and I'm not convinced that the a's are actually a's, when you look closely, they could be u's. But the summer is over, and the sunglasses will do for anything autumn has to throw at me.

Securing myself a quiet desk at the back of the library, I get to work. It shouldn't be difficult finding material on the Millfords, or wolves. If I get time, I might even google potential journals that might be interested in the story of Carolyn's last manuscript. Perhaps this extra day on the island will serve me well. I'm about to fire up the library PC, when my phone buzzes with a text from Marco.

> You do know I'm not a pharmacist, right?

My fingers fly over the keypad.

> Yes. But you DO KNOW your medicines?

A series of blinking ellipses swirl in the chat line before the text settles again.

> Not something I'd advertise on my Tinder. You DO KNOW you are odd, right?

I chase hearses to boost my income so, yes, I do get that I'm on the odd spectrum, a little weird around the edges, but this is getting us nowhere. I set my fingers on the keypad again.

> The medicines? What are they?

The text comes back.

Didn't realise I'd become your PA now.

There's a pause. It's a dramatic pause. Sometimes, Marco seriously does drive me up the wall.

Well?

The first two are easy. So easy I'm amazed you couldn't just google it.

He delivers a frowny face emoji.

Roxicodone is a painkiller. On the strong side. And Heparin is an intravenous. Helps stop clotting.

Tim had very little autonomous movement, so neither of those medications prompts warning bells. Another text hits the thread.

The third one is odd. Denzomipropine.

I know the spelling is right. I didn't text him the names; I sent photos, so I can't have got it wrong. He's still texting.

It's not on the market at the moment. All I can find is that the name's under copyright.

I feel my forehead crease into a frown, then text back.

What does that mean?

The pharma industry hasn't unwrapped it yet.

I place the phone down on the wide library desk. I don't know what I'd expected, but not this. Then I remember the overheard conversation: Erica saying she wanted to get rid of things in Timmy's room. She knew something wasn't right. Maybe Oscar had form. Maybe that's why he stopped practising medicine. Perhaps he didn't leave – he was pushed, his indiscretion covered up.

'Kernow police?' A young woman answers, the question mark already ironed into her voice – nobody rings the station for a quick chat.

I'm standing outside the library. My coat and bag still holding my place. I just felt I needed to pass on whatever it was, Marco's turned up. 'Could I speak to DS Graham?' I ask.

'In connection with?'

I feel my shoulders rise in irritation. I hate gatekeepers.

'It's Kirstin Conroy. I have information.'

'Putting you through.'

Thankfully, he's there.

'Kirstin?' If there's an element of surprise in Graham's voice, he's not letting it leak through. Nothing seems to ruffle this man's feathers.

'I found some medicine in Timmy Millford's room this morning. I…'

This is awkward. How can I explain that I took the liberty of sending them to a friend so I could stick my nose up close and personal into other people's business? I decide this is a time where making it simple will work best. 'I think there may be something odd about them,' I bluster on, 'because I overheard Erica Millford saying she was going to clean out Timmy's room today. Could I just send you some images of the labels so you can check them out?'

'Sure.'

There's a pause.

'And you're still at the house?'

'No. I've ah...'

I think of the coke in Luke's bedside drawer, the account book, Luke's odd mood swings. I have no intention of telling the DS any of that.

'Just waiting for the ferries to start.'

I go into my photo app, put a check on all the photos detailing the medicines. All of them, even the ones that I think are probably the usual stuff, and send everything over. The ball is in DS Graham's court now. Then I call Julia and ask if we can meet up. I want to find out about Carolyn and the adopted children, and that kind of secret is no way going to appear online. Not yet anyway, because once I leak the manuscript, that side of the story is going to be all anyone wants to hear, and I need to make sure all roads lead back to me standing with a story I can sell. But first, I need to find out what the library has to offer.

26

JULIA

I PUNCH the day code the librarian gave me into the computer. The gods must be smiling because on my very first hit, I discover an article about the estate, accompanied by a head and shoulders shot of an unsmiling James Millford, Carolyn's father. The sharp eyes, hard as flint and the lips a narrow unsmiling line. According to the news clipping there were two brothers, James and Mathew. James was the eldest, so most likely, he inherited the entire estate. That's the way it tended to work back then in the UK. European countries divide the estate up between the children. But for the British, the estate is more important than the offspring. It needs to be kept intact and going by the lack of coverage on Mathew, it would seem that poor old Mathew Millford was given the traditional British elbow. Sadly, this is as far as I get. A good two hours later, elongating my neck, listening as my bones crunch back into shape, I can't help but feel disappointed because nothing I've turned up is giving me any hints as to what is going on in the here-and-now. Hopefully, Julia will have a few more leads.

It's the same receptionist at the desk in the Ship. She still looks as lopsided as the surroundings, standing one shoulder up, one shoulder down as she eyes me cautiously along the length of her angular nose. I give her a swift smile on my way towards the lounge.

'Still here?' she calls after me.

'Looks like it.'

She leans her body over the counter as if we're close friends, and she'd like more of an update.

'They're saying it's a murder investigation?'

'I know. Crazy.' My gut instinct is to tell her to mind her own business, but I'd rather be staying at the Ship tonight than with some woman I barely know, so friendly is best. I turn back towards her, rustling up a smile that looks halfway genuine. 'You don't have a...'

'Room?' She smirks as she completes my sentence. 'Nada.'

'I ordered tea for us and a plate of sandwiches.'

Julia's already in situ. The lounge has a different vibe than the à la mode fish-bowl of the restaurant. It's old-school – soft cushions, beamed walls and the crackle in the wide grate of a real fire.

'Do you always think of everything?' I say, glancing at the low table perfectly laid for a light tea and realising I'm starving.

Despite the red rims engrained around her eyes, Julia smiles. 'You'd get tired of my fussing soon enough.'

'Never.'

I slide into the armchair opposite, its low arms circling my body, as I rest my newly prized fake sunglasses on the table. 'I've been at the library most of the morning.'

'Oh?' Julia asks, acknowledging the waitress with a short, kind smile while still not taking her interest away from me.

'Yes. Looking up the family.'

'The illustrious Millfords.' She sighs.

'Exactly. I didn't realise Carolyn's father had a brother.'

'They fell out. Oh, my goodness, years ago. And there was a lovely niece as well.'

'Was?'

'Families.' She fusses with the teacups on the tray. 'Any news at the house?' Pausing in her task, she stares over at me, her gentle, watery eyes looking intent and nervous.

I sometimes forget I'm a newcomer here, but the house and the Millfords, that's been Julia's entire life, of course she'll have questions for me.

I draw in a deep breath, helping myself to a sandwich. 'To be honest, it's difficult to keep up.'

'I heard Timmy's been taken into hospital.'

I nod, curious as to how the information got out so quickly.

'I've a friend at ICU,' Julia explains. 'She called me when Timmy came in, concerned I'd be...' Julia hesitates. 'Upset.'

I reach out a hand towards her. She grasps it gently with her small, warm fingers.

'How's he doing?' I ask.

Yet again, Julia appears to have the information. She draws in her bottom lip, taking herself a deep breath before continuing. 'A bit better today. To be honest, there's a part of me that's relieved. I know Oscar has medical training but...'

I lean forward a little in my seat. 'But?'

'No, Kirsten.' She raises the palm of one hand, as though to stop me. 'Come on. Let's have our tea and get some food into you. Now... Have you got your car back?'

'No.' I take the cup and saucer from her; she's shaking a little, attempting to cover her pain in domestic bluster. The raw loss only visible at the very margins of her being; the red eyes; the shaking hands; the slight breathiness in the voice.

'So, what time will Luke be coming to take you back to the house?'

'Actually, Luke and I, we've fallen out a bit.'

She looks surprised. 'Oh. I'm sorry. I thought you were good for each other.' She pauses, eyeing me cautiously. 'You know Kirstin,' Julia continues, 'people aren't always simple.' Her voice sounds weary, as if it's being dragged over a life of finding little that sparkles. 'They maybe have sides we'd rather forget. I know that from experience.' Blushing, she fusses over the tea tray, moving the sugar bowl from side to side when there is absolutely no need. 'I've been involved with someone who had…' She hesitates. 'Problems, shall we say.'

I find myself readjusting my mental image of Julia. Despite the overhaul of her apartment, I'd had Julia firmly fixed in the spinster camp. I realise now this is ridiculous. She's in her fifties and still pretty, with her kindness and warmth. Julia would be an easy person to love.

'I didn't realise,' I say.

She glances up at me, an amused smile crossing her lips. 'Why would you?'

I'm happy for her. No one should be going through what she's having to face alone. I want to ask more about her partner; how long has it been going on? Is he local? Is he being supportive now? But Julia picks up her saucer, leans firmly back into her chair with an attitude of finality and glances philosophically into the hot brown liquid swirling in her cup. 'People are who they are, Kirstin.'

'I guess.' I examine her face carefully. Does she know about Timmy, the details of what happened? 'I was wondering, Julia, about Timmy's medication.'

'Oh, that's not my area. Rose or I just administered what we were told.'

I reach for my phone, flicking through the images I'd taken of the medication in Tim's room until I arrive at the Denzomipropine.

When I hand the phone over, she frowns. 'I don't remember this one. But his condition got a lot worse after Carolyn died and, as you know, I wasn't there for very long after the funeral. Doctor Meerson may well have switched things around.' She reaches for her handbag and takes out her reading glasses, holding the phone at arm's length while enlarging the label on the screen.

'Hmm.' She looks concerned. 'No, I definitely haven't seen these before. Perhaps you should take it to the police.'

'Already done.'

'Good.' Julia leans back, brushing imaginary crumbs from her skirt, her eyes lowered. There's something she's not telling me.

'Julia?' I press.

'Oh, Kirstin. I don't know.' Her face has lost any spring it had. She looks genuinely exhausted.

'Is it to do with Oscar?' I ask.

She shakes her head. 'Let's leave it, Kirstin. If the police have all the information, they'll deal with it.'

'You knew this was going to happen, didn't you?'

Tears prick her eyes. 'Not *knew*, no. No, of course not. I just felt Timmy was vulnerable, and Oscar, well, you probably didn't know but he studied medicine.'

I don't bother to tell her that, yes actually, I'm up to speed on that one.

'Then he just gave it up? I've always thought it was odd. One minute he loves medicine, then he arrived back at the estate very... preoccupied. Kept reading the papers every day. Scanning all the major ones. It was as if...' She raises her eyes to mine as though willing me to understand, before lowering her voice. 'Something had gone wrong, and he was waiting for it to blow up.'

I lean forward, not wanting to air this too loud before I have all the facts. 'You think he got struck off, rather than leaving voluntarily?'

She doesn't reply, just shoots me a knowing look.

'And the adoptions. It wasn't just Miri was it.'

There's a moment of what I think looks like shock, before Julia's features cloud over, impenetrable. 'I'm sorry, Kirstin.' She clears her throat. 'I think you've asked enough questions. I'm tired.'

It's clear that I'm getting nothing more from Julia. There's a loyalty to the family which, despite all, I'm not going to break through. But she's confirmed my suspicions. Oscar killed his sister and had a shot at Timmy's life, and apart from Luke, the siblings are in blissful ignorance that they're all adopted. Hurrying back through reception, the cogs in my brain won't stop whirring; the newspapers are absolutely going to want my side of this story. This is my way out.

'WOW!' The receptionist shrieks as I head through the lobby. She's holding one finger frozen in the air: paused while scrolling.

I have to stop. The '*wow*' was so completely and utterly over the top. 'What?'

'This.' She slides the phone towards me.

At first, I'm not sure what I'm seeing. It's a photo of a young woman and a man in a restaurant. 'Sorry?'

She scrolls through the images. It's like one of those flick books. The shot gets closer, as do the characters on view till finally it's all crystal – on the screen I see Miri. She's sitting opposite a sandy-haired, chisel-chinned young man.

The image might be clear, but I'm still not sure why the thing is important. 'Not getting it,' I say, peering closer at the loving couple.

The receptionist raises her wonky eyes as if I'm a first-class idiot. 'That was not her fiancé,' she says, savouring the sentence as though it's one of the best dishes she's tasted in a long while.

'Well, she wasn't a nun. She would have been dating people before she got engaged.'

With a palpable air of satisfaction, the receptionist places one polished nail on the feed again. 'Before? That's the day Malcolm Tanner's car went up in smoke.'

Suddenly it all makes sense. Someone was blackmailing Miri. That's what I'd seen at the wake. These photos would have ruined her. I flick through the feed, the receptionist watching with an unsettling kind of glee. The trolls are already out and keen for blood. The fact that the poor woman is dead is making not one jot of difference; their teeth are bared with indignation, and it's all aimed at poor, dead, Miri.

My head's spinning as I find myself once again on the quayside. I thought my life was complicated enough before, but now it's hitting a whole different level. My phone buzzes. It's a text from Luke.

Can we talk?

If I text back, I'll just keep pumping oxygen into this relationship, and that's no good. He's going to hate me when I sell my story. Rightly so, he's desperate for the manuscript; it could save his publishing business. But the man is a crook. A pusher. He might not have committed murder, but he doesn't deserve my sympathy. Frustratingly, there's still nothing from AJ. I'm unsure how long I should leave it before I start to pester. I feel a wave of exhaustion wash over me. This is all too much. I glance down the street, squinting as the sun bores into my eyes. My sunglasses, I think. At least one irritation is easily solved. Opening my bag, I realise the glasses aren't there. I'd left them on the table by the tea tray. Sure, they were only cheap, but they did the job. Retracing my steps, I pull open the heavy door to the inn.

'You're back,' the receptionist pipes up cheerily. 'List's no shorter.'

'Sunglasses,' I explain.

'Don't,' she chuckles, 'they should come with homing devices.'

I don't bother to reply, pushing on past a woman with far too many suitcases for your average individual, on my way to the lounge. I go to pull the glass door open, then stop. Julia's not alone. I fall back out of sight, my breath catching in my throat. There's a man sitting opposite her, one I know all too well – Fordham. Somehow Oscar's being framed. Fordham's violent. I know that from bitter experience. He has motive, access and looks every inch the killer. I've taken the whole investigation off on a tangent. I've been duped!

'I need to speak to DS Graham,' I splutter into my phone, when I'm standing safely quayside. Clutching my mobile to my ear, I hear a muffled sound as, at the other end of the line – someone puts their clammy hand over the receiver.

'It's her again.'

They're making me feel like a timewaster, but if they were doing their job, I wouldn't be here in the first place.

'DS Graham.' His voice sounds neutral, as though he has no idea who he's talking to.

'It's Kirstin.'

'Yup?'

'I've just seen Fordham in the Ship with Julia Catalow.'

Silence. I can't believe he's not getting this. I'm going to have to spell it out. 'Don't you see? There's a connection. Fordham would have been able to get into the house.'

I had trusted Julia completely; she was so sweet, maybe too sweet. I can't believe I've been duped.

DS Graham takes a moment to clear his throat. 'Fordham's been cleared, Kirstin. He's innocent.'

Irritation floods my brain. 'Do you mind my asking who gave him the alibi?' It has to be Julia.

Another pause. I get the feeling Graham is sizing me up, assessing whether I'm trustworthy enough to hold a little more information. 'Okay. He was at the Fighting Cocks, passed out on a bench all night. We've got a roomful of witnesses.'

'He attacked me.'

'He says, he bumped into you.'

This is infuriating.

'Look, Kirstin… I wouldn't normally do this, but I feel I owe you. The photos you sent this morning.'

'Timmy's medicine?'

'Yeah.'

'Well, that was kind of the missing piece we were looking for.'

Medicine. I can't help but feel irritated – we are back on the medicine track when I just know we should be putting more pressure on Fordham.

'The Denzomipropine,' DS Graham says calmly. 'It's still in development.'

That's odd. If the drug wasn't readily available, then only someone with access to medicine could get hold of it. Julia had just told me she had a friend at the hospital. Could she be working with Fordham? Surely that couldn't be right. She couldn't have killed her own daughter? Although, maybe that wasn't part of the plan. Perhaps something went wrong. A mistake. Fordham had somehow bungled it.

'The same person tried to harm all the siblings,' I say, decisively. 'Carolyn's dead, fallen from the cliff by Fordham's secret hovel. Timmy's only just clinging on. I'd been attacked,' I say, flinching at the memory. 'Mistaken for Luke. And...' I gasp. 'Someone tried to get at Erica; tampering with *her* car. Fordham would know about cars.'

'And young Miri?' he asks.

'Has to be a mistake. If she's Julia's daughter, it has to...'

'The same drugs were in the shake.' DS Graham clears his throat. 'Fordham doesn't fit. Think about it, Kirstin. What this actually proves is that someone with access to a pharmaceutical environment was administering drugs to Timmy – drugs that were still under trial.'

'But hospital... if someone had a friend at a hospital...'

'No,' he cuts me off, 'Fordham's a handyman at best, though some people would take issue with that, especially after he's had a drop. But the point is, Fordham doesn't have access to these kind of drugs. Denzomipropine isn't currently available.'

I stare out over the water, trying to fit all the pieces together. 'So, it is Oscar?'

There's a pause. 'We've brought Oscar Millford in for questioning.'

I feel my body slump and realise that deep down, I'd wanted it to be Fordham too badly. I didn't like the man. He scared me. 'I heard that Oscar dismissed the regular carer, Rose,' I mumble. 'He must have needed her out of the way so he could get rid of Timmy.'

'Right. Okay...' The way Graham draws out the okay makes me think he didn't know about Rose. 'Thank you, Kirstin. That's helpful.'

I like the sound of being helpful to the DS – of DS Graham owing me one. I need to move on it before he forgets. 'Okay, so... I've got this situation.' I take in a deep breath. 'My brother, he...'

'Andrew John Conroy,' DS Graham chimes in. 'He's in Holloway.'

I laugh. I know it's not funny, but there I was, thinking nobody was interested in me.

'Don't be offended, Kirstin. I do this for a living.'

I smile. 'Okay. No offence taken but, could you do me a favour? His parole got recalled. I just think there's something odd about it.'

27

GULL POINT

As soon as the taxi rounds the high, cliffside bend, I can see why Niamh wasn't worried about giving me her full address. *Gull Point* is all you need to know. It's a hut-like affair; a mixture of white-washed stone and clapperboards. The kind of house you might see in Kent, wind-washed and rustic, but this place certainly has a point of difference. There's a lighthouse standing tall and straight out of its side. In truth, there's probably way more *light* than *house*. It couldn't be more of a contrast to the Millford estate.

'This place is amazing,' I say as Niamh pulls open the door, a giant smile on her round face.

Before I'm even over the threshold, I can smell supper. Something wholesome and slow-cooked bubbling away on the stove.

'Well, thank you.' She reaches out for my bag then stands back, ushering me through the narrow doorway straight into the kitchen. Everything inside the house is crowded. There's barely a space that isn't cluttered with books, magazines, papers and a multitude of spider plants.

She glances proudly around the room. 'I bought the house in the eighties. It's fun, I think.'

'You're not kidding.'

I have to stop myself from doing the estate agent overhaul thing. Such a bad habit. My mind is constantly white-washing walls and sticking up extensions where they just do not need to go.

'I'll get the tea on,' Niamh says, already filling an old-fashioned kettle from the tap before placing it with a reassuring thud on the hotplate of the Rayburn. 'Did you have a good day?'

I don't know how to answer that. I decide to plump for short and sweet. 'Yes,' I say. 'It was... fine.'

'Wonderful. Let me show you to your room. You're in the tower; I call it the tower. Come through, come through.'

She steers me through the house, shoving a chair out of the way as we pass. I resist the itch to explain to Niamh that smaller furniture would make this place appear a whole lot bigger. The feng shui at Gull Point has definitely gone to pot; then again, maybe she doesn't want the room to 'appear' larger. Maybe she's happy with oversized comfort.

'I'm afraid I use the spare room as an office, so...' Her voice fades away, unable to explain. In my head, I picture chaos.

There's a small hallway just before the sweep of the lighthouse begins in earnest. We cross it in two short steps, Niamh pulling open a door, revealing a tiny, cramped bedroom. A small window, its frame white-washed, curving neatly into the wall. The room smells of geranium oil. I love geranium oil, but the space is so small, and the door was so tightly shut that the smell is overpowering. The bed takes up most of the room, which would also be fine, but I'd have a job getting in under the sheets which are currently covered in a haphazard blanket of loose paper.

'Ah.' She blusters forward, hastily collating piles of documents before glancing around as if wondering where to put them. The only other item of furniture is a small chair. It's set so close to the bed, there's barely any knee room to sit properly. 'I'll just stash these here,' she says, dropping the papers onto the chair.

The sitting problem has been sorted – it's no longer an option. I can't help but wonder how this woman and Carolyn could ever have become close friends. They seem so different: Carolyn so ordered, Niamh absolute anarchy. Perhaps it was just the bridge thing? Maybe nothing else mattered.

'I'm upstairs,' she indicates back out into the hallway and the bottom step of a curved stairway which must actually curl around the room we're in, 'and, right at the top, there's the light.'

'Can I see it?' I've never seen a lighthouse up close before.

She smiles, opening her arms as though extending the welcome. 'It's part of the tour.' She steps back out of the room into the hall.

'Does the light still work?'

'Technically, yes.' Niamh indicates a large wooden box sitting on the wall by the base of the stairs. 'It's all digital these days, although even with that, we've been superseded. One of the little uninhabited islands has a small beacon on it now.' She opens the box at the base of the stairs. 'Shame really, because it wasn't so difficult to operate from here – flick of a switch.'

I can see the switch. She doesn't press it though, just closes the box over with an endearing note of sadness.

'But the glass, Kirstin, the glass is still truly magnificent,' Niamh says lightly, as she mounts the curved stone steps. 'We have someone come out every year; check us over.'

Again, the 'us' – Niamh and the lighthouse? It has to be. I follow her as we circle around the stone stem.

'We're grade two-star listing,' she announces proudly.

My heart normally sinks when I hear this. Grade two is bad enough. Stick a star on the end and it means you're not going to be doing anything with the structure, nothing with any imagination at least. With this place, what you see will be pretty much what you get.

We continue corkscrewing our way upwards, passing occasional slit-like windows that cast lightsaber rays across the steps in front of us.

'My room,' she says breathlessly when we reach a small landing. 'I like it better up here. There's more of a view. I feel like I'm up with the gulls.' She laughs, throwing open the door.

The room is, in fact, even smaller than mine, no doubt because the tower is narrowing. Although there's no chair in here, so the space is a little better managed. I'm not sure the view is an improvement though. The white window frame contains nothing but a clear block of blue sky. Niamh remains undaunted.

'But, really,' her eyes sparkle, 'the best view is from the light.'

We continue to climb.

'Most days, I come and sit up here. The sunsets are fantastic.'

We round the last corner, finding ourselves in the small room at the top of the tower. Instantly, I'm won over. The light is enormous. Hundreds of tubes of glass, fixed at different angles. Even without automation, the glass vials fracture each image and ray of sun that happens to fall across them. Niamh smiles proudly at it.

'Rather beautiful, don't you think?'

'I absolutely do.' Glancing around me, taking in the 360-degree view I see that the sea surrounds us as though buoying us up, offering us to the gods.

'Sit here, if you like. Bring your tea up. Dinner won't be till seven thirty. I hope that's okay?'

'That's great.'

'I eat late and too much,' she says, glancing down cheekily, like a child caught out in a terrible faux pas. 'I know it's not best for your metabolism, but…' she winks at me, 'at my age… who cares.'

I take my tea from the kitchen, grab Tim's journal from my bag and head back to the light room. There are two high stools up there so you can sit at the windows and look out over the sea. It really does feel as though I'm up with the gulls. The sound of their constant calls, the cackles and shrieks, skirt around me. It's not hard to see how you would fall in love with a place like this. It hasn't got all the mod cons, but maybe mod cons are a con? What are we all doing, I wonder as I stare out over the sea, hamster-wheeling ourselves into mortgages we can never pay off? All just so we get the latest *look* for living, before becoming so run-ragged with work, we forget the life bit. What would happen if everyone just said, *Do you know what, I'm happy with this? I'm content*. Okay, so I would probably be out of a job. Then again, I already am.

I flick through Tim's journal, looking for entries about The Wolf. But there's nothing. The places Tim visited sound amazing: a bay with magnificent rock features; caves made of marble, the floors so slippery when wet that he saw two people slide and fall; a restaurant in Laos – a world heritage site, set on a massive lily pond. But not one Wolf. I turn to the last page. He's arrived in Cambodia. Angkor Wat sounds incredible. Temples woven with tree trunks. Structures that tower like the Himalayas out of the jungle. Then, suddenly, I stop my eyes, pausing over Tim's neatly written words – The Wolf has arranged a trip for him, a trek through the jungle. A temple very few visitors get to see. The tickets are booked for the following day. He writes with enthusiasm. He's excited to see something away from the crowds, so excited he can barely sleep. I turn the page. It's blank. There are no more entries. I can guess what happened next – the landmine.

My mind is buzzing. Did The Wolf send Timmy off on a trip, knowing it would end in tragedy? Who would do that? I think of poor Miri. I think of the recent attempt on Timmy's life and realise I have my answer – someone who wanted more of a share of the will. Oscar? I close the book, feeling an overwhelming sense of sadness. I'll hand it in to DS Graham in the morning before I go. Which reminds me, I need to keep an eye on the boat situation.

Back in the spare room, I check my phone. The ferries are back on tomorrow. With a few clicks, I reserve a place on the 10.30.

There's another text from Luke.

Kirstin. We need to talk.

We need to talk. Does he know I'm onto him? Then, suddenly, I feel a wave of nausea. Did I close the drawer in his bedroom? I scan back through my memories. I must have done. Surely, I must have. But I don't remember sliding the thing shut. Luke would have been able to tell someone had used his shower. I'd left it tidy, but there would have been fresh water on the screens. Nobody else would have been using that shower. Most of them were out, and besides, everyone had their own. If I'd left the drawer open, Luke would have realised I'd seen the drugs and his accounts book. No wonder he felt we needed to talk.

Exhausted, I throw myself back on the bed, but there's something under the pillow. More of Niamh's papers. I pull them out, glancing at them as I do. Instantly, my heart falters as the stability of my entire world slides from under my feet. It's a proposal – details for a new port. They're addressed to Councillor Niamh Corbet. She's on the council. Niamh is behind this port, could she have an interest in shipping illegal substances? My God. She could easily be working with Luke. With a sickening gut punch it all starts falling into place. Niamh's a writer. She's a friend of the family, but was her connection primarily with Luke rather than Carolyn? They're in the same industry. And the earring I found in the snug; it was hers. She'd told me she didn't go to the house for the bridge club, that happened at the Ship. She must have been meeting Luke: talking about the port. I scan through the documents. There are three proposed sites. One is to extend Kernow. The other is a small cove, Carbis Bay. It's a tourist attraction. I can't imagine that would go down well. I flick to the last page, and my heart sinks. The Millford estate. The house is still there but the wide cove between the church and the house, the one that stretches out just the other side of the steep hill I climbed on my cliff-top walk, the one I felt would provide some great promo shots – that's the third site.

Flicking back through the document, it's pretty clear that the Millford estate is the only site proposal that makes any sense. I may not have all the facts, but I know one thing for sure. This is a mess. Am I in danger? There were drugs in AJ's cell. If he'd got parole, maybe I'd have got myself off the island a bit quicker. The bad news about my brother had wrapped me in inertia. But why would it suit anyone to have me here? I don't know these people, and why had Niamh been so keen for me to come to her house? Somebody tampered with my car. What if they weren't after Erica at all? I know about the drugs. And the hushed conversation between Miri and that mystery person that I'd overheard. Perhaps Miri wouldn't agree to sell off the land for the port? I'd witnessed the blackmail attempt. What if somebody saw me come out of the blue room? They saw me, but hadn't realised I couldn't identify them. They'd want to keep me quiet.

I've got to get out. I can call a taxi, go back into town. I'll go to the police station, tell them everything. I've had enough of secrets. My phone buzzes. I grab it. It's a text from DS Graham.

> That favour you wanted? Your brother has no
> history of dealing or selling drugs.

AJ must have been set up. Somehow, this is all connected, and Niamh and Luke are behind it. I throw my things back into my bag, wondering if I can remember the name of the cab company.

Mabel's, or was it Mavis? I can't even think straight anymore. My mind is spinning. I'll google it.

Suddenly, there's a knock on the door. I freeze.

'Kirstin, can I come in?'

She doesn't wait for a reply but even though Niamh glibly pulls the door open, she stops dead in the frame. Her face falling in an attitude of shock. 'Kirstin, what's wrong?'

'I...' The words won't come, they're hidden somewhere deep behind panic and fear.

'What is it?'

I step back. She glances down. She can see the documents on the bed. The plans for the port, all waiting there, ready for her signature.

'Ah...' A wide smile spreads over her face. 'Just what I was looking for...'

Should I give them to her? But she doesn't wait, snatching them up.

'Need to get that objection in. Tomorrow is the deadline. They'll be sticking container ports all over the islands if I don't. What a ridiculous idea.' She glances at me again, concerned. 'Kirstin, is there something you want to tell me?'

At which point I burst into tears.

I sit in the kitchen, my body bent over the large tea-ringed table as Niamh hands me another mug. She insists on putting sugar in. What is it about old people and sugar?

'It's good for shock. Clinically proven,' she says. 'Don't argue. Just drink. Okay, start at the beginning.'

I take a deep breath. 'I'm not actually sure I know where the beginning is.'

Niamh helps herself to a chocolate digestive, chewing on it

loudly as she thinks the problem over. 'Okay, start at the bit that you think makes the most sense.'

That seems like a plan. I draw in a deep breath. 'Okay, so the police think Oscar was giving Timmy medicine which was still under trial.'

'Oscar?' She looks truly shocked.

I nod.

'Well, I mean, he hasn't practised medicine for years.' Her eyes narrow as she tries to make sense of the information. 'Maybe he heard of something, some new drug and thought it could help?'

I run one hand over my forehead, warily. 'They found the same drug in Miri's shake.'

'They told you this?'

'Not in so many words, but... That's what killed her.'

'Seriously?'

I nod.

Niamh shifts uncomfortably. 'Oscar, though? I just wouldn't have thought...'

'I'm not sure who's implicated and who's not, but I found cocaine in Luke's room.'

'Oh, dear. That's not good.' She sighs, dunking her biscuit in her tea till the chocolate coating begins to slide off its base. She shakes her head pragmatically. 'Then again, Kirstin, I may be old, but I do know that many young people take recreational drugs these days.'

'No, Niamh, you don't understand. Luke had an accounts book with the drugs. It was too much for personal use. That's why I was scared when I found the port approval documents in your guest room.'

'I'm trying to stop it.' Her voice sounds a little wounded and all on the defence.

'I know that now, but I thought you might be in on... something.'

'New port facilities would mean more containers, more ways of getting illegal items in?'

'Maybe.' I shrug. 'And there's this...'

I push Tim's notebook over the table towards her. 'It's Tim's travel journal, from just before he had his accident. He was doing a lot of long-haul stuff. Actually...' I hesitate. 'He was pretty much doing Asia's golden drugs triangle.'

Her face pales. 'Timmy? But it doesn't mean...'

'Someone paid for his trip. Someone called The Wolf.'

I scan her face curiously, hoping it might light up in recognition. It doesn't. 'Niamh, do you know if any of the family members was called The Wolf? Maybe a nickname?'

She bites her lip apologetically. 'I never really got that close to them. I don't have kids myself, so... I'm not that good with them – have no idea how their minds work. To be honest, I'm not sure Carolyn did either. You've read her book?'

I shake my head.

'Well, it's not really the book that's the problem. Most of it's normal enough stuff. Discipline, reward, a sense of loyalty to the family. Although I always think Carolyn added the loyalty bit because of the Millford name. The *good name* was everything to Carolyn. If you ask me, loyalty should come with respect. Sadly, I'm not sure respect was something that went both ways with Carolyn Millford.'

'Meaning she didn't respect the children?'

'Exactly. And that was part of the problem underlying her ground-breaking theory.'

'I'm sorry?'

'Chapter Three. *The Golden Child*.'

The Golden Child. This rings a bell. Hadn't Miri said something about it?

'Carolyn believed that in a group of siblings, one child was the golden child and deserved ultimate respect. Her own father had the same warped notion. He inherited the estate. His brother

Mathew got nothing, as far as I know. Difficult to tell. I tried to do some research on Mathew for the historical society, but there's barely anything. There was some local story.' She squints her eyes tightly as if trying to squeeze the memory out of her brain. 'I can't remember exactly what – but locals say James had Mathew... what was it? Washed over? Painted over? Painted out?'

I'm not sure I understand. Niamh doesn't look like she does either. After a moment, she shrugs dismissively. 'James had enough money and influence to do anything. Anyway, Carolyn had this idea that one child in each generation was *chosen*.'

'Do you know who she chose?'

'No. If she did choose one of them. The book came out in the late nineties. It caused a sensation. She didn't think you should do the traditional firstborn thing – let the eldest inherit the estate. She felt you should, oh, I don't know, audition the children in a way. Switch the attention around to see which would thrive under the spotlight. Oscar's the eldest. According to tradition he would be the obvious person to inherit everything. But...'

'But?'

'I'm not sure, in Carolyn's eyes, Oscar ever lived up to his promise. He left his medical studies.'

'Do you know why?'

'Hmm...' She sucks in her cheeks as if mulling over whether or not to spill, before nodding sadly. 'One of his patients died. A young lad. I think it was haemophilia. Oscar failed to get consent from the parents for a transfusion. Not his fault, but Oscar felt disillusioned, powerless.'

So, he wasn't struck off. 'What about the others and this *star treatment*?'

'Erica was favoured for a little while. But... she's very uptight. Overthinks. Over-plans. She likes organising people. I think Carolyn found that infuriating.'

'Luke, then?'

'Luke, I don't know. He seems so charming, but… and I remember this because it is so odd; Carolyn always said he wasn't perfect. That was the thing she said about Luke if we ever spoke of him.'

'What did she mean?'

Niamh shrugs. 'I'm not sure. I told her no one's perfect, although I think there was more to it. But, golden child? No, he wasn't that. Certainly not in Carolyn's eyes. Timmy was absolutely the golden child. Then when Timmy had his accident, that changed. Carolyn seemed to think they'd all disappointed her. She switched her attention to Miri.'

'A different generation?'

'I suppose, yes. Families…' Niamh laughs. 'Best not to have them.'

I think of AJ. I think of all the heartache we've been through and how I worry constantly about him, but I'd never, in a million years, say my life would be better without him. 'And what about Erica's marriage. Were there children?'

Carolyn's second will had said blood relatives should inherit.

'No, no children. Erica's marriage was very brief.' Niamh pours herself another tea from the pot. 'All the others had subsequent relationships after their divorces, but Erica, no… just one disastrous marriage. He turned out to be a gambler, I think. Stole things from the house.'

'Ah.' I can't help feeling sorry for her.

'Think that probably put her off relationships for life.'

'I did see her with a man in town.'

Niamh looks surprised.

'It was on the street where we met earlier – Fore Street. A red-haired man around her age, maybe a little younger.'

'Ah.' Smiling, Niamh leans towards me, curious.

'I think his name might be Mark Hitchin?'

Her eyes sparkle with amusement as she loses control of her tea mug; thumping it down a little too hard onto the table, so the hot liquid spills onto a carved corner of the wooden grain. 'Mark Hitchin? That's my nephew. No, he's definitely not seeing Erica.' Niamh laughs. 'He's a PI. Private Investigator. I think he had worked for Erica.'

'Look, Niamh.' I perch forward in my chair. 'I hate to ask you this, but could you contact Mark and see if you can find out what Erica was looking into?'

Her large round face sinks back into her neck, tortoise-like. 'That doesn't sound very ethical.'

'I suppose not,' I say sadly.

'But...' Her smile beams. 'He can always say *no*.'

28

THE VISITOR

I DECIDE TO TAKE A WALK. It'll be dark soon, but I need to get things straight in my head. So much has happened, and I still don't know how it all fits together. So I skirt along the cliff-top path, gulls screaming in my ears, the wind battering my face, throwing my hair around as if it wants to shake me. In my pocket, my phone gives out that familiar buzz. It's DS Graham.

'Kirstin?'

'Yes?'

'I can barely hear you. Where are you?'

'Gull Point.' I raise my voice. 'A friend of Carolyn's is putting me up.'

'Niamh Corbet?'

'How did you know?'

'Brilliant detective work.'

I laugh.

'All right. Not so brilliant. In case you hadn't noticed, there's only one house up at Gull Point.'

I glance around. He's right – this could be the edge of the moon.

'I was ringing to say Oscar Millford is in custody.'

'Wow.' Just for one moment, I find it difficult to collect my thoughts, but I still have a million questions. 'Why did he tamper with my car?'

'He's confessed to nothing yet.'

'Did you find the medicine in Timmy's room?'

'Eventually. Not in his actual room, though. Had to look through all the bins. We're treating Oscar to a night in the cells. We might get more sense out of him in the morning.'

'You know he's friendly with a solicitor at Longbow and Mclean. The people who had Carolyn's will?'

'Yes, we're already looking into that.'

'I found Timmy Millford's travel diary,' I say.

'Hmm?'

'It's from when he went to Cambodia. That's where he had the accident.'

'Right? Wasn't that years ago?'

'Yes, but in the journal, he talks about somebody called The Wolf. I know it sounds stupid, but maybe Oscar's got some sort of split personality.'

'Wolf in sheep's clothing?'

'If it helps you focus.'

'I'll try asking him, see if he bites.'

I laugh. 'And before you go… my car?'

'Should be able to get it back to you soon.'

'I'm leaving tomorrow.' The wind flicks a spray of hair across my face; I clutch it back behind the nape of my neck. 'Do I need to book it on the ferry?'

'Best go on foot, Kirstin. If they're all done and dusted with it in the morning, I'll drive it over to the boat myself.'

'Okay, and I…' I hesitate. I'm thinking about the drugs in Luke's drawer and the accounts book, could this, in any way, be connected? I'm not sure if straight-laced Oscar would be capable of murdering his family in cold blood. Then again, I'm not sure of anything anymore.

'Yes?'

'No, nothing. Just a red herring. You've got your big fish.'

I push open the door to the lighthouse, a gust of sharp seawatery wind following me through to the warm kitchen.

'You were in luck,' Niamh calls out brightly from where she's standing at the range. 'My nephew Mark says he can't see that it would hurt – me telling you what he was investigating. To be honest, he said he'd never work for Erica again. Very stressy. Mark told me she had him looking for any family members that might still be around. People that were related to Mathew Millford.'

'James Millford's brother,' I offer.

'That's the one.' Niamh jabs the wooden stirring spoon towards me. 'Erica wanted my Mark to find out if there had been any grandchildren.'

'Because in one will Carolyn stipulates that blood relatives will get the inheritance?'

Niamh looks at me thoughtfully. 'That, I didn't know.' She sticks the spoon into the stew once again, gives it a stir then pops the heavy casserole lid back on. 'Are you starving?'

Then it dawns on me.

'Kirstin?' Niamh's eyeing me with genuine concern.

'I've just realised. If Erica had Mark hunting for Carolyn's uncle, that has to mean Erica knew about the other will. And what about Mark, did he turn anything up on Carolyn's missing uncle?'

Niamh pushes an errant strand of hair back into its tortoiseshell clasp. 'He did. He said he'd fax it over later.'

'Fax?' I laugh.

She screws up her eyes, her face mock-serious. 'I spent five hundred pounds on that machine, back in the day. It may be old-fashioned, but it means everything gets printed out. Very useful for the parish council. Email threads always get far too busy. I like hard copies.'

I remember the piles of paper stacked up in the guest bedroom – she's not kidding.

Niamh fills a small, white china ramekin with nuts, pushing it across the table towards me. 'Keep you going. I think we're about half an hour off.'

'Sounds good.'

Suddenly, she glances out of the darkened window, her brow knitting. The day has disappeared, but a set of headlights are piercing the darkness.

Niamh looks puzzled. 'Were you expecting anyone, Kirstin?'

I shake my head. 'No one knows I'm here, well, apart from DS Graham.'

She peers again out into the night. 'Odd,' she says, brushing her hands across her apron. 'Why don't you just wait in your room till I get rid of whoever this is. It's probably council business, and they do tend to go on.'

I do as I'm told. I seriously can't be bothered with company, only I don't shut the door, which, as it turns out, works to my advantage.

'Oh, Niamh. I'm so glad you're here.' Erica's sharp tones waft through the building from the doorstep.

Immediately I'm curious.

'Are you okay? Come in.' Niamh's voice sounds gentle, full of concern.

'Thank you.'

The front door closes, and I catch a light thud as Erica dumps what must be her heavy wool coat over the back of a chair. 'Sorry, you're about to eat?'

Oh no, I think. Please don't tell her I'm here. Uptight Erica is about the last thing I need right now.

'Not at all,' Niamh says without a wobble of over-explanation. 'It's stew. It's ready when I am.'

'I just...' Erica's voice cracks. 'I didn't know who else to talk to. It's my brother, Oscar.'

'Oh?' Niamh is giving nothing away.

'Oscar's been arrested,' Erica blurts. 'They say he murdered Miri and made an attempt on Timmy's life.'

Suddenly it hits me. Gareth, Oscar's friend, he was the guy in the photo that Marco had sent me. The one who had been passing himself off as one of the sons. They are definitely working together.

'Oscar killed Miri?' Niamh says, her voice full of curiosity. 'And you believe that?'

Erica sighs. 'I don't know what to believe anymore. This whole thing is a mess. And I'm so worried about Luke. I thought he might be here?'

There's a pause.

'Why would he be here?'

'Something about a container port?'

Another pause.

'I think that's what he said.' Erica picks up the conversation again. 'I could be wrong. I know he's keen on backing the scheme.'

Niamh clears her throat. 'He has spoken to me about it,' Niamh says hesitantly, unsure perhaps if she should be keeping this confidential. 'He does have a valid point. He feels it would bring jobs to the island.'

There's a beat in which, no doubt, a bit of sizing up is going on. When Niamh speaks again, I get the distinct impression she's fishing. 'As a family, Erica, I'm sure they would have made it worth your while financially to sell?'

'I think it was my mother they approached. I have no idea about the figures. I'm just worried about Luke. Worried he might do something stupid. You know he's bipolar?'

My heart slides into my throat. That's what Carolyn must have meant by *he's not perfect*, and hadn't Luke almost confessed as much? He'd done the genetic test to find out if the condition he had was hereditary – this must be the condition. I'd certainly seen two sides to his personality. Just like a wolf. I wonder. Would he really describe himself as that?

'I didn't know he was bipolar,' Niamh says softly. 'These last few days must have been very difficult for him. Poor Luke.'

'He's on medication, but I think he's been taking... other things. No, sorry,' Erica corrects herself, 'I know he's been taking other things. Oscar's arrest could easily push Luke over the edge. He's been acting so strangely. Then there was that girl from the funeral.'

'Kirstin? Nice young woman.'

I smile to myself, glad to have Niamh in my corner.

'Yes, I'd hoped...' Whatever she *hoped* gets lost, tangled in a web of overthinking. Through the crack in the door I catch a glimpse of Erica's slender body as it leans in, and she lowers her voice to a whisper. 'She's also disappeared.'

Another pause. I think that at any moment, Niamh's going to say, *'No. She's here.'* But, for whatever reason, my new-found friend brushes the comment aside.

'I'm sure she's fine, Erica. There have been problems with the ferry. Besides, goodness, dear, you've got enough on your mind without worrying about people you barely know.'

'It's just Luke... sometimes he forms odd attachments,' Erica stutters.

'Yes?' Niamh asks gently.

'Oh, nothing.' Erica's voice sounds weary as if it's all too much. 'He's...' She laughs. 'Different.'

'I like a bit of *different* myself,' Niamh says lightly. 'People often say that I'm different. It would be a boring old world if we were all the same.'

'Hmm.' Erica puffs, as if she doesn't necessarily agree, but is working up to something bigger. 'I don't suppose you would have the details of this proposed port?'

'Of course. It is on the parish website.'

'Yes, but if you had a hard copy, that would be great. I'm trying to work out what Luke's interest is.'

I feel my knees give just a little. I get the feeling that I'm all too aware of what his *interest* is.

'As I said before,' Niamh says gently. 'I think it is to do with employment. And he does have a point. The island doesn't have enough industry. Our young people are always having to leave, get jobs elsewhere.'

'But, from an environmental position,' Erica says, her voice clipped, 'it's so wrong.'

'Everyone should be allowed to voice their opinion, but tomorrow is the deadline for getting comments in.'

Erica sighs. 'Then a hard copy would be great, thank you.'

A chair scrapes backwards over the tiled floor. 'Wait there. I'll get it.'

Niamh's shadow stands, momentarily blocking the crack in the kitchen door before pulling it open wide. I sink back onto the bed as Niamh crosses the small hallway and comes into my room. She smiles a small, secret smile, before grabbing a copy of the port proposal from where she'd thrown it earlier on the chair. We say nothing.

'There you go.' Back in the kitchen, Niamh hands the brochure to Erica.

A second chair scrapes back over the floor. 'Thank you. I'm sorry to have bothered you. It feels like my family is falling to pieces.'

'Well, if you need to talk,' Niamh's voice is soft, full of reassurance, 'you know where I am.'

'You were such a good friend to my mother.'

'Friends are supposed to be good.'

I hear another scrape of chairs and ruffled material as Erica slips back into her coat.

'Oh, and Erica? I meant to ask,' Niamh says casually.

'Yes?'

'Silly, really, but I've always been curious. Your mother, she used to say one of you was called The Wolf.' The woman should seriously get an Oscar for her performance. It's delivered so naturally. 'A nickname perhaps,' she continues. 'I just wondered, would that have been Oscar?'

'The Wolf. Oh, my goodness.' Erica laughs. 'We used to have this stupid game. Luke. It was Luke who was The Wolf.'

Of course it was.

'If I've learnt one thing from the parish council,' Niamh stirs the stew with a large wooden spoon, 'it's that people like to say their bit.' The table is set. We're almost ready to eat. 'Voicing opinions,' Niamh continues, 'is often more important than having some kind of action on an item.' She draws two glasses of water from the tap. 'Personally, I hope Erica's in charge of the disposal of the estate. Sounds as though she'll be against selling it to some shipping magnate.'

Niamh ladles the stew onto my plate before seeing to her own.

'This smells incredible.'

She pulls out a brightly coloured napkin, shakes it, and sits down, placing the purple cotton square across her lap. 'Erica's clearly worried about Luke.'

I think of the barrage of texts on my phone from Luke. I'm getting them every twenty minutes. He seems so insistent. He must know I've seen the drugs. But if he is The Wolf it's not only the drugs which are the problem… hurting Timmy, and what about the others? – the man is brutal. Perhaps he's been egged on by the feeling that he's the outsider. The adopted child. If only he'd known that none of the Millfords belonged.

'I appreciate you not telling Erica I was here,' I say, filling my fork with stew.

Niamh smiles. 'Feeling a bit like a spy at the moment. Tomorrow, I will enjoy a return to normality, but two visitors in a day, that's pretty much a record.'

After the plates are eaten, we push back into our chairs. The evening lying ahead of us. The warmth in Niamh's kitchen making me feel safe and wanted. 'Do you think maybe I should tell DS Graham about the drugs in Luke's drawer?'

Niamh gives me a long hard stare. 'It's probably best to lay everything on the table. He's going to need all the pieces if he wants to understand how it all fits together.'

'You think Luke knew what Oscar was doing?'

She shrugs. 'I don't know, but best to be on the safe side.'

'Can I just make a quick call?'

I scuttle out into the hallway. As it turns out, the call is really quick. DS Graham is not around. His voice tells me to leave a message.

I take a deep breath before launching in. 'Hi. Me again. Kirstin Conroy.' I don't really know how to say what I need to say, so I just deliver it fast. 'I discovered drugs in a drawer in Luke Millford's bedroom. They're in his bedside cabinet. There's also an accounts book. I… should have told you earlier. I'm sorry.'

I put the phone down, hoping to God I've done the right thing.

Over coffee Niamh tells me all the funny stories about the parish council. The container port has been the first proper thing they've had to vote on in years. Normally it's home extensions and island squabbles. She has some hilarious tales. It's so easy, being in her kitchen. There is no pretence here. She's determined that although everyone is entitled to voice their opinion, the port is not going to happen.

It may only be 8.30, but the warmth of the kitchen, the heavy stew, the red wine, it's all making me feel sleepy. I start clearing plates from the table when a grating, squeaking noise fills the air.

'That's the fax,' Niamh says, delighted. Leaving the dishes she goes to a cupboard, pulling open the creaking doors. Inside stands a relic of a different age – the fax machine. 'Mark must be sending the details of the lost relatives.'

I go to stand next to her and pull out my phone. Damn it, there's a message from AJ. I could kick myself. I've missed having a direct talk. Thank goodness he's left a text.

The fax machine continues to chug the image out of its wide plastic mouth as I scan my eyes across AJ's message.

> Sorry, sis. Keep missing you. Making the most of a shit hand here. Enjoying my family history class. The lady teaching it found this photo of Mum. I knew you'd appreciate it. Sorry for telling you all those years ago it didn't matter. Of course it does. Do you know who the other woman is?

I glance at the JPEG as it downloads on my phone. Suddenly my heart pounds double-time in my chest. It's the photo on the digital frame in Timmy's room. My mother is the other woman. Not Maya. Maria.

'There you go,' Niamh says, oblivious to the whirlwind rocketing around my brain. She tears a slip of printer paper from the fax.

'This must be the niece. Oh.' Suddenly she stops. She holds the paper a little closer to her eyes. 'I don't understand.'

She stares at me, twisting the image in her hand so I can see it too.

I gawp in disbelief as my head starts to spin. Niamh is holding a picture of me.

29

LONG WAY DOWN

THERE'S a blast of cold air. A door must be open somewhere. Something nudges my body hard. I can hear the sound of dragging. I don't know where Niamh is anymore. She's not beside me. The warm press on my arm has gone. I feel sick. My vision is blurred as though my eyeballs are smeared in wax. I squeeze my eyes tightly closed till the shuffling and dragging stops. I don't want whoever it is to know I'm conscious. As soon as it all goes quiet, I try to open my heavy eyelids again, try to stand, but I can barely see straight through the blur, and my legs refuse to work. It's as though I have no legs. I look around for my phone, but the room won't stay fixed in place. The dull-coloured tiles of the floor warp and cascade over my eyeballs. Through the open door, I can hear something happening outside. Movement. Car doors being opened. Something heavy being dragged. Someone grunting. I need to get help. It's The Wolf. He's found us. He's going to destroy us. But I don't know where my phone is, and I can't even get to my feet. I manage to roll onto my front, my body heavy as a loaded sack. I lie there, beached as a floundering fish after the tide's slipped out. I have to move. I have to get help. Pushing my heavy arms in front of me a little, I press them against the hard floor and slide forward on my stomach, my body shifting slowly but surely like a drunken worm. Every inch is an effort. My arms ache as though they've been carrying lead, and my ears ring with warnings…

'He's different.'

'Are you Irish?'

'Where are you, Kirstin?' How many times has he asked me that today?

From the moment I'd met Luke, he must have known my name. He knew who I was – that as a blood relative I was more entitled to a share of the will than he was. Luke must have got hold of Erica's files. I need to get out. My arms reach ahead of me, desperate to grab anything that might be able to jettison me forward. My fingers clasping on something soft. There's a coat on the back of a chair. My coat. It must have been here all evening; Erica would have seen it when she was in the kitchen. She must know I'm here. She could help. She'll at least be able to tell the police. Luke can't get away with this. I grope around the tails of the coat, find a chair leg and pull myself across the floor in another slow but firm slither. My head hurts as if it's been split in two. But I know I'm in danger. I saw too much. That's why Erica had come here – to warn me. She knew Luke would be after me. She was worried that the killing was not going to stop. I inch my hands out in front and try desperately to clutch onto something solid again. Nothing. This is hopeless. My body slumps. I want to cry. I'm about to melt into a blithering mess, when suddenly I think of my brother. If I don't survive, there will be no *us* ever again. No normal; however fucked up our normal might be, it's ours and worth fighting for. Niamh's house is as cluttered as hell. There has to be something here that can help me. I reach again. Success. This time my palms clasp a hard surface. Possibly the edge of a large armchair. It doesn't matter. It holds firm. I fix my fingers around it and pull my body forward. If I can get to my room, I might be able to find something: nail scissors, a pair of tweezers. Anything sharp will do. If I go for the eyes, I'll be fine. I have one chance. I reach out again, needing to grasp one more thing that will help pull me along. The cold blast of air from the open door fades behind me as I slide forward. I can still hear noises from outside, but they're muffled now. I have to be quick. My hands fumble towards the doorframe leading out into the hallway. I pull. I'm through. It can't be more than four feet to my room; less than the length of my body. I'm almost there. The smeary-looking door to my bedroom is open. I can do this, despite the blurring images and the constant ringing in my head. I just need to... A car door slams. I don't have time. I glance behind me.

My vision still warped, the lighthouse stairs nightmarishly slanted and concave. Then I see it, a wave of hope rushes through me; the box! Sitting at the base of the stone steps, fixed to the wall, is the motor for the lighthouse. I throw my left arm towards it. The catch on the lock loosens. My fingers grope frantically for the switch. If I can just get the light on. If I can switch on the light, surely help will come. People will know something is wrong. I reach and reach, willing my fingers to grow. I'm almost there. Almost safe. Suddenly I'm sliding in the opposite direction. Someone is pulling my legs across the floor. My jellified body follows. The light switch has not been pressed. The lighthouse remains dark. My muscles slump into pulp, as my head bumps hard on the doorframe and I'm pulled through it into the cold night air.

The next thing I know, a seatbelt is being yanked firmly across my body. I hear it clunk into place. *Good,* I think. *I'm too drunk. Someone is looking after me. That wine was strong. I should have eaten something.* Then I realise; I did eat something. None of this is normal. I force my eyes open. I'm in a car. It's not my car. I'm in the passenger seat. Niamh is in the driver's seat, but not in the right position. Her head hangs down, lolling over her body. She won't be able to see the road. This is bad. I try to say something, but my vocal cords have frozen. The car door beside me bangs shut with a hermetically sealed thud as a black shape flits past outside the window. I want to call out, to say, 'help', but I can't. It's then that the car starts to move; juddering at first, small hesitant jerks. I have to reach the handbrake, but my arms aren't working. I'm paralysed. Paralysed, just like Timmy. My God, it is all Luke. Oscar had nothing to do with this. Or maybe they were working together? I don't know. I want to scream. I've been so naïve. It all makes sense now. Luke knew I was related. He knew I could be getting a piece of the will. That's why he was so interested in me at the funeral. He wasn't flirting. He wanted to get me back to the house. The night of the wake, Miri said her brother tore out of the drive, driving too fast. It wasn't an accident. Luke wanted to mow me down. He probably would have done, but the place where I fell, that's where Fordham's path started. Fordham was watching. I had seen his eyes in the undergrowth. That's why Fordham was trying to contact me on the cliff path – to warn me. But the car is moving faster now. I'm strapped inside a sealed bullet. It's dark outside. The silhouettes of trees lining one side of the cliff road rush past. Their inky fingers clutching idly at the speeding vehicle. I know there's a sheer drop coming soon. A turn in the road where the edge peters out, falling away into the deep, cold sea. If we keep racing forward, nothing will stop us. We are going to die. BANG. Everything goes black.

30

ALL IN THE SPIN

'I THINK SHE'S COMING AROUND,' I hear someone say, from the cobwebby edges of my brain. My eyelids are so heavy. It feels as though someone has superglued them together. The sliver of light that manages to slip through when I finally do manage to peel my eyes open pierces my brain, cruel as a set of sharpened knives.

'Oww.'

'Kirstin.'

I recognise that voice. Oscar?

'Kirstin. You're all right.'

Tears flood my eyes. Now there's no chance of opening them. I start to sob.

'Christ.' I hear DS Graham's embarrassed mumble.

'That's not very helpful,' says a woman. A voice I don't know, and I hear the soft scrape of a starched uniform accompanied by the gentle, reassuring touch of a female hand on my bare arm. 'It's okay, love. You're safe now.'

'Did you catch Luke?' My words stick in my throat, sounding croaky and unnatural.

'Um, no...?' It's Luke's voice!

'What...?' I wrench my eyes open. The pain is unbearable. But when the light in the room finally stops battering my retinas, I realise that Luke's standing over my bed. I shrink back deeper into the pillow.

'Luke Millford had nothing to do with this,' DS Graham says.

'Yeah,' Luke smirks, 'I hope that's not a disappointment. You've my sister to thank for the sore head.'

Erica? And once again I'm out.

Two days later, the headache has finally gone, and I've begun to get a grip on the events. I was lucky. Really lucky. Niamh is in a worse state than me. She's in the same hospital. I've been to visit her a few times, navigating my wheelchair down long hospital corridors amidst that smell of disinfectant and pressure-cooked air. I would be fine on my feet, but the nursing staff are cautious about my recovery. Even though I got off lightly – a fracture to my right leg and a few fresh bruises that I picked up to replace the ones I'd acquired courtesy of Luke's car that first night. But considering everything, physically I'm not doing too bad. Although I'm still under what the medical staff have termed 'observation'. The drug Erica slipped into the stew when Niamh was out of the room to get the port proposals hadn't been through clinical trials. Niamh, myself and Timmy are now unwitting focus group participants. I can't speak for the others, but my blood pressure is still unnaturally high, and I'm pretty sure that's because of the drugs but I'm not complaining. I came out of this okay. Niamh wasn't quite so fortunate. The steering column hit her hard when we crashed. Her face exploded in bruises. Her nose is broken, and she's got a couple of cracked ribs to add to the mix, but her smile is still warm.

Actually, my hospital schedule ends up being pretty busy. I soon learn that Timmy is also squirrelled away in the same hospital. The family tried to put him in a private room, but he refused. He'd had enough of ivory towers; they're not all they're cracked up to be. I think this is a good sign. Him refusing to be pushed around means he's in a better state than he was the last time we met.

On day three, I scoot along to see him. I've got so many questions. But when I get to the ward, my bravado seems callous. My courage evaporates. I don't go in. Instead, I sit outside, staring through the large glass observation window trying to pluck up courage. I've never really met Timmy, not properly at least. I wonder if he'll think it odd that I've come wheeling all the way over here. He may not even know who I am. It feels somehow wrong to have looked at a face so closely, to know it so well, and have doubts that the person owning that face will recognise you back. But as I stare through the fish-bowl window into the room, I can't help but smile. Despite having survived a cardiac arrest, Timmy's looking so much better than he was. He's got a hint of colour to his cheeks and is sitting up in his hospital bed with his come-get-me buzzer lying on the blankets but he's not twitching for attention. Not one bit. He's looking intently at something across the ward and I'm not sure, but I think he may actually be smiling. I narrow my eyes, peering closer. He's watching an old guy in the bed opposite. The old man is chatting to a little kid, a boy. So I guess the old guy has to be the granddad. The kid is showing off some home-made, cardboard robot. A school project, hastily painted in garish, poster paints. Despite the fact that the bits of box are barely holding together, for all the praise Granddad is heaping on it, the kid could be showing off a NASA-style humanoid that he's spent every second of his short life building. The interaction is sweet and heartfelt, Granddad twisting the robot in all directions, admiring the jerky tilt of an arm and the curious angle of the antenna sticking out precariously from the robot's head. Timmy's smiling at the two strangers, enjoying the chat, even though he's outside of it. And I can see immediately why he wanted to be on a ward. This is life, the small things. The smiles. The caring. Suddenly, his features change. He's aware he's being watched. He's aware of me. My heart skips as he turns his head towards my window. But I needn't have worried. As soon as he sees me, he lets loose another one of those smiles, open and wide and welcoming. My eyes well up.

'You knew, didn't you?' I say gently. 'You knew I was your cousin?'

'I'd had that digital frame on for years. I knew every inch of every face on it. Apart from Aunt Maria.'

'My mum?'

'We all thought she was dead. That was the family story. Ran off with some Irish guy.'

'Liverpudlian actually, but there must have been Irish somewhere along the line.'

'The details we got were pretty sketchy. It was *black sheep of the family* stuff. All that filtered down to us was that she ran off and it all went bad. The guy was a drunkard.'

I give an ironic snort. 'Sadly, that part's right.'

'I think Carolyn kept in contact with your mother.'

I know now that's true. She kept in contact for all the wrong reasons. Unable to have kids, she 'bought' my mother's first child. Oscar. But I have no intention on spilling the beans. Certainly not at the moment. All of that can wait. Besides, I'm not done with my questions.

'When did you start being suspicious about Erica?' I ask.

He takes a deep breath. 'I knew something was up. After Cambodia, I mean. I didn't think my own sister would have actively tried to hurt me deliberately, but…'

'You had a niggling doubt?'

'She was very competitive, and mother had this thing about *The Golden Child*. There could only be one.'

'I heard. So, in short, you didn't trust Erica?'

'Not one hundred per cent.' He pauses, looking me straight in the eye. 'You've met her right?'

He's funny.

'Did you call her The Wolf?'

He laughs. 'She liked to call herself that. I always thought it was odd but, hey, she paid for my trip to Asia, so...' His voice fades. It's obvious, now the facts are sliding into place, that the trip has had a whole new paradigm shift for Timmy. He was manipulated. Erica played him for a pawn.

'A wolf,' he mumbles. 'Yeah. Maybe that's exactly what she is; the old wolf in sheep's clothing. At the wake, I saw her tampering with the chandelier. I couldn't work out what she was doing. It had been overhauled recently. Then I saw you walking up the steps to the house, and to be honest I nearly had the heart attack then. Because it was the exact same face as in the frame.'

'You think so? I didn't see it at all.'

'You didn't look at the image hard enough.'

Or maybe I just hadn't expected any likeness to be there.

'At first, when I saw Erica tampering with the mechanism for the chandelier, I didn't get it, but then when I saw you, and I knew whatever was happening, it wasn't good.'

Like a match sparking in my brain, everything comes together. 'I wasn't in the right place.' It all starts flooding back. 'I helped Julia with the coats. I broke the line.'

'Maybe. I saw Erica panicking a bit, well, maybe not panicking but flustered at least. She was probably trying to re-secure the mechanism. You weren't in range. She thought she'd done it, but I...'

Even though I know that I'm safe now, my body has gone icy cold at the thought of what almost happened.

'I can't thank you enough.'

He waves the air dismissively. 'Hey, you were with me when I went into arrest. You got me out of that house. You were my lifeline.'

On my scoot back to my own ward, I decide to drop off at the news kiosk but, no sooner is the edge of one of my wheels through the door, than I start to regret it. I can see the headlines. That beacon of journalistic mundanity – *The Island Journal* – is shouting the loudest. It's all front-page proprietorial stuff: *Erica Millford. An extreme plan to save the island.*

I grab a copy off the rack and start to read.

'You got to pay for that,' a voice says.

'Sure,' I shoot back, not even bothering to look up. My eyes can't keep up with my brain as I pore over the squiggles of black ink. The story has been spun to perfection. A lone woman, driven to insanity by corporate shipping giants and their plans to turn '*our beautiful island*' into a container port. To destroy the nesting habitat of the rare sea urns. To drive away tourism and concentrate instead on industry. To cover the peaceful island in a blanket of diesel fumes and emissions from tankers that stand taller and sit wider than any current building on the island. The sale of the Millford estate would have let the developers get their foot in the door. The story I am reading is a story of absolute self-sacrifice, a woman putting the needs of the planet before those of her family and herself.

I pay my money. On my way out of the shop, I thrust *The Island Journal* into the bin. If the newsagent is surprised, he doesn't look it. That woman has spun herself from psychopath to saint.

Wheeling back to my room I find Luke sitting in the hard chair beside the window. It's the first time he's visited since that initial hospital wake-up call. I can't blame him, if the roles were reversed, I'd do the same. Although, my stupid heart still vibrates a little too quickly at the sight of him.

'Sorry, didn't mean to doorstep you, but I'm driving out to the house. Do you fancy a trip?'

'I knew about the blood relative thing,' Luke says, threading the steering wheel through his hands. 'It's written into the deeds of the house. Dealing in antiquities, you come across all kinds of arcane laws, and other dealers knew I was always on the lookout for stuff about the family. Couldn't believe it when I came across a book that my "grandfather" had written.' He smirks awkwardly. 'At the time, I didn't think it was a big deal, but then a couple of years later, the DNA test came back. I only did myself and Oscar, that was enough. Course, that's not important anymore. Nobody's directly related to the estate. Apart from you.'

'Oscar and AJ,' I say helpfully.

He laughs. 'Yeah, who would have thought? Oscar was your mother's firstborn. I can't imagine how irritated that would have made Carolyn, not being able to have her own child, but having a black-sheep cousin who was as fertile as the garden of Eden.'

Who stands to inherit the estate is still not clear. It'll be stuck in the courts for years. There's only one thing that's sure, myself, AJ and Oscar are a genetic family bundle. Then it dawns on me. 'Luke, could we take a detour?' I may not want a slice of the inheritance, but I do want answers.

'What are you looking for?' Luke asks, following in my wake as I walk quickly down the aisle of the old church.

'The picture.'

'Picture?'

But I'm not stopping. 'If I'm right… Can you help me bring over a pew? I'm not tall enough.'

He's still looking confused, but he helps anyway. It's only when I'm standing on the pew in front of the large canvas over the altar that I can get a good look. Carolyn the birds and her father are on the left side, but the right side of the picture, it's dark as tar.

'Have you got anything sharp?'

Worry creases Luke's forehead. 'Kirstin, I'm not sure…'

I take my phone out of my bag. It's a new phone, but all hooked up with my old data. I flick quickly through my photos till I find what I'm looking for – two images; the first is the dark textured photo of an oil painting. The only thing we had from my mother. The second image is the back of the exact same photo. Only this time there's the cursive handwriting, *The true cost*. The true cost is to be painted out. To be silenced.

Holding the photo of the painting up against the mural it's easy to see these are the exact same brush strokes. 'You see!' I can hardly contain my excitement.

'Sorry but, absolutely lost here.'

I scratch at the paint with my nail, just a little to the right of the image of Carolyn.

'Kirstin!'

'It's here. It's somewhere here.'

And sure enough as the paint flakes, the image of a woman starts to appear, the same young woman I saw in the digital photo frame. Carolyn's cousin, my mother.

Back at the house, the downstairs rooms are quiet. The party is most definitely over. As I amble through the empty house I can't help wondering, did Carolyn disapprove of her father's harsh decision? She had clearly gone against him. Carried on meeting my mother at least until Oscar, AJ and I were born.

From the windows of my yellow bedroom I spot Luke down on the beach. He's building a bonfire yet again. I take one final look around my room. There's the picture still hanging there. The pretty Dutch master. How could the Millfords have all these treasures lying around and not value them? Not even notice them.

'Brought something for you,' I say, throwing a stack of broken wood onto the burning pile.

'Thanks. Thought I'd burn it all up,' Luke says, gazing at the flames. 'Feels like we've come to the end of something.' He throws a large branch up to the top of the stack. It holds.

'Well, there is family baggage and…' I glance over at him, his clear skin raw in the sea wind, his perfect chiselled face, his bright dancing eyes. 'And then there's what you Millfords have, which is in a whole different league.'

'Hey. You're part of it now.' He laughs.

'I'm happy to do Christmas but if you could just leave me out of the Agatha Christie-style day-to-day shitshow. Speaking of which: have you spoken to Erica?'

He draws in a deep breath, spiralling his body around in the wind. 'Trying my best to avoid her.'

This makes perfect sense; she'd tried to put Luke and Oscar in the frame. 'How did she even get those drugs she was giving Timmy?'

'You knew she was in PR, right?'

'Yes, but I don't see how…'

'That's exactly what she was relying on. She thought that if the deaths were related to medicine, Oscar would be in the line of fire. But PR, it's not all about trying to persuade people to drink Diet Coke. The company that she runs. Sorry,' he corrects himself, 'ran. A lot of her contracts were for the big pharmas.'

'Pharmaceuticals?'

'Yeah. She took some trial samples. Actually, so did you, Timmy, and Niamh.'

'The way we *took* them was a bit different.'

'Don't complain. Didn't you ever wonder why you were getting such stellar care back at the hospital? I wouldn't say... lab rat... but.'

'Lab rat.'

He smiles. 'Yeah. I'm sorry I was so... off the wall,' he says, glancing down awkwardly. 'You know. Erica, my loving *sister*, had swapped my medication, so some of the time I was high as a kite.'

'And the drugs I saw in your drawer?'

'That woman's love of detail is beyond reproach. She'd bagged up baking powder, wrote an entire notebook of drugs accounts which I found, incidentally. I seriously wish my handwriting was that neat. That morning when you used my shower, she put all the evidence in place. She must have seen you go into my room.'

'She was talking ten to the dozen. A regular monologue.' Then I remember her conversation about Rose, how Oscar had let Rose go. Before that I'd thought Luke had acted inappropriately. Had he? 'I just... I was wondering about Rose?'

He looks blank.

'The live-in carer that got "let go of" just before the funeral.'

'Oh, right. Rose?'

'Did you...?'

'What?'

I say nothing, letting the thought dawn on him.

Suddenly his face lights up in amusement. 'No.'

'So what happened?'

'I don't know. Erica accused her of taking something, earrings? A necklace maybe? I'm not up on all the specifics. Why?'

'Erica implied Oscar had let her go, and I thought Oscar implied...'

He laughed. 'This is all a long jump too far. Rose was in her fifties. If she was a day.'

I could kick myself. 'I should have been suspicious.'

'Where Erica is involved, it's always best to be suspicious.'

When he drops me off later at the hospital there's an odd silence, too heavy for words. Eventually he gets out, goes around the car and opens my door.

'So, I'll see you around then.'

'Weddings and funerals?'

He smiles back at me. 'Weddings and funerals, only hopefully not our own.'

When they check me out, I go for two last visits. Timmy and Niamh. I give them my address and a hug. I don't just hope we will stay in touch; I know we will. Then I stand in the hospital reception, which is hot as a subtropical rainforest, waiting for a lift to the ferry. My car is out of order, yet again. DS Graham had been driving it up to Gull Point so that I'd have it for the next day. We had literally bumped into each other. If we hadn't, at the next bend, Niamh and I would have been over the cliff. We would have been part of what Erica would have been so neatly spinning as Luke's story. The story Erica had for Luke was supposed to be about drugs and angling to get a container port built. According to Erica's story, Luke was trying to get rid of Niamh – the councillor who was so against the port. I would have just been collateral, although, in fact, I was the main target. You have to admire Erica for her balls.

'You ready then?' DS Graham saunters through the sliding doors, bringing a welcome hint of fresh island air along with him.

I must admit, I'm surprised to see him. 'Thought it would be one of your minions.'

'I don't have minions.'

'Well, I appreciate the lift.'

'That all you've got...' he says, stooping to pick up my canvas bag.

'I only came for the day.'

He laughs.

We get into his car, and I belt up, a cold shiver passing down my spine as I hear that clunk-click securing me.

'I still have questions,' I say, as we draw away from the hospital and head out along the winding coast road towards the port.

'Go for it,' Graham says, not taking his eyes from the road, which I am more than happy about.

'The wills? Which one is the right one?'

'Now you've got a vested interest?'

'Seriously, I'm almost beyond caring.'

He nods. 'Okay, well from what we've ascertained, and this is off-record?'

'Sure.'

'There were always two wills. Carolyn liked to play games with people.'

'Like some kind of Russian roulette deal?'

'Whichever will the solicitors had in their possession at the time she died, that was the one they would most likely go with.'

'So I'm probably out of luck as far as inheritance goes?'

'I think the brothers feel that would be wrong. If it weren't for you, the outcome would have been very different.'

'But Erica must have known that the will which divided the money between the 'siblings,' that was the one that the solicitors had? You don't think she pushed her own mother over the cliff, do you?'

He shrugs. 'I doubt we'll ever know; there are no witnesses and Erica's not confessing. But, to answer your question, yes, she knew which will was at the solicitors.' He smiles, threading the steering wheel through his hands. 'She also had herself a plan B, just in case it all went belly-up.'

'Oh?'

'She attempted to blackmail Miri.'

Of course.

'Miri was having an affair. Erica must have got hold of some pictures. Miri's fiancé Malcolm died in a car crash, there was an outpouring of public sympathy and, more to the point, job offers for Miri. But Miri's fiancé was driving too fast because he'd just seen the photos of her with another man. He was mad at his fiancé.'

I think of the feed that the receptionist at the Ship showed me. The level of hatred in the comments had been palpable. 'Who leaked the photos?'

'Anyone can take a photo. They probably didn't even realise what they had on their phone until Miri died. We think that Carolyn had invited the family down for the weekend, because she was going to announce she had terminal cancer.'

'With everyone in the same place, Erica decided it was time to take action?'

He taps the steering wheel under his hands, as if in tune to some inner rhythm. 'And now Erica's painting herself as a saint. She claims she's an environmentalist and that the port would have been an ecological disaster.'

'I read the article in *The Island Journal*.'

He takes a moment to give me an ironic look, before glancing back quickly at the road. 'Yes. Well written that article. Better class of journalism than the normal day-to-day *Island Journal* tripe.'

'I got the feeling the newspaper had been given a helping hand. You think Erica genuinely felt that the environmental ends would justify the means?'

DS Graham draws in a deep breath. 'It's all very well trying to justify our actions. Trying to put them into some wider moral framework so it looks like you might be following the higher path, but boil it down and it's all about arrogance. Erica had already knocked one family member off the favourites list. She saw herself as the golden child.' He shoots me another quick look. 'You know about Carolyn's *Golden Child* theory?'

'Yeah.'

'Chances are, for Erica this wasn't a money thing, or an environmental thing. It was a power thing.'

'Erica liked organising them all.' I'd been told that before. 'Golden child. How obnoxious.'

'You got that right.'

'Poor Timmy,' I say. 'Her first victim. I guess that's going to be really difficult to prove.'

'You'd be surprised, Kirstin. There was another incident, a kid at school, Bristow. Suspicious suicide.' He takes a moment to clear his throat. 'I promise you; she won't be smelling of roses by the time we've finished with her, however fancy her spin is.'

The car turns the corner onto Fore Street, the main artery towards the quay. I can see the ferry in the distance. There's an odd sense in which I feel like this has all been some kind of bad dream and that once I'm on that boat, I can leave it all behind forever. I glance out of the window, at the neat parade of shops, at Captain Jack's, the door continually opening and shutting like a gossip's mouth as people spill in and out. Then my eyes light up. Julia. It's Julia. She doesn't see me. I rap on the window, but she can't hear. She's smiling as if wallowing in the aftermath of an amusing conversation.

'Julia,' I say, excitement bubbling over but that excitement soon does a whole sea-change. 'And Fordham?'

DS Graham peers out of the side window. 'He's in safe hands now.'

They're both smiling at each other, Fordham reaching chivalrously for Julia's shopping bag which is bursting with treats from local delis. Oblivious that she's being watched, Julia's smile is as bashful as a schoolgirl's.

'Ms Catalow had been having a relationship with Fordham. That all finished when he got hooked on the drugs, courtesy of Erica. She was, apparently, very helpful with supplying him. Didn't even ask him for money.'

'The stories of Erica just keep getting worse.'

'Don't they. Anyway, now he's clean.'

So, that was what Julia had tried to tell me in the pub that day; people weren't perfect, but that didn't mean you gave up on them. Everyone has their problems.

'Speaking of clean,' I say as a new thought hits me. 'Could Erica have planted the drugs in my brother's cell?'

Graham laughs. 'Seriously, Kirstin?'

'Okay,' I say with a sigh. 'It was worth a try.'

'Not everything's going to end up at that woman's door, most of it but…' His voice trails away in thought, before he smiles, a small simple smile of admiration. 'It's a damn shame that woman was a crook. The logistical mind on her, she would have made a great cop.'

'Actually,' I say, fixing him with my eyes. 'You did all right.'

He beams, as if he's genuinely touched. 'I'll take that.'

'There's still so much that I just don't get – I mean, me being here, that was all just coincidence?'

He laughs. 'Oh, come on, Kirstin. You see how meticulously this thing has been planned and you're talking about coincidence?'

He's got a point.

He breathes out heavily. 'We know about your little scam.'

'What?'

'Please don't bother protesting. The funeral thing. Your boss knew as well and have yourself a guess on who he went to school with?'

Ah, now I get it. 'Erica?'

'Exactly. When she started tracing you, she found out you weren't even a million miles away and working for a mate. Well, she gets talking to him. He tells her what you're up to. She was already paying a lad at the solicitors to keep an eye on the fluctuating will.'

'Gareth?' Oscar's friend. The one who came to the beach party.

'That's the one. She also paid him to "befriend" Oscar.'

'Ew, that's unfair.'

'Yes. That must have hit Oscar Millford pretty hard. Never nice to find out your mates are on the payroll. Anyway, Erica got Gareth to go to the same clubs as your partner Marco and spill the beans about the funeral.'

'Marco's not my partner. He's just a mate.'

'You want to get yourself some better mates.'

'You don't have to tell me that.'

When we pull up at the terminal, DS Graham gets out, grabs my bag from the back seat, then walks around the car to pull open my door.

'Aren't you the gent.'

'Always,' he says, fishing into the back seat again and pulling out my walking poles. I hook the handles into my palms and edge myself forward on to the side of my seat, ready for the push up. I'm getting pretty good at this. I'm on my feet in seconds.

'So,' I say, taking in a deep breath of salt and seaweed as I look out over the port and the waiting ferry. This is it. It's all done, apart for one last thing. I look back towards DS Graham standing there beside me. 'I guess I need to thank you for saving my life.'

He shies away slightly, one hand waving the air dismissively. 'That's what I live for.'

I scrutinise him for a moment, is he taking the piss or serious? I have no idea, so I simply turn my back and start to shuffle away. The sea wind is so fresh, so welcome, after all that hospital air. It feels like a beginning, not an end.

'Wait.'

I turn back to see Graham striding towards me holding something up high in his hand.

'You dropped this.'

It's the large sparkling earring. The one I'd found forgotten on the shelf back at the estate. Idiot, I think. There's not even two of the damn things. I should have left it where it was. But I don't say any of that.

'Thank you. Would have been lost without it.' And it's in my pocket before he can get a closer look.

I turn and head towards the gangplank, relieved he didn't check my bag and find the neatly rolled painting of the flowers from my yellow room. It had broken my heart to smash up that antique frame and stick it on Luke's bonfire. Broken my heart a little, but not enough to stop me doing it. I'm not sure yet if the painting is a souvenir, or something I'm intending to sell. I can't keep holding on to all these damn things when I don't even own any walls to hang them on. Then again, I'll get settled one of these days, with or without a cut of the will. AJ will be out sooner or later. He's served enough time. The drugs in his cell were a minor offence. He certainly doesn't know where that painting is. AJ's not the brains of the family. I may not play bridge, but I do keep my cards close. I've got a lot of things to sell now. My story, Carolyn's manuscript, I'll be able to set myself up anywhere, even without the Lowry.

I guess I should be feeling pleased with myself, as I take the handrail and step up the gangway onto the ferry but in reality, I'm getting tired of playing *clever*. Clever is a lonely business. Things have to change. This is no kind of life, just like the woman in Lowry's infamous Punch and Judy picture, I'm on the inside looking out. I draw out my phone and tap in a number. 'Hi, Janice?'

'Kirstin?' She sounds confused.

'Fancy going to the cinema. Didn't we say Wednesday?'

There's an excited, 'Absolutely,' from Janice.

'Great,' I say with genuine warmth. 'Only, I don't suppose you like comedy?'

I figure I've had enough horror to last me a year or two.

THE END

ACKNOWLEDGEMENTS

As well as the Escalator team, I'd like to thank Breck for their wonderfully insightful comments, Betsy Reavley for her advice on cuts, Ian Skewis for the scrupulous editing, Shirley Khan for proofreading and all the Bloodhound team.

ALSO BY SHIRLEY DAY

The Insect House

Reap What You Sow

A NOTE FROM THE PUBLISHER

Thank you for reading this book. If you enjoyed it please do consider leaving a review on Amazon to help others find it too.

We hate typos. All of our books have been rigorously edited and proofread, but sometimes mistakes do slip through. If you have spotted a typo, please do let us know and we can get it amended within hours.

info@bloodhoundbooks.com